Backyard Burial

Janet McGuire Hendershot

PublishAmerica
Baltimore

First printing

At the specific preference of the author, PublishAmerica allowed this work to remain exactly as the author intended, verbatim, without editorial input.

This book is a work of fiction. Names, characters, places, and incidents are products of the author's imagination or are used fictitiously. Any resemblance to actual events or locales or persons, living or dead, is entirely coincidental.

ISBN: 1-4241-3372-6
PUBLISHED BY PUBLISHAMERICA, LLLP
www.publishamerica.com
Baltimore

Printed in the United States of America

To Ivan, my first love and ultimate hero

ACKNOWLEDGMENTS:

I need to thank Dee Gatrell, Pat Williams and Becky Crawford Hendershot for their hours and hours of proof-reading, Ivan Hendershot for advice on security procedures, and Melinda Hendershot Sprague for advice on yachting and harbors.

Chapter 1

The partygoers gathered around Lucifer, a gray German Shepherd who had dug a large hole in John Fleming's rose garden. Mrs. Gunthrey, John's housekeeper, stood with her hands on her hips and scowled at the animal. Matrina McCoy put her hand to her mouth in shock. How could her sister allow this dog to tear up John's backyard?

Granted, the dog did belong to Andy Douglas, Rosie's latest flame, and Andy did look a lot like Tom Cruise, drop-dead gorgeous, only taller. How long the flame would last would be anyone's guess. Matrina shook her head in acceptance of Rosie's latest escapade.

"Rosie," she said, "you guys can't allow that dog to dig up John's yard like this."

"We can't stop him," Rosie said. She sipped her wine cooler and moved away from the dirt that flew from Lucifer's efforts. She stood closer to Andy. "He's a cadaver dog that they use at the Sheriff's Department where Andy works. Lucifer only digs where there's something dead."

Matrina wished she could stop the worry that enveloped her when it came to Rosie. Their mother died in their eighteenth and eighth year, and after that, Matrina assumed the surrogate mother role. Their busy dad allowed it, and through the years, two decades of them, the worry had not subsided. Matrina prayed for Rosie daily, but so far, God held to His "hands off" policy.

Matrina had to admire Rosie's ability to roll with life and have fun no matter what the situation, the immediate situation being the destruction of John's backyard on their first visit to his home.

"Andy says there's something buried here, and we have to let him find out what it is," Rosie said.

"It's probably an old dog someone buried years ago."

"No. It's got to be pretty current, and it's got to be a human."

"Oh, Rosie," Matrina said. "John? A body buried in his backyard? Get real."

"You never know. Sometimes still waters run deep," Rosie said.

John went over to speak with Andy. They exchanged views on the digging, and John agreed to allow the dog to continue. The host continued across the yard to Matrina and Rosie.

"I said the dog could keep digging," he said. "Your Andy says this dog only reacts to human remains. How can I refuse? If I've got a body buried in my backyard, I guess I need to know about it."

David Rogers crossed the yard and stood beside John.

"I didn't know my move into your area would be so exciting," he said. "Usually being a deacon in the Baptist church means you just stand around and deacon. Here we are having a bar-be-cue with church members and some dog thinks you have a body buried back here?"

"That's the rumor," John said. "This dog is a cadaver dog owned by the Sarasota Sheriff's Department. Matrina's sister, Rosie's boyfriend, Andy's a deputy, so I'm letting the dog dig. If there's a body out here, I certainly don't want it to stay here."

"How would it get here?" David said.

"Must have been here since before I moved in," John said. "I've been here over a year, and I know for sure there's been no bodies buried since I've lived here."

The frenzy of the dog faded, and he stopped the storm of dirt. John walked over to the gapping hole. Andy already stood beside the hole to oversee the dog's work.

"There's a body down here," Andy said. "I have a duty to report it." He dialed nine-one-one on his cell phone. "Since I work for Sarasota County," he said to John, "and you live in Manatee County, we'll have to call Manatee."

"Call away," John said. Matrina watched him wrinkle his brow. She wondered what he thought of all this. Matrina's year-long friendship with John, based on their common interest in investigative work and their trials as widowed single parents, had not yet crossed the threshold to shared brain waves.

Darkness encompassed the yard, except for the intervention of the yard lights strung to give the yard a festive glow. In the glow of the gentle, swinging lights that tried to push back the struggling shadows of night, Matrina watched as John tried to make out the image of the man down in the hole.

The body wore a plaid sport shirt and beige khakis, and the back of his head showed through the disturbed soil. He had dark hair. John peered through the blotchy darkness, and Matrina watched as a faint glimmer of recognition painted John's face with an element of disbelief.

Matrina moved closer to where John stood. "There really is a body down there?" she said.

"Yes," John said. "And it's not been buried long either, maybe a week."

"How's that possible?"

"Wish I knew."

"John, you could be in real trouble here."

"Oh, Matrina, who would think I had anything to do with this? I'm a church-going security guy, with a good job and nice kids. Nobody would hold me responsible for this, whatever it is."

"It's not every day you find bodies in your backyard," she said. She moved a loose stone with her foot and it fell back into the hole. She winced.

"Body," John said. "Only one body, not bodies."

"Only one. Now I feel better." She rolled her eyes upward in frustration.

Sirens wailed and uniforms filed through the house to the hole in the backyard. An ambulance arrived, and men lifted the body from the shallow grave.

The Manatee County Sheriff's Department officials pulled the body out of the grave. Matrina moved closer to the grave for a better look. She saw the corpse had been shot in the back of the head and buried face down. She turned away. Her hand touched John's shoulder and felt his neck stiffen. He inhaled out of step with his breathing.

"Do you know him?" she said. She sensed the reaction of familiarity.

"Yes. He's Robert Walker. He goes to our church. We all know him. We called him, 'Slats.' How crazy is this?"

"Someone you know?" David said. He came to join John and Matrina.

"Someone you know, too," John said. "It's Slats. Robert Walker."

"From church? How can this be?"

"I have no idea," John said.

"I think we ought to go to God with this," David said. "People, let's have moment of silent prayer for this brother who is no longer with us."

The picnickers gathered about the opened grave and bowed their heads. The blooms of the surrounding roses bent to the sultry evening breeze, and Matrina felt tears in her eyes despite the fact that she had never known the deceased man. The uniformed officers paused and bowed their heads as well.

"Amen," David said. "Carry on, gentlemen." He spoke to the officers. The men loaded the body onto a gurney and strapped it down.

9

"Guess I'd better get back to my grill," John said. His husky voice sounded grim. "At least that's something I understand."

Matrina nodded her head and felt helpless. No intelligent words made their way from her mind to her mouth.

Burgers and steaks crackled on the grill, and people stood about and waited for the picnic to continue. Petunias lined the fence around the backyard, and Matrina suspected this to be the work of Mrs. Gunthrey. John didn't seem like a petunia kind of guy.

John flipped the burgers and removed the steaks. "Well, these will soon be crispy critters," he said.

"No one will care," Matrina said. She held the plate for the steaks. "Just dish it up, holler, 'Soup's on,' and hit the deck."

"Soup's on," John said. He smiled at Matrina as his three children stormed out of the house. "How'd you do that?"

"I'm a mom," Matrina said. She held another plate for the burgers. "I know this stuff."

While the emergency staff finalized the removal of the body, the church people filled their plates from the buffet lined up on one of the picnic tables. No one seemed to mind the overdone meat. A somber, quiet mood overcast the backyard bar-be-cue.

John approached a fifty-something couple who sat at one of the other picnic tables scattered about the backyard. The couple sipped cans of Dr. Pepper and munched Cheetos from a small bowl. Their plates of steak and salad were before them.

"Matrina," John said, "I'd like you to meet David and Ida Rogers. David is a deacon in the church, and they're new in our area."

Matrina held her plate, and Ida patted a place at the table for her to sit.

"Please, join us," Ida said. She smiled at Matrina and put A-1 sauce on her steak. Matrina climbed over the bench of the table and sat down. She put catsup on her hamburger and studied David Rogers and his wife.

They smelled like they had stepped from a Dial soap commercial, and his plaid cotton shirt and Docker trousers were impeccably pressed. Mrs. Rogers wore a crisp flowered sun dress. All the other ladies present wore jeans or shorts and sport shirts, which included Matrina, who wore comfortable Wranglers and a short-sleeved tee shirt.

"Glad to meet you," Matrina said. She extended her hand, and the Rogers accepted her hand and smiled back at her.

"Do you live in Bradenton?" David said.

"No," Matrina said. She shook her head as she spoke. "I live in Sarasota."

Dee-Dee, John's twelve-year-old daughter, carried a tray of canned sodas and juice among the guests. Matrina accepted a can of Diet Coke and smiled at Dee-Dee as their eyes met.

"You go to the Baptist church down there?" David said.

"Actually, no," Matrina said. "I know John from security work. You probably already know, he works for the Publix grocery store chain, and I work for Apex Cyberspace Security. We don't know each other from church."

"Oh," David said. His smile faded. "So, where do you attend church?"

"I don't actually attend anywhere right now," she said. "I'm kind of between churches at the moment."

"I see," David said. He used his very best, disapproving deacon tone of voice. "And your husband doesn't attend church either, I would assume?"

"I'm a widow. My husband died on nine-eleven. He was a firefighter, and he died at the twin towers."

"Oh, I'm so sorry," David said.

"So am I," Matrina said. She tried to think of something to break the silence that followed. "So, where are you from, since you just moved here?" That ought to be a more comfortable subject.

"We're from Jamestown, New York," Ida Rogers said. She seemed to join Matrina in the attempt to change the subject.

"You're kidding," Matrina said. She cut her hamburger in half. "My mother was from Jamestown."

"Isn't that something," Ida said. "Did you hear that, David? This lady's mother is from Jamestown."

"That's quite a coincidence," David said. "Does she still live in Jamestown?"

Matrina shook her head. "Oh, no," she said, "my mom, and my dad passed away several years ago. But she lived in Jamestown when she was a little girl. Then she met my dad, and they moved down state to Long Island. That's where I was born."

"So, you're from Long Island?" David said.

"Yes, until recently. After Mike's death, I felt the children and I needed a fresh start, so we moved to Florida, to Sarasota last winter."

"And you're happy with your move?" David said. Matrina figured he always played the role of counselor, always the elder, always happy to offer aid and advice.

"Yes," Matrina said. "It's been very good for all of us."

"You said you work," Ida said. "You said security, like John?"

"Yes. I'm an investigator for Apex Cyberspace Security. They call it ACS."

"That sounds interesting," Ida said.

"It is," Matrina said. "Sometimes it can be too interesting."

"Have you been dating John long?" Ida said.

"Oh, we don't date," Matrina said. "We're just friends because we have so much in common with our jobs and our kids. We're both still married to people who aren't here anymore. I still wear my wedding rings, and so does John. I guess you've noticed that. Neither one of us is ready to date anyone. I don't know that I'll ever be ready for that."

"Nine-eleven had to be a terrible experience for you, for all of us, but you especially," Ida said. "Were you able to provide a proper funeral for your husband?"

"No. Nothing of him was found, except for his wedding band which surfaced in the debris from the site. I wear it around my neck." Matrina hauled the band of gold from inside her shirt. It hung around her neck on a gold chain.

"I see," Ida said.

"Your job sounds like a dangerous job for a woman," David said. He cut a piece of his steak and put it into his mouth.

"Not really," Matrina said. "I don't carry a gun or anything like that."

"You don't?" David sounded surprised. He chewed his steak and ate a forkful of potato salad.

"No," Matrina said. "I told them that for the money they pay me, if there's a crisis, my plan would be to run to the nearest phone and dial nine-one-one."

John came and stood beside the picnic table. "I know her boss," he said. "And I can attest to that being her exact comment."

Matrina wanted to take her leave of these religious people before she dug herself into a deeper hole. "Well," she said, "its been so nice meeting you. But I guess I'd better go and see if I can help Mrs. Gunthrey." She neglected to add that she had already offered to do that and been kicked to the curb.

"Yes, of course," David said. He added salt to his potato salad.

Ida smiled at her. "It has been nice chatting with you," she said. "I do hope we'll get a chance to chat further."

"I'm sure we will," Matrina said. She smiled back at Ida, picked up her plate and left the table.

* * *

Matrina walked back into the house, and John followed close behind. They went through the utilitarian kitchen. No curtains fluttered at the kitchen windows, and no multi-piece canister set on the sink shelf. The counter did boast a coffee pot and a microwave. The clean dishtowels didn't match, and no rug lay in front of the sink on the beige tiled floor. Mrs. Gunthrey, still on duty, made coffee and grumbled orders to whomever stood within earshot.

"...between churches?" John said in a low tone of voice at the back of Matrina's head.

"It's all I could come up with on the fly," Matrina said. She put her used paper plate into the plastic bag that lined the trash can.

"I told you we wouldn't fit in with your friends. I feel embarrassed I even came to this party."

"That's ridiculous. They need to loosen up. You're fine. You and I are good friends. They can understand me better by getting to know you better."

"Right. And once they get to know Rosie, they may have more understanding than they can handle. You may have more understanding than you can handle."

"Rosie's fine. You worry too much."

"Did you notice she brought wine coolers to a non-drinking Baptist Church bar-be-cue?"

"That's okay. Different strokes. I don't care who drinks what. I'll drink what I like, and they can drink what they like. What difference can it make?"

Matrina walked into the neat living room. Brown carpeting lay beneath sturdy furniture. A couch upholstered in ecru fabric stood beneath scenic pictures on the walls. She saw no flowers or knickknacks, but crocheted or embroidered doilies rested on every end table.

The coffee table sported a large circular crocheted doily with a variety of tiny crocheted mauve flowers splattered over it. She paused and studied the lovely table coverings. Had Delores, John's deceased wife, made these? They were the solitary touches of femininity in this otherwise masculine home.

A large screen TV sat in one corner of the living room and an expensive sound system in the other corner. Music must be John's one vice, big time.

The small dining room contained a large, round oak table that occupied the center of the room. The table took up too much space and a pale pink, round, embroidered tablecloth covered it. No centerpiece sat in the middle of the table, and six oak chairs sat around it. The computer crammed into a corner of the dining room rested on a small table rather than a computer stand.

"So, the sound system, that's your big hobby?" Matrina said. She touched the embroidered tablecloth and admired the workmanship. "That and my gun collection," John said.

"You have a gun collection?" Matrina said.

"Yes. Come on. I'll show it to you," John said. "I think it's a classic. All cops, well, ex-cops, have gun collections, you know."

"I guess it's an occupational hazard," Matrina said. "I had forgotten you used to be a cop. You have that in common with Andy."

"Yes, that's interesting," John said. "Maybe I'll get to swap cop stories with him one of these days."

"That should be fun," Matrina said.

John led the way into his den where his gun collection sat in a glass cabinet.

Red leather furniture filled the den, and beneath the furniture lay the same brown carpeting that covered the rest of the floors in the house. Trophies for marksmanship sat around on several side tables on the every-present crocheted doilies, and a large picture of a pheasant that cruised over a field of wheat hung on the far wall. Piles of file folders lay on the large, highly-polished desk that sat in one corner of the room.

Matrina noted the extensive display of guns in his gun cabinet. She felt awe-struck. The firearms looked like new.

"So, do you know what any of these guns are?" John said. He opened the cabinet with a key he removed from the center drawer of his desk.

"Of course not," Matrina said. "I don't think I ever took 'Guns 101' when I worked in security for Wal-Mart back on Long Island. I just had to catch shoplifters, and I didn't need a gun for that. A whistle would have come in handy, and maybe a baseball bat, but I didn't have a gun."

John removed one of the guns. "This one is my favorite. This is a 1902 American Eagle Luger. Very rare. It's worth over four thousand dollars. Dee bought it for me at a yard sale for a hundred bucks. She had no idea of its value, and neither did the seller, obviously."

"I've never even seen a gun that looks like that," Matrina said. She reached out, but withdrew her finger without touching it.

"Dee brought it home and gave it to me, and I was just dumbfounded. She got all upset because she thought I was mad because she'd paid so much money for a gun. She started to cry, and offered to take it back."

"She didn't know what a good deal she had gotten?"

"No. She didn't have a clue, and I was so shocked she would know to buy such a valuable gun. But she said she thought it was 'different.' Boy, she was right in that aspect of it."

"She must have loved you very much."

John paused and caught his breath. He caressed the barrel of the gun. "So, anyway, I felt guilty about paying so little for the gun. I couldn't pay what it was worth, but I wanted to give the people who sold it to Dee another couple of hundred bucks more anyway."

"That was nice of you."

"I didn't want God to get me for being unfair, so we drove back to where the yard sale was, but they were gone, lock, stock and barrel. They had been set up in the little trailer park outside Little Falls, and we guessed they just sold what they could, packed up everything else and moved on."

"What did you do then?"

"I looked for them for weeks in other towns around the Mohawk Valley, and I never did find them. They probably never knew what they had, or they would have sold it for more."

"So, what are these other guns?" Matrina said.

"This one here is a 45 Long Colt, Hartford Model, and this one is a 1873 single action."

John continued through his collection and explained each gun to her.

"Do you worry about John and Matt being around guns like this?" Matrina said. She would have worried to have two young boys in the house with all these firearms. She would worry to have her twelve-year-old son, Turner, in a house with all these firearms.

"Oh, I don't have any bullets in the house," John said. "The guns, I love. But I don't have much use for bullets." Matrina chuckled. They left the den and she followed John back to the backyard and the subdued partygoers.

* * *

After the police left, and the ambulance left, and the deacon and his wife left, and the other church guests left, and Rosie and Andy removed Andy's dog and left, Matrina sat at a picnic table with John over a cup of coffee. Mrs. Gunthrey brought a cup for herself and joined them.

The capable housekeeper, usually quite vocal about the happenings in John's life, sat beside the gaping hole in the backyard and said nothing. Matrina sat there as well and enjoyed the evening breeze that had dropped the late June temperature a few degrees. No words came to her mind either that would make any difference.

After a few minutes, a thought came to her. "We need to tell George," she said. She patted John's hand as he picked paint from the picnic table. "George might have some insight into this situation."

"George is just your boss and my friend. I don't see how he could help."

"He's ex-FBI. He's got connections. They could come and sweep the yard for DNA and other evidence."

"The Manatee Sheriffs will do that."

"Well, if they do, that'll be good," Mrs. Gunthrey said. She sipped her coffee. "They'll find all this has no connection to you."

"I knew him," John said. "He was found dead here in my back yard. He appears to have been shot. I have guns. That's what they call means and opportunity."

"What about motive? There's certainly no motive," Mrs. Gunthrey said.

The space of silence that stopped the conversation made Matrina uncomfortable. She never knew what to do with awkward silences.

"Yeah, they might come up with a motive," John said. He continued to flick chips of paint from the table top. "It would be a weak motive, at best. I really don't think anyone could put me in the loop on this."

"What kind of a motive would anyone have?" Matrina said.

"We didn't get along well, Slats and I. He always borrowed money from me and never paid me back."

"You're not the type person who would kill someone over an unpaid debt," Matrina said. "You're not the type of person who would even get angry over an unpaid debt."

"People have killed people over less."

Now Matrina generated the silence. Mrs. Gunthrey continued to sip her coffee, and Matrina noticed her bright gray eyes looked sullen and dark. When elderly women worry, their eyes betray them.

Chapter 2

"You're sure you want to do this," Matrina said to John a week later.

"Sure, why not?" he said. "It's not like we were going on the actual fourth of July. That would be nuts. But the crowds ought to be manageable on the sixth."

They drove in her white Astro van up the interstate to Disney World. John's three children and her two children sat on the two rear seats where they listened to headsets and played hand-held video games. Matrina's Turner instructed John's younger boys, John and Matt, on the prowess of conquering the current baseball video game they now owned.

"I just thought maybe we ought to find out who murdered your friend, Slats," Matrina said. Her concern over John's indifference about who killed Slats clouded her mind. Why couldn't he see he might be the easy prime suspect?

"Let the sheriff's department do that. I don't have anything to do with his murder. They have to know that," John said. He steered Matrina's van into a less crowded lane of traffic. "I've got one huge element on my side."

"And what would that be?"

"I didn't do it," he said. "Case closed."

"Simple solution to complex problem."

"You've got it. That's why no one has even questioned me about it. They know it, too."

"I hope you're right."

* * *

Three hours later, they sat at glass-topped tables at an outdoor ice cream parlor on Main Street in the Magic Kingdom. They battled the Florida July heat that sabotaged their banana splits. A trash can meandered up to their table and spoke to them.

"So, how come your sneakers are green?" the beige trash can said to

17

seven-year-old Matt Fleming. Chocolate ice cream from Matt's banana split filled his mouth.

"My sneakers are not green," Matt said to the trash can. His twelve-year-old sister, Dee-Dee, took a napkin from the dispenser on the table and helped him mop up the cascading chocolate ice cream that wound up on his orange gator shirt. "They're white."

"They're green as grass," the trash can said.

"No, they're white."

"You can't tell your colors yet?" the trash can said.

"Dad, what color are my sneakers?" Matt looked at John for validation.

"They're white," John said. He helped mop up the chocolate mess. "The trash can will be able to tell colors when it grows up. Right now, it's a little color blind."

"You gonna put that napkin in the trash can like a good girl?" the trash can said. It whirled its attention in Dee-Dee's direction.

"Of course," Dee-Dee said. She deposited the napkin into the swinging lid. "Look at me, Dad. I've reduced myself to talking to a trash can. What next?" She shook her head in disbelief.

The trash can whirled its attention to Matrina. "And so, who's this pretty chick with the silky blonde hair?"

"Tell him your name, Mom," Turner said. Matrina's twelve-year-old son out-ate the tropical heat and devoured his frozen treat.

"Yeah, Mom," Michelle said. "Tell the nice trash can your name." Matrina's fifteen-year-old daughter, whose dark shiny curls bounced in glee around her ivory skin, and whose clear blue eyes sparkled in amusement waited for her mother's response.

The trash can began to croon. "Are you allooooone?" It said. It swung its lid back and forth at Matrina's elbow.

"Okay, that's it," Matrina said. She fished in the pockets of her Ralph Laurens. "Where's my Mace. I know I have it here somewhere." She winked at Michelle and waited to see if she had gotten a rise out of the trash can.

"Sheewwwww," the trash can said. Matrina watched as it moved away from her. "Beautiful smile, cranky disposition."

At that moment, a very pretty girl in red short shorts and a white tank top walked past and headed into one of the sidewalk shops. The trash can gave out a loud, low wolf whistle. The girl turned and gave John a dirty look.

"It was the trash can," John said. He shrugged his shoulders." Matrina and the children collapsed in laughter, and the girl flounced off.

"This trash can thing really is a neat stunt," Matrina said to John. "Where's the dude?"

"Over your right shoulder, against that stone wall about fifty feet behind you," John said. "See? He's got the remote in one hand and a microphone in the other."

"Oh, yeah." Matrina smiled at the operator.

At that moment, John's laughter faded into seriousness, and he bolted from his seat. He sent his chair into the air.

"Tell the trash can we have a Mayday," he said to Matrina. He left the group and darted across the concourse and tackled a large middle-aged man who wore a heavy coat. With one swift motion, John body-slammed the man to the ground, face down. A black oblong object flew from the man's hand, and John yelled to the gathering bystanders, "Don't touch that remote."

"There's a Mayday at eleven o'clock from your location," Matrina said into the trash can. "The tackler is the good guy."

Within minutes six security guards with weapons drawn swarmed the scene. John held the man in the coat on the ground and hollered for someone to hand him their belt. A black, middle-aged man did, and John quickly secured the man's hands behind his back with the snugly pulled leather accessory.

"Want me to help you get him up?" offered a bystander.

"No," John said. "Don't touch him. Don't move him. Somebody guard that remote to be sure it isn't touched either." The bystanders made an ever-widening circle around John, the remote, and the tethered man, not sure what would happen next.

With one swift movement, the man on the ground contorted his body and landed on his feet. He bolted through the crowd, which parted as he plowed through them. He disappeared into the Haunted House exhibit. Matrina watched the scene as if she were in a movie and played a bit part as an onlooker.

* * *

John stood and dusted himself off. When security descended on the scene, John said to the officer in charge, "That man is wearing a bomb. I could feel it beneath his clothing. It must be a backup device, as that remote over there on the ground can no doubt trigger a more serious bomb. That bomb is here somewhere. I would suggest you check out that twin stroller under the magnolia trees. The one side has a giant panda in it, and the other side has a kid who is probably what, three or four years old?

John continued. "This kid hasn't been awake for hours, ever since this guy has been in the park. We've passed him several times, and the kid hasn't even moved. He's still not moving despite all this commotion that's around him. Something's seriously wrong here."

The speechless security guard's eyes grew larger with each word from John's mouth, and he looked at the giant panda with suspicion. The other five guards, who accompanied him to the site, stood in a group, and John figured they all treaded water in the deep end of the pool on this one.

John understood the guards knew they had to neutralize the situation and not violate anyone's civil rights. They had to decide if the man who fled the scene threatened the overall safety of the parkgoers, or could the guy who pleaded for immediate shut down of the park be the troublemaker.

John figured he had violated a whole slew of civil rights already, all on his own. He could read in the eyes of the guards they knew heads would swing over this, no matter what they did.

"You have to shut down the park," John said. He hoped someone would heed this advice before something tragic happened. "The guy who ran into the Haunted House is wearing a bomb, and I'll bet the farm that the panda over there is wearing one as well. And you'd better guard that remote until a bomb squad gets here, or we could all be headed to paradise."

Security moved the crowd to another area of the park without the creation of a panic. John noted Matrina and the kids moved to the exit gate and would probably wait for him there. The trip to the land of magic and adventure had taken a sudden turn into the twilight zone.

Within the half hour, the Orange County Sheriff's Department and two representatives of the FBI arrived on the scene. The sheriff's department deputies trotted into the Haunted House to look for the escaped dude who wore the heavy coat. Other deputies removed the sleeping child, who even when removed from the restraints of the stroller did not awaken. Scary. John watched the scene and felt uneasy as to its outcome. He would feel better to see the deputies exit the Haunted House with the coated guy in tow. They came out empty handed.

One FBI agent retrieved the remote control device that still lay on the pavement. He placed it in a protective container. A bomb squad swept the giant panda with a Geiger counter, and bagged the huge, fuzzy toy in a lead container. They hauled it through the employee's entrance to a safe location.

One of the FBI agents walked over to John who stood on the sidelines.

The agent extended his hand to John. "Carl Randolph," he said.

"John Fleming," John said.

"That was amazing work," Carl said. He scratched his head. "What alerted you to this situation?"

John felt embarrassed and sheepish. "I'm an ex-cop," John said. "I'd been watching this guy in the big coat ever since we got here—Florida—month of July—hundred and two in the shade—and this guy's dressed like the middle of winter. Then there was the kid, constantly asleep, in Disney World? Give me a break."

"How did you know he was ready to make his move?"

"When I saw the remote. Doesn't take much brain power to tie it to the panda."

"Did you realize he wore a body bomb when you tackled him?" The FBI guy wiped his brow with his handkerchief.

"I suspected it, but didn't know for sure until I had him on the ground."

"Weren't you afraid of setting it off?"

"No. I figured he would have to detonate it, since he had the clicker. He'd want to be sure the bigger job was done."

"Wonder why he wired himself with a bomb on top of the panda bomb?"

"Probably as a backup plan, in case he got made with the panda. He could still take out a few dozen people on his way to Utopia."

"So you assume this is al Qaeda?"

"Don't you?"

"There are so many nuts running around these days. Hard to nail it down until we know for sure."

"Wonder why he didn't plan this for the fourth? Wonder why he chose this day for his attack?"

"They have more people here today than on the fourth," the FBI agent said. "People avoid the real holidays as they figure Disney will be too crowded. They flock here on these off-days, especially if it's sunny."

"That makes sense," John said. He moped his brow with his handkerchief as well. "Whatever was going on, I'm glad I was here to toss a monkey wrench into the plans."

"Me, too," Carl said. "So, what outfit are you connected with in law enforcement right now?"

"None right now," John said. "I used to be a cop in Little Falls, New York. But for the past few years, I've just been chasing shoplifters and hot check artists for Publix down in Bradenton."

"Ever think of getting back into law enforcement?"

"No, not really," John said. "I'm pretty happy where I am."

"Well, let me do my paperwork thing," Carl said, "and then you can go." He walked over to the bench where the stroller had been parked and sat down. He opened his briefcase. He pulled out a folder that contained information forms and asked John for his vital statistics.

* * *

Another half hour later, Matrina watched John as he made his way to the gate where she and the children waited. John walked with a weary gait. Everyone stayed quiet, open-mouthed, wide-eyed.

"Oh, stop it," John said. "It's like you never saw anyone tackle a homicide bomber before."

"And speaking of that," Matrina said, "where'd you learn to tackle like that? You were like a flying fortress."

"Four years at Central Connecticut State University," John said. "Blue Devils. Offensive lineman. Tough coach."

"Wow, Mr. Fleming," Turner said. "You were awesome."

"Like Superman, Dad," John said.

"Yes, could you be like Superman, Dad?" Matt said.

"No, don't be silly," Dee-Dee said. "Dad's just Dad, and it looks like that was enough for today."

"Yes," Matrina said, "it certainly was more than enough for today. Could it have been a nuclear bomb?"

"They don't know," John said. "They think it's possible. It tested positive on the Geiger counter, whatever it was. I think it might have been one of those suitcase bombs. Those are easy to make. You can find directions on the internet."

"If it turns out to be nuclear, it could have enough explosive to equal one kiloton of TNT. That would leave a crater here in Disney World about a half-mile wide," Matrina said. She shook her head in refusal to accept such a scenario.

"I know," John said. He sighed a deep sigh.

Matrina looked for an opening in the crowd to get through the exit gate and out to the parking lot. The exiters kept marching, jam-packed and endless. She leaned back against the outside wall of the concession stand where they stood and bowed her head. She could feel the hot tears that scalded her eyes. She tried to pray. God should know she appreciated the final outcome, but why did He allow the situation to start with?

22

The twin towers had to be enough. The loss of Mike and his colleagues to these madmen had to be sufficient. What would bring the end to all this terror and fear? Tears escaped despite her effort to control them.

John walked over to her and ran his hand over her hair as if he stroked an injured animal. The stroking didn't relieve the pain, but at least it conveyed the fact that he understood and cared. Matrina wished he would hug her, not out of physical attraction but out of compassion. Sometimes a person needs a simple hug to put a Band-aid over a gapping hole in their heart.

Mike filled Matrina's mind, and nothing could ease the emptiness in her soul. She understood John's sympathy. He, too, had lost a mate, but Delores died of cancer. Mike died in perfect health because duty called, and he answered. "Too close for comfort," John said into her hair.

"Only close," she said. "Close is good. Better than right on target."

Chapter 3

The next day, Matrina headed to work. The outcome of her current assignment, an insurance fraud case, seemed to be up in the air. She concluded the workers comp claimant had a valid case and should be awarded whatever workers comp would pay.

George, her boss, would not like that. He liked all their insurance company clients to be victorious, and all the claimants be guilty as sin.

Matrina stopped at a light and looked at the cross streets to get her bearings. Her cell phone paged her from the bottom of her purse. She dug down into her purse to find it.

"Hello," she said.

"Hey, where are you?" John Fleming's voice filtered into her ear.

"I haven't a clue," she said. She looked once more at the cross streets. "Somewhere south of the hospital on the Trail."

"Close enough. Want to do lunch?"

"Where?"

"Subway. It's on the Trail in the Gulf Gate Shopping Center."

"That's cool," she said. "I'm headed to Gulf Gate today, so actually, that's perfect. You must be working the store down there?"

"Yeah, they think they've got somebody waltzing out of here with booze, and I've been watching the camera all morning until I'm cross-eyed. Maybe our boozer doesn't drink until afternoon. But right now I need a meatball sub break."

"Sounds good. I think I'm about ten minutes away."

"See you soon."

Matrina thought of John as thoroughly enjoyable company. She looked forward to lunches with him. She appreciated his dedication to his family, his church and his job. He must have been a fabulous police officer in Little Falls, New York.

She wondered why he hadn't continued on the policeman trail when he moved to Florida. What made him switch to industrial security? He hadn't volunteered his motives, and she hadn't asked. A lot of things in each other's lives remained in the unknown shadows. Their friendship hinged on the occasional lunch, intermittent e-mails and instant messages. She pulled into the Gulf Gate Shopping Center parking lot and saw John's blue Jeep Wagoneer parked in front of the Subway sandwich shop. She got out and pushed her "lock" button.

On her way into the sandwich shop, she noticed a newspaper dispenser that displayed the *Sarasota Herald Tribune,* and John's handsome face grinned up from the front page. She felt a giggle rise in her throat. She inserted two quarters, removed a paper, and walked into the shop. John sat in a booth at the back of the shop with two meatball sandwiches and two sodas in large paper cups in front of him. He stuck a straw in the top of each soda through the plastic cover.

"Oh, Mr. Fleming," she said. She gushed her words and batted her eyelashes. "Would you be so kind as to give me your autograph on your picture so I can frame it and hang it in my laundry room?"

"Oh, no, not you, too," he said. He moaned and put his head down on the table. "I've been getting this all morning. The next bomber I spot, I'm going to tell myself, 'Not your job, John.' No more heroics for me."

Matrina laughed folded the paper and sat down. She took a sip of her soda.

"Diet Coke," she said, and her element of surprise surfaced. "How'd you know I drank Diet Coke? On our other lunches, I was always there from the get-go, and ordered my own stuff."

"I'm an ex-cop. I pay attention," John said. "Hope you like cheese on your meatballs."

"My jeans probably won't fit me when I waddle out of here, but yes, I'd probably put cheese on everything if I had no conscience."

They bit into their sandwiches and sipped their sodas. Matrina scanned the article in the paper about the Disney World incident. Constant conversation between them could wane without that uncomfortable feeling. The need to impress each other had never been present. They felt no stress over how the relationship stood. No relationship existed, except for that of two friends who rowed similar boats over the same stormy sea and flashed friendly signals at each other that sunnier days hovered on the horizon.

"Wow, check this out," Matrina said. She turned the paper so John could read what she had read. "Did you know the would-be bomber is a guy named Christopher O'Brien?"

"Christopher O'Brien?" John said. He knitted his brow in disbelief and put his sandwich down. He looked at her as if she said the moon had become blue. "You're making that up."

"Haven't you read this?"

"No. I got too sick of everyone kidding me about it at work."

"You don't watch the morning news?"

"I didn't watch it today. Don't tell me I was on that, too."

"Of course, you were on it. You were it, almost all of it. You're quite the celebrity now."

"Great."

"And you truly haven't read this about the bomber."

"No. Did they finally catch him?"

"No. That's the bad part. He got away, but they know who he is through fingerprints and DNA. Read right here." She pointed to the words in the article. "His father was William O'Brien, native of Ireland, migrated to the United States, became a United States citizen. He went to Israel in 1970 on a fact-finding mission. He was writing some kind of a book about the Islamic religion.

"He met an Israeli girl named Nyisha, married her, and in 1972, they had Christopher. William and Nyisha were killed in a private plane crash in 1982, and little Christopher went to live with some of Nyisha's relatives who lived in Afghanistan. Christopher got connected to Osama Bin Laden, and whalla, a decade or two later, you have Osama's hero of the hour in an attempt to blow up Disney World and earn his seventy-two virgins."

"Wow, he sure didn't look like a 'Christopher,'" John said. He took the paper from her and read the article for himself. "He looked like the typical profile of middle-eastern culture from head to foot."

"I guess he is, on the outside. But his genetics say he's half Irish." Matrina bit into her sandwich, and wiped her mouth with a paper napkin.

"So, how's your world going?" John said. He added salt to his sandwich and munched a potato chip from the opened bag that he had put in the middle of the table.

Matrina noted a swift change of subject. "My world?" She figured she'd better not give him the long version, how Nick at Nite played for hours in the bedroom to stamp out the loneliness. And how she prayed that tomorrow would dawn and reveal this had all been a bad dream. Tomorrow morning she'd awaken and find they lived back home in Hempstead, and Mike would be alive. "Oh, everything's fine," she said. "The kids are doing well in school, which was over a month ago, of course. Thank goodness for summer school, which they're both doing for extra credit."

Matrina continued. "When summer school's over, I'll have to consider someone like your Mrs. Gunthrey to look in on them. Michelle's fifteen, and all of that, but I don't like the latch-key-kid syndrome. Rosie can't fill in much anymore. She has her job and this a new fellow."

"Yeah, her new fellow is something else, isn't he?"

"Rosie dating a cop. How strange is that?"

"Where'd she meet this guy anyway. Was he working vice at some bar where Rosie was hustling pool?"

"Close. They met at this Casey's Lounge on Lido Beach. That's close to where Rosie's condo is, and Casey's has a pool table and line dancing. She didn't know he was a police officer in the beginning."

"I'll bet he didn't know about her in the beginning either," John said. He took another potato chip from the opened bag of chips and slid the bag toward Matrina. She shook her head in the negative, rolled her eyes and patted her stomach.

"Probably not," she said. "She's not too tightly wrapped at times, but I'm sure he's got that figured out by now"

"Probably."

"I hope he's not all glitter and nothing more. They've only been dating a couple of months." Matrina dabbed at her chin with a napkin, found it did not do the job and took three more napkins from the dispenser.

"How long's he been with the Sarasota County Sheriff's Department?"

"Three years, I think."

"Where's he from?"

"I don't know," Matrina said. "I've asked Rosie, but she doesn't know. She's always gushing about how much fun he is, and what they did the night before, and how he comes through her cashier line at Winn Dixie with donuts and fruit, and how much he looks like Tom Cruise, and then it's back to how much fun he is. We're not down to the nonessentials like where is he from; is he married, is he an illegal alien, is he on 'America's Most Wanted,' superficial stuff like that."

"You think he might be married?"

"Who knows, the way the world is today. I certainly hope not, as Rosie is head over heels for this one." Matrina took a sip of her Diet Coke and stirred at the ice with her straw.

"She never checked?"

"No. She asked him if he were single; he said, 'Yes.' End of story. You know how she is."

"What's his name again?" John said.

"Andy. Andy Douglas. Ring any bells?"

"No. Never crossed paths with him before last Saturday night," John said. He took another bite of his sandwich, and popped a couple more chips into his mouth.

"And then there are the day to day crises with Michelle. You know how teenage girls can be." Matrina weakened and tossed a potato chip into her mouth.

"Not exactly," John said, "but I have Dee-Dee coming up to that level soon, and without my Dee here to guide her, well, I hope Mrs. Gunthrey will be able to remember the pitfalls."

"Me, too," Matrina said. "Of course, the rules keep changing, so if you know what's going on today, tomorrow will be a whole new story."

They finished their subs and Matrina rose to leave. She gave her chin one last swipe with a napkin and dumped her sandwich wrap and napkins into the receptacle. "They should provide manuals for these kids when we bring them home from the hospital."

"Would that they could," John said. He got up from his seat as well. He put their soda cups inside each other and tossed them both in the trash. They walked to the front of the shop. John held the door open for Matrina as they walked out onto the sidewalk.

* * *

They paused on the pavement. John gazed at Matrina and tried not to think about her clear blue eyes and her shiny blond hair. Christ would have plenty to say about that line of thought. "It's been fun," he said. He picked his teeth with a toothpick. "What kind of a case are you working on today?"

"It's a worker's comp case. The insurance company hired us to blow this supposedly injured lady out of the water, and I've been working on it for a week now, and I think the lady's really hurt. I don't think she's faking it."

"Ole George will love that," John said. "No margin of profit in proving your client's wrong."

"I know. I hate that, but if she's hurt, then she's entitled to the benefits. What can I say?"

"So, how're you going to prove it, one way or the other?" John moved back into the shade of the building to avoid the merciless July sun.

"I'll do something creative to either bring her out of her wheelchair, or prove she can't get out of her wheelchair."

John smiled and mopped his brow. "Oh," he said, "I heard about how you did that with your first case, that dude who lived down from the hospital in Sarasota, where you faked being hit by the car. The guy came roaring out of his wheelchair to do the 'knight in shining armor' bit. Case closed. I don't think the guy who drove the car even stopped."

"How'd you know about that?" Matrina said. Shock cloaked her as she joined John in the shady shadow of the building.

"George told me. He thought it was quite innovative."

"George knew I did that?"

"Sure."

"How? I never told anyone about that little charade. I had Michelle with me to film the claimant getting out his wheelchair. I didn't bother with details."

John said, "You didn't really think George would send you off on your first assignment and not have you watched, did you?"

"He had me watched?"

"Sure. Tyler Sanders watched you. He almost choked on his Big Mac when he saw you go down beside that cruising station wagon. Then he spotted Michelle in your van with the video camera rolling, and he figured what you were up to."

"The guy was faking. I knew it. He knew it. It was just a matter of time until he slipped up. I go for truth, win, lose or draw."

"That's always been my battle plan," John said.

"Well, guess I'd better go and try to suppress more crime. See you," Matrina said. "Thanks for lunch. I enjoyed it." She began to walk away.

"Hold on a minute, Matrina," John said. He reached out to touch her arm and keep her attention. "I have something to show you. It came in the morning mail."

Matrina stopped and held her vehicle keys in one hand and shaded her eyes from the incandescent Florida sun with the other. The sun seemed to have figured out she stood in the shadow of the sandwich shop, and it moved its position enough to invade her shade. "Something good in the mail I hope?"

"Let's say, it's interesting," John said. He reached into his shirt pocket and handed Matrina a folded envelope addressed to him in black crayon. Inside, she found a piece of paper that had been torn from a spiral notebook. It, too, sported black crayon.

Matrina took the envelope and removed the scribbled note.

"Oh mercy, John," she said. She spoke in hushed tones. "This is a death threat."

"Seems so," John said. "What do you make of it?"

"I make of it what it says," she said. She read the words again. "You go to the police with this?"

"No," John said. "That would be silly. I thought I'd show it to George tonight when we go bowling and see what he thinks about it."

"I can tell you right now, he'll have a cow that you haven't already gone to the police. This is serious."

"Is it?" John said. "Or is it just a prank because my picture's in the paper. All this notoriety I've gotten tends to bring out the fruitcakes, you know."

Matrina studied the note and repeated it to herself, one more time. It said, "You have interfered with the holy jihad. You have put yourself and your family in great danger. You should go back where you came from and stay out of the way." No signature appeared below it, of course.

Matrina studied the envelope. An American flag stamp flashed in the upper right hand corner.

"Nice stamp," she said.

"Yes, I thought that was a bit over the top," John said. "So, you think this is for real?"

"Don't you?"

"No, not for sure. My first reaction was that it was a prank."

"You'd best report it, no matter what, and I guess you have a plan for keeping an eye on the kids."

"I have a password a person would have to know to pick them up at school. And Mrs. Gunthrey is with them after school. The boys have to play in the backyard, not the front yard, and Dee-Dee is an inside-the-house kid, watches TV and reads. I don't know what else to do."

"Are we contaminating this note with our fingerprints?" Matrina said. She tried to hold the envelope by the tip of one corner.

"Probably," John said. "But I'm sure whoever did this wore gloves. They took such care to write in crayon and use such childish scrawling, they surely wouldn't have done something stupid like leave fingerprints on it."

"You ought to have George run it through the FBI lab. He still has connections there. And there might be a fingerprint where the stamp is. They might have worn gloves for the preparation of the note, and even the sealing of the envelope, and then stamped it at a later time. There might even be DNA on the envelope, if they licked it."

"That's a good thought," John said. "I'll just show all this to George tonight and see what he thinks." John took the note and envelope back from Matrina, put the note back inside the envelope and folded it over and put it in his pocket.

"Please be careful," Matrina said. She patted his arm, and John noted the deep concern in her eyes.

"You bet," John said. He stroked her hand as it lay on his arm in return. "I've been around the block a few times, you know. I don't think these yahoos are for real. But I'll let you know what George says about this little epistle."

"I already know what he's going to say," Matrina said. She removed her hand from his arm. "I already told you. He's going to have a cow. He's going to rant and rave, and you'll be lucky if you bowl a hundred tonight"

John chuckled and walked with Matrina toward the parking lot. She unlocked her van, and he held the door for her as she climbed inside. She clicked her seat belt and cranked up her engine. She spun the air conditioner control to high tilt and pulled out of her parking space. She smiled at John and waved good-bye.

John waved good-bye and got into his jeep. He watched her drive out of the parking lot, and he felt a twinge of regret that lunch had passed so quickly. Her opinion of the letter tweaked him. Did danger lurk around the corners of his life?

Chapter 4

The next morning, nine A.M., Matrina walked into the office of Apex Cyberspace Security in Sarasota. Franny, the elderly, gray-haired, chunky receptionist, who held ACS together greeted her.

"Hi, Matrina," Franny said. "Want some coffee?"

"Oh, yes, thanks," Matrina said. She walked back toward George's office.

"How about a Krispy Kreme?" Franny's voice drifted down the hall from the kitchen.

"No. I'd love one, but I need to pass," Matrina said over her shoulder.

Matrina walked into George's office, but she didn't see him anywhere. "Where's George?" she said. She hollered back to Franny who washed cups at the sink in the kitchen.

"He isn't there?"

"No, unless he's hiding under the desk."

"Did you look?"

"I couldn't have driven him that nuts already this week. It's only Wednesday."

"Then, he must be in the little boy's room," Franny said. She brought Matrina's coffee into George's office. "Black, right?"

"Yes, good girl, Franny. Thanks." Matrina sat down across from George's desk. She noticed her e-mailed report on her current worker's comp case that she had sent to him last night on top of his morning paperwork. And beside her report she noticed the threatening letter John must have given George during their bowling tournament. John actually did what she suggested. How about that?

Matrina set her coffee on the corner of George's wide desk and pulled the black-crayoned letter out from the stack of papers by one corner so she would not put any unnecessary fingerprints on it.

She hurried around the corner to the copy machine which seemed to take forever to crank out a copy of the ominous letter to John. Once she had folded the copy of the letter and put it into her slacks pocket, she carried the original letter back to George's desk. She sat back down and sipped her coffee, and moments later, George came back to his office. He carried his latest copy of the *Conservative Chronicle.*

"Hi, George," she said.

"Hi, Matrina," George said. He rounded the desk and sat down behind it.

"I see John gave you the letter," she said. She tried to sound casual. "What a good boy."

"Yes," he said. He picked it up and also put his fingers on the corner, and laid it down again. "He thought you were making too much over it, but I thought it was worth looking into."

"Suppose it's real. He and the kids could be in real danger."

"Yes. It's probably a prank, but I'm going to have a friend at the lab look at it and see what comes from it. Fingerprints, anything that might identify the writer, you know, a thorough analysis." George got up and adjusted the blinds to shut out the blazing mid-morning sun. The air conditioning churned cool air from the vents in the ceiling. Matrina wished the air would not blow down right on her head. No matter. She wouldn't be here that long.

"Good. That might tell us something," she said.

"If it's a professional job, there won't be any fingerprints or anything else on it," George said. "Just the lack of lab results will tell us a little bit about the people who sent it."

"That's nice of you to help." Matrina moved her chair so as to avoid the onslaught of blowing air. "So," she changed the subject. "I guess I need another assignment."

"It would seem so, "George said. He pulled her e-mailed report to the top of the pile of paperwork that cluttered his desk. "You're sure this lady is really injured?"

"Yes, George. She's for real. I'm sorry, but that's the way the cookie crumbles."

"How can you be so sure she's really injured?" George said. He matched his five fingers from each hand together and tapped them back and forth while he lounged back in his executive desk chair.

"I did a little test on the injured woman's situation. Nancy is her name. And I overheard a conversation between her and her daughter. The daughter's name is Edith."

"What test? What conversation?" He stared at her, and she knew he wanted concrete answers.

"Well, the conversation made me believe the Nancy wasn't faking. I saw Nancy as she sat on the front porch in her wheelchair. She just sat there and cried. And then Edith, the daughter, came out and actually yelled at her mother for being a 'Whaa-whaa' person.

"She said something like, 'You just sit there in that chair, keep your mouth shut, and let the lawyer get this through the courts. Then we can all celebrate. Why are you trying to ruin everything by wanting to get out of that chair?'

"And Nancy said something like, 'Because I hate sitting in this chair. Easy for you to say. You're free to walk around. I just want to get better so I can walk around, too, and get back to my life.'

"And Edith said, 'That's the most selfish attitude I've ever heard. You're just thinking of yourself.'

"And Nancy said, 'That's true. I'm thinking of myself, and how I want to get out of here and go back to work. That's all. Just to be able to go back to work. That's all I want.'

"So Edith said, 'Wait until this is all settled, and you can go back to work.'" Matrina sipped her coffee and shifted in her chair. George studied her intently.

"And Nancy said, 'I can't. I can't walk.' She sobbed as she said it, Matrina said.

"And Edith said, 'Well, maybe you'll get better someday. Meanwhile, we'll be comfortable and rich while we wait for you to get on your feet.'

"And after that, Edith went back into the house and slammed the door behind her. She left Nancy to sob into her hands on the front porch while she sat in her wheelchair."

"So what did you do to find out the truth?" George's fingers continued to tap in cadence.

"I'd hate to tell you," Matrina said. She sipped more of her coffee and hoped George wouldn't press the issue. He pressed the issue.

"Tell. I'm the boss. I need to know these things." Fingers continued to tap.

"I had a plastic shopping bag with two dozen eggs, loose from the carton and twelve tea glasses. I set the video camera on the dashboard of my van secured with a clamp. I flicked the switch that got it rolling, and checked to be sure it was focused in the area from Nancy to the sidewalk in front of her house."

Matrina gulped and watched George. Maybe she could gauge his reaction to this story. He sat at his desk, poker-faced.

"Then what?" he said.

"I walked down the block so as not to seem obvious, and then back up on the side of the street where Nancy and Edith lived. Once I was in front of their house, I slammed my foot into the uneven sidewalk seam, screamed and tossed the plastic bag up into the air."

"And?"

"And I went down in a heap, and glasses and eggs shattered all about me. What a mess. And Nancy reacted just as I thought she would. She cried out in distress, hollered for Edith to come outside, and tried with all her might to wheel herself to my aid. George, she couldn't even get the wheelchair to move. There's a handicapped ramp on the porch, but she couldn't even get to it. She was so concerned over my fall, I know she would have come to my aid, if she'd been able. No, she and that wheelchair are a set."

"What did you do after that?"

"Hauled myself up, brushed eggs and glass from my slacks, apologized to Nancy, and by then Edith had come out of the house to yell at me for making so much noise and such a mess. I apologized to her as well. She got me a broom, and I swept up my mess. Dumped the whole concoction into the plastic bag, took it with me and walked back down the street. Case closed."

"Hummm," George said. "And you'd state in court that she really is crippled from her fall at work?"

"She's crippled from something. That's all I know. She'll need a ton of money, a good therapist and a baseball bat to control her daughter to cope with this accident."

"Okay. That's what we'll go with." George sighed, and Matrina could feel his frustration. He pulled out his file drawer in his desk and removed a file folder. "Here's something you can work on. This is a restaurant and lounge on Anna Maria Island called the Trade Winds. The manager has contracted us to find out why he's losing money and his inventory is all out of whack. He's barely taking in enough right now through his register to pay the piper, and he used to make a good buck off this business. He wants to know what's going on."

"Okay, George," Matrina said. She breathed a sigh of relief that he no longer questioned the conclusion to Nancy's case. She took the file folder and got up to leave. "I'll go see who's hauling what out the back door."

George did not answer her, but returned his attention to his *Conservative Chronicle.*

Chapter 5

Ten days later, Matrina cruised up the Trail to Bradenton. She had made this trip daily for the past week to run surveillance at the Trade Winds Restaurant. As she drove, she rolled down her window and inhaled the salty breeze. The Floridian temperature this July ballooned toward one hundred, but somehow, along the Gulf, it seemed to invigorate her. She felt the damp, Gulf warmth as it tossed her shoulder-length, blonde hair, and she took a deep breath and smiled over nothing in particular. Smiles came with more ease these days.

She loved this ride up the beach to the restaurant, and the comfortable slap, slap, slap of the Gulf tide could lull her to sleep, if she weren't driving and on duty. And the clues which might solve the problem at the Trade Winds had begun to jell, however she didn't like the picture they formed. She hated to go to George and inform him that, once again, the client turned out to be the bad guy. This morning, Matrina dressed to blend with the Anna Maria Sunday crowd. She wore a white pants suit, with a lavender silk blouse tucked into her pants and a deep purple scarf lazily tossed around her jacket. Three gold chains lay on top of the silk blouse. One of the gold chains sported Mike's wedding band. Her fingers caressed the circle of gold, and her finger traced the inscription, "M & M forever," Matrina and Mike. Forever had come too soon.

Small gold earrings dotted her earlobes. She wore low heeled white dress shoes, and between the bottom of the trousers and the tops of her shoes panty hose were in evidence. Ten minutes after she embarked on this journey, Matrina knew the panty hose were a mistake. They already stuck to her body. She should have worn her jeans, as she had on all the other days this past week.

The manager dude at the Trade Winds claimed his profit picture had slumped. Matrina wished George had gotten more information. She wished she could have interviewed the manager herself and asked him some pertinent questions.

George's FBI background led him to ask important questions. He made sure all employees had drug tests and checked to be sure all supplies are carefully checked in so the vendors can't take the client to the cleaners.

However, George failed to ask such things as how many waitresses existed on child support payments from deadbeat husbands who now lived with other women who lived off child support payments from their ex-hubbies. Someone needed to ask how many employees had to dodge the used car repo guy because they stayed three weeks behind in their payments on their 1990 Pontiac Gran Am. It would be helpful to know how many employees had to haul something edible out the back door at the end of their shift to feed their three preschool children who had nothing to eat that day.

In her ten years experience in loss prevention at Wal-Mart, those were the things that caused shrinkage, not the exciting element of drug addiction or big-time crime. Theft erupted as a side effect to quiet desperation. Oh, well, she would sit on the Trade Winds one more day and see what hatched.

* * *

A few blocks before the restaurant, Matrina noted the Holmes Beach Marina filled with boats, some of them so luxurious a person could live on them and not need a home anywhere else. She wondered how many people who owned those kind of boats did that, and spent their twilight years sailing, sailing, sailing…

Matrina turned into the Trade Winds parking lot and parked her vehicle. The Sunday lunch hour rush filled the parking lot with expensive, late-model cars. Matrina's 2004 white Chevy van blended in well enough.

The weather-worn restaurant building boasted wide walkways lined with marigolds that led up to the glass front door. Some laboring landscape guy had planted the blossoms and hoped his efforts would still be note-worthy in a month. Sadly enough, the dancing flowers could be gone in a week. The deciding factor would be the irrigation system that tried to beat off the efforts of the southern sun to deep-fry the colorful blooms that nodded in the tropical Gulf breeze.

Once inside, Matrina no longer noticed the interior of polished wood with fishing nets that hung over expansive walls. An aquarium filled a space in the center of the dining room with various tropical fish that plummeted here and there and looked for food that had not yet been sprinkled.

The barefooted hostess wore a skimpy floral wrap-around skirt and a halter top. She carried an armload of large, plastic-coated menus, and she approached Matrina. The shiny, straight, black hair of the hostess cascaded down her back. She would have made a great poster girl for Fiji. This gal seemed a little too much for Manatee County. This gal would be a tad too much for any kind of county.

"This restaurant is all non-smoking, of course," the hostess said. "And you are alone?" The hostess did not waste the dazzling smile on Matrina. The smile targeted the four men who stood in line behind her.

"I'm glad this is all non-smoking," Matrina said, "and no, I'm not alone. I'm expecting someone to join me." Matrina shot an involuntary look upward. She hoped God would understand the need for a cover story when on surveillance, and a detained dinner partner justified the need to linger longer at her table than if she were dining alone.

"Very good," the hostess said in a professional, icy tone. "Right this way."

Matrina followed the slender girl whose hips swayed to the gentle rhythm of some kind of absent music. She led Matrina to a table for two in a dark corner of the room. Two menus settled on the table, and the hostess looked to Matrina for approval.

"Could I have that table-for-two over there, by the window?" She did not add, "by the cash register."

The hostess picked up the two menus with a huff, and led Matrina to the table by the window. She placed the two menus down, and turned to leave so she could concentrate on the four upwardly mobile gentlemen who awaited her in the lobby.

"Your waitress will be here shortly," she said over her shoulder to Matrina. She gave no more opportunity for Matrina to complain.

Matrina sat down at the table covered with an immaculate white tablecloth and looked out the window at the Gulf waves that foamed along the shoreline. She wished the windows could admit the refreshing breeze. The air conditioning seemed to recycle only stagnant air, no doubt partially attributed to the abundant flow of alcohol sipped by the noon-time diners.

The waitress appeared, and Matrina ordered a grilled grouper sandwich and a Diet Coke. She had to change her order every time she entered the restaurant this past week, so the waitresses would not remember her. She also sat in different sections so she would be attended by different servers.

She informed the waitress her companion would order when he arrived. The waitress nodded and took one of the menus away and left the other one for Matrina's guest.

The server wore a similar wrap-around skirt and halter top, and she, too, had straight black hair to her waist. The island theme at this Trade Winds restaurant seemed to be complete.

Matrina scanned the room and four waitresses could be seen carrying trays of beverages and food. All of them wore this island costume, and all had long black hair, although three of the four could attribute their darkened strands to Clairol.

Then Matrina switched her attention to the cashier. This cashier had manned the register all week. She even worked double shifts. In fact no other person approached the cash register.

The young, slender, tall cashier dressed in a turquoise, full-skirted, below-the-knee skirt and a matching tube top. She had long hair, slightly curly and dazzling red, and it, too, appeared to be compliments of Clairol. The cashier had a killer smile that displayed bonded teeth and sparkling eyes. Her flawless makeup set off her large, hoop earrings. She wore no other jewelry, no bracelets, no chains of gold around her bared neck and no rings. Her artificial, French-style, flat-shaped, white-underlined fingernails boasted no polish. Very striking. Why did she deviate from the island costume?

Matrina wished she could take notes, but if this "let's beat the system" caper involved professional-type thieves, note-taking would be a definite red flag. She would have to remember all the pertinent factors, and record them as soon as she got back to the van. The notes so far caused a rise in her chagrin at the direction this case had taken.

The grilled grouper tasted fantastic, but then, it should at twenty bucks a pop. Matrina ate the meal and watched as the system for collection of payment at the cash register played out its game. She knew the system by heart.

It never varied, and the system itself showed Matrina that the cashier tapped the till and recorded her proceeds with pennies. The redhead kept two cups of pennies by the register, and whenever she would under ring a sale, a penny moved from one cup to the other. Each penny would mark the extra money in the till, usually five dollars for each penny. Matrina did the math on that one, to figure out how much money the redhead could pocket at the end of her shift and not come up short.

It helped that many customers ate in groups where cocktails before the meal melted into wine with the meal and slid into brandy after the meal. Laughter and back-slapping escalated, and the host seemed all too eager to finish the celebration and melt plastic with the wave of his platinum Visa card.

Many hosts scribbled their signatures on credit card slips and put their receipts in their shirt pockets or purses and didn't bother to look at them. After all, this perk with their company would be the problem of some little bookkeeper who worked for minimum wage to tally up later. Right now, the gayety of the party and the pleasure of the clients could be measured by the amount of the tab, and the more affluent and nonchalant the host appeared, the more affluent the company must be. Right? And affluence generated confidence, and confidence generated profits.

After a spurt of about a dozen tickets, the cashier moved pennies from the one cup to the other cup. Huummmm.

As Matrina watched the action at the register, her phone rang from the bottom of her purse. She fished it out.

"So, do you care what came in yesterday's mail?" John's voice.

"Probably. How come you didn't call me yesterday when the mail first came?"

"Because you're not going to like it. And I thought I'd give myself another day's reprieve before you hollered about it."

"I don't holler."

"Maybe not on the outside. But you holler a lot on the inside."

"Okay, so lay it on me."

"It's another crazy letter."

"A threatening letter?" Matrina lowered her voice to almost a whisper.

"Well, let's just say it's not a fan letter."

"What does it say?"

"It says, 'You are not paying attention. Don't stay here until you are missing Dee-Dee. Once she is wearing a burqa, you will not be able to find her.'"

Matrina took a deep breath. The waitress came to her table.

"Are you all right, Ma'am?" she said.

"Yes, thank you," Matrina said. She struggled to produce a smile for the waitress.

"Is your guest still expected?"

"No, I guess not."

"Will you require anything else?"

"Yes. A cup of coffee, if you don't mind."

The waitress removed the remaining menu and flounced away.

"You there, Matrina?" John said.

"Yes. I'm at work, and one of my subjects is displaying intense disapproval of me."

"That can't be good."

"In this case, it's okay." Matrina paused. "John, go to the police with all this."

"I might at least get back with George. I still think it's a prank."

"Threats to Dee-Dee is no prank. Cops, John. Go to the cops."

"I am going to send the kids to upstate New York for a few weeks to be with Dee's parents," John said. "They're leaving Friday."

"Can I come over tonight and see the letter?"

"Come on down."

"It'll be late. I have to be here through closing, which is nine."

"We'll be here. I'll put the coffeepot on."

"No, no coffee. I'll be up all night. Water will do nicely."

"We have water, and I'll leave the porch light on."

"Okay. See you then. I want to look at that letter for myself."

The phone clicked off and got dumped back into Matrina's purse. She focused on the cash register once again. She noticed more pennies migrated from one cup to the other. She also noticed the closed-circuit video camera that circulated overhead. How does the light-fingered cashier compensate for the video? Double huuummmmmm. Minutes later, Matrina took her cell phone from her purse and phoned home. The waitress returned with her coffee.

"Hey," Matrina said to Michelle, who answered the phone. "What's up?"

"Nothing," Michelle said. "Aunt Rosie's here and we're playing Scrabble."

"You're letting Turner play?"

"Of course," Michelle said. Her voice reflected the frustration in her reply. "We always let him play."

"That's nice. And everything's okay?"

"Of course." More pained tone of voice. "We really don't even need Aunt Rosie, you know, Mom. I could baby-sit with kids right now at my age. I don't need an adult to be here when I only have Turner to watch."

"I can watch myself." Matrina could hear the young male voice in the background. "I don't need some ole girl to baby-sit me. What a hummer dummer."

"Which is why we need Aunt Rosie for these days when you are home alone all day," Matrina said. Her voice had a controlled quiet tone.

"We do fine after school," Michelle said.

"That's true, but that's only an hour or two. This is all day. I'm just more comfortable if Aunt Rosie is there. And you like being with her, so it's good for everyone. Okay?"

"Yeah, it's okay," Michelle said with more lilt in her voice." Aunt Rosie's fun. We're having fun."

"Yeah, and I'm winning," Turner's voice again.

"You are not." Michelle had to dispute the fact.

"I am, too. Look at this word I just made."

"That's not a word."

"Is too."

"Aunt Rosie, is that a word?" Michelle begged to be validated.

"Hello," Matrina said. "I'm still here, if anyone cares…"

"Hi, Matrina," Rosie said. A giggle laced her voice as she took the phone from Michelle who hurried to find the dictionary. "We're having a ball. I ordered a pizza, and we're going out for Dairy Queen when this game is over. And I wondered if it would be okay if I took the kids over to my place to swim. That okay with you?"

"Yeah, that's fine," Matrina said. She sipped her coffee and watched the next wave of payment folders being presented to the cashier.

The Trade Winds lunch hour business seemed very lucrative, and people stood in the foyer as they waited for tables. The lounge stayed packed with diners who imbibed mid-afternoon cocktails. "Rosie," she said, "you want to go home because Andy is coming over?"

"Yeah. That's no big deal, is it?"

"No, I guess not. You'll not get distracted with the kids in the pool or over at the Gulf, will you?"

"Matrina," Rosie said in her serious tone, "I have been baby-sitting these kids since they've been born, and I haven't lost one of them yet. Why are you such a worry wart?"

"Wait until you have your own kids. Then you'll see."

"That could be in my not-too-far-distant future, if things keep going like they are," Rosie said. Another giggle sailed over the airwaves to Matrina's ear.

"What are you talking about?"

"Andy, Dunce."

"Andy?"

"Yes." Then in lower tones. "He told me he loved me last night. Can you believe it, Matrina? A guy that gorgeous actually loves me?"

Matrina felt her eyebrows knit with concern. "Oh, Rosie," she said. "Don't go too fast on this one. You've only known him, what, two months? That's too soon to be in love."

"You're so old-fashioned. When are you going to get into the twenty-first century?"

"Never, I hope," Matrina sighed and glanced out over the sparkling Gulf.

"Well, this could lead to wedding bells, and a home with grass to mow, and I could borrow recipes from you to cook in our crock pot, and evenings of watching TV in our pajamas, evenings of watching TV without our pajamas, (Matrina could imagine the sly glance shot at Michelle, and Michelle's eyes rolling toward the ceiling), and children, and trips to the Caribbean, and growing old together. The whole nine yards, Matrina. Please be happy for me."

"Of course, I'd be happy for you, Rosie. Just be careful. Don't charge into this at a full gallop."

"When do I ever charge into things at a full gallop?"

"Every time you get into a relationship. You're just so anxious to believe everything these guys tell you."

"And you don't believe anything anybody tells you."

"That's probably true. Well, somewhere between you and me there has to be a balance."

"Okay. I'll be sensible. Got to go. Michelle has found the word in the dictionary, or not found it, I'm not sure, but whatever it is, we have to put on our striped shirt and do our referee bit."

"Good luck."

"Just pick the kids up at my place when you're done."

"It'll be late. Probably midnight. This'll be a long shift and then I was going to run over the John's for a minute."

"Over to John's for a minute, she says." Matrina could feel the sarcasm in Rosie's voice. "And one minute could lead to two, and two to an hour. Something going on there, Sis?"

"No, nothing's going on, Rosie. John got a letter and I'm curious about it. That's all. It's strictly business."

"Knowing you, that's probably true," Rosie said. "If you'll be that late, then just let them spend the night. We'll rent a video and pop some popcorn."

"Rosie?"

"Yes."

"Um, Andy doesn't, like, sleep over, does he?"

"Sleep over? Sleep over? Are we playing *Leave it to Beaver* here? Nobody refers to having an affair as 'sleeping over.'"

"Whatever the name of the game is this century."

"To answer your question, no, Andy is not 'sleeping over.' And even if he were, I wouldn't have him there with the kids over. You should know that. He's just coming over for supper, and he may stay through the video."

"Okay. No scary videos, okay?"

"Okay. No Stephen King. No Harry Potter. Wow, your kids are growing up so deprived."

"Good. I hope to keep it that way."

"See you in the morning. I go to work at three in the afternoon, so you can come get the kids any time before that."

"Gottcha. You have breakfast food?"

"Sure. Wine coolers and Cheese Crunchies. That sound like enough food groups for you?"

"How about oatmeal and bananas?"

"How about eggs and toast?"

"Deal. And Rosie, be sure Turner feeds Tramp before you go, and let's him outside to go potty. Then put him in the garage so he can get out of the rain if he has to, but he can still go outside when he needs to."

"Okay. That forty pounds of canine fuzz has a better life than lots of kids."

"He's been part of the family for so long, he thinks he is one of the kids."

"See you tomorrow," Rosie said. Before she hung up, Matrina heard her tell Michelle and Turner, "I got ya sprung from the warden. You can swim at my place, and we can stay up all night and watch videos and eat junk food." Matrina heard the shrieks of delight from her children, shook her head in defeat, and punched "end send" on her cell phone. An hour later, the red-haired cashier had several pennies switched from one cup to the other by the register. Matrina would guess perhaps twenty pennies had made the trip.

The waitress presented Matrina with her black folder, and Matrina put a Visa card into the folder and returned it to the waitress. The adding machine tape stapled to the guest check screamed twenty-seven dollars and thirty-two cents. George will frown at that. She should have passed on the coffee. Three bucks a cup. Oh, well, that's next week's problem when she turned in her expense account.

Matrina scanned the room for someone who ate a meal for which she knew the price. She spotted a young man two tables over. He had a grouper sandwich and a Coke.

Matrina did the math for the sandwich and the drink, added the tax and lingered at her table as she dug in her purse for her tube of lipstick. The waitress brought the guest check to the young man, he gave her a twenty and a ten, and the waitress took the payment back to the cashier.

The cashier rang up the sandwich and the drink. The amount should have been twenty-three-thirty-nine. She rang up eighteen thirty-nine. A penny passed from one cup to the other. So for sure each penny would be worth five bucks.

At that moment, Frank Lowell, the restaurant manager, came to the cash register from the back room. He walked behind the cashier and touched her waist as he passed her. She looked over her shoulder and smiled at him.

He reached over her and checked the pennies in the one cup. He put the cup back in its place and returned to the back room.

Triple hhhuuummmmmmmmm.

Chapter 6

All afternoon that same day, Matrina sat in the parking lot of the Trade Winds and watched the clientele come and go. She watched the limousine shuttle from the Holmes Beach Marina bring wealthy yacht owners from their castles-on-the-sea to the Trade Winds to enjoy a perfect prime rib or the catch of the day. Among all these customers, an air of frivolity and unashamed wealth framed their enjoyment of the American dream.

The Trade Winds shift changed at three P.M. all week. From the employees who came and left, this shift change appeared to include everyone, waitresses and kitchen help. The redheaded cashier did not leave, however. She evidently worked from the lunch shift through the dinner shift every day.

Matrina took out her yellow legal pad and made note of how many waitresses and kitchen help changed out at three P.M. She figured most employees thought life at the Trades Winds would be a bowl of cherries. Their slumped shoulders and shuffled steps belied this hope.

The restaurant closed at nine. Matrina planned to make another meal run back inside around seven, if not for food, certainly for coffee. At that point, she should have concrete evidence on the under ringing of sales and the great penny caper. She needed to have something solid on paper for George early this coming week.

The afternoon shift seemed to provide a complete change in waitresses. No one would recognize her. She doubted the cashier would take note of her. As insurance, she would remove the white jacket and the purple scarf, pull the lavender blouse outside of her trousers and put her hair up in a scrunchy.

Matrina cranked the van to provide a little air while she waited. She parked in a crowded section of the parking lot so she wouldn't be noticed. She checked her watch. She needed to report to George. He wanted communication from her every day. Matrina hauled her cell phone out and dialed George at home.

"Hi, Sarah," Matrina said to George's wife who answered. "Is his royal majesty at home?"

"Hi, Matrina. Yes. Let me summon him from his royal television set."

"Thanks."

Moments later. "Hi, Matrina," George said. "Everything going okay?"

"Oh, sure. I'm here sitting on the Trade Winds, out in the parking lot. I did another internal evaluation earlier, and I'm going back in for a further look see around seven. Then I plan to do another check on their closing system.

"Right now, I haven't come up with anything that will fly, but maybe I will be the end of the evening. I know the cashier is under ringing sales, but she has to validate the guest checks, so I have to figure out how she's overcoming that little hiccup. I'll send you an e-mail when I get home."

"Good girl. I'll look for it in the morning."

"George, speaking of morning, tomorrow is Monday and the restaurant here is closed, but I need to drop by the office and speak to you about something."

"Okay. I'll be there. What is it?"

"Did John tell you he got another threatening letter?"

"No. He got another letter?"

"Yes. Did the FBI lab come up with anything on the first letter?"

"Actually, they did. I'll explain it to you in the morning when you stop by. I don't know what it means, but there is something. I'll have them check out this new letter as well."

"Good. Not only that, but I guess he told you about the body in his backyard?"

"Body in the backyard? Someone found a body in his backyard?"

"Yeah. I can't believe he hasn't told you about it. It's been a couple of weeks now."

"This is a joke, right?"

"Afraid not. A genuine, bona fide, for-real, dead body."

"What made anyone even look?"

"My sister, Rosie, has this new fellow, and he's a cop in Sarasota, and he had his cadaver dog with him, and he tied the dog up in John's backyard, and the stupid dog dug up a body."

"Rosie's cop boyfriend brought a cadaver dog to a backyard party..."

"Actually, he had picked the dog up from the vet, and he lives in Sarasota. So, if he had to take the dog all the way home, and then come back to John's in Bradenton, the bar-be-cue would have been half over. So, he decided to just tie the dog in the backyard until he was ready to go home. He asked John; John said okay; end of story."

"You sure you're not making this up?"

"I wish I were. And you know John. He's not taking any of this seriously. He should have called you right away so you could look into all of this. Especially now that he's received this second threatening letter."

"You know, you could stop by John's tonight after the restaurant closes and get the letter and bring it with you in the morning."

"Good idea," Matrina said. "In fact I already asked him if I could do just that, and he said, 'Fine.'"

"And you say he still thinks all this is just a prank?"

"Yes."

"Including the body?"

"Well, no, that's for real. Even he's got to know that."

"But the body has no connection to John, right?"

"Actually, there is a connection."

"John knew the dead guy?"

"Yeah. It's some guy who went to his church. The man appears to have been shot, and John has this gun collection. He knew the guy, and they didn't get along, and that's probably not good. But you know John. Everything's beautiful, and all's right with the world."

"Why didn't they get along?"

"The guy was a deadbeat. Borrowed money from John and never paid it back. Hardly a motive for murder."

"No, but these days, anything goes. He needs to check into how he stands on this issue. I'll see if I can rain on his parade."

"Thanks, George. And I don't want to invade John's life, but I think we need to launch an effort to find out what's the deal on the dead body, and also find out where that would-be Disney bomber is right now, and if he could be involved in sending these threatening letters. I don't suppose there's any connection between the letters and the body, but both issues need to be resolved."

George's sigh could be heard over the connection. "I don't like the sound of any of this. I wonder if the letters and the body could be connected."

"I don't know, but if you wanted to mess up a guy's life, nothing would do it better than getting him involved in a murder. Especially if you could make him a suspect."

"The body and the letters can't be connected because the body was found before the Disney thing happened."

"True."

So, John's got a double-fronted war going on. And for him to be a suspect in a murder is laughable."

"I would say so, but then you and I know him better than the police do."

"And the letters, you think they're connected to the Disney incident?"

"That would be my guess, since they both refer to terrorism issues."

"Do they even know if the body was a murder victim for sure? Maybe the guy died of natural causes."

"That's possible. But people hardly ever shoot themselves and then bury themselves in someone's backyard."

"That's true. They're sure the victim was shot?"

"I don't know. That's what everyone was saying, that he had a hole in his head. I didn't look that closely at it when they removed the body. But somebody probably knows by now. Think you could find out?"

"Probably. Let me call in a few favors. I'll let you know in the morning if I do any good. And Matrina?"

"Yes."

"Thanks for coming to me with all this. John hasn't said a word, but somebody needs to be watching his back. He's just too trusting."

"Yes. For an ex-cop, I find that amazing."

"Little Falls, New York, isn't exactly the crime capital of the world. He probably didn't run into enough gross stuff to harden him."

"Yes, that's probably it. Well, see you in the morning."

"Okay. Don't work too hard."

"You'd be better off telling me not to eat too much. Wait 'til you see my expense account. You should see the prices I'm paying for the food I'm eating in this place."

"Go to MacDonalds. Take a doggy bag into the Trade Winds. Order coffee to go with your doggy bag."

"Coffee's three bucks a pop."

"Order water."

"Right, George. That wouldn't make me look obvious or anything."

"Okay, order water with ice and lemon."

"Good-bye, George. See you tomorrow." Matrina clicked on "end send" and put her cell phone back into her purse.

* * *

As the sun waltzed over the water-soaked horizon, and the oven-baked

49

breeze faded to a tepid flutter, Matrina left her van and walked once again into the Trade Winds. Once again, an island-attired girl with black hair to her waist greeted her.

Matrina requested a table by the window, with full view of the cash register, before the hostess had a chance to lead her to an obscure table in a corner. The hostess placed two menus on the table since Matrina had once again invented her phantom guest.

The agenda called for one action. Watch the little ole red-haired gal. Matrina needed to figure out how the cashier validated the guest checks and pilfered under rung money before she wound up on a diet of peanut butter sandwiches in the van to keep King George happy.

The menu presented the usual twenty-dollar grouper sandwich, among other items, and a side salad at four-ninety-nine. The side salad would do and coffee.

Matrina placed her order and feigned a look out over the Gulf as she watched the cash register from the corner of her eye. The system never changed. Bring the batch of guest tickets to the register. The cashier would add items on the ticket on the adding machine, staple the tape to the ticket, ring up the guest check, validate the guest check and spindle it. Throughout this procedure, pennies would drift from one cup to the other on either side of the register.

Twice in the hour, the cashier made a quick run into the ladies' room. Upon her return, she continued to process tickets. She ran adding machine tapes and stapled them to guest checks. She did not ring up these tickets, or validate them. Why? After she stapled the tape to the ticket, she spindled them. Why did she run adding machine tapes on guest checks, staple the tape to the ticket, spindle them and not ring them up? Strange.

"More coffee?" the waitress said to Matrina, poised with the pot over her cup.

"Please," Matrina said. "Say, I have a question."

"Okay."

"Do you know the cashier there?"

"Kind of. She's from the Trade Winds up by Regetta Pointe. She's been here a couple of weeks for training."

"She looks familiar to me. I was wondering if she might be the same person I knew from my hometown."

"She's from Las Vegas. She used to work in the change room at Circus Circus out there. Is she ever quick with her hands," the chatty waitress said.

"You ought to see her count money. You can hardly see her fingers move. And she can sort the bills on the fly. It really is awesome. I've seen magic acts where the magician's hands aren't that fast."

"Really? How interesting. Well, I thought I might know her. Do you know her name?"

"Kiran Kirkland. Do you want me to tell her you'd like to speak with her?"

"No. I'll just pop up and surprise her as I leave," Matrina said. "Thanks."

So, she used to work in a change room in Las Vegas. And she has hands that fly faster than those of a magician. Now isn't that an interesting skill to have mastered. Wonder if she can appear to put money into the drawer or spindle tickets when in reality she could stash them in those deep pockets she has in her skirt.

Matrina sipped her coffee, and watched the cashier. The cashier appeared to make one of her casual trips to the ladies' room, and Matrina followed at a safe distance.

Once inside the ladies' room, Matrina noticed the cashier sat in one of the stalls. Her full skirt brushed the floor above her shoes. A sound came from the stall that Matrina could not quite recognize, although her mind told her she had heard that sound before, a clicking sound, followed by a rustle of paper. Click, rustle, click, rustle, click, rustle...

After about ten repetitions of this sound, paper would crumple and the toilet would be flushed. The cashier rose to her feet and walked out of the stall. Matrina entered another stall so she would be out of sight when the cashier left. The red-haired girl left the ladies' room, and no evidence of water running or hand washing in the sink could be heard.

Matrina left the ladies' room and returned to her table and her coffee. The cashier added up guest checks on the adding machine, and stapled the tapes to the tickets. Then she hunched forward as if to hide her actions from the video with her body and spindled the tickets without ringing them up.

At that moment, a stack of black folders arrived at the cash register, and the cashier began to ring up and validate the new guest checks. Matrina watched the action, and then the scheme became clear.

The cashier did not spindld all of the tickets. When she rang up a ticket that prompted her to move a penny from one cup to the other, she moved her fingers as if to slip the ticket on the spindle, but the ticket did not slide into place. The cashier made a deft movement toward her pocket. Matrina's guess would be the ticket slipped into the deep pocket. Why? The cashier did this with several guest checks. More strange behavior.

This movement had to perk in Matrina's mind, and then the pieces clicked, clicked, clicked into place, like pieces of a Rubik's cube. Matrina had heard this sound often at ACS. Franny produced this sound when she pulled staples from paper with a staple puller.

So, the cashier pocketed the under rung guest checks. Since she tracked these sales with the pennies, the tickets could be altered, and leave extra cash in the register for her to remove at the end of the day.

These tickets would have a stapled adding machine tape in one corner that proclaimed one amount, but the validated amount would not match the tape. She would have to remove the old adding machine tape, alter the tickets to whatever had been actually validated, and staple the new tape to the corner. She would simply cross out an item of food, change it to an item of food that matched the new dollar amount, an "eight" could become a "three," a "five" a "zero," a "seven" a "two," and no questions would be asked.

Matrina paid her bill and walked outside into the humid July evening. The incessant breeze off the Gulf blew at her blouse and her hair.

* * *

Matrina's watch said eight-thirty. She knew she had to sit in her van until nine. When they shut down the outside lights, she walked up to the front of the restaurant and peered in through the front windows. Her station near the front glass doors would be safe since no outside lights blared to give her position away.

The shut-down mode kicked itself into high gear. The waitresses vacuumed floors, filled salt and pepper shakers, cleaned windows and wiped the chairs down.

Kiran Kirkland removed the money from her drawer and counted the bills in each denomination. She jotted the figures down on a yellow form. Her hands moved with skill, and any bank teller would be hard pressed to match her dexterity.

She stopped in the middle of the count and took the pennies from the cup on one side of the register and appeared to count them. Then she dumped the pennies back into the cup on the other side of the register. Kiran seemed to do this with her body in front of the camera. She completed the count of the bills, tapped them on the counter, put a rubber band around them and placed them in a zippered bag, all very fluid, very rapid, very slick. If she kept any of the bills out, Matrina didn't catch it. But as swiftly as her fingers flowed over the bills, she must have manipulated the money faster than the naked eye could record.

Matrina returned to her van and watched the rest of the nine o'clock closing procedure. The employees filed out the front door once again, somber and weary. They trudged home to houses they had no time to clean and cranky children who should have been in bed hours ago.

All except Kiran. She came through the front door about nine-twenty, and she had a bounce to her step and tossed her long red locks in the wind. She lingered by her red Acura and pretended to unlock it. It had to be pretense, as Rosie could have picked the lock and hot-wired the engine in the time it took Kiran to get her key into the door.

Then from behind the cashier, Frank Lowell, the restaurant manager, appeared. He grabbed Kiran around the waist and extracted a quiet giggle from deep within her. Kiran turned within the circle of his arms and kissed him, long and deliberate, her arms entwined around his neck. They embraced for several moments after the kiss, and whatever he whispered into her ear brought the quiet giggle to her lips once again. The man patted Kiran on the rear, and she got into her car. She cranked the engine, and he got into his white BMW. She followed him out of the parking lot. They stayed a car-length apart down Gulf Drive until Matrina saw the taillights disappear.

Matrina pulled around the back of the empty parking lot to see if any suspicious boxes or containers could be spotted. These might be left for pickup in the middle of the night. She noted the trash container parked in the far corner of the lot that was made of wire. It had a few white plastic garbage bags in it, but the bags appeared to contain garbage, nothing more.

Well, come Tuesday, this case will slide to its logical conclusion. The evidence had mounted, and things didn't look good for Kiran. The solution had jelled, and come Tuesday, Matrina would be able to dump Frank Lowell into the mix. She needed to understand his game plan, and another day of concentration on him should reveal it.

Her watch said quarter to ten, and Matrina pulled out of the parking lot and headed to John's. She wished the day hadn't left her so sweaty, so tangle-haired, so brain dead. But she had to get the new letter, exchange a few pleasantries with John, and then she'd be free to drive home to a bath of lavender bubbles, a glass of warm milk and another evening of non-stop Nick at Nite.

Chapter 7

John stood in the open doorway of his home as Matrina came up the walkway.

"Hie thyself into yon castle, fair maiden," he said. He made a gracious bow, and Matrina chuckled and walked past him into the house. A tiny black and white long-haired Chihuahua barked at her as she entered the living room. He looked like a tiny yak with hair down to the floor.

"And you must be Oreo," she said to him. She tried to stoop to pet him, but he backed away from her and continued to bark.

"You're a stranger," Dee-Dee said from the dining room table. "He'll have to get to know you, and then he'll like you. Right now, he's our watch dog, and you're a stranger." Dee-Dee sat before a Sequence card game board on the table, and it appeared she and John were in the middle of a game.

"Okay," Matrina said, "someone should get him a mirror so he can see how much he's capable of watching. I think he's overshooting the runway a little bit here." She straightened up, and Oreo hunkered down and watched her with suspicion.

"What are you playing?" Matrina said. She walked into the dining room.

"Sequence," John said. He followed behind her. "It's a great game. Dee-Dee and I are at it tonight, but it's simple enough that even the boys can play."

"Neat," Matrina said. "How does it go?"

"You get cards," Dee-Dee said. She showed Matrina her hand. "And the board has all the pictures of the cards on it, and you find a place to put a chip on a card that you have in your hand, and when you get five chips in a row, that's a sequence."

"And two sequences wins the game," John said. He pulled a chair out for Matrina to sit down.

"Sounds easy enough," Matrina said.

"It's not as easy at it looks," Dee-Dee said. "And when the boys play, we do teams. It's my brother, John, and I against Dad and Matt."

"Yes," John said. "And we keep score for a month, and the losers have to buy the winners a Dairy Queen."

"Wow," Matrina said. "Cards and gambling. I'm shocked."

"Let's table this game for tonight," John said to Dee-Dee. "We'll finish up tomorrow."

"Okay, Dad," Dee-Dee said. She got up and kissed her father good-night. She hugged Matrina, which took Matrina aback. "Good night, Mrs. McCoy. Good to see you again."

Dee-Dee walked down the hall to her bedroom, and Matrina could hear the bedroom door close. "She's such a mannerly young lady," Matrina said.

"Let's hope it lasts," John said. "I'm not sure how long Dee's influence will stay in her mind."

"You have Mrs. Gunthrey. That should reinforce whatever training Dee was able to give her."

John nodded and moved the playing board to a corner of the dining room table. "That letter is on my desk, if you want to get it," he said. "And you don't want coffee or soda? Just water?"

"Yes, water is fine."

Matrina walked down the carpeted hallway to John's den. She looked through the piles of papers on John's desk and retrieved the new threatening letter. Once again, black crayon written on a piece of paper pulled from a spiral notebook glared up at her. Once again, black crayon with John's address wandered across the envelope, and once again a flag stamp sat in the right hand corner as postage. She read the letter. It said: "You are not paying attention. Don't stay here until you are missing Dee-Dee. Once she is wearing a burqa, you will not be able to find her."

Matrina held the page by one corner, and felt her heart accelerate as she read the words. She put the letter and its envelope into an empty file folder.

Before she left the den, Matrina noticed the picture of a very pretty, slender young woman in a pale pink organdy dress in a silver frame on the edge of John's desk. The young woman fought a prevailing breeze, one hand on her billowing skirt, the other hand trying to corral a tangle of long auburn curls. There was a childish giggle on her lips, and a look of adoring love in her eyes. She wore high heels, and a picture hat sailed away behind her.

Dee, Matrina thought. No doubt, this was Dee. He has her framed in a silver frame, and it's the only picture on his desk. She's so pretty, and so sweet, and looks so kind, and so gentle. No wonder he misses her so much. Matrina had trouble drawing herself away from the picture. How could someone so lovely be so dead? How could Mike be dead? What kind of a stupid world has us captive like this anyway? When she was this tired, her negative thoughts seemed to take over her mind with more ease.

Matrina carried the file folder out of the office and returned to the dining room.

"This must be it," she said to John.

"Yes, that's it. What do you think?"

"I think you'd better hie thyself and thy offspring to yonder castle in upstate New York and stay there, lest this fate come upon thee."

"Well, offspring, anyway. I told you, they leave Friday."

"George said to bring it in tomorrow and he'll have a check run on it. He said they did find something on the first letter."

"Really? What?"

"He didn't tell me on the phone. Didn't want to run up my cell minutes. You know George. He'll tell me tomorrow when I report in."

"How's your investigation going?" John put a glass of ice water on the table, and Matrina sipped from it but did not sit down. She wanted to get out of here and home, the quicker the sooner.

"The manager, the dude who hired us says his profits are down, yet his business is up. The business part appears to be true. So why are his profits down?"

"You've been sitting surveillance all week. What's your guess?"

"My money's on this cute little red-haired cashier who looks like she's using that old trick of tracking under-rung sales with marching pennies."

"That's been done to death, but I guess it still works."

"But there's a huge question in my mind about that."

"What?"

"There's closed circuit video. There's a camera aimed at the register. The restaurant manager is no doubt the one who mans this, and that would mean he would pick up the actions of the cashier. Why hire ACS for an investigation that is so obvious? He could watch the tape, bust the cashier, and solve the problem. What's this really all about? And then there's another issue. He's playing footsy with the cashier."

"So is that why he's letting her slide?"

"If so, why hire us? I keep going round and round and round with this. I know she's tapping the till, and the boss knows she's tapping the till, and they have this little thingy going on the side. So, all in all, what's the bottom line?"

John knitted his brow and drummed his fingers on the back of the dining room chair. "One thought comes to mind," he said. "Maybe he wants to know how good she is at this till-tapping escapade. He hires you to catch her, if you can. If you can't, then he knows she's good to go and do this little number somewhere else."

Matrina looked at John, and her tiredness faded. She gulped her water and coughed over it. "Oh, John," she said, "you may have hit the nail right on the head. The Trade Winds is a corporation of fourteen restaurants up and down the Florida west coast. They're head quartered in St. Pete. Some guy named Raymond Willard is CEO, more commonly known as 'RW.'"

"Okay, so?" John sat down in the dining room chair. He drank cold coffee from the cup that had been there from his card game with Dee-Dee.

"This cashier, Kiran Kirkland, is in training from another restaurant in the chain. I got that information from a waitress who seemed to know the system. Maybe the manager of this restaurant on Anna Maria is setting her up to skim money from the other restaurants in the chain, once he's sure she's good enough to get away with it at his restaurant."

"Not a bad idea," John said. "She puts extra money in the cash register that she tracks with the pennies, and makes up for it by altering the guest checks. But how does she do that? Do you see her with a pen changing numbers on tickets at the register?"

"Not at the register," Matrina said. "But she pulls the adding machine tapes that add up the guest checks off the tickets in the ladies' room. And five will get you ten she alters the tickets there. Then she reruns the adding machine tapes, and the new tapes match the prior validation where she under rung the sale." Matrina could barely contain her excitement. "That's it. Oh, John, you've supplied the missing piece to the puzzle. This clown is training her to tap the till at other Trade Winds restaurants."

"Not any more," John said. He smiled in amusement. "You just busted her butt."

"No, you just busted her butt, but I'll get the credit for it. That works for me."

"Glad to be of service. You'll have to find out if the same system works at other Trade Winds restaurants."

"I already planned to check out the one that's on the way to Sneads Island, near Regatta Pointe. That's the restaurant the cashier is supposed to be from. It's bigger than the restaurant on Anna Maria, so there's probably more action there."

"Probably."

"The girls at Anna Maria all dress in tropical island costumes, and have long, straight black hair, but this flaky cashier has long red hair and dresses in a tube top and a full skirt. I'll see how they dress up at the Trade Winds near Regatta Pointe."

"Sounds like you have a plan."

"I'll run it all past George tomorrow, and if he thinks I have a plan, then I can go with it. Thanks again, John. I'm not sure I would have thought of that angle on my own."

"Sure, you would have. Your brain is just in overdrive tonight."Matrina walked toward the front door. She wrapped the second threatening letter in a tissue and put it down in her purse. "This goes to George tomorrow as well."

"Good." John followed her to the door.

"Well, good night," Matrina said. She stood in the opened doorway. Oreo sat on the couch and continued to watch her, however now he was silent about it.

John put his hands on either side of her face, and his lips touched hers in a gentle kiss. Matrina felt a charge of electricity surge through her body. Emotions she thought were permanently dead sprang to life. She closed her eyes and wanted the kiss to last longer.

"I'm sorry," John said. He cleared his throat and shook his head. "I don't know what's the matter with me. That was out of line."

"No, it wasn't" she said. She spoke in a whisper. She lowered her eyes to the carpet, afraid of what he might see in them if she met his gaze. She leaned toward him and kissed him on the cheek. Then she fled from the doorway and the house and sped down the Trail to the safety of home and lavender bubbles.

Chapter 8

The next morning, Matrina walked through the front doors at the Apex Cyberspace Security office. She awoke from a good night's sleep, the result of a long soak in lavender bubbles and the droning of Nick at Nite. John's kiss simmered in the background of her mind like the wallpaper on her computer screen.

"Hi, Franny," Matrina said. Since the kids were at Rosie's overnight, she felt the impact of the empty house, and she longed to speak face-to-face to another human being. Franny presented a port in the storm.

"Hi, Matrina," Franny said. "Coffee?"

"Yes, please. Could you bring it back to George's office?"

"Sure. I think he's waiting for you."

"Good. At least, I hope that's good. You never know with George."

"Ain't that the truth," Franny said. She ambled down the hallway to the kitchen.

Matrina stopped at the copy machine and made a copy of the second threatening letter. She folded the copy and put it in her purse, along with the copy she had made of the first letter.

"Hi, George," Matrina said. She accepted the ceramic cup of coffee from Franny on her way through the door.

"Coffee, George?" Franny said. She hung onto the door frame as she spoke.

"No, thanks, Franny," George said. "I'm coffeed out. Hi, Matrina."

"So, here's the second letter," Matrina said. She sat in the chair in front of George's desk and passed him the paper. "See? It's torn out of a spiral notebook, like the first one, and it's written in black crayon, like the other, and the envelope has a flag postage stamp on it, like the other." She passed the envelope to him as well.

"Hum," George said. He handled the letter and the envelope with thumb and forefinger, and held them by the corners. "I'm sure there will be no fingerprints, like the first, but just in case…" George laid the letter down on his desk and handled it no further. He read the words:

"You are not paying attention. Don't stay here until you are missing Dee-Dee. Once she is wearing a burqa, you will not be able to find her."

George read the words again, and his brow furrowed into tiny creases. He shook his head.

"I thought the first one was perhaps just a hoax, but now, with this, I'm not so sure. What do you think?"

"I'm not sure either. What would be behind sending these to John? If the sender is that Christopher O'Brien from the bomb threat at Disney, what would be his purpose? John messed up the goal of bombing at Disney. That's a done deal. Why would they want him to move? That's what these letters say, move or pay. It's not like John is plugged into al Qaeda and knows what they're next move would be."

"That's my question, too," George said. He got up and adjusted the blinds behind his desk, which emitted the brilliant eastern sunlight that reflected off his desk set and made the letter difficult to read. George always messed with the blinds. Matrina wondered why he didn't leave them closed when he left at night and be done with it.

"You said the FBI found something on the first letter that was interesting?" Matrina said. She sipped her coffee and crossed her legs. She wore an older pair of Levis and a light blue shirt. Mike's wedding band bounced on her chest tethered by the single gold chain.

"Yes," George said. He opened his brief case.

George wore a starched and ironed yellow sport shirt and pressed khaki trousers. Matrina always marveled at the effort Sarah put into George's clothes. He always looked pressed and fresh, evidence of Niagra starch and a steam iron. He took the first letter out of a file folder he removed from his briefcase.

He flashed the letter toward Matrina. "No fingerprints, of course," he said. "No surprise there. No fingerprints even on the envelope or the stamp. No DNA on the flap of the envelope. The moisture used to seal the envelope was evidently a sponge soaked in normal city water. Plenty of chlorine, lots of fluoride."

"Well, the lack of evidence tells us something," Matrina said. She put her half-full coffee cup on the floor beside her chair. "Whoever did this knew what they were doing. They knew not to leave fingerprints, anywhere, or DNA. They don't live in the country. The moisture to seal the envelope comes from city water, not well water. Would people in al Qaeda be up on all that kind of stuff?"

"Probably," George said. "There was a clue that they didn't think about, however."

"Really?" Matrina almost floated from her chair with enthusiasm. And she knew that George would let her twist in the wind, for as long as she would allow, which wouldn't be much longer. The clock ticked away at her patience.

"Yes, and I'm not sure what it means, but it's all we've got."

"So, what?"

"It's vague, and I'm sure they didn't know they left this clue behind."

"What? What?" She motioned with her outstretched hands for George to give it up.

"It's not something that can be detected with the naked eye. It took lab instruments to discover it."

"George, are you going to tell me what it is, or just dangle it out there and have me play twenty questions?"

George smiled. "The dangling and the twenty questions appeal to me," he said, "no contest. But I won't get any work out of you today if I don't tell you. You'd just launch a great quest and figure this thing out on your own."

"Probably."

Silence. She settled back in her chair. She could wait him out. She'd done it before.

"Do I need another cup of coffee for this?" she said. Her tone remained sweet and soft.

"No," George said. He dug deeper into the file folder and retrieved a printout of the lab report. He passed it over to her.

"Thank you," she said. The sweet demeanor remained prevalent in her tone. She flipped the paper in a fanning gesture and read the words. "Oh, George," she said. Excitement broke through and overshadowed the sweetness. "This is good. This is a really good break, isn't it?"

"I don't know," George said. "What does it mean?"

"I'll have to think about it," she said. She read the report again. The report said the numerals two-three-nine appeared faintly on the paper beneath the black crayon. Apparently, before the writer wrote the note, the numerals two-three-nine had been written in a large, scrawling hand that covered half the sheet on the page above. And these numerals had been etched into the page beneath, and were still there when that page became the basis for the letter, not visible to the naked eye, but visible to evidence equipment.

"Two-three-nine," Matrina said. "What do you think? A safe combination? A safety deposit box? A storage box at an airport, bus station?"

"A PIN number for an ATM card?" George said. "I've been running the possibilities."

"No. I think PIN numbers have to be at least four digits."

"Okay, a date, February 3, year ending in nine? A time sequence, two hundred thirty nine days from when...the attempted bombing at Disney? Then another attempt will be made somewhere else?"

"Maybe. How about two hundred and thirty-nine days into the year. That would be late August, early September?"

"Good," George said. "We'll just have to make a list of all the possibilities and start checking them out when we don't have anything else to do. We still have to pay the bills at ACS, you know."

"Yes, George, I know that," Matrina said. "But at least, we have a lead." Matrina handed the report back to George, and he put it back into the file folder and back into his briefcase.

"It would seem so. Give it some thought, run it past John, and we'll see what we can come up with."

"Okay. It has to be important because the person wrote it down so he wouldn't forget it."

"True. So, how are you doing at Trade Winds?"

"I've got some ideas, nothing to take to the bank, but by tomorrow, I should have something concrete. What does this manager look like?"

"Frank Lowell? Tall, late thirties, early forties, clean cut, nice guy, drives a white BMW."

"Uh, huh, "Matrina said.

"Why?"

"Just curious. But that tracks. And he's our client?"

"Yes. He wants to know why his profits are suddenly down. Sales are up, but he keeps buying the same volume of food and drinks. The Trade Winds is a corporation, and they have about fourteen restaurants and lounges, but he wants to solve this on his own, and not go to corporate with the problem. He's afraid it will look bad on his management record if they have to jump in and solve it."

"Uh huh," Matrina said. "That tracks, too."

"Which means..."

"Oh, nothing. Just me thinking out loud. They're closed today, but I'll be back up there tomorrow. Maybe I'll have a report for you then."

"You logging your hours?"

"Of course."

"And saving your receipts for expenses?"

"Yes." The struggle to keep the sound of exasperation out of her voice failed. "I'm even logging my mileage."

"Oh, good girl. I forgot about that one."

"So, guess I'd better go and claim my offspring before my sister has them diving for gold off the coast."

"Not a bad venture," George said. "Don't be so quick to throw rocks at people who walk to the beat of the different drummer."

"I don't think Rosie walks to the beat of any kind of drummer." Matrina laughed and picked up her empty coffee cup and headed to the door. "Of course, there might be one in her head that none of us knows about."

"See you," George said.

"Later," Matrina said. She left George's office and went to the lounge area and washed her coffee cup. She put it back on the counter, walked past Franny, gave her a discreet wave of farewell and left the office.

Within minutes, Matrina drove over the John Ringling Causeway to Lido Beach and Rosie's condo. The condo proved a little pricey for Rosie's income as a cashier at Winn Dixie, but she wanted to live there. She drove a 1990 Ford Escort, and ate lots of beans and hot dogs in order to manage her tight budget. The living room/kitchen combination in the condo would fit into some people's closets, and the tiny bedroom and tinier bathroom would be smaller than any other room in most people's houses. Closet space, well, what closet space? How about hooks on one bedroom wall?

Michelle and Turner took no notice of the cramped living conditions. They enjoyed the beach, the pool, the recreation room with the computer games and Ping-Pong table and sleeping on the floor in front of the TV in the living room. Life with Rosie meant party-time, nonstop.

When Rosie stayed with them at Matrina's house, there might be pizza and Dairy Queen, complements of their mom, but that didn't compare to time with Rosie, on Rosie's terms, in Rosie's world. They incurred no rules, no lectures and no punishments.

Matrina tried to tell them that life with Rosie twenty-four-seven would bring on plenty of these things, but they never believed that.

Rosie's parking lot loomed ahead, and Matrina parked next to Rosie's white Ford Escort. She noticed Rosie had left the driver's side window rolled down. She made a mental note to ask Rosie if her A/C had blipped out again. Matrina could float her a loan to get it fixed. After all, in Florida air conditioning in one's car could be critical, not optional. The climb up the stairs revealed waves of laughter from the opened windows of Rosie's apartment. Ah, the troops were in camp.

"Yoo-hoo." She called through the screen of the opened door. "The wicked witch of the west is here."

Michelle hurried to unlatch the door and let her mother in. "Oh, Mom," she said, "you're not the wicked witch of the west. How silly."

"Hi, Mom," Turner said. They sat at the small table by the stove, and a boisterous game of pinochle rocked the room. Rosie kept score. "I'm winning," Turner said.

"Great," Matrina said.

"Want to play?" Rosie said. "We can deal you in and play partners."

"Well, maybe," Matrina said. "How much more do you have to go in this game?"

"Probably one more hand," Michelle said. "Turner has just been so lucky. He's been doing really stupid stuff, Mom, and it's been working out for him. I can't believe it."

"That's the way life is sometimes," Matrina said. She hugged Michelle as she entered, and kissed Turner on the top of the head when she got to the table. Then she kissed Rosie on the top of the head as well. Bowls of popped corn sat on the floor by the table, and cans of opened soda sat on the table.

They finished that game, pulled the table away from the wall to make room for Matrina. They started a partners game. Matrina took Turner as her partner, and Michelle paired herself with Rosie.

The breeze that floated through the opened kitchen window fluttered the white lace curtains and blew a few paper napkins across the table. Turner reached down, picked them up from the floor and put them beneath his soda can.

"So, did Andy come by to see you yesterday?" Matrina said. She shuffled the cards and dealt out four hands.

"Of course," Rosie said. She picked up her hand and sorted her cards. "And he's just so cool. Honestly, Matrina, I don't think I have ever been in love before now. I'm just nuts about this guy."

"He's really nice, Mom," Michelle said. She went to the refrigerator and got her mother a can of Diet Coke. "Do you want a can of pop, Aunt Rosie." Michelle spoke with her head in the refrigerator.

"No, thanks," Rosie said, "maybe later." Matrina sorted her hand and smiled at Turner.

"I'll have a can of Coke," said Turner. He put his hand in suits face down in front of him on the table in four piles.

Michelle handed him a can of Coke. "You shouldn't do that, Turner," she said. "People can tell what you have by how many cards you have in each pile."

"They can not." He popped the top on his can of soda.

"Yes, they can. Look you have bunches of cards in those three suits, and only two cards in that one suit. That tells us you're three suited."

"Maybe so, but you don't know what suit I'm out of," he said.

"We'll know after you play one of those cards from those two after you put them in your hand."

"You shouldn't look that closely," Turner said. Indignation shaded his voice.

"Don't worry, Turner," Matrina said. "They won't be able to remember what you play after a few hands. Trust me. It'll be a big blur after a while."

Michelle sat back in her chair with a huff, and Matrina knew that her daughter understood this topic of conversation had ended.

"Andy paid for our video rentals last night," Michelle said. She sighed, and she sorted the cards in her hand, "and he brought us bar-be-cue for dinner. He said we could call him, 'Uncle Andy.'"

"How about that?" Rosie said. "Uncle Andy, no less." A note of triumph rang in her voice.

"Sounds too fast to me," Matrina said.

Rosie popped a few kernels of popped corn into her mouth. She offered the bowl to Matrina, who waved her off. "Michelle," Rosie said, "you will be at least thirty before she lets you even date. You've got quite a row to hoe ahead of you."

Michelle nodded, grimaced and looked at her hand to calculate her bid.

"And you aren't worried about this thing with Andy happening too fast," Matrina said. The bidding in the game began.

"Nope. This is the real thing. I can just feel it," Rosie said. She smiled as she spoke.

"I hope you're right. I would be so happy for you if it turns out to be true."

"It's true," Rosie said. "So, just get used to it. You're going to be a sister-in-law."

"It'll be fun having an uncle who looks like Tom Cruise," said Michelle. "Everyone will think he's a brother or at the very least, a relative of some kind."

An hour later, they heard two sets of footsteps clump up the stairs. Andy and his partner, Kenneth Stephens, appeared at the screen door.

Andy hollered through the screen, "Anybody home?"

"Everybody's home," Rosie said. She got up to let them in.

Andy kissed Rosie when he walked past her, and Kenneth followed Andy and pretended to do the same.

"Watch it, Buddy," Andy said. "This is my girl."

Kenneth laughed. "I keep forgetting," he said. "I keep thinking maybe there's a chance for me to take her away from you, but if not, oh, well."

"She has a sister," Andy said.

"No kidding?"

"Yeah. And here she is. Matrina, this is my partner, Kenny Stephens," Andy said.

Matrina smiled in hello and nodded her head. Kenny Stephens, early forties, black hair that didn't show much gray, tall, filled out his Sarasota Sheriff's Department uniform well stood by the table and studied Matrina with interest.

He looked over at Rosie. "You didn't tell me you had a sister," he said.

"I didn't want you distracted from trying to take me away from Andy," Rosie said. "I have to keep him on his toes, you know."

"That boy's on his toes all right," Kenny said. "No need to worry there. We're just on our half hour lunch break, and he had to beat feet up here to just say Hi to you."

"Good. That's the way I like to keep them," Rosie said, "tired and hungry."

Andy produced a bag of Big Macs and a couple of sodas. He and Kenny sat on the couch and ate their lunch.

"I'm sorry," Andy said, "I didn't know you had company or I would have brought more food. I did bring a hamburger for you, Rosie. I guess you could share it. I didn't even know the kids would still be here."

"Thanks," Rosie said, "but you guys can split it up, I'm sure. We had lunch earlier." Rosie put down her cards and turned to pay attention to her visiting cops.

"Don't stop your game on account of us," Andy said. "We're just stopping by. We have to eat and run. I'll be back tonight. I'll bring dinner."

"It'll have to be late," Rosie said. "I work three to eleven tonight."

"Oh, I forgot that," Andy said. "I'll come by for your dinner break and we can catch some Boston Market. How's that?"

"Great. I'll probably go at six."

Andy nodded in agreement.

Two hands later, the men tossed their remains into Rosie's trash can and left. Andy kissed Rosie good-bye and trudged down the steps.

Kenny flashed his most winning smile at Matrina. "Glad to have met you, Matrina," he said. "Maybe we can double with Andy and Rosie sometime."

Matrina smiled back in a noncommittal way. "Maybe," she said.

"Andy will talk to Rosie, and we'll set it up," Kenny said.

Matrina continued to smile in silence. Kenny followed Andy down the steps back to their squad car.

"I think I know his daughter," Michelle said. She sorted her current hand and checked the score.

"Really?" Rosie said.

"Yes. I think she's in my English class. Her name is Kendra Stephens, and she says her dad works for the sheriff's department. You wouldn't think there would be two guys named Stephens working there. And Kendra could be a name like her dad's."

"That's true, and he's got a daughter in Sarasota High, so it's probably her," Rosie said. "Don't you think it's an omen of some kind, Matrina?"

"What's an omen?" Matrina said. She sorted her hand and put some popped corn into her mouth.

"That Kenny has a daughter in Michelle's class."

"An omen for what?"

"That the two of you have girls the same age."

"And that would mean?"

"That you might have something in common."

"Rosie, I have things in common with almost every man I meet. And I don't go out with any of them. And I'm not going out with Kenny, okay?"

"Okay. Don't get your knickers all in a knot. I think it's neat that he seems interested in you. That's all."

"Kenny seems interested in everything in skirts."

"Or Ralph Laurens."

"Whatever."

"So, dating is out of the question?"

"Yes."

"Until when?"

"Until I say so. I'm still married. My husband just isn't sharing the same planet with me at the moment. That's all." Matrina thought about John's kiss and hoped Rosie could not see what galloped around in her mind.

"Okay. What's trump?" Rosie said.

"Hearts," Matrina said.

"Yes." Turner said with enthusiasm.

"Don't ever go to Vegas, kid," Rosie said. "We're fixin' to get creamed," she said to Michelle, and Michelle nodded in agreement.

Chapter 9

Matrina pulled into the Trade Winds parking lot the next morning, Tuesday. She wore an older pair of Levis and a blue knit shirt with "Go Gators" written on it in orange. The overcast skies threatened rain, and the breeze from the Gulf smelled like fish. Her cell phone summoned her from the bottom of her purse. She parked her Chevy Astro and answered her phone.

"Mom," Michelle said, and Matrina knew this was the continuation of an emotional battle that had begun at home before she left. Michelle did not want Wendy Byrd, a Junior from the University of Miami, who lived with her parents next door to the McCoys, to look in on them during the day throughout the rest of the summer. Michelle made it very clear she wanted to be the baby-sitter in charge.

Matrina had to be strong. She needed to do this. This was too dangerous a world for school-aged children to be home alone at any age. Wendy would look in on the kids. This was not the same as the employment of a baby-sitter, she didn't think.

"Hi, Michelle, "Matrina said. She spoke with a smile in her voice and cut the engine to her van.

"We didn't finish our conversation," Michelle said. Hurt feelings laced her voice.

"Yeah, I think we did," Matrina said. Her tone was gentle and soft. "Wendy isn't a baby-sitter. She's just a mature friend who will look in on you guys to be sure everything is okay. You may even enjoy her. She'll tell you college stories, and she probably knows tons of stuff about makeup and clothes and all the latest music. Turner will probably develop a crush on her. She's really cute."

"I know she's cute," Michelle said, "and I don't care if Turner falls in love with her. I could baby-sit in my own right, and I just don't see why I need anyone to 'look in on me' at my age."

"What?" Matrina could hear Turner's exclamation in the background. "Who am I supposed to be in love with?"

"Michelle," easy does it, Matrina told herself, "if you were baby-sitting, it would be for an evening, or an afternoon, and the children would be quite young. That's different from leaving a teenager your age and a twelve-year-old unsupervised for eight to ten hours all day long. It's just different. She's not baby-sitting. She knows it, and now you know it. She's just making herself available in case there's a problem. That's all there is to it. And it's a done deal, so as long as you plug your blow dryer into my electricity, you'll have to live with it. Sorry, Babe."

Silence came across the cell phone connection. Then a deep sigh.

"All right," Michelle said. "But I don't like it."

"You don't have to like it," Matrina said. "I don't like a lot of things I have to do in life, but I do them because I have to. It's called growing up."

"See you tonight."

"Have a good day."

"Sure." Another sigh came over the connection. And then the ominous click of the connection broken.

Matrina put her head back on her seat and closed her eyes. They're growing up so fast. Why is it always 'on the job training' with parenting? It's never clear if the right decisions are made until it's too late.

The cell phone rang again.

"Shut up," Matrina said to the inside of her purse. She picked up the phone and waited for Michelle to begin round three.

"Are you there?" the male voice said.

"Oh, yeah," Matrina said. She recognized the voice of John Fleming.

"I'm having a little parent/child skirmish with Michelle, and I thought she was ringing me to begin round three. I think we tied in round two, not sure. What's up?"

"Meatballs at Subway, twelve-thirty, Cortez Road, be there."

"My kind sir," Matrina said. The smile in her voice crept over the phone connection, "do you know where I am at this very moment?"

"No. Should I care?"

"I am anticipating my midday repast at the illustrious accommodations of the Trade Winds on Anna Maria, ala ACS. And I should pass on that to gobble a sandwich at Subway?"

"Certainly." John's reply was immediate. "Because Subway has one thing that the hoitsy-toitsy Trade Winds doesn't have."

"And what would that be, my good man?"

"Me."

"Oh, well, if you're going to use cold, calculated logic on me, how can I refuse?" Matrina said. "Twelve-thirty it is."

"Good."

"Hey, John?"

"Yeah?"

"Could I downgrade my meatball sub to one of those low fat jobbers? That sweet onion item is good, or a turkey breast, something like that, no extra oil, no mayo?"

"Sounds boring, but they're your taste buds."

"Thanks. See you in a few."

"Copy that," he said and broke the connection.

After a morning of surveillance at the Trade Winds, Matrina drove back down Cortez Road to Subway at twelve-thirty. Drizzles of rain marked the morning, and she had to run her wipers on low as she drove. She pulled into the parking lot at Subway, killed her motor and her wipers, and got out. She locked her van and walked inside the sandwich shop.

John sat at a table by the window. His red plaid cotton sport shirt testified that Mrs. Gunthrey could still swing a mean iron, and his gray Haggar slacks and black Florsheim shoes screamed with newness. His traditionally cut light brown hair with invading streaks of gray shone of shampoo in the invading sunlight. Two sandwiches and two sodas, one of which was a diet Coke, sat on the table before him. A bag of chips lay on the table from which he munched as he looked out the window into the parking lot.

Matrina stood for a moment and gazed at him. The memory of his lips on hers lingered like a thunderbolt in her mind. She felt like a school girl in her first crush. This had to be too crazy. She still grieved for Mike. How could another man make such an impact on her emotions?

She had to get over this attraction. She had to be careful she did not allow John to look into her eyes and see into her heart. Don't make eye contact. Walk over to the table and be calm. There had been dozens of lunches with this man over the past few months. This was just one more.

She sat down across the table from him. "Mercy," she said, "you look distressed." She noticed his disconnected demeanor. "Are we a bizillion miles away or what?"

"At least," John said. He pushed the chips in her direction. "Rough morning. How's life on millionaire's row?"

"Not bad, actually," Matrina said. She pushed the chips back in his direction and checked her sandwich, smoked turkey, no mayo. She smiled to herself. "I'm getting ready to drop the hammer on these folks. They're both up to something. All I have to do is prove it. That's coming soon."

"Good on you," he said. He sighed and sipped his soda.

"You're so down in the dumps today," Matrina said. She took a bite of her sandwich. "Suppressing crime isn't all that much fun today?"

"No," he said. He took a bite from his sandwich and mopped up tomato sauce that dripped onto the table with a paper napkin. He crumpled the napkin and put it on the table near the window. "Suppressing crime is never much fun. Sometimes I wonder why I bother with it. Sometimes I wonder why you bother with it. Sometimes I wonder why anyone bothers with it. Suppressing crime always rocks somebody's world. No matter how you look at it, someone's going down."

"That's true," she said. She put a little salt on her sandwich. "I tell myself that if I can stop the thieves who steal from other folks, it will let the merchandise and money stay with the rightful owners. You know, the dudes who take the risks in business and are responsible for all the debts."

John nodded. "That's a good philosophy," he said. He gazed out the window and watched the flow of traffic through the parking lot.

"Why are you so preoccupied?" Matrina said.

"I'm sorry," he said. He shifted his eyes in her direction. "I'm a terrible lunch buddy today. I just had a big rumble with a suspicious produce manager, and I'm kind of depressed over it."

"You? A rumble?" Matrina giggled and wiped her mouth with a paper napkin. "I should have sold tickets to that."

"You probably could have," he said. He smiled in spite of himself. "This guy jumped my case, big time, and I was only trying to do my job, checking stuff out, you know, the stuff the suits pay us for doing."

"He got in a huff over security doing its job? That makes him sound a little more than suspicious," Matrina said. She sipped her soda. "That makes him sound downright guilty. Of what, I couldn't say, but guilty of something."

"His name is Vince Haynes, and he's the produce manager at the Publix near here. I know what he earns, and his lifestyle is head and shoulders above that. I was just trying to clarify some things about him. That's all. He got wind of it, and he went postal on me."

"Maybe he's just having a bad day. Maybe his wife is bugging him about things as well. Maybe everyone is asking nosy questions, and it's just making him crazy."

"His wife is what started it all," John said. He popped a couple of chips into his mouth and wiped his fingers on another paper napkin. "Vince drives a Kia to work, conservative car, relatively low-priced, something he could afford on his salary. No big deal. Then this morning, here comes his wife, cruising through the parking lot in a brand new white Lexus. Gold lettering, all the extras. I mean, we're talking sixty grand, maybe more. I almost fell over, right there in the parking lot. Sixty grand. How can he afford that?

"Then I asked around, and the chatter is that he owns a boat also. I'm talking BOAT! Like thirty feet of cruiser, downstairs cabin, too big to moor at the marina at Holmes Beach. I understand the name of the boat is the-*Fly-by-Night*. And he lives on Key Royale."

Matrina raised her eyebrows. "Whoa. They probably require you to drive a Lexus to even look for land on Key Royale."

"Really. That's my point."

"So, why'd ole Vince get on your case?"

"Because he found out I was asking questions about him. He said his finances were none of my business."

"Hum. Sticky situation. Too bad you got caught checking up on him."

"Yeah. The meat manager and the payroll clerk are blabber mouths."

"Wonder why they would bother to tell him you had asked about him?"

"Because being security doesn't help your popularity. They all see us as the enemy. You know that."

"We're above cost and scheduling. That's usually enough to bug most folks."

John nodded his head and took another bite of his sandwich.

"One thing's for sure," Matrina said. She took another bite from her sandwich, chewed it and swallowed it. A chip found its way into her mouth in spite of her reluctance. "If he's living beyond his means, the money is coming from somewhere. And Publix is as good a guess as any."

"That was my first thought, and my last thought, and all my thoughts in between." John finished his sandwich, stood up and gathered their trash and put it into the trash receptacle. Matrina wrapped the last of her sandwich in a paper napkin and added it to the trash. She rescued her soda cup and sipped on it. A gaze out the window revealed two Manatee County Sheriff's Department cars parked next to her van. Their roof lights flashed red and blue around the parking lot.

John walked back to the table from the trash can. "Looky here," she said.

"Hum. Someone in this strip mall must have stopped a shoplifter." John watched the four policemen leave the two cars and walk toward the Subway shop. They entered the shop and walked over to the table where Matrina and John prepared to leave.

"John Fleming?" one sheriff's deputy said.

"Yes," John said. He stood beside the table. Matrina waited for the policemen to explain their presence.

"You are under arrest for the murder of Robert Walker."

John threw up his hands in despair. "Oh, give me a break," he said.

"You have the right to remain silent. Everything you say may be used against you in a court of law."

"Yeah, yeah, yeah," John said with disgust in his voice. "I have the right to an attorney, and if I can't afford an attorney, one will be provided for me. I could recite this Miranda thing backwards."

Matrina patted him on the arm while she kept her eyes on the four sheriff's deputies. "Maybe you shouldn't say anything to these guys right now, John," she said.

"That's right, Sir," one of the deputies said. He prepared to put handcuffs on John. "Better listen to the pretty lady."

"So, how am I supposed to have killed this Robert Walker?" John said. He held out his hands to be voluntarily cuffed.

"You shot him, Sir," the deputy who snapped the cuffs on John's wrists said.

"Let me guess," John said. He walked out of the sandwich shop between the first two deputies, and the other two followed behind. The drizzle had grown to a light sprinkling, and the droplets landed on their heads and their shoulders. "I supposedly shot him with a 1902 American Eagle Luger."

"John," Matrina said. Her tone voiced a definite reprimand. "Please. Don't say anything more."

"If I were going to frame me, that's how I'd do it, with one of my rare guns from my collection; steal it, use it for the murder; sneak it back into my house."

"They did determine that Robert Walker's death was murder, then?" Matrina said to the deputy closest to her. They walked through the strip mall parking lot in the lightly falling rain.

"Yes, Ma'am," the polite deputy said. "Single gunshot wound, back of the head, bullet lodged in the brain."

"Not much imagination there," John said. His voice was tart and sarcastic.

Matrina shot him a menacing look, and he went silent.

"Who can I call for you?" Matrina said to John when they neared the police cars. "Do you know any lawyers?" She followed behind the last deputy in the line.

John sighed. "Yeah," he said. He bent into the back of the sheriff's department police car. "Call Nathan Caldwell. He's a lawyer, goes to church with me. Mrs. Gunthrey will have his number. I might even have it, on my desk in my phone directory."

"Okay," Matrina said. "I'll call him, and I'll tell Mrs. Gunthrey to stay with the kids until you get bonded out."

"Thanks. And Matrina?"

"Yes?"

"If you're going to Regatta Pointe sometime soon, could you please look for the *Fly-by-Night* at the marina? Get the ID numbers off it for me? I wanted to go check it out this afternoon, but I seem to be otherwise detained."

Matrina shook her head in helplessness. "John, forget Publix for the moment. We got serious fish to fry here."

"So, fry up the fish, and dish up the hush puppies. Meanwhile, see if that boat is at Regatta Pointe. Okay?"

"Okay," she said. She watched as they closed the car door behind John. She watched the police cars roll out of the parking lot, and reached into her purse for her cell phone to call Mrs. Gunthrey for the number of Nathan Caldwell.

Her mind sorted out the past few minutes of her life. This Nathan goes to church with John? That's his total credentials? Are those credentials enough?

Chapter 10

As soon as Matrina got back into her van, she called Mrs. Gunthrey. She wanted to call Nathan Caldwell and get him going on John's case as soon as possible, but couldn't get past Mrs. Gunthrey to learn the phone number. The elderly housekeeper would call Nathan herself, and she would do it right now. She said John's arrest appalled her.

Well, the whole situation appalled everyone. But this realization didn't get John off the hook. He had attracted an adversary, big time. Who and why loomed over the situation like night over the sunset.

Could there be a connection between the threatening notes and Robert Walker's murder? Did John have one enemy or two? Why did someone like John have any enemies at all?

Christopher O'Brien would be a likely enemy, since he still maintained his freedom after the Disney incident. And now, Vince Haynes might be another one. Would Vince retaliate if he feared John could wreck his future? All these thoughts danced around in Matrina's head as she drove to Regatta Pointe. She found her destination and pulled into the Trades Winds parking lot.

Wow, she thought, this Trade Winds made the one on Anna Maria look like chump change. She pulled into a larger parking area, in front of a bigger, fancier building, surrounded by more landscaping and wider walkways. She could hardly wait to go inside and see what that had going for itself.

Raindrops filtered through the clouds and splashed the petunias that lined the walk as she got out of the van. Matrina walked down the flower-lined pavement and smelled the sweet odor of freshly mown lawn that surrounded the restaurant. She entered through the front double-glass doors, and what she saw dumbfounded her. She hoped her mouth had not gaped open.

Where the Trade Winds on Anna Maria Island required all the waitresses to look like island maidens, the waitresses here all looked like Kiran Kirkland. They all had long red hair, flowing skirts, tube tops, all pastel colors, bare feet.

Okay, so little Kiran would fit right in here, no problem. No doubt she would be scheduled to score a nice retirement fund for Frank Lowell, and she might pick up a few coins for herself.

Matrina maneuvered the hostess to seat her ten feet away from the register. The comfortable turquoise leather seats against the crisp white linen table cloths and folded white linen napkins screamed elegance. A single fresh red rose towered above a slender crystal bud vase in the middle of the table. Tall-stemmed crystal glasses awaited the inevitable splash of ice water from the young, white-shirted, black bow-tied water boy. Thick turquoise, beige and white marbled carpet showed carpet dents where the chairs had been moved about. The carpet looked new. From the color scheme, Matrina imagined they must have to change it out every six months.

She ordered a cup of coffee and a piece of key-lime pie. George would gag a maggot when he saw she paid eight dollars for a piece of pie, plus three dollars for a cup of coffee. Her scale at home would gag a maggot when she hopped on it tonight after all this dining out. It could be worse. She could have had meatballs for lunch.

Matrina watched the cashier at the register do her job. The system seemed to work the same as on Anna Maria except pennies did not leap from cup to cup at the register, and tickets went on the spindle, not in the pocket. The cashier made no dash to the ladies' room. In fact, no one dashed anywhere, more confirmation that the actions of Kiran Kirkland should generate suspicion. And after suspicion, actions became criminal, but Matrina didn't want to come down on Kiran and incriminate her alone. Matrina wanted to land good ole Frank in the net as well. She couldn't let Frank become the prize fish that got away.

A glance through the wall of glass to her left at the foamy waves of the Gulf that crashed on the rocky shore relaxed her. The shore gave way to the Regatta Pointe Marina where a weather-beaten dock meandered down to dozens of slipped boats. The impending summer storm hung in the clouds and restricted its rain to misty dew.

When the guest check arrived, Matrina paid it and walked outside and down toward the marina. She had never seen so many large, luxurious vessels all in one clump before, and she admired their beautiful craftsmanship. They all displayed highly polished wood, flawless paint, gleaming brass, sparkling windows, and deck furniture that showed no wear to mar the vista.

She scanned the berths and looked for the *Fly-by-Night*, but so many vessels looped their ropes over these tie posts, it could be here, and she might overlook it. Row upon row upon row of very expensive boats sat beside the docks, unlike the Holmes Beach Marina, whose the patrons had tastes that drifted toward sailboats and catamarans.

Matrina walked up and down the docks and checked the names on the vessels, and then it came into view. The *Fly-by-Night* waited two docks away. It danced in the wake of sister boats that churned down the Manatee River from Tampa Bay.

The thirty-foot long *Fly-by-Night* looked like it might be new. Matrina walked around to the dock and copied the ID number from the front of the boat. When she got back to the office, she would have Franny run the ID and find out more about the owner.

For a preliminary surveillance visit, Matrina felt she did quite well, so she returned to her van and left Regatta Pointe before the storm broke.

* * *

An hour later, Matrina walked into the ACS office. She needed to give George the scoop on John's arrest and the update on the great Trade Winds caper. Neither news bulletin would receive applause from George.

"Hi, Franny," Matrina said.

"Hi, Matrina." Franny looked up from her computer. "What's shaking?"

"Me, or at least, I will be once I lay what I have on good old George. Is he in?"

"Yes, he's back in his office. Want some coffee to fortify yourself?"

"No, I guess not." Matrina walked past Franny's desk. "I guess I'll go this cold turkey and see how I fair."

"Your news is that bad?"

"Afraid so. Two doses of bad news."

"Just toss it out there and hit the deck."

"Good idea." Matrina walked past Franny's desk and then returned to her. "Franny," she said. She reached into her purse to find the ID number of the *Fly-by-Night*. "Could you run this ID for me and see what turns up?"

"Sure," Franny said. "Might be tomorrow before I can get to it."

"That's fine. Thanks." Matrina walked away from Franny and down the hall to George's office.

George sat at his desk and sipped from a bottle of water. He pondered reports in a thick file folder. He looked up when Matrina entered.

"Hi, Toots," he said. "You rescue the world for mankind one more day?"

"Hardly. I kind of tossed the world to the wolves, although I did solve the Trade Winds issue."

"Really? Great. We can prepare our report for Frank Lowell, and collect our big bucks. Good job."

Matrina sat down across from George's desk. "No, not good job," she said. "Frank Lowell is one of our bad guys."

"Come on, Matrina," George said. He closed his file folder with an element of harshness. "Why do you keep finding out our clients are the bad guys? How're we going to pay the rent around here if the guys who pay us to work keep turning up on the crooked side of the ledger?"

"Not my fault," Matrina said. She raised her hands in defense and crossed her legs. "I can't help it if the guys who hire us are playing silly games. All I do is investigate. That means lift the lid and see what's there. What's there at the Trade Winds on Anna Maria is rotten to the core."

George took a deep breath and settled back in his high-backed chair. "So, what's the story?" he said. He folded his hands.

Matrina nutshelled the facts for him. He shook his head in frustration.

"So, what's your recommendation? Do we call Frank and say, we solved your case. Too bad you're the crook? How come you hired us to catch you? Did you forget you were the felon?"

"No," Matrina said. "But I do have an idea. The Trade Winds restaurants are a chain, you know. They are owned by the Salt and Sea Corporation; headquarters are in St. Pete. They have fourteen restaurants up and down the west coast, plus a few marinas, and some dive shops." Matrina leaned toward George and hoped she could keep his attention.

"Raymond Willard is the CEO. How about I call him and make an appointment, trot my bones up there and lay all this on him. I could offer to blow Kiran and Frank out of the water. Once Kiran is back to work at Regetta Pointe with her pots of pennies she'll feel safe." George didn't interrupt, so Matrina continued.

"If her application for employment doesn't reflect her Las Vegas background, that pulls Frank Lowell into the picture, as he was the one who got her the job at Trade Winds. In fact, it wouldn't surprise me if he had a little Vegas in his background as well."

"And…" George said. He looked at her with stern eye contact.

"And I could get Mr. Willard to check Kiran's references with Circus Circus in Vegas, and if they say she did work in the change room, and her application doesn't reflect that, hello, we have a winner. Mr. Willard might be really impressed at what we found. And that, George, might lead to a contract with Salt and Sea to run register checks in all fourteen of their establishments, plus whatever else we could arrange in their other ventures. What do you think?"

George rocked back and forth in his chair and rubbed his chin with his fingers.

"I don't know, Matrina," he said. "That sounds a little risky, doesn't it? The contract we have now is with Frank Lowell, on his own. If we go over his head to the corporate headquarters, we risk not getting paid for what we have invested so far."

"And if we don't, George, we risk not landing the contract to do security on the whole Salt and Sea empire. And I, for one, can't prepare a report for Frank Lowell and tell him his little red-haired cutey pie is a thief, and she's in this on her own."

George let that wash over him for a moment. "But you could go to St. Pete and handle this whole thing? Meet with this Mr. Willard? Explain the situation to him? Convince him this might be going on in some of his other restaurants?"

"Sure. No big deal. George, I'm from New York City. I've gone to lots of board meetings when I worked for Wal-Mart."

"You weren't like this a year ago. You were afraid of your own shadow when you first came here."

"I know. Something died inside me when Mike died. But time seems to have healed that wound. My self-confidence seems to have surfaced again."

"Okay. Call this Willard fellow and set it up. You're absolutely certain this is what's going down on Anna Maria?"

"Yes. And it's not just Anna Maria. Frank's sending Kiran back to the restaurant near Regatta Pointe. She's only in training on Anna Maria."

"Okay. Go get 'em, Tiger."

"Thanks, George." Matrina smiled and rose from her chair. "Oh, and one more thing."

"What's that?" He was preoccupied once again. He sipped his water and read his material.

"John Fleming is in jail up in Manatee."

"What?" Full attention now.

"They arrested him this afternoon. We were lunching at Subway on Cortez Road in Bradenton, and the sheriff's department just swooped down and hauled him off."

"What for?"

"Murder One. Robert Walker."

"The guy they found in John's backyard?"

"Yes. They have enough evidence against John to get an indictment."

"How's that possible? What do they have?"

"I don't know for sure. John had me tell Mrs. Gunthrey to call a lawyer, so I guess he'll look into it."

"Oh, good. He knows a good lawyer then?"

"Some guy who goes to their church."

"That's it? Some guy who goes to church with them?"

"I guess so. At least, that's what John said."

"Where'd this lawyer go to law school? How long's he been in practice? How many murder one cases has he handled? How many of them did he win?"

Matrina shrugged her shoulders. "I'll know more when I talk to John again. I'll call up there this evening and see what I can find out. And I'll call Mrs. Gunthrey and find out more about this Nathan Caldwell. That's who the lawyer is."

"Nathan Caldwell?"

"Yes. That's his name."

George pulled a phone book from his top desk drawer. He flipped to the yellow pages.

"There's no Nathan Caldwell listed under the 'Attorneys' section."

"Maybe he's just connected to a law firm where he's not an actual partner."

"Like a junior executive, or an intern."

"Yeah."

"Oh, my," George said. He put his head down on the desk and put his arms over his hair. Then he sat back up. "I'll run up to Manatee tonight and check into this, too. Let me know what you find out, and I'll swap you for what I find out."

"Okay. See you after my trip to St. Pete. I'll call before I leave here and try to get an appointment for tomorrow. I'll tell Mr. Willard it's of the utmost urgency I talk to him."

"Good. Let me know."

Chapter 11

The trip to St. Petersburg the next morning over the Skyway Bridge exhilarated Matrina. She wore her sky blue tailored suit, with a tailored white blouse, Coach shoes and matching purse. She had piled her hair up on her head in a French twist. Lots of mousse and hair spray kept it up there.

When she telephoned Mr. Willard yesterday, he seemed to be interested in what she had to say. When she mentioned Frank Lowell, he became more than interested. He became intense, and he agreed to an appointment this morning at eleven A.M.

Matrina prepared her report on the Trade Winds, Anna Maria Island, and inserted it in a plastic report cover. She put the report in a large white envelope. Words on paper hammered home facts like no other medium.

She parked in the parking garage of the Salt and Sea building in downtown St. Pete and paid her three dollars for the privilege. She figured she could get validated somewhere in the building, but if not, oh, well. It would be item seven on her expense account. She rode the elevator up to the eleventh floor, got out and walked down the mauve-carpeted hallway to Mr. Willard's office.

Ethan Allen furniture upholstered in beige filled the outer office. She introduced herself to the slender receptionist who had long blonde hair and professionally manicured fingernails painted Christmas-candy red.

The receptionist ushered Matrina into Mr. Willard's private office where the mauve carpet got thicker and the furniture more expensive. The upholstery went from beige to blue. She extended her right hand to Mr. Willard for a handshake. He shook her hand and motioned to a comfortable chair in which to sit.

Forty-something Mr. Willard stood five-foot seven, the same height as Matrina. His portly build complemented his balding dark hair and piercing dark eyes enlarged by thick bifocals. Matrina handed him her white envelope that contained her report along with one of her ACS business cards.

She sat back in the comfortable chair, crossed her legs and made sure her conservative skirt stayed tucked beneath her thighs. Womanly wiles could not cloud this case. She had worked hard on this case and had the goods on Kiran Kirkland and Frank Lowell. She wanted credit for her mental effort, not her dedication to *Caribbean Workout.*

Mr. Willard flipped through the report and speed-read through the pages.

"So you think this Kiran Kirkland is tapping the till, and you think that Frank Lowell is knowledgeable of her actions," Mr. Willard said. He gazed at her with suspicion over his thick glasses.

"Yes, Sir, I do," Matrina said. She met his gaze with confidence and ignored the wide-bodied jet that cruised past his large expanse of window on its way to the airport.

"He brought her to us, you know," Mr. Willard said. He closed the report and rocked in his well-upholstered, high-backed desk chair.

"That doesn't surprise me," Matrina said.

"He said she'd be perfect for our facility near Regatta Pointe. She even had her hair dyed red for the position."

"Yes, I noticed that."

"He said he could take a couple of weeks to train her, and then she'd be good to go."

"Did he say how he knew her? Anything about her background?"

"I have her application for employment here in our files," Mr. Willard said. He got up from his chair and pulled a file folder from the top drawer of his file cabinet. He glanced through the dozens of applications for employment and pulled out Kiran's.

"Do you have Frank Lowell's application for employment there as well?" Matrina said.

"Yes. Is there a reason to look into that application, too?"

"It might come in handy," she said. She decided to play the hunch she had nursed all week. Frank Lowell and Kiran seemed to be on a more intimate basis that a two-week acquaintanceship would justify.

"Here they are," Mr. Willard said. He sat down once again and handed the applications to Matrina. She took them and looked them over. She committed both their social security numbers and their previous places of employment to memory.

"There's no reference to Circus Circus in Las Vegas on her application," Matrina said.

"No. It says she came to us from Albertson's in Orlando where she was a cashier."

"Why would she lie about not being from Las Vegas?"

"You're sure Las Vegas is part of her past?"

"That's what the local grapevine says, and it has been my experience that the workplace grapevine can be very valid."

"All her references are from Florida. I don't know how much credence one can place on the local grapevine."

"There is one way to find out," said Matrina. "May I use your phone?"

"Mrs. McCoy," Mr. Willard said. He sat back in his comfortable chair and brushed imaginary dust from the edge of his highly polished desk. "I don't know who you are, or what you hope to accomplish by this visit, but we have a very well-oiled machine here in our administration. Believe me, no one can become employed at any of our establishments without thorough scrutiny. If Kiran Kirkland's application says she has always worked in Florida, there is no way she could have any history in Las Vegas in her background."

Shock rocked Matrina down to her trendy Coach sandals. "So, you're saying I don't have your permission to check out these references." She felt cast adrift in unfamiliar turbulent waters, and she struggled to surface and get back to shore.

"That is correct," Mr. Willard said. His icy tone informed Matrina that this interview had ended. "There is no point in wasting time on checking out things that have already been verified by experts."

Matrina rose from her chair. "Thank you for your time, Mr. Willard," she said. She extended her hand for a parting handshake. "I am sorry my report fell on deaf ears. I feel you will live to regret your decision, but it's your decision to make. Good-bye." She walked out of the office in a daze, past the receptionist who buffed her perfect nails.

Matrina caught the elevator back to the parking garage. She jotted Kiran's and Frank's social security numbers and their declared places of prior employment down on a note pad from her purse. What's this all about?

* * *

Back in her van, before she pulled out of the parking garage, Matrina dialed information on her cell phone and got the number for Circus, Circus in Las Vegas. She dialed the number.

"Circus Circus." A crisp, efficient voice answered the phone.

"Personnel," Matrina said.

"One moment, please," the efficient voice said.

"Personnel." Another efficient voice.

"My name is Matrina McCoy and I'm calling from Apex Cyberspace Security in Sarasota, Florida, and I would like to verify an employment history of a previous employee of yours."

"Certainly. What is the name and social security number?"

"Kiran Kirkland." Then Matrina stated the social security number she read from Kiran's application for employment.

"One moment, please."

"Yes," the efficient voice said. "She worked here from January, 2004, until May of 2005. Her performance was adequate and she is eligible for rehire."

"Could you give me a reference on one more person?" Matrina took a deep breath and hoped her hunch about Frank Lowell's knowledge of Kiran from somewhere in the past had foundation.

"Yes. Just give me the name and social security number."

"Frank Lowell." Matrina read the social security number and held her breath.

"Mr. Lowell did work for us from March, 2004, through January, 2005. He was a dealer. He was dismissed from his position, and he is not eligible for rehire."

"Could you tell me the nature of the dismissal from employment?" Matrina said.

"I'm sorry. That is confidential information. It would be a violation of Mr. Lowell's civil rights to disclose the details of his dismissal to you."

"I understand. Thank you for the information you have been able to pass on to us. We appreciate it." Matrina said. She clicked "end send."

They both worked there. He came here in January, and she followed in May. He got hired as a manager at Trade Winds because he lied on his application, and she got hired as a cashier because he vouched for her. Her application also boasted lies, which no one checked, despite Mr. Willard's assurances.

Frank got her hired in at Regatta Pointe, then brought her to his restaurant on Anna Maria. He taught her how to under ring sales and track the difference in pennies. It would be nothing to pull a hundred dollars a day from the drawer, maybe a hundred and fifty. She could double that in Regetta Pointe.

To verify her conclusion, Matrina dialed Albertson's in Orlando and K-Mart in Tampa and of course, no one ever heard of either one of them. So, what to do about all this? One thing blared across her mind. No way could she throw in the towel, turn in a generic report to Frank Lowell, recommend he fire Kiran, and collect the money he owed ACS for surveillance. No way. She had to bait a trap, catch them both in it and tell George about it later.

One problem loomed before her. Once she snagged her prey, who would care? Where could she go with that information? She'd have to think that one over, and she had until Kiran returned to Regetta Pointe to come up with an idea.

What she could do would be tell Frank that Kiran proved to be squeaky clean, and ACS could find nothing wrong in his organization. Matrina smiled to herself. She would do that right now, unofficially, of course. Couldn't bring George into the picture until all her ducks marched in a row. If she called Frank, he might send Kiran back to Regetta Pointe, and by Sunday, she'd be ripe for the picking.

She dialed Frank on her cell phone.

"Frank."

"Yes. Who is this?"

"Matrina McCoy from Apex Cyberspace Security."

"Yes. How is the investigation going?"

"Not extremely well. We really haven't come up with anything at the moment, but we're still working on it We have plans to attack the problem from another angle. We have cleared all your inside employees, so we are looking at your vendors now. Perhaps there is something going on with their business ethics."

"Yes, yes, that's a good thing to check into. I never know what these guys are doing half the time. They come in the back door and put merchandise in the frig, or on the kitchen floor, we check it all in when we have time, and they get paid, and who knows exactly what's been delivered."

"Exactly. That will begin tomorrow. Then we should have something concrete to show you."

"Okay. Thanks, Mrs. McCoy. I'll see you tomorrow."

One more bridge to burn. She dialed Mr. Willard's office.

"Mr. Willard, Matrina McCoy."

"Mrs. McCoy, I thought I made it very clear our interview was over."

"You did. That's why I'm calling. I must apologize for my incorrect evaluation of the situation at Trade Winds. I had no idea you had such an intricate organization, and that you checked your employees out so thoroughly. I am evidently in error about Kiran Kirkland and Frank Lowell. Please forgive my intrusion on your time."

"Of course, Mrs. McCoy. No problem. Thank you for your concern. Good day."

Click. Problem solved. She had to get Mr. Willard off the scent before he alarmed Kiran and Frank that they fell under suspicion. Matrina hoped she nailed that necessity down with this phone call.

A smile weaved its way to Matrina's lips. This would be fun, until George found out. Then it would be a walk over hot rocks. Meanwhile, Kiran and Frank would coast on her radar screen.

She thought of George. She had to do something to divert him as well, or he might tip her hand before the clock ticked to ready.

"Hi, George."

"Hi, Matrina. How'd St. Pete go?"

"Not bad. George, I wanted to ask you a favor."

"Shoot."

"You haven't mentioned anything to Frank Lowell about what I found at Trade Winds, have you?"

"No. I was waiting for your final report."

"Good. I may have been a little hasty in my evaluation of the troubles at Trade Winds. I'd like another week to round it out. Then we can do a final, complete report to Frank. That sound okay with you?"

"Sure. Glad you're having second thoughts about him. I won't do anything until I get your word."

"Good. Thanks, George."

"When are you going back to Trade Winds?"

"Tomorrow. I'm going to do a vendor search."

"That sounds good. Let me know how it goes."

"Okay." End send.

What to do now? Michelle visited school friends, and Turner had gone to Busch Gardens in Tampa with the family of a friend from his soccer team at school. Both involved spending the night. That meant dinner and TV alone with only the sounds of Tramp's toenails on the marble floor to interrupt the silence.

She had to be a grownup, go home, watch TV, take a long, hot bath and go to bed. No big deal. This had gone on for months and months and months now. Matrina wondered, will the months and months and months ever end? No, they won't. She had to learn to live with it.

Of course, Bradenton loomed between here and home, so maybe it would be nice to stop at John's house and take pizza. That would delay the trip home. She'd better phone Mrs. Gunthrey and see if such a visit would be considered an invasion.

She might even get to meet Nathan, the churchy lawyer. George said Nathan had planned to go before the judge sometime this week and see if he could bond John out of jail. Everyone doubted that would be possible since murder one hung over him.

With a new element of resolve, Matrina cranked the van and drove to the Pizza Hut near John's home. A Wal-Mart stood behind Pizza Hut in the same shopping plaza.

She ran into Wal-Mart while they built her pizza and bought an embroidery set for Dee-Dee, complete with needles and thread, and two hand-held computer games for Matt and John. Armed with pizza and gifts, she drove down John's street. She called Mrs. Gunthrey to let her know the plan to invade her domain. Mrs. Gunthrey sighed a deep sigh of acceptance, but at least she didn't say, "No, don't come." That's as close to an invitation anyone would get from Mrs. Gunthrey.

Chapter 12

Matrina felt a little unnerved as she pulled her Chevy Astro into John's driveway. Mrs. Gunthrey had not been thrilled over the news that dinner had become pizza. It took convincing to show Mrs. Gunthrey the pizza would be a blessing, not an attempt to storm the castle and usurp her reign.

The interloper carried the hot pizza box up the walk with her purse over one arm and the blue plastic bags of gifts over the other. John, Jr., spotted her from the front window.

"Wow, pizza," John said. He opened the front door for her. "Thanks, Mrs. McCoy. This is neat."

"Let's hope," Matrina said. She entered the living room and scanned the house for Mrs. Gunthrey. Oreo bounced up to her and instead of the usual "big dog" bark, he wagged his tail and sniffed her shoes.

"He's getting used to you," John said. "He hasn't nipped at your toes or anything."

"There's good news," Matrina said. She scrunched her toes in her open-toed sandals away from the edge of the shoes and the wet nose of the little dog.

Mrs. Gunthrey came from the kitchen and dried her hands on a green striped kitchen towel. She wore a white starched apron over her pink flowered, starched, cotton, short-sleeved dress. Pink Rick Rack edged the apron, and the bow in the back of the apron had been puffed, and the ties hung at exactly the same length.

She grumbled something under her breath and took the pizza and put it on the dining room table. The delicately embroidered tablecloth had been removed and folded, and now it lay draped over one of the dining room chairs.

"Thanks," Matrina said. She smiled at the elderly lady. Mrs. Gunthrey did not smile in return.

"I was going to fix dinner," Mrs. Gunthrey said. "Something healthy, but I guess this will do."

Matrina patted Mrs. Gunthrey's arm. "You work so hard," she said. "Maybe this will give you a little break."

"I don't need a break," Mrs. Gunthrey said. "I need more hours in the day." She walked into the kitchen area to get plates and forks and napkins. She put them out on the table in a "serve yourself" manner. She returned to the kitchen and brought out glasses for water or soda. "I can make coffee. You want coffee?" she said to Matrina.

"Oh, no. Please, don't bother. Soda will be fine," Matrina said. "I don't suppose you have any Diet Coke?"

"Yes, we do. John puts that on my list every week, and I have no clue why. Nobody around here drinks it. I just ignore him, as we have most of the first six-pack of Diet Coke I ever bought."

"I drink it, so it's nice you have some. Where are Dee-Dee and Matt?"

"Dee-Dee just got a phone call, and Matt is watching something on the Western Channel back in John's bedroom, I think. John, go fetch your brother and sister."

John scurried down the hall and came back with his brother.

"Come on," he said to the fair-haired, seven-year-old Matt. "We've got pizza. Aren't you excited about that?"

"Yeah," Matt said. He looked around and spotted the square box. "It's in here?"

"Sure is," Matrina said. Hamburger, cheese, mushrooms, no green peppers." She made a face with her nose and shook her head when she commented on the peppers.

"Cool," Matt said. "I hate green peppers."

"I remembered," Matrina said. "That's why I didn't get any."

"Dee-Dee." Mrs. Gunthrey called down the hallway. "Dinner's up."

"Okay," Dee-Dee called back from down the hall. "I'm coming." She wore cut-off jeans shorts of a conservative length, and a lemon-yellow tee shirt. Gold-colored barrettes controlled her mousey hair, and the lack of other jewelry or makeup set an example of a young girl who teetered on the brink of womanhood, but clung to a childhood she did not want to see disappear.

She hurried up the hall and deposited the portable phone into its cradle. She turned the corner into the dining room and came to a complete stop.

"Wow, Mrs. McCoy. I didn't know you were here. It's nice of you to stop by, and you brought pizza? What a treat. And look at you. You're all dressed up. I don't think I've ever seen you look so spiffy. And those are Coach shoes?

I'd just die if Dad would let me get some Coach shoes. Do you have the purse, too?"

"Yes, as a matter of fact, I do. And a tote bag for my laptop computer."

"You are so in style. Does Michelle have any Coach stuff yet?"

"Not yet. But she's working on it."

"Pizza is such a treat. Mrs. Gunthrey doesn't like us to have things that are not homemade, and Dad is a meat and potatoes kind of guy."

"I thought maybe we all needed a treat today." Matrina sat down at the table and waited for Mrs. Gunthrey to dish up the pizza. Once everybody had a piece on their plate, Mrs. Gunthrey asked John to say a prayer.

"Dear God," John said. "Thank you for the pizza. Not that what Mrs. Gunthrey fixes wouldn't have been really good, but this is a treat." John had developed an air of political correctness, it would seem. "And please get Dad out of jail. He couldn't have killed anyone, God. He doesn't even get mad at people, or even get into fist fights, or throw things at anyone. No way could he have killed someone, especially Slats. Everybody liked Slats. I can't imagine anyone wanting to kill Slats. And for sure, Dad didn't do it. Amen."

"Mr. Walker," Mrs. Gunthrey said. She sat down at the head of the table. "Children need to call adults by their proper names." She aimed the comment in John's direction, and placed a can of Diet Coke at Matrina's elbow.

"Mr. Walker," John said in a repentant tone.

Mrs. Gunthrey nodded approval.

"John mentioned that Robert Walker's nickname was Slats," Matrina said. She popped the top on her soda can. "Why was that?"

"Not sure," Mrs. Gunthrey said. She passed cans of soda to each of the children. "I guess it was because he was so tall and so lanky. I think he was like, six foot three, about a hundred sixty pounds. Really tall, really skinny."

"Oh," Matrina said. She picked up her piece of pizza and chewed a chunk from the narrow end. "Then Slats would certainly fit him."

"Will Dad get to come home soon?" Dee-Dee said.

"We certainly hope so," Matrina said. "I suppose Nathan Caldwell is working on bonding him out?" She looked at Mrs. Gunthrey for a reply.

"Yes, he is," Mrs. Gunthrey said. She chewed a piece of pizza and sprinkled Parmesan cheese on the piece left on her plate. "The judge who will set the bond and make the decision goes to our church, so that ought to help. This judge would know that John is definitely not a flight risk."

"That sounds positive," Matrina said. She nodded acceptance and put Parmesan on her remaining pizza. "Do you know what the bond will be?"

"No," Mrs. Gunthrey said, "but it will be high. That's for sure."

"Does John have the means to come up with a really high bond?"

Mrs. Gunthrey shrugged her shoulders. "I don't know," she said. "Nathan is supposed to stop by later this evening and let us know where we are, so maybe he will have some good information by then."

"Mind if I stay and meet him?" Matrina said.

"No, not at all," Mrs. Gunthrey said. "You'll like him. He's very nice."

Very nice. Not exactly what this situation requires. It might be better if he could be described as a despot with a whip and chair in the courtroom. But if "nice" described him, then "nice" will have to do.

Dee-Dee giggled into her soda can. "He's short," she said.

"Short?" Matrina said. She sipped her Diet Coke.

"Yeah," Dee-Dee said. "He's like five-foot-four."

"Really?" Matrina looked to Mrs. Gunthrey for verification. The best John could do for a hard core a lawyer, a nice, short guy who goes to their church?

"That's unkind," Mrs. Gunthrey said. "God does not judge us by our outward appearance."

Maybe not, but juries sure do. Maybe John's jury will consist of nice, short, religious people.

"Five-foot-four?" Matrina quizzed Dee-Dee.

"Yeah. That's what I am, and he's my height, so he's got to be about five-foot-four."

"I'm almost as tall as he is," John said. Matrina watched as he struggled to keep his giggle silent lest Mrs. Gunthrey erupt in his direction.

"Well, Mrs. Gunthrey's right," Matrina said. She wiped her mouth with a paper napkin. "Mr. Caldwell's height may be of great concern to others. Maybe he feels really badly about it himself. So we certainly don't want to react to it, and for sure, we don't want to comment on it. Okay?"

"Okay," the three Fleming offspring said. Matrina could see Matt felt a little fuzzy as to why they couldn't comment on something so obvious. Silence draped over the dining table for a good minute and a half.

"Mrs. McCoy," Matt said, after John whispered something into his ear.

"Yes, Matt?"

"What's in those blue plastic bags over there in the chair?"

"Oh, thanks for reminding me," Matrina said. She got up to get the gift bags. "I almost forgot." She could feel the ripple of apprehension run through the younger set.

"Just a little something I picked up for you guys today at Wal-Mart."

Matrina passed the embroidery set to Dee-Dee and the hand-held computer games, one each, to John and Matt. Squeals of glee drifted up from the table.

"This is great, Mrs. McCoy," Dee-Dee said. Her eyes sparkled in anticipation. "My mom used to embroider a lot, and I was wondering how I would ever learn, now that, well, you know, she's not here to teach me."

"Yes, I thought as much," Matrina said. She helped Mrs. Gunthrey clear the table of the dirty dishes and empty soda cans. "I noticed the doilies on all the tables, some are crocheted, but some are embroidered, and the dining room tablecloth here is so beautifully embroidered."

Mrs. Gunthrey wiped the table clean, and Matrina took the folded tablecloth from the back of Matt's chair, shook it out, and floated it back in place. Dee-Dee placed a bowl of fruit in the center of the tablecloth.

"Do you think I can figure out how to do this?" Dee-Dee said. She looked at the table runner in her embroidery kit and the hoop and all the samples of brightly colored thread.

"I'm sure you'll have no trouble," Matrina said. She dug down into the bag and pulled out a "how-to" embroidery book. "See? It gives you all the instructions right here in this book. All the different kinds of stitches, how to tie knots, how to start off, how to finish up, everything is right here."

"Oh, great," Dee-Dee said. She took the book and flipped through it.

"And it even tells you what colors to use on this piece, in case you want to follow that instead of making up your own color scheme."

Dee-Dee scanned the first few pages of the embroidery book, and John and Matt concentrated on their beeping computer games. Mrs. Gunthrey rolled her eyes to the ceiling over the constant sound made when one moved the tiny computer heroes about the tiny computer screens.

"Sorry," Matrina said in Mrs. Gunthrey's direction. "I didn't realize these games were wired for sound."

"It's okay," Mrs. Gunthrey said. She put grounds and water into the coffeepot. "It's almost Gene Autry time on the Western Channel. That will override the games. Then we can do baths and pajama time."

Matrina made no further comment. "Sorry," had been said.

"Mrs. McCoy," Dee-Dee said. "Would you like to see some of my mom's embroidered stuff?"

"Oh, yes, Dee-Dee," Matrina said, glad to put distance between herself and Mrs. Gunthrey.

"Come on into my room. I have bunches of it stashed in one of my drawers." Dee-Dee led the way down the hallway to her room.

The ice pink bedroom provided a nice backdrop for the pink and cranberry striped window curtains and matching bedspread. Cranberry ruffled pillows splashed across the top of the bed. White wicker bedroom furniture sat on the basic brown carpeting that covered the rest of the house. A CD player sat on the dresser surrounded by CD's, some of which Matrina recognized since Michelle had the same artists in her collection.

A white wicker chair sat at the desk, with the striped material made into a cover for the cushion on the seat. Several library books crowded the CD player, and Matrina flipped through the books.

"Oh, I see you like Laura Ingalls Wilder books," she commented. "That's nice safe reading for someone your age."

"Yes, my dad and Mrs. Gunthrey really check up on what books I get from the library, like I'm going to smuggle Stephen King books in and hide them under my bed."

"I do the same with Michelle." Matrina chuckled and patted the books in approval. "I know it's a pain to have us adults hovering over you like we do, but we just have to keep an eye on you. It's our job."

Dee-Dee sighed. "I know," she said. She rummaged in a dresser drawer, hauled out several pieces of embroidered doilies and table runners and laid them out on the bed.

Matrina surveyed the room further and noted pictures of Dee-Dee's mother on one wall, thirty photographs, all framed and placed in order by year, almost a shrine. They dropped off the year she died five years ago. Matrina felt a magnetism toward them like a beautiful sunset draws its admirers to its altar and makes the earth seem to stand still.

While Dee-Dee separated the needlework, Matrina studied each photo of Delores. She wanted to touch the frames in reverence but resisted the impulse.

"She was so beautiful," she said. She spoke in a whisper.

"Yes, wasn't she?" Dee-Dee said. "I put the pictures all up on the wall because I'm afraid I'll forget what she looked like. John's already not sure what she looked like, and Matt has forgotten her completely. But then, he was only two when she died."

"You'll never forget her," Matrina said. My mother died when I was eighteen, and I remember her like she was here yesterday."

"I hope so. I wish I looked more like her. She was so delicate, and all that neat reddish-brown hair. None of us got that pretty hair. We have sandy-colored hair, like Dad. She and Dad both have blue eyes, but Dad's are a lighter blue, and we have those, too, not the darker blue like Mom had."

"Yes, your dad's eyes are almost a gray," Matrina said. She couldn't tear herself away from the pictures on display. "I see all these pictures are of your mom in a dress. Were these church occasions, or did she always wear dresses?"

"She wore dresses. Dad always liked her in dresses, so she almost never wore pants or jeans. She just wore dresses, lots of them she made herself. She really liked to sew."

"The dresses here are lovely. She must have been very talented."

"Yeah, she was," Dee-Dee said. She smoothed the doilies and table runners out on the bed.

"How did they meet?" Matrina said. "Your mom and your dad."

"At church. My grandparents used to bring my mom to church, and Dad met her there."

"Bring her to church," Matrina said. She wondered about the strange choice of words. "You mean like she needed help getting to church? Couldn't she make it to church on her own?"

"Well," Dee-Dee said. She paused to ponder her words. "There was one little thing wrong with Mom, but Dad doesn't like us to talk about it. And we were definitely never to tell anyone about it."

Matrina felt herself back off. "I didn't mean to pry. I just wondered. She must have been in her twenties when she met your dad, and it is curious that her parents would be bringing her to church. That's all."

"She was hard of learning," Dee-Dee said. Her voice had a softness to it, as if the words spoken in such low tones would cancel the actual meaning of them.

"Hard of learning?" Matrina copied Dee-Dee whispered tone. "You mean she had a learning deficiency?"

"I guess that's what you call it," Dee-Dee said. "Sometimes it feels good to talk about it. Dad said she was just intellectually challenged. He tried to teach her things as we went along. He was teaching her to read more complicated books when she got sick. And he was teaching her to make change with money, well, I helped with that. We used to play store every other night or so, but she just couldn't get the hang of that."

Dee-Dee traced one of the embroidered flowers on a doily with her finger, and she seemed to be talking to the doily, not anyone else in the room.

"But she must have shopped. She bought your dad that nice gun he's so proud of."

"Oh, yeah, she shopped. She bought groceries, and charged them. Then

95

Dad would pay the bill at the end of the week. When she bought the gun, she was spending money given to her by her mom and dad, and she didn't really know how much money she was spending. Turned out, she did really good, and brought home a bargain."

Matrina laughed. "I'll say," she said. "I'll bet your dad had to sit back and take notice of that."

"He tried to find the people and give them more money, as she got the gun way under what it was worth. But they had already moved on, so she got to keep the bargain."

"That's what he told me," Matrina said, "that he felt badly your mom had gotten the gun for such a cheap price. And all the time, your mom didn't have any concept of exactly how cheap it was. How wonderfully ironic."

"I really miss my mom," Dee-Dee said. She plopped down on the edge of the bed. "She wasn't smart, but she was so nice, and she loved us so much. She never raised her voice, or got mad, and she tried so hard to learn how to do things that other moms did. Once, Dad bought her a cookbook written for children, figuring she could maybe learn from that, but she couldn't. It was too hard for her."

"But she sewed, and crocheted and embroidered," Matrina said. She scanned the beautiful pieces of needlework that covered the bed. "She would have had to follow instructions to do that."

"Exactly," Dee-Dee said. "That's why Dad thought she should be able to read other stuff, but she just couldn't figure some things out. It really bothered her. She could read the Bible, and the sewing stuff, but cookbooks, or newspapers were just too much for her. And she used to cry over it all the time."

"How sad," Matrina said. She picked up one of the pieces of embroidery and turned it over. The reverse side looked as perfect as the front side. "She would have learned more things, eventually, I would think. Look how perfect this sewing is. It takes a lot of intelligence and patience to sew like this."

"I hope I can learn to sew like she did."

"I'm sure you will." Matrina replaced the doily. "If your mom couldn't master the cooking part, what did you do about meals?"

"Dad taught her to do some things, and my grandma would come over and help. Grandma and Grandpa lived just down the street. So, my mom could do hot dogs, or hamburgers, or heat up soup, make salad, stuff like that. But once Dad gave her that cookbook, she wanted to make things from that, and she just couldn't. Once, she caught the stove on fire, and the neighbors called the fire department."

"That must have scared your dad to death. Being a policeman, they probably called him to come home, too."

"They did, and he was all upset, and he took the cookbook away from her She put her head down on the kitchen table and sobbed. I was only six, but I remember that day. That was the closest my mom and dad ever came to having a fight."

"Do you still have the cookbook?"

"Yes. It's here in my dresser." Dee-Dee opened another dresser drawer and pulled out the cookbook with cartoon pictures and large print with recipes for things like macaroni and cheese, chili, and peanut butter cookies.

Matrina flipped through the cookbook. Smudges of tomato sauce and butter marred the pages. She felt a closeness to Delores, and wished she had been able to know her and help her conquer this challenge. Then through her mind galloped another abstract thought. Would she tell her about her attraction to her husband before or after attempting to help her overcome life? Matrina shook her head to erase the thought from her mind, as one would shake an etch-a-sketch to clear the screen.

"Do you get to see your grandparents very often now that you live in Florida?" Matrina said. She closed the cookbook and put it back in the dresser drawer.

"Yes. They come down every Thanksgiving. I love it when they come down. Makes me not miss Mom quite so much."

"Maybe your grandmother could give you some advice on the sewing."

"Maybe. She has e-mail. I'll e-mail her tonight about my new project. Maybe she'll have some suggestions."

"Does she e-mail you often?"

"Every day. She's so cool."

Mrs. Gunthrey knocked on the bedroom door. Then she opened it a crack and stuck her head inside.

"Nathan's here," she said. "Coffee's ready, in case you want some, Matrina. Dee-Dee, you get ready for bed. Please stay in your room and read or something. John and Matt are going to their rooms, too. This get together is just for the adults. If you children could entertain yourselves, it would really help out."

"Okay, Mrs. Gunthrey," Dee-Dee said. Matrina felt Dee-Dee wanted their chat to continue. She hoped they would get another chance to chat some other time.

"Oh, goody, Nathan's here," Matrina said. She spoke in quiet voice to Dee-Dee out of Mrs. Gunthrey's hearing. "Now I get to meet our nice, short person. Hope he's a giant inside so he can get your dad out of this trouble."

"Me, too," Dee-Dee said. She put the doilies and table runners back into her drawer. She smiled at Matrina and gave her a hug. "Thanks for talking with me, Mrs. McCoy. I really like it when you visit."

"I like it when I visit it, too, Dee-Dee. We'll talk again, and you can tell me some more things about your mom. Talking about her will help you to remember her better. My sister and I talk about our mom and dad, and that helps us remember them."

Dee-Dee closed her dresser drawer, and Matrina left the room to walk down the hallway and meet today's nice short person who held John's future in his hands.

Chapter 13

Matrina followed Mrs. Gunthrey back down the hall from Dee-Dee's room and into the dining room. She expected to see Nathan Caldwell somewhere within her eyeshot. Nathan and four other people sat at the dining room table. The embroidered tablecloth had been left on the table this time, and cups and saucers were in place. Freshly brewed coffee brimmed in each cup.

Nathan Caldwell sat at the head of the table with briefcase opened. Two yellow legal pads lay beside the briefcase, and two pens waited on top of the pads. Nathan did lack stature and his brown hair looked as if it hadn't seen a comb all day, maybe not all week. Matrina wanted to lick her fingers and smooth his cowlick.

Nathan wore a clean, white shirt, but the effort made by an iron had missed its mark, the insignia of a single man. His tie might have been knotted this morning, but now it hung from his neck, loosened and askew.

Samuel and Liza Hancock, the church minister and his wife, sat to his right, and David and Ida Rogers, the deacon and wife for whom John had thrown the welcoming barbecue the night the body had been discovered, sat on his left. Liza and Ida wore correctly modest sun dresses in lime green and lilac gingham, respectively, pressed with the liberal use of spray starch.

Mrs. Gunthrey went into the kitchen and brought back another pot of coffee and checked to see how empty the several cups had become. The guests must have been there long enough to have sipped some coffee before Mrs. Gunthrey summoned Matrina. Possibly a little prayer meeting had been held before the non-church-going person showed up? She forced the negative assumption from her mind and smiled in hello.

Matrina stood by the table, unsure where she should sit, unsure whether she should even be here.

"You must be Matrina McCoy," Nathan Caldwell said. He still riffled through his briefcase, but stopped long enough to stand up and extend his hand in welcome. His shortness didn't seem to interfere with his commanding demeanor.

"Yes," Matrina said. She shook his hand. "I hope it's not an intrusion that I'm here."

"Not at all," Nathan said. He got his notes in order and closed his briefcase. "If you weren't going to be here, I would've called you. John says you're the best investigator he knows, and it's his wish you do all the investigation necessary to form a solid defense for him."

"How nice," Matrina said. She continued to stand by the table and felt the scrutiny of the four sets of eyes of the four on her.

"I bowl with John and George, your boss, and I've already cleared this plan with George. He says you can work it in with your regular ACS duties, and if you run into a conflict, just talk to him."

"Good," Matrina said. She walked to the empty chair at the end of the table opposite Nathan. Mrs. Gunthrey put a cup of coffee on the table at her place. She wished she could swap it for another can of diet Coke or a glass of water.

"You'll need this," Nathan said. He slid a yellow legal pad and a pen down to her. "We'll go over what we have on this case, and decide what we need to find out."

"Okay," Matrina said. The agenda of this meeting had begun to take on a legal air, and she felt herself relax under the familiar atmosphere. This Nathan may be short, and he may be a tad on the disheveled side, but he seemed to be a dynamo at dining room table conferences. She hoped he would be as aggressive in the courtroom.

"Now," Nathan said. He sipped his coffee. "Great coffee, Mrs. Gunthrey."

"Thank you," Mrs. Gunthrey said. She put a plate of homemade peanut butter cookies in the center of the table beside the bowl of fruit.

"Okay," Nathan said, "listen up. Let's start from the beginning. By the way, we'll be informed of everything the D. A. has on this case in discovery. I told him if he tried to hide anything, I'd throw him under the bus so fast, he'd wonder why he even wanted to be a prosecutor. He has no real evidence. He can't put John with Slats any time prior to the finding of the body, except for church activities. They have not yet determined the time of death. So much time had passed, a guesstimate is as good as they can do."

"That sounds good," Matrina said. She jotted a note to that effect on her yellow pad.

"There are no witnesses. The murder weapon is a joke. Why would a guy, an ex-cop, totally knowledgeable about firearms, chose such a hokey weapon from his total collection of firearms? I mean, let's get real. A 1902 American Eagle Luger? It has 'come and get me; I'm using this collector's item so you can pin this murder on me, and only me' stamped all over it. And the motive is even more laughable." Nathan sipped some more coffee and reached for a cookie. "Great cookies, too, Mrs. Gunthrey." He muttered the comment while he munched the cookie.

Mrs. Gunthrey nodded from the kitchen. She wiped the kitchen counter shelf, and Matrina figured the elderly housekeeper tried to appear busy so she could stay within earshot.

"What kind of a motive do they have?" Samuel Hancock, the minister said.

"Yes," David Rogers, the deacon said. "John involved in a murder is just so bizarre. He's such a patient, gentle person."

"Is it supposedly over this Robert Walker owing John money?" Matrina asked.

"No," Nathan said. "They say it was over a woman." The lawyer shook his head in wonderment and reached for another cookie.

"A woman?" Everyone at the table spoke almost in unison.

"What woman?" Mrs. Gunthrey said. "There're no women in John's life."

"According to the D. A. there is," Nathan said. He spoke between bites of cookie, "and according to the woman there is."

"There's a woman who says John is interested in her, and might have killed someone over her?" The shocked words came from David, the deacon. He reached for a cookie, perhaps out of hunger, perhaps out of the need for something to do to fill an uncomfortable void.

"This is ridiculous," Samuel said. "This woman is lying. Who in the world is she? Anyone we would know?"

"Yes," Nathan said. He sipped more coffee. "We all know her. Alice Toney."

"Alice Toney?" more unison echoes by everyone except Matrina.

"Who's Alice Toney," Matrina said. She jotted the name on her legal pad.

"Alice Toney is a young woman who attends church with us," Liza Hancock said to Matrina. "She's in her late twenties, has a son about Matt's age. She works as a librarian here in town. She's a very intelligent woman. I think she has a master's degree in library science."

Matrina jotted all the information down on her pad.

"Matrina," Nathan said, "how about you talking to Alice, since you don't know her. She may be more candid with you. And for sure, you would be more candid with her than any of us. Find out why she is claiming John is interested in her. She gave a statement to the D. A. that said they had been dating, and when she started dating Slats, John tried to talk her out of it."

"Oh, for Pete's sake," Mrs. Gunthrey said. She walked toward the table with the soapy dish rag in her hand. "That ditsy girl. As Liza said, she does have a boy Matt's age. John thought it would be good for the child to join little league with John and Matt. Alice doesn't like to drive in the evening by herself, so John used to pick her and her son up, drive them to practice, and buy them a hamburger on the way home. He was fulfilling the advice in the book of James to visit the fatherless and the widows. That's all there was to it. It certainly couldn't be considered dating."

"Was he negative about her dating Slats?" Nathan said.

"Of course he was negative about her dating Slats," Mrs. Gunthrey said in adamant tones. "Who wouldn't be? I was negative about her dating Slats. Slats was a nice, pleasant man, but he wouldn't have the brains God gave geese about being married and raising a youngster. John didn't want to see them both make a huge mistake."

A silence prevailed over the table. Matrina sensed that no one wanted to comment on Mrs. Gunthrey's assessment of the situation.

"Okay, as I have said before," Nathan said. He wiped his mouth with a paper napkin he had pulled from a dispenser Mrs. Gunthrey had placed on the table. "Let's start at the beginning, one more time."

"I have a question," Matrina said. She pushed her cup of coffee away from her legal pad. "Do we have a definite day of death? Maybe we can come up with an alibi for John, if we know when they think Mr. Walker was killed."

"They have the day of death set for the third Friday in June, in the evening, around nine P.M. give or take five or six hours. John was camping with the kids in Myakka State Park that weekend. He left mid-afternoon on Friday and came home on Sunday."

"So the kids were with him all weekend?" Matrina asked.

"Not only were the kids with him," Mrs. Gunthrey said, "I was with him."

"You were with him?" Nathan looked at the housekeeper like she had become a statue of pure gold.

"Yes. And we did leave Friday about three and returned home Sunday after lunch."

"So you could be John's alibi," Matrina said. "You could vouch for the fact that he was with you all weekend and couldn't possibly be here at the house with Mr. Walker."

Mrs. Gunthrey lowered her soapy rag and studied the floor.

"What's wrong?" Nathan asked the question, and it came out laced with the concern.

"Well, I hate to say so," Mrs. Gunthrey said. Her voice shifted to a lower tone, "but John did leave the campground once."

"What do you mean, 'He left the campground once?'" David now in the quest for answers.

"He took his hurricane preparedness kit with us," Mrs. Gunthrey said.

"He always takes that kit camping," Samuel said. "He brings it on church outings. He has everything in there, flashlights, batteries, first aid things, portable radio, everything you could need to survive a hurricane or a trip into the woods."

"Yes, that's true," Mrs. Gunthrey said. She put her soapy rag back into the sink. "Only this time, all the batteries were missing."

"What do you mean, 'All the batteries were missing?'" Nathan paused, cookie in mid-air.

"Just that," Mrs. Gunthrey said. "The batteries were all gone from the kit. Even the ones that had been in the flashlights."

"How'd that happen?" Matrina tried to put the pieces together.

Mrs. Gunthrey shrugged. "We don't know. John thought the children had gotten them to use with their computer games or CD players."

"They wouldn't be the same size battery," Matrina again.

"That's what they said," Mrs. Gunthrey said.

"What did John think about that?" Matrina said.

"He didn't know what happened. The batteries were just missing." Mrs. Gunthrey returned to the sink as if the subject had run itself out.

"So, John ran to the store and got batteries," Nathan said. Another cookie found its way into his mouth.

"He got in the Jeep and drove to the store," Mrs. Gunthrey said. She hesitated with the rest of the story.

"And…" David encouraged her to finish.

"He was gone almost two hours," Mrs. Gunthrey said. Her voice hovered near a whisper.

"Two hours?" Unison from the dining room table.

"Just to find batteries?" Nathan had to get to the bottom of this.

"Yes. He said he drove to three convenience stores near the park, and they were all out of flashlight batteries."

"All of them?" Matrina's mind stumbled around this fact.

"It's the middle of hurricane season, you know," Mrs. Gunthrey said, "and I guess the stores just kept selling out of batteries."

"Wonder why they wouldn't keep their stock up on such items?" Matrina, still on the hunt for facts.

Mrs. Gunthrey shrugged. "We don't know."

"So John eventually found batteries?" Samuel asked the question.

"Yes, and he brought them back to camp, but he had to drive clear into town before he found any. The fourth store he went to had some."

"And he was gone two hours," Nathan said. He had to repeat the time for verification. His disbelief seemed to rattle his confidence.

"Yes. It was almost dark when he left, and way past the children's bedtime before he got back." Mrs. Gunthrey looked at Nathan, and he looked away.

"Plenty of time to ice Slats and bury him in the backyard," Nathan said. He verbalized what everyone else thought.

Mrs. Gunthrey sprayed Windex on the toaster

"Anybody hear any digging on Friday night?" Matrina could not let this new fact pass unchallenged. "Any of the neighbors? Anybody?"

"Nope. Nobody saw anything. Again, in our favor. Some things are concrete facts, such as someone definitely shot Slats in the back of the head with a nine millimeter bullet. The bullet was still lodged in the front of his brain. Then they buried him in John's backyard. But there is nothing to tie that to John except his collector's gun has proven to be the murder weapon, and it uses nine millimeter bullets. As I say, their case is weak." Nathan sipped some more coffee.

"I'll say," Matrina said beneath her breath." And I suppose they came with a search warrant and definitely proved John's gun was the murder weapon.

"You bettcha," Nathan said. "Absolutely no doubt about it."

"Fingerprints on the gun? Probably only John's?" Matrina again. Nathan nodded.

"Okay, people, one more time," Nathan said. He swallowed his coffee and tapped his pen on his blank pad. "We need to start at the beginning. We seem to be having a little trouble getting to the beginning. No offense, Matrina, your questions are well taken. But we have to establish a timeline here, so we can get a handle on what's going on. Someone's after John, and this's not a game. They killed Slats, and they set John up for it. The frame is not tight, but it's firm enough to get an indictment."

"So," Samuel said. He seemed to bow to Nathan's leadership. "Where do we start?"

"The third weekend in June," Nathan said. He jotted that phrase down on his legal pad. "Matrina, do you remember anything out of the ordinary John might have commented about concerning that weekend, other than being out of batteries?"

"He never even commented on that," Matrina said. She shook her head and gave Nathan a blank look.

"There've been the threatening letters since then, of course. They're certainly out of the ordinary."

"The threatening letters," Nathan's pen wrote a comment on his legal pad.

"What threatening letters?" Samuel said. Shock creased his face.

"Threatening letters?" David said. Shock knitted his brow as well. The wives gasped in surprise.

"When were the threatening letters received?" Nathan said. He spoke to Matrina, since she seemed to be the only at the table who knew about the letters. Matrina knew Mrs. Gunthrey knew about the first one, but she doubted the elderly lady knew about the second. Mrs. Gunthrey made no comment.

"The first one was received just a few days after the incident at Disney. The second one a couple of weeks later, more recently. I took both letters to George, my boss, and he had them analyzed."

"Were there any fingerprints?" Nathan said.

"Of course not," Matrina said. "These were professionally done. They left no fingerprints, no DNA from saliva, nothing, except for a faint indentation on the first letter from another piece of paper which must have lain on top of the page on which the letter was written."

"Indentation?" David said. "What indentation?"

"First of all," Samuel said, "what did the letters say?"

"Yes," David said, "what did the letters say?"

"I have copies of them in my purse," Matrina said. She rose to get her purse from where she had left it in the living room. She pulled the copies from her purse and slid them across the table to Nathan. He glanced at them and slid them to Samuel, who read them and slid them to David. The wives read over their husband's shoulders.

"Oh, dear me," Ida said.

"Yes," Liza said. "'Dear me,' says it all."

"Why didn't John tell us about this?" Samuel said. "We could have had a prayer request for the safety of the family made at church."

"Because he doesn't take any of this seriously," Nathan said. "He's the ultimate optimist. Philippians four, verse eight is his favorite Bible scripture. You all know that."

"Yes," Samuel said. He nodded his head in agreement. "That's where it says, 'Whatsoever things are good, and pure, and fine, *et cetera*, think on these things.'"

"Exactly," Nathan said. "He thinks everyone's nuts, and there's no way these letters could be for real, and for sure, they can't convict him of murder. They interrogate him, and he laughs at them. He can't believe they're serious, which is actually working in our behalf. The D.A. is inclined to allow bail to be set in this, because John wouldn't be a flight risk if he doesn't think he's in serious trouble."

"So, he might actually get out on bail?" Matrina said. Hope sparkled through her voice.

"Could be. We go before Judge Newton day after tomorrow, Friday, so we'll see how it goes."

Samuel smiled. "Oh, that's Barry," he said. "It should help that he's in church with all of us."

"Not really," Nathan said. "Doesn't hurt, but doesn't help, as Barry can't be prejudiced. What helps is the D.A. is not fighting us on this one."

"That's a blessing in itself," David said.

"Yes," Nathan said. "Okay, back to the timeline." Nathan rolled his eyes to the ceiling and shook his head.

Matrina figured Nathan's desire to get this group to stay on target paralleled lining up fifty chickens on one side of the chicken coop. She watched as he sighed a deep sigh of determination and heard him continue. "The letters talk about things going badly for John and his family in the first letter, and things going badly specifically for Dee-Dee in the second. What does anyone make of these threats?"

"Sounds like it's a direct tie-in to the Disney incident," Samuel said. "The folks who wanted to blow up Disney are upset that John thwarted that little escapade. And the would-be bomber is still free, I understand. Do we know anything about this guy?"

"A little," Matrina said. "The newspaper gave the name of the bomber as 'Christopher O'Brien.' His father was Irish, and his mother Israeli. Christopher was orphaned at an early age, and grew up in Afghanistan, and was associated with Osama Bin Laden."

"Matrina," Nathan said, "could you look into this Christopher O'Brien's whereabouts since coming to the States, and see if there's a tie-in between him and the notes? Find out where he is now."

"Yes," Matrina said. She jotted the name on her note pad. "I've been wanting to do that ever since I heard about him. This will give me the incentive to get it done."

"Oh, and Matrina," Nathan said, "what was the indentation found on the first letter?"

"The numerals two, three and nine," Matrina said. "The paper on which the letter was written was torn from a spiral notebook. On the page above it, someone wrote 'two-three-nine,' with enough force that the page beneath bore the indentation of these numbers. Also, the envelopes were stamped with the same type of postage stamp, an American flag stamp, and the same black crayon was used in both letters."

"So, we could assume both letters were written by the same person," Nathan said.

"That would be my guess," Matrina said.

"And there was no DNA where someone licked the envelope, nothing like that?" Nathan said.

"No," Matrina said. "Both envelopes were moistened with a foreign moistener, like a sponge, that contained city water. There was fluoride on both envelope flaps."

"Okay, so whoever did this lived in the city, not the country, as the flap was not moistened with well water."

"That's correct," Matrina said. "They might not actually live where they prepared the letters, but wherever they prepared the letters, they used city water, not well water."

"Okay," Nathan said, "it would also appear the letters are connected to the Disney incident. Are we all agreed on that?"

Nodded heads confirmed the assumption. Nathan jotted notes on his pad.

"Matrina," he continued, "could you check into the two-three-nine issue? See if there's any connection to Christopher O'Brien."

Matrina nodded, and jotted that on her pad.

"The next problem we have is that the death of Slats is not connected to the Disney incident," Nathan said.

"How do you figure?" David said.

"Because the death occurred before the Disney incident."

"Oh, yeah." David nodded. "I didn't think about that."

"So, we have at least a two-fronted war going on here," Nathan said.

"Some of which may overlap; some of which may not. So, let's talk about how the gun got out of the house."

"Gun out of the house?" Samuel said.

"Yes. Someone obviously took the Luger from John's gun cabinet, used it to kill Slats, buried Slats in the backyard, wiped all the fingerprints off the gun, and replaced the gun in the gun cabinet."

"Was the murder committed here on John's property?" Matrina said.

"Good question," Nathan said. "No, as a matter of fact, it was not. There wasn't enough blood in the shallow grave to require a Band-Aid. The search warrant allowed the sheriff's department to comb John's premises for blood, and they found zip. They did find the gun, however. No surprise there. They did not find any bullets. That may help us, not sure yet."

"So," Matrina said, "we're looking for someone who had access to the house so he, or she, could remove the gun. And then they'd have to have access to the house to put the gun back."

"That seems to be a good scenario," Nathan said.

"So, there would probably be more than one person involved in doing this," Matrina said. She jotted a doodle of a four-pointed star on her note pad.

"Why do you say that?" David said.

"Because one person couldn't have carried Slats from a transporting vehicle to the backyard without a great deal of effort. Struggling with a body might attract the attention of passersby. The killers would have no way of knowing when a car might drive down the street past the house, or a neighbor would be walking a dog. They would have had to move Slats into the backyard quickly and smoothly."

"Good point," Nathan said. He jotted that down on his note pad.

"So John would have had to be out of the house during the burial." Matrina spoke and looked at Nathan.

Nathan let that thought wash over him. "He was out of the house. He was camping," Nathan said. He chewed on the end of his pen.

"Would the killer have known he was camping?" Mrs. Gunthrey spoke while she polished the microwave.

"Yes," Matrina said, "the killer would have to have known John would be gone all weekend so he could dig the grave and bury the body."

Silence enveloped the dining room table. The killer had to have known John's plans.

"Does John remember the gun being missing before they went to Myakka to camp?" Matrina broke the silence.

"No," Nathan said. "But then, he doesn't look at the guns every day, so it could have been taken long before it was actually used."

"There was no forced entry into the house?" Matrina said.

"Not that John noticed."

"So, that means what?" Matrina said. "The gun was taken by someone he knows?"

"Oh, I doubt that," Samuel said. "John's guests are mostly church people, not hooligans. No one in our circle would steal anything from anyone, much less kill anyone with it."

"Well, someone stole something from John," Matrina said. She tried to sound matter-of-fact. "And they did it very well, and they put it back, and they didn't leave a trace. We're dealing with someone very professional here."

Nathan nodded. "That's true," he said. He took another sip of his coffee, which had to be cold by now. "I guess they could have jimmied a lock, or gotten in with a credit card. Lots of ways to get into a house and not leave any clues."

"The credit card angle is a myth," Matrina said. "I've known policemen who say they've tried and tried to use their credit cards to trigger locks, and it just doesn't work."

"These guys used something, because they got in and stole the gun, and then put it back," David said. He sipped his cooled coffee and added more sugar.

"What about there not being any bullets?" Nathan said. "Did John ever mention having bullets missing?"

"He didn't keep bullets in the house," Matrina said.

"He had guns, and no bullets?" Samuel was surprised.

"Yes," Matrina said, "because of the children. He didn't like bullets around the house."

"That's true," Mrs. Gunthrey said. She moved with her Windex bottle to put a shine on the kitchen window on the inside.

Nathan scribbled on his legal pad. "So our perpetrator would have had to buy bullets somewhere, to fit the rare gun."

"Yes," Matrina said. She jotted that fact on her pad.

"That gun uses nine millimeter bullets," Samuel said. "John and I discussed that one day a while back."

"Matrina," Nathan said, "could you research how we would investigate the purchase of nine millimeter bullets during the third week in June? Our murderer couldn't have the gun out of the house too long before the murder, or he would risk John missing it. He might have bought the bullets on that Tuesday or Wednesday before the day of the murder. Sound like an impossible task?"

"No," Matrina said. She made note of it. "Time-consuming, maybe, difficult for sure, but not impossible."

"I want to take a look at the gun cabinet," Nathan said. He got up from the table. "Come on. Let's go into the den and look at it. The Luger is missing, of course. The cops confiscated that when they searched the house."

"And I suppose they found John's fingerprints all over it," Matrina said. She followed him to the gun cabinet.

"Of course," Nathan said. "The killer wiped the gun clean as a whistle, and John said he got it out of the cabinet the day of the barbecue and showed it to you. So, that put his prints back on it."

"Too bad I didn't handle it, too," Matrina said. "That would have put my fingerprints on it as well. That would have thrown a nice little monkey wrench into the physical evidence works."

Nathan chuckled. "Yes, too bad you didn't."

The troop wandered down the hallway to John's den used as an office. They stood in front of the gun cabinet. Mrs. Gunthrey brought up the rear.

"Okay," Nathan said. "You can see where the Luger used to be kept. That space is empty. Why choose that gun, when there are all these other, more common guns? That will be a good item in the defense. Oh." He stopped suddenly, and looked over at Mrs. Gunthrey. "Mrs. Gunthrey, there appears to be another gun missing, a thirty-two caliber snub nose. Do you know anything about that? The cops only took the murder weapon."

Everyone turned to look at Mrs. Gunthrey, when she plopped down in a big brown-leather chair nearby and put her head down into her lap. Her shoulders heaved up and down, and she wept into her apron.

"Mrs. Gunthrey," Matrina said. She went to her and put her arm around her shoulders. "What's wrong?"

"Oh, I didn't want anyone to know," she said. She tried to subdue her weeping. "My son, Jared, was here last week, and I think he took that gun."

"You have a son who visited here?" Matrina said. She stroked the elderly lady's back. Then she knelt before Mrs. Gunthrey, and tried to look up into her face to reassure her.

Mrs. Gunthrey continued to weep. "Yes," she said, "Jared. And he has been such a troubled young man. He means no harm, and he's a good boy. He just falls into temptation so easily." The sobbing found new depth, and she buried her face more deeply into her apron. She tried to avoid Matrina's eyes.

"How old is your son?" Nathan said. He tried to absorb this new information.

"Thirty-two," Mrs. Gunthrey said. She spoke between sobs. "He came one day last week, and he was angry because I won't let him move back in with me. I want him to get a job and support himself. He can't see that. He thinks I should support him. He thinks I'm being mean if I refuse. He keeps saying he's just down on his luck at the moment. He keeps thinking that some pot of gold is at the end of some rainbow just around the corner, and only fools actually work for a living, like me, I guess."

"You're making the right stand," Nathan said. "You keep telling him what's what. Eventually, he'll catch on." Nathan bent over Mrs. Gunthrey and patted her on the back. "And we don't know for sure he took the gun," he said.

"Yes, we do," Mrs. Gunthrey said. "It was missing right after he left. I told John about it right away. He said not to worry about it. He's so nice about Jared. He worries about him, too, like I do."

Everyone stood silent and looked at each other. Matrina avoided everyone's eyes. She feared someone would read her thoughts. Jared Gunthrey. Did he steal the Luger? Did he know Slats? Did he have a reason to kill Slats? Did he steal the gun for someone else who had a reason to kill Slats?

Matrina stood up, and Nathan got into her path and caught her eye. He motioned for her to make a note of this on her pad that still lay on the dining room table. Matrina nodded, and made a mental note to look into the background of Jared Gunthrey, and where he was on the few days before the camp out the third weekend of June.

The little group filed back to the dining room table. The mood had shifted from dedicated action to morbid realization. They all hoped against hope that Jared Gunthrey had a solid reason to prove no involvement in all of this. They resumed their seats at the table, and Mrs. Gunthrey made her rounds with a new pot of hot coffee. Only Nathan accepted a refill.

"You mentioned bond," Samuel said. "Did they say how much the bond would be, if they do let John bond out?"

"How high is up?" Nathan said. He shook his head. "Like five hundred thousand dollars."

Sounds of discouragement came from the table-sitters.

"Does John have that kind of money to post a bond that high?" David said. He pushed his half-consumed, cold coffee into the middle of the table.

"No," Nathan said, "but he hates to post the ten percent and hire a bonds person. That would be fifty thousand dollars down the drain. He wants to post the whole thing and then just get it all back when he's acquitted."

"How much can he come up with?" Matrina said. She jotted down the figure on her legal pad.

"About two hundred thousand," Nathan said. "This house is paid for, and he could borrow an equity loan on it, and he has about a hundred thousand in the money market in a college fund for the kids. This all comes from insurance money, of course, from his wife's death."

"I'm in about the same financial situation," Matrina said. "I'd be willing to put up another two hundred thousand. I could get a loan on my house, and I have about a hundred thousand in my kids' college fund."

"You'd do that for John?" Nathan said. His mouth dropped open in surprise.

"Yes. He's a friend. He's not guilty. He's not a flight risk. He's going to beat this. I'm just sure of it."

"That would sure help," Nathan said. He jotted figures on his pad. "That would leave us a hundred thousand short. Any way the church could help?" he asked of Samuel.

Liza darted a quick look of refusal to Samuel, and shook her head at the same time. She traced one of the yellow flowers on the tablecloth with her right index finger.

"I'm afraid not," Samuel said. "I have to be so careful of the church money, and what money we have of our own has to go to pay off debts so we can start a family. Sorry."

"Just thought I'd ask," Nathan said.

"I'll help," David said. Ida sat by his side, and did not react. Matrina tried to read if she was in favor of this decision, or had reservations about it. She was impossible to read. This showed years of practice in control over her emotions, no doubt.

"Really?" Nathan said. "Could you come up with fifty thousand? If you can, I think I can scrounge up the other fifty."

"Yes. I can do that," David said. "Just let me know when the bond is set and you need the money."

"Great," Nathan said. "So, we're good to go, if the bond is approved."

"Let's all pray our Judge Barry has a good week going for him, and he'll be easily entreated," David said.

"Amen," Samuel, Liza, Ida, Mrs. Gunthrey and Nathan together.

"Amen," Matrina said in her mind.

Chapter 14

Matrina walked into the ACS office the next morning, dressed in white slacks and a lime-green flowered blouse. Franny grabbed printed sheets that poured from the printer and seemed to read them with interest.

"Whatcha got, Franny?" Matrina said. She stopped at the front desk to check out the object of Franny's attention.

"Your information on that boat ID you gave me a few days ago. It's pretty interesting."

"What's it say?" Matrina said. She called back to Franny as she walked to the kitchen area and the coffeepot. "Want a cup of coffee?"

"Yeah. I haven't had a chance to get one yet today. Cream and sugar."

"Gottcha." Matrina poured two cups of coffee, and doctored Franny's with a plop of sugar and dump of milk. Hers, as usual, stayed black. She carried both cups back to Franny's desk.

Franny took her coffee and handed Matrina the report on Vince Haynes' boat at Regatta Pointe. The information on the boat leaped up at them from the printed page.

"Wow," Matrina said. "Mrs. Haynes is a Van Brighton? Of the Long Island Van Brightons?"

"Yes. She's Ethel Van Brighton Haynes, as in 'deep pockets' Van Brighton." Franny smiled. "I'm surprised all she drives is a Lexus. I'd think she'd have a Bentley."

Matrina hovered at Franny's desk and scanned the report. "She probably does," she said. "The Lexus is probably just her 'tooling-around-town' car, and the Bentley is at home in the garage."

"This's kind of sudden wealth, though," Franny said. She pointed to several items in the report. "See? They lived in a track house in Palmetto up until last year, and their only car was his Kia. Then all of a sudden they sold that house, bought the one on Key Royale, bought the big boat, bought the Lexus."

"I see that," Matrina said. "She must have come into some kind of inheritance. No way could Vince have pilfered enough money from the Publix produce department to justify that much change in lifestyle in a year. He's all aggravated with John for looking into his affairs. Wonder why he wouldn't just explain it to John? Why would it be such a big secret?"

"He probably thought it was none of John's business," Franny said. She brought a box of Pecan Sandies out of her top left-hand desk drawer. "Cookie?"

"No, thanks," Matrina said. "Well, I'll just give this report to John, and he can figure out what it means, assuming he gets out of jail sometime soon. The hearing for bond is set for Friday."

"Friday? Oh, that's good," Franny said. "I'm sure they'll let him out. He's such a nice, squeaky clean type of guy." Franny paused. "There's one more thing about this Haynes couple."

"What?"

"Well, the house they had for years in Palmetto was in both their names. And the Kia is in both their names. Then the Palmetto house was sold, and the house on Key Royale was purchased. The Key Royale house is in Ethel's name alone, and the Kia was transferred into Vince's name alone. The Lexus and the boat are both in Ethel's name alone. What do you make of that?"

"Sounds like trouble in Paradise," Matrina said. She raised her eyebrows.

"Sounds like trouble somewhere," Franny said. She sat back down at her desk and sipped her coffee. She put the box of cookies back into her top drawer.

"Where's George?" Matrina said.

"He's out at the industrial park checking guard meters. He wants to be sure all the guards are punching their cards. You know how he is. Runs a tight ship, and all that."

"Oh, yes," Matrina said. "Been there, lived through that. I feel for the poor guards, if they've missed any check-in points out there. The fallout won't be pretty."

Matrina walked away and headed to her cubicle. She wanted to begin her investigation into the elements of John's case. Nathan really loaded her up with assignments. She hoped she could uncover something useful.

Where to begin? To quote good ole Nathan, the beginning is as good a place as any. So, that would be Christopher O'Brien, the would-be Disney bomber. Come on, search engine, do your stuff.

Matrina brought up the program that searched into people's past, what they owned, past addresses, police records, marriages, and inserted her password.

Then she typed in Christopher's name. Scant information flashed on the screen about Christopher O'Brien. His attempted mayhem at Disney showed up, of course, and his date of birth, parents names, dates of their deaths, slight reference to his schooling in Afghanistan, and the date he entered the United States, which occurred six months ago. And of course, since then, his star had risen and splashed across *America's Most Wanted.*

He had no listed employment, so how did he survive here with no income? He had a bank account, and that showed steady deposits and transfers of funds, mostly from Switzerland. No surprise there. It gave his last current address as Laurel Drive in North Fort Myers, Florida. Even a phone number popped up. Hummmmmm.

Christopher had a phone listed in his own name. He rented a house trailer on Laurel Drive, and the record gave a phone number for the landlord as well. Additional information showed Christopher had no lapses in his insurance coverage on his vehicle, and no late payments on his credit cards or utility bills, and he had city water. Another hummmmm.

Matrina wondered what postmark the threatening letters bore. She hadn't thought to look at that until right this minute. And she hadn't thought to make a copy of the envelopes. She got up from her computer, left her cubicle and walked down the hall to George's office. She rummaged through the file folders on top of his desk and found the one that had simply "John" written on the tab.

Inside were the two letters, and the two envelopes, along with the official reports on the findings of the lab analysis. The postmark on both envelopes stated, "Bradenton, Florida." The zip code indicated the mailer used the post office not far from John's house. She wished it said, "North Fort Myers." Too much to ask.

Matrina returned to her station and dug further into Christopher O'Brien's life. This guy led such a straight life, someone should nominate him for sainthood, if they had such a classification in the Muslim religion.

He served soup in the soup kitchens, served as a volunteer at the local nursing home and helped out with little league baseball. Little league players and parents loved him. Of course, as a well-trained international terrorist, that's the way he'd play it—Mr. Model Citizen.

Matrina jotted Christopher's phone number on the yellow legal pad she had gotten from Nathan. She paused a moment, and then pulled her cell phone from her purse. She decided not to use the ACS phone on her desk. George might complain this was not ACS business. And then when the call went through, the caller ID that flashed at the O'Brien home might raise red flags. Her cell phone will just flash, "Alltel," and nothing more.

She dialed the phone number of Christopher O'Brien's home. Of course, he would not be home, but he might have someone there to keep the home fires burning. The number was 941-555-9842. The phone rang. Then a computer interrupted the call.

The voice said, "The area code which you have dialed has been changed. The new area code is now two-three-nine. Please make a note of this for your records. Thank you for using AT&T."

While her mind assimilated this new information, she dialed the number again, using the new area code, two-three-nine. The phone rang in her ear. After twelve rings, she hit, "end send." No one answered. Maybe Christopher lived alone. Maybe whoever shared his living quarters had left for the morning. No matter. Then the importance of the new area code, two-three-nine, tromped across her brain, and created a ground swell that almost made her dizzy. Two-three-nine.

Matrina sat in her chair, stunned, pen in hand, unable to record the new area code, two-three-nine. One piece of the puzzle seemed to slam into place. Did the writer of the threatening letters jot this new area code down in his spiral notebook? Did he tear out the next page and write the ominous letter? He wouldn't need to record the whole phone number, just the new area code, two-three-nine.

She could call Christopher's landlord and see how he stacked up as a tenant. Before Matrina dialed the number, using the new area code, she already knew the answer.

The landlord answered his phone, and responded to her questions. He seemed weary, probably due to the hundreds of phone calls he had received since the Disney incident.

He confirmed that Christopher had been no trouble as a model tenant, paid his rent on time, threw no wild parties, didn't do drugs or even alcohol, to the landlord's knowledge. He didn't smoke. He had no pets and no visitors.

The landlord, who lived next door, never knew when Christopher came and went. Matrina thanked him for his help, said her good-byes, and hit "end send."

As she sat there in her desk chair, still holding her cell phone, it rang. She jumped at the sound of the instrument that twittered in her hand.

"Hello?" She said. She expected the voice of either Michelle or Turner, already bored with summer vacation and full of plans to hitch-hike to Sea

World, or Busch Gardens. Thankfully, Wendy, the next-door college girl, not a baby-sitter, would be the voice of reason.

"We got trouble." The voice belonged to Nathan.

"What?" Matrina. She sat erect, and her forehead creased in concern.

"The D.A. can put John with Slats on the day of the murder."

"Oh, come on. How could he do that?"

"Easy. John told him about it."

"You're kidding."

"Nope. John just remembered Slats came to Publix Friday morning, that third Friday in June. He borrowed twenty bucks from him to take Alice out to dinner that night."

"And John, being John, went right to the D.A. with this new information."

"Yeap. He just thought of it, and he was afraid if he withheld it, the D.A. would come across someone who saw John with Slats in the parking lot, and it would look like he was being cagey."

Matrina sighed a deep sigh of frustration. "So, now they think John shot Slats in the Publix parking lot in the middle of the morning with hundreds of shoppers present?"

"Something like that. They got a search warrant for his Jeep Wagoneer, and they're out there now, even as we speak, going through it with a fine-toothed comb."

"Honestly, what next. Well, if Slats had a date with Alice Friday evening, then she could testify that he was alive when they went out to dinner."

"Nope. He never showed up for their date. He should have been there at six, and when it got to be seven, she called his apartment. No one answered, and none of his neighbors at his apartment complex saw him come home that afternoon at all."

"So, what we have is that John was the supposedly last person to see Slats alive?"

"You got it, Sweet Pea."

"Well, I might have a little good news to balance this out," Matrina tapped her pen on her pad where she jotted down the two-three-nine area code beside Christopher's phone number. She crossed out the nine-four-one, and wrote two-three-nine above it.

"I could use some good news. Lay it on me."

"There's a possible explanation for the two-three-nine impression on the first letter. Christopher O'Brien lives in North Fort Myers, Florida. He even has a phone in his own name. The area code used to be nine-forty-one, but it's been changed, and now it is, guess what?"

"Two-three-nine." A twinge of excitement edged Nathan's voice. "Cool."

"I thought so. I called, and there's no one home, however."

"Of course not. If he has a roomy, they're probably out blowing up bridges or something. Try again later. Even terrorists have to sleep, or eat, or take a shower once in a while. But the two-three-nine could very well be the jotting down of the new area code on the spiral notebook."

"I thought so. I'll keep calling. Thanks for letting me know the latest."

"Sorry it wasn't more positive."

"This won't effect John's bonding out, will it?"

"Heavens, no. If anything, it goes the other way. The D.A. thinks this guy is true blue, except for the fact that he murdered Slats, of course. Pray they don't find any DNA from Slats in the Jeep. Was Slats ever in John's jeep to your knowledge?"

"I really wouldn't know. John would know, of course. What did he say about it?"

"He didn't think Slats had ever been in his vehicle. Slats always drove his own vehicle to church and Bible studies, things like that. John couldn't remember any occasion where he had ever picked up Slats for any reason. Hope he doesn't come up with an incident while he's running all this through his memory bank."

"Me, too."

"So, later, bye."

"Thanks, bye."

Matrina walked back to the kitchen area to refill her coffee cup. This had definitely grown into a two-cup morning.

"More coffee, Franny?" she hollered down the hallway.

"No, thanks. I'm good," came the reply.

Once back at her desk, Matrina decided to jump into round two. Jared Gunthrey. She punched his name into the search engine, and up popped six pages of past arrests, eviction notices, bad check charges, traffic tickets, delinquent payments on just about everything and revocation of his driver's license. The records showed nothing serious, however; nothing to indicate he might be a murderer.

Matrina did a search to see if Robert Walker, AKA Slats, could be connected to either Christopher O'Brien or Jared Gunthrey. That would have been helpful, but nothing popped up. In fact, the data on Robert Walker proved to be sketchy. It gave his current address, phone number, banking information, credit information, all of the data painted him as mediocre at best. He had lived in Bradenton for four years. He apparently held an irrigation and landscaping license. He had a truck in his name, a valid Florida driver's license, and paid-up vehicle insurance.

Before that, it gave the names of towns where he had lived, but no solid addresses. His date of birth showed up as April 10, 1967, Jacksonville, Florida. The hospital listing offered no parents names. Huh? Maybe they got this information from the census or county directory listings, and Slats hadn't bothered to fill in the questionnaires. Whatever, there seemed to be no place he would have crossed paths with either Christopher or Jared.

One item of interest haunted Matrina, however, but she had no idea how to classify it. Slats had been a Catholic at birth, and attended the Catholic church while growing up, but now he belonged to the Baptist Church where John attended. She wondered why the change?

She sat back in her chair and closed her eyes to put her mind into another gear. Why would a person switch from being Catholic to non-Catholic? What could possibly account for that? At that moment, Matrina heard voices in the foyer by Franny's desk.

"So, is she here?" the giggly voice of a woman. Rosie. Oh, mercy. She didn't have time to mess with Rosie today and hoped her little sister didn't have something major on her agenda.

"So, here you are," Rosie loomed in the doorway of Matrina's cubicle.

"Yes, here I am." Matrina tried to look cheerful and belie the fact that her plate of pressing tasks overflowed her morning and splashed into the afternoon.

"We're just stopping by." Rosie made room for Andy to share the doorway with her. Andy wore casual clothing, no uniform today. His plaid short-sleeved shirt matched his casual slacks with the same shade of blue, and Rosie complemented him in her blue peddle pushers and blue plaid button-up-the-front blouse. They looked like Tweedle-Dee and Tweedle Dum from *The Wizard of Oz*, except thinner, and one of them looked like Tom Cruise.

"So, where are you bound?" Matrina said. She hoped the comment would indicate they should be headed someplace other than her office.

"We're out shopping for rings," Rosie said. Andy stood beside her and nodded affirmation. He smiled broadly and hugged Rosie around the waist.

"Rings. Are you serious?"

"You bet we're serious." Enthusiasm warmed Andy's voice. "We're shopping for rings, and then we're going house-hunting. Rosie wants to stay on the beach, but we're not sure we can afford that, if we go to a regular house. I don't want to live in a hole-in-the-wall like she does, just to say I live on Lido."

"So, we're compromising," Rosie said. She beamed with happiness, and her tone glowed with a sparkle of glee. "We're looking for a house, inland, within ten minutes of the beach."

Matrina managed a smile. "That sounds sensible," she said. She got up from her chair and rushed over to Rosie and hugged her tight. "I'm so happy for you." Matrina hugged Andy, too. "Congratulations. I couldn't be happier for both of you. Have you set a date yet?"

"We're talking about Labor Day weekend," Andy said.

"And you'll have a regular wedding?" Matrina said. She moved back to her desk chair.

"We're not sure," Rosie said. "We're still talking about it. We don't want to spend money on a big wedding, when we want to get into a house, buy furniture, stuff like that."

"That sounds very sensible. My flaky little sister, being sensible, getting married, being normal. How wonderful is that?"

Andy chuckled. "It's been a long row to hoe, but finally, I think I've got her straightened out."

"Thankfully, you came along." Matrina joined him in his chuckle.

"Hey, you two. There's nothing wrong with me," Rosie said, hands on hips, stance gone military.

"No," Matrina said. "Nothing that the love of a good man, solid home, bright future, and direction in life couldn't solve."

"And thankfully, I'm just the dude to bring all that into her life." Andy pulled her to his side once more.

"Thankfully," Matrina said.

"Well, we're on our way," Rosie said. "Got rings to buy, houses to reject."

"Let me know," Matrina said.

"If we find the right house, you'll be the first to know," Andy said. He whispered something private into Rosie's ear, and she giggled. They left the office arm in arm.

Matrina sighed a sigh of acceptance. She wished she could feel the exhilaration she displayed at Rosie's happiness. Why did she have to put on such an act? Why couldn't she feel approval and elation for real? She feared she had lost control over Rosie. She rejected that thought. A person can't lose something they never had.

Chapter 15

That same day, later in the afternoon, Matrina drove up the Trail to Bradenton to talk to Alice Toney. She had called her at noon and arranged to meet her at her apartment. Matrina had offered to meet her at the library where she worked, but Alice opted to meet at her home.

Alice sounded curt on the phone, and Matrina hoped she hadn't alienated her with the fact that she needed information about her relationship with John. A "none of your business" persona presented itself over the telephone wires. Why shouldn't she want to cooperate? Given enough spin on her Chevy Astro tires, Matrina would soon know.

Alice's apartment complex proved to be modest two-story dwellings, four beige stucco units per building, no flowers in front, no trees to offer shade. The aged sidewalk framed the area where the vehicles of the tenants parked along the curb in the lumpy parking lot.

Matrina looked at the vehicles present and tried to figure out which one would belong to Alice. She spotted a license tag that said, "Save the whales," and speculated that might be a good fit. A 1993 Dodge Neon, white, sat beneath the specialty tag. She'd better wait for the interview and not jump to hasty conclusions.

John's investigator parked her van and got out. She walked up the cracked walk, avoided the grass that peeked through the cracks, and walked through the front entrance. The odor of brewed coffee and simmered beans wafted out at her, along with the sound of afternoon soap operas.

She found apartment three and knocked on the wooden door. The beige paint on the door matched the inside hallway walls and the outside of the building. Someone must have stumbled on a huge sale of beige paint, bought it up and used it without restraint.

These apartments must be townhouses, as all four units had entrances on the ground floor. Matrina knocked again. A small boy with blond hair and brown eyes, around age seven, opened the door and smiled up at her.

"Hi," Matrina said. She wondered why he would be allowed to open the door without knowledge of who stood on the other side. "Is your mom home?"

"I don't know," the child said. "I'll go see."

"Please do," Matrina said. Strange answer. Does he think he might be home alone? She didn't want to go there. She needed to stay focused on why this woman gave the D.A. a motive for John to have killed Slats. What she did with her child would be another issue for another day and another visitor. Nothing to do with her. She needed to let it slide.

"Oh, Mrs. McCoy," Alice said. The woman came to the door behind her child who led the way. "I didn't hear you knock. Please, do come in."

Alice Tony wore beige slacks and a beige blouse, and she appeared to be all elbows and knees as she led Matrina into the living room. To say she looked like a poster woman for an eating disorder rang as an understatement. She wore her brown hair smoothed back into a tight bun, and her adequate makeup added no color to her face. She wore no jewelry.

"Thank you, Mrs. Toney." It would be good to get to the "Alice and Matrina" level, but if formal names have set the tone, so be it. One way or the other, Matrina had to find out why this woman has taken such an illogical stand. "It is so good of you to see me."

"Yes, well," Alice said, "I haven't the foggiest idea why you would want to see me."

"I'm helping Nathan with John's defense," Matrina said. She waited for the invitation to sit down. She had a long wait in store.

"Yes, well, what does that have to do with me?" Alice said. She stood in the middle of the living room beside Matrina and did not invite her to be seated.

The nondescript beige carpeting matched the nondescript beige walls, and went well with the nondescript blonde furniture. The beige table lamps that adorned the room added light, but no color splashed anywhere except for what flashed from the *National Geographic* magazines spread on the blond coffee table.

"May I sit down?" Matrina said. She tried to establish an air of camaraderie in an atmosphere of nonchalance. What could explain this unresponsiveness? If she thought she had a romance going with John, wouldn't she be glad to help in his defense?

"Do you think you'll be here that long?" Alice said. The little boy stood by his mother, clung to her beige slacks and peeked at Matrina from behind her leg.

"What's your little boy's name?" Matrina said. She sat down on a Danish modern beige chair. Alice didn't tell her not to sit down, so why not?

"Adam," Alice said.

"Hi, Adam," Matrina said. She smiled at the cute, small child. "You're a fine looking young man."

"So, what is it you need to know?" Alice said. She sat down on the edge of the beige Danish modern couch.

"I need to know why it is you think John has a romantic interest in you, and why you think he was against your dating Slats?"

"Because John's in love with me, and he did try to break up my relationship with Slats. I guess that's why he killed him."

Matrina struggled to maintain control. The remark stunned her as if it had been a slap in the face.

"Excuse me?" She wanted to twist her fingers in her ears to clear her hearing.

"Yes. It's clear as a bell. The District Attorney realizes this was a crime of passion. Why can't you people see it as a crime of passion?"

"Alice," like it or not we're going to Alice and Matrina, "that's absurd. John would never harm anyone, for starters, and he didn't realize that you were misinterpreting his intentions. He was simply extending the hand of Christian fellowship to you and Adam. If he were negative about your relationship with Slats, it was because he didn't think Slats could support you, and provide adequate guidance for Adam."

"That has no bearing on his intentions." Alice snapped her response, and Adam sat down on the couch beside his mother.

"I'm thirsty, Mom," he said. He tugged on the sleeve of her beige blouse. "Get me a glass of juice."

"I'll be right back," Alice said. "I have to attend to the needs of my child right now."

"Come on, Sweetheart," she said to Adam. "Mommy will get you some juice. We can't have Mommy's boy thirsty, now, can we."

They left the living room and returned shortly with Adam toting a glass of red-looking liquid. He placed the glass on the coffee table. Alice resumed her seat on the couch, with Adam beside her. He did not touch the juice.

"Alice," Matrina said. She leaned toward her and entreated her to understand, "your assertion is extremely dangerous. You are accusing John of murder. The District Attorney can build his case on your testimony. You have misunderstood circumstances and come up with a false conclusion. You have no facts to support your assumption. Please, for John's sake, reconsider your stand on this issue."

"You reconsider your stand on this issue," Alice said. "John loves me, and he is going to ask me to marry him. You people need to learn to live with that. He couldn't stand it when Slats became interested in me as well."

"Has he ever made any romantic advances toward you?" Matrina said.

"Of course not. We're religious. We wouldn't become physically involved before marriage. What a question to even ask."

"Did he ever give you any reason to believe that his friendship with you was anything other than platonic?"

"I just told you. Religious men don't express their attraction for a woman they plan to marry the way men in the world do. John has always been a total gentleman. Any romantic expression of affection would be saved until after the wedding."

"Another thing," Matrina said. She made serious eye contact with this slender enemy and hoped to escalate her desperate attempt to make a connection with this woman's totally inane mind, "you realize that John is old enough to be your father. Don't you think the age difference would eventually effect your relationship?"

"He is not old enough to be my father," Alice said. She laughed and shook her head.

"How old are you?" Matrina said. She fished for direction in this nebulous arena.

"Twenty-seven," Alice said.

"John is forty-four," Matrina said. "You've got a master's degree. Do the math."

Alice paused for a moment. Matrina hoped this would be a revelation for her to ponder. John didn't look forty-four. That could be part of the problem. His actual age might be news to Alice.

"Mommy," Adam said. "I'm hungry. I want some cookies."

"Yes, Dear," Alice said. She rose from her seat. "Excuse me once more. My child needs attention." She walked toward the kitchen. "Come, Adam. Mommy will get you some cookies. What kind would you like, Dear?"

"Oreos," Adam said. He skipped beside Alice on their way to the kitchen. Within minutes they returned to the living room, and Alice carried a small plate of Oreo cookies.

She placed them on the coffee table beside the untouched juice. "There you go, Sweetheart."

124

"Alice," Matrina said. She felt a need to redirect this trip through the looking glass and come at her from another direction, "even if John were in love with you, and he were jealous of Slats, why would you think he would be capable of murder? Isn't that quite a leap?"

"No," Alice said. "Men often commit crimes of passion over the women they love. It's not unusual at all."

"Do you love John?"

"That is none of your affair." Her icy tone bounced off the austere walls.

"Well, you like John, don't you?" Matrina rephrased the question. "You don't hate him?"

"Of course not. He's been wonderful to Adam and me."

"All right, then," Matrina said. Maybe we can make a tiny amount of progress here. "So, because of your testimony to the District Attorney, John may get the death penalty for this crime, leave his children orphans, be put to death in the prime of his life. Is that what you want?"

"Of course not," Alice said, "but I can't help what measures the law takes. I can only tell the truth. What happens to John after that is out of my control."

"What you're saying represents the facts as you perceive them." Matrina continued to lean in toward Alice in an attempt to make her grasp the situation. "Other people will interpret the facts in a different light, and come to a different conclusion. Can you make allowances for that?"

"No. What I perceive is the truth. Anyone who does not perceive the facts as I know them to be true is not accepting the truth."

"No way you can be wrong."

"No way."

"How can you impute motives with such assurance?"

"Because I've been aware of how John felt for weeks now. And I have been aware of how Slats felt about me. I have been waiting for God to show me which man would be correct for me to marry."

"Did Slats mention marriage to you?"

"Yes, as a matter of fact, he did." Alice picked up three crumbs Adam spilled on the carpet and wiped them from her finger with a tissue from her pocket.

"Did you give him any encouragement?"

"Not really. I was waiting to see what John was going to present to me by way of a proposal. And I would rather not discuss the issue with you. It's none of your affair."

At that moment, Adam took his hand and swiped at the cookies and juice and knocked them from the coffee table into Matrina's lap.

"I don't want these kind of cookies any more," he said. His loud aggressive tone might have generated a call to nine-one-one from another apartment. Matrina reminded herself to listen for oncoming sirens. "And this juice is all warm now. I need peanut butter cookies and a glass of cold milk. She's distracting you, and you're not taking care of me. She's making you a bad mother. Make her go away."

"Yes, Dear," Alice said. She reached for him to cradle him in her arms. "Mommy will get you the cookies you like, and some milk that is cold. Don't worry, Darling. Mommy is here for you."

Adam began to cry. He wrested himself away from Alice, threw himself on the couch and kicked his feet in her direction. Matrina stood up and brushed red liquid from her white slacks. She shook her dripping hands toward the coffee table, which harbored soggy *National Geographics* and red juice that cascaded to the carpet.

"I guess I'd better go," Matrina said. She sighed in defeat. She made pinkish footprints as she sloshed toward the door in her juice-filled shoes. "I can see you have your mind made up to crucify John, and that's a shame, after all he's done for you. I would think your church would teach you to love one another."

"We do love one another," Alice said. Her eyes and her voice snapped at Matrina. She tried to get Adam back into her grasp, but his kicking feet and flailing arms made that impossible. "We are also taught to tell the truth. I would think you would respect that. And yes, I think you should go. You have upset Adam terribly."

"I can see that," Matrina said, almost beneath her breath. "I'll let myself out."

"Here, Darling," Alice said in the direction of her thrashing son. "Let's go into the kitchen and see if we can find those peanut butter cookies and some nice, cold milk."

"Okay," Adam said. He sniffled back tears and left the couch. "They'd better be fresh cookies and really cold milk." He wiped his nose on his sleeve and took his mother's extended hand. "And she's going to leave, right?"

"Yes, Dear," Alice said. Matrina sensed an attempt on Alice's part to denote an element of calmness in her voice. "She's leaving right now. Please close the door behind you as you depart, Mrs. McCoy." Alice spoke in Matrina's direction.

"Glad to," Matrina said. She couldn't wait to close the door on this little episode, glad to close the door on meeting Alice and Adam, glad to close the door on sticky juice and crumbly cookies. If someone had told her people like Alice existed, she'd have said, "No way, get out of town."

Matrina closed the door to apartment three, and went back to her Chevy van. She hoped to mop up enough red juice with the roll of paper towels under her seat that her light upholstery and floor carpet would escape the red stains. Probably not possible, ran her thoughts, unless she could drive home barefoot and standing.

Chapter 16

The Saturday after the skirmish with Alice Toney, Matrina sank into the blanket of iridescent bubbles ebbing and flowing in her square garden bathtub. The afternoon sun made rainbows on the white tile covering the bathroom walls as it filtered through the apothecary bottles lined up on the ledge of her high bathroom window.

This large garden bathtub drew her to this house last year when she first moved down from Long Island. However, life turned out to be so hectic, she seldom had the time to use it.

Today, it felt scandalous to luxuriate like this in the middle of the afternoon, but she told herself she had earned this little break in life. She had deliberately culled out these precious moments to soak and do nothing. She sighed a deep sigh of contentment, and turned to the next page of the current Janet Evanovich novel.

Stephanie Plum, the heroine of this novel, paraded across the pages with her usual hilarious escapades. Matrina laughed out loud, and it occurred to her that she could laugh again, something she thought nine-eleven had removed from her life forever. The laughter had resurfaced. How neat. Laughter, and peace and quiet. What a wonderful afternoon. Then the peace and quiet dissolved into an interruption. Bummer.

"Mom," Michelle hollered while she knocked on the outside of the bathroom door. "Are you okay?"

"Yes, Dear," Matrina said. She giggled to herself and turned the page of the book with a soapy hand. "Why do you ask?"

"Because you're laughing, and you're in there all alone. What are you laughing at?"

"Oh, it's just this book. I don't know how this writer thinks up all this funny stuff."

"Is it a book I can read?"

"Probably not this year. It's a little mature for you right now, but someday."

"Oh, pooh." Michelle paused, and Matrina knew she still stood outside the bathroom door. "Aunt Rosie called."

"What did she want?"

"She wants to bring Kentucky Fried Chicken and some mashed potatoes for supper."

"She doesn't need to bother. I'm doing sloppy joes, something simple."

"She wants to bring the chicken. She says she won't take 'no' for an answer. She already hung up on the phone. She'll be here around five."

"Well, I hate for her to bother, but if she thinks she has to bring chicken, I guess we'll let her bring chicken. Do you want to toss a salad together?"

"Yeah, I can do that. And I should set the table?" Matrina heard Michelle as she shuffled outside the door.

"Yes, but just use the paper plates. That movie we're watching on 'pay-for-view' is on at eight. We don't want to get bogged down with kitchen work."

"How about I use our everyday dishes? I hate paper plates."

"Okay. Not the good dishes, though. Just the dishes that can go into the dishwasher."

"I will. We're watching *Miss Congeniality 2,* right?"

"Yes. That Sandra Bullock movie."

"That's going to be so cool."

"Be a pal and let me lounge here a little bit longer, will you, Michelle?"

"Sure. I'm sorry. I didn't mean to bother you. I just wanted to tell you about Aunt Rosie calling, oh, and I almost forgot, Turner wants to have Buddy over for dinner and the movie."

"Does he know what we're watching? It's not really a boy's movie."

"Yeah, he knows. He says it's okay. He got to pick the last movie when we had a coupon. Remember, we watched *Mission Impossible II?* Besides, he's got a crush on Sandra Bullock."

"I do not." Turner's voice drifted down the hall. "I just like her because she's a good actress."

"You love her, and what kind of an actress she is has nothing to do with it."

"You take that back. You're always accusing me of stuff I don't do."

"I won't take it back." Michelle hollered in return and walked down the hall toward Turner's room. "You're just always trying to worm out of things."

"I do not." Turner stood at the bathroom door now and knocked. "So, Mom, can I call Buddy and invite him over?"

"Yes, I guess so," Matrina said. She closed her book and stepped out of the tub. This shouting back and forth through the closed bathroom door had shattered her peace.

She thought she had hog-tied life, wrangled it into the barn and corralled it for an afternoon. However now it had lunged to freedom and circled the bathroom. She toyed with the bubbles and wished she could enjoy the unhurried novel a bit longer, but life demanded her back in the saddle again.

"Can he come for dinner before the movie?" Turner said. He leaned on the door.

"Yes. Tell him to come around five."

"Can he spend the night?"

Matrina had to think that one over.

"I guess so. But no tricks, Turner," she said. She dried herself off and hung the towel on the rack. "No pranks on Michelle in the middle of the night. Nothing, you understand? You and Buddy have to go to bed at a reasonable hour and stay in bed, and go to sleep. If not, it will be a long, long while before Buddy is able to spend the night again, got it?"

"Got it." Turner sighed and walked back down the hall and into the living room to call his classmate.

The white chenille bathrobe covered Matrina's body, and she trotted barefooted into her bedroom. Casual blue slacks and a matching blue tee shirt replaced the robe, and she ran a brush through her shiny blond hair. A blue hair band held the hair in place. She pulled on a pair of bedroom slippers and marched into the living room. Turner had hung up the phone from his conversation with Buddy.

"His mom says he can come," Turner said. "If we get bored with the movie, we can play Turismo."

"That sounds fine," Matrina said. She reached for the portable phone. She plopped into the comfy flowered recliner in front of the TV which broadcasted *So Little Time* and dialed John's phone number.

"Hello," came John's calm voice.

"How's it feel to be out?" she said. She tried to sound cheerful with encouragement.

"Great. You should have been here last night for the grand homecoming."

"I thought about it, but it seemed like it should be a family affair."

"It was that, complete with banner that said, 'Dad's out of jail, hurrah.'"

"I bet the neighbors loved that."

"I think the neighbors helped the kids paint it. This neighborhood hasn't seen this much excitement since hurricane Donna came through and blew down the drive-in."

"So, you're doing okay?" Matrina changed the channel and put the TV on Fox News.

"Yeah, as good as can be expected. Right now, I'm working on flying the kids to Dee's parents. I hate to take any of this mumbo jumbo seriously, but I can't gamble with the kids welfare. Slats really is dead. There's some strange stuff going down. I had this trip for the kids nailed down before I got otherwise detained, and they missed their flight. I have to reschedule it."

"That's the truth. You're doing the right thing with the kids. And they'll love it. So will Dee's parents."

"Yeah, they're all really excited about it. It'll only be for a month or so, until I get this thing sorted out. I have them flying out of Tampa tomorrow morning. After that, I've really got to kick this defense into high gear. There's actually going to be a trial. Can you believe it?"

"And you're sure Nathan is your best defense attorney?"

"Oh, you bet. I've seen him in court. He can send prosecuting attorneys to the corner to cut out paper dolls and entire juries to tread water in the tears they weep over his closing arguments. He may be short of stature, but he's long on charisma."

"That sounds good. Did Nathan tell you the latest on Christopher O'Brien?"

"Yes, and the two-three-nine connection. Good work. Makes sense, doesn't it?"

"It's a possibility. Not the only answer, of course, but a possibility."

"Sounds likely to me. The terrorist could have jotted the new area code down so he wouldn't forget it."

"Nathan said the authorities were checking into your seeing Slats on the day he died." Tramp wandered over and put his head in Matrina's lap. She scratched his ears, and he sighed with contentment and looked up at her with large syrupy eyes.

"Yeah. They strip-searched my Jeep. They didn't find anything, thankfully. I didn't think Slats had ever been in my Jeep, and I guess he hadn't. Nathan told me he had you go and do battle with Alice Toney."

"It wasn't much of a battle. I left covered with what I think was grape juice, *a la* Adam."

"Isn't that kid a trip?"

"Doesn't she realize she's ruining him with all this smothering?"

"She doesn't realize the world is round. That's why I became involved with her, to try to get the kid into sports so he would see the world doesn't revolve around him."

"She equated that to dating."

"She equates my standing next to her at church and sharing her hymnal to dating."

"I did my best to rattle her cage, but she's having none of it. She says you murdered Slats because you love her and want to marry her, and that's the name of that tune."

"Did you tell her I was only trying to help her out with Adam? Be kind to her? And I only bought her a hamburger on the way home from the ballpark so she wouldn't go home hungry?"

"I said she misunderstood your motives. I even told her you were old enough to be her father, and there couldn't be a romantic interest on your part, that she was too young."

"How'd that logic go?"

"Nowhere. She thinks age is not a factor." A commercial came on TV, and she triggered the mute button.

"And she told the D.A. I killed Slats over her?"

"Yeap. She admitted that to me. She's not ashamed of it. In fact, she's wearing the murder like a merit badge. She thinks it was a crime of passion."

"Oh, give me a break."

"I did my best, but she stayed so focused on Adam and his juice and milk and cookies, I'm not sure she'd even know who I was."

"I guess I'll have to go and see her myself and try to reason with her. I'll pull out all the stops and make her see what's happening here."

"Don't go alone. Take Nathan with you. She'll say you came to see her as soon as you got out of jail to declare your love, or whatever she has garbled in her mind. How can someone so smart be so obtuse?"

"Mystery to me. Of course, it's actually my fault. I was too oblivious to her reaction when I showed interest in her and Adam. I thought it was obvious what I was doing. I was wrong."

"She thinks you and Slats both wanted to marry her. She was waiting for God to show her which one of you she should choose. Of course, she sees the death of Slats as you leveling the playing field." The commercial finished, and Matrina put the TV on low volume to follow the latest debacle in politics.

"Marry her? Oh, wouldn't that be a good idea. Then, she could raise my children like she's raising Adam. And somewhere down the line, while Adam is out knocking over convenience stores, John or Matt can drive the get-a-way car."

"Yes, and Dee-Dee can polish their artillery. Scary thought, eh?"

"Yes. How'd she get so far off track like this?"

"She just got the female fantasy going, and somewhere along the line, her mind jumped the track, and now fantasy is reality."

"We have to get her back on track, and soon. I'll take Nathan and go see her, and if we can't reason with her, I'll sic Samuel on her. That might cause her some embarrassment."

"Let's hope so. So, are we on schedule with planning your defense?" Matrina gave Tramp a final pat on the head and walked with the portable phone in hand into the kitchen. Michelle had everything under control so she walked back to the living room. By now, Tramp had crashed in front of the news channel.

"Who knows. I'm starting Monday collecting register tapes from all the stores in the area that sell nine millimeter bullets. I figure I'll check the Wednesday and Thursday before the day of the murder. I plan to start with Thursday. The folks who killed Slats had to buy bullets someplace. There has to be a paper trail."

"Sounds huge. Nathan had that on my list of things to do."

"It's way too much for you to do with your job. Publix is okay with me working on my defense right now, so let me collect the tapes, and you can help me screen them, if you like."

"I like."

"If we find the purchase of a box of nine millimeter bullets at Wal-Mart or Kmart, or any other department store, we can get the security video tapes for that day and see who was at that register at that time. Maybe Lady Luck will jump up and pat us on the head."

"Let's hope so. Oh, by the way, I got the information on that boat you wanted, Vince Haynes' boat, remember? It was the biggest problem you had going back before the world went completely nuts?"

"Oh, yeah. What's the scoop?"

"Vince is married to money, I mean deep pockets money, old, musty money, real money. I don't know what was up with them living in Bradenton on the brink of mediocrity for so long, but suddenly, she took the reins, and they moved to Key Royale; she bought the Lexus; she bought the boat, and she is living the life fantastic. Maybe Vince is just not willing to admit that they're living this new life on her money. I don't think he's tapping the till. I think she's footing the bills, all of them."

"Hum. I'll have to check that out. Thanks for running the I.D. from the boat. If I ever get out of the murder-thy-neighbor trick bag, maybe I can get back to suppressing crime at Publix. You have this info on Vince in hard copy?"

"Yes. It's all in a file for you. I'll give it to you whenever I see you."

"Sounds good." There was a pause in the conversation. Matrina waited for him to say, "Good-bye," and hang up. Instead, he said, "Matrina?"

"Yes?"

"Thanks for helping to bail me out."

"No problem. You'd do it for me," she said. She felt embarrassed he knew about her contribution.

"Yes, I would. And Nathan has some change for you. He didn't need quite all of your two hundred thousand."

"Really? They came down on the bond?"

"No, the kids kicked in their life savings, twenty-one dollars and seventeen cents. So your part came to one hundred ninety-nine thousand, nine hundred and seventy-eight dollars and eighty-three cents. You have twenty-one-seventeen coming as change."

"Goody. That'll take us all to Subway one of these days."

"Look forward to it."

"I've got Rosie and a friend of Turner's coming to dinner and a movie, so guess I'd better go and prepare to feed my flock, although Rosie's bringing chicken."

"That sounds good."

"Yes, talk to you later."

"I'll let you know if I do any good with the bullet search."

"I'll get with you and take part of the tapes. I'll be happy to help scan them. We'll split up the load."

"I ain't heavy; I'm your brother?"

"Something like that," she said. She laughed and he joined her. The laughter sounded nervous. "We're going to beat this, John."

"Thanks. Have a good evening with your chicken and your movie."

"I'll try. Talk to you probably tomorrow."

"Copy that."

"Yeah, copy." Then the dull thud of dial tone rang in her ears. She held the phone for thirty seconds and replaced it in its base. She patted the phone and sighed.

Rosie waltzed through the front door with a bucket of chicken and a couple of tubs of mashed potatoes. She put them on the dining room table. "Hello, the house," she said.

"Wow, this sure smells good," Turner said. He inhaled over the buckets and grinned.

"And here's the salad," Michelle said. She brought the brimming glass bowl of fresh veggies to the table, along with three bottles of dressing. "This is all the dressing we have, though. I hope it's enough."

"Looks fine," Rosie said. She removed the lids from the chicken and potatoes.

"We're so glad Uncle Andy is working tonight so you could come see us," Michelle said. She gave her aunt a warm hug.

"If the guy is going to take on another mouth to feed, I guess he'd better put his shoulder to the wheel and earn some big bucks," Rosie said. She hugged Michelle in return.

"Let me see your ring," Michelle said.

Rosie proudly displayed the solitaire diamond that decorated the third finger of her left hand. "Ain't it a douzzy?"

"Oh, Aunt Rosie," Michelle said. "It's truly beautiful. I'm so happy for you. When's the big day?"

"The Saturday before Labor Day, at sunset, whenever that is."

"Let's eat," Matrina said. She sat down and hoped everyone else would follow suit.

"Oh, boy," Turner said. "I'm starved, but Buddy isn't here yet."

"We'll save some for him," Matrina said. She motioned to Turner to take his seat. "This isn't a formal dinner. He doesn't have to be here on time. We won't let him starve."

"Turner, would you like to say grace?" Matrina said.

"Okay," Turner said. He bowed his head. "Dear God, thank you for the chicken, but next time, please let Aunt Rosie bring pizza. Amen."

Michelle rolled her eyes to the ceiling, and Matrina shot her a look that warned her to not allow her thoughts to find their way to her mouth.

"It's nice you can tell God exactly what you're thinking," Matrina said to Turner. "But it would be good not to complain about the food God has given us. We need to be grateful we have any food at all. And chicken is above and beyond what a lot of people are sitting down to eat tonight."

Turner nodded and helped himself to a chicken leg.

Matrina noticed Tramp whimpered at her side. He had resurrected himself from his unconscious position in front of the TV and moved to Matrina's elbow to promote what he could from the barrel of chicken. He sat erect, and moved his front feet up and down so his nails clicked on the marble floor.

"You are tilting at windmills," Matrina said to him. "You're wasting your effort on the wrong family member." She resisted her impulse to pat him on the head. She hated to get dog dander mixed up in the fried chicken. "Turner," she said, "Could you please take Tramp out on the back porch and give him some Kibbles and Chunks? And close the door on him so he stays there until we're finished eating."

"Okay," Turner said. "Come on, Tramp. I'm the one who's starving, and you get to eat before I do. Something's wrong with this picture."

The boy grabbed a small piece of chicken that had no bone in it and walked out of the dining room with Tramp on his heels. Matrina could hear Turner as he led Tramp onto the back porch and dumped Kibbles and Chunks into the dog's bowl. He made a detour through the kitchen to wash his hands before he returned to the table.

Matrina sighed a small sigh of victory that he washed up without the usual reminder. A small victory here, a small victory there, and perhaps she would win the battle before her son turned thirty-five.

"So, Rosie," Michelle said. She passed the bucket of chicken to her mother, "Where's the wedding to be held? Are we all invited?"

"Of course you're all invited," Rosie said. "Andy and I talked about where to have the wedding, and Matrina, don't have a cow, but we've decided to have it on the boardwalk at the beach." Rosie took the bucket from Matrina, removed a chicken breast, and put it on her plate. She licked her fingers after she put the chicken down.

"At the beach?" Matrina said. She tried to conceal her shock. "Rosie, this is your first, and hopefully, last wedding. You don't think you should do it in church?"

"No," Rosie said. She drew out the "no" as she pronounced it. "Neither one of us are churchy, and it seems hypocritical to go to church to get married when you don't go any other time. God is at the beach just as He is in church. So, it'll be on the boardwalk, at sundown, and Matrina, I was hoping you'd be my matron of honor, unless you'd rather not because it's not in a church."

Matrina sighed. "Oh, Rosie, of course, I'd be thrilled to be your matron of honor, no matter where the wedding is. I assume we're all wearing bathing suits? Or maybe jogging shorts and Nikes?"

"No." Long, drawn out, "no" once again. "I'm wearing a pale, pale, pale aqua dress, barely off-white, but into the aqua color scheme, and I thought you could wear a nice, long, satin dress of a deeper aqua, and maybe a picture hat."

"And lots of hat pins to fight off the sea breeze," Matrina said.

"Yes, if necessary," Rosie said. "And my dress will be long, and satin, and I'll have a matching veil, not white, but off-white into the aqua, and I'll carry one white rose, and you'll carry a bouquet of aqua-dyed chrysanthemums. Andy will wear an aqua tux, and Kenny, his partner, will wear the same. Kenny's his best man, and we're hoping that at the reception, you and Kenny will become friends. He really likes you, you know."

"Reception? On the boardwalk?" Matrina stopped eating, fork suspended in air.

"Of course not." Matrina felt sorry she had irked Rosie, but she wasn't on the same page, as usual, and things between them often required longer explanations. "It's at Casey's Lounge on Lido, not far from the boardwalk. That's where Andy and I met."

"A bar?" Matrina's chagrin surfaced and hung over the table for a full moment.

"It's not a bar," Rosie said. "It's a respectable lounge with a pool table and line dancing. And they have a private room that can be rented for special occasions, and this is our special occasion. We'll have a deli buffet with corned beef and hickory smoked turkey and Alpine Lace Swiss cheese on Kaiser rolls, coffee, tea, soda, and a cash bar."

Matrina hoped her concerned sigh hadn't surfaced out loud. "Sounds nice," she said aloud.

"Yes," Rosie said. She took a bite from her chicken breast. "It's going to be wonderful. I cannot believe I've met someone as wonderful as Andy, a cop, with a steady job, who's handsome, and kind, and generous, and thoughtful. I have to pinch myself every day to believe it's really happening."

"Who's performing the wedding ceremony?" Matrina said. She put French dressing on her salad.

"I was hoping you wouldn't ask," Rosie said. "Our assistant manager at work is a notary public, and she's doing the ceremony. That's legal in Florida, you know, for a notary public to perform weddings. Besides, it's not who performs the ceremony that counts. It's the vows the people take. It's kind of like being out to sea, and the captain of the ship can perform the ceremony. It's all legal, and it's better than getting a preacher who doesn't even know us."

"You don't have to be so defensive about it," Matrina said. She put a good clump of salad on her fork. "I didn't say a word. It's your wedding. You have the right to whatever you want." She put the forkful of salad into her mouth.

"Well, I know you," Rosie said, "and I can feel your disapproval bouncing off all the ceiling of this room."

"It's none of my business," Matrina said. She tried to sound sincere. "I'm happy for you, Rosie. And if this is the kind of wedding you want, then that's what you should have. We'll all come and be happy with you."

"Yes, it sounds like fun," Michelle said.

The doorbell rang, and Turner dashed to let Buddy in. He fixed Buddy a plate and handed it to his freckle-faced, red-haired pal from school. He picked up his own plate and caught his mother's eye.

"Can we take our plates and go eat in front of the TV?" he said. "I think there's a Roy Rogers movie on the Western Channel."

"Sure," Matrina said. "I guess wedding talk is a little boring for boys."

"No kidding," Turner said. "And we know the big movie is on at eight, so we won't get into any show that goes past eight."

"Good," Matrina said.

"Save room for dessert," Rosie said. "I brought Breyers, butter pecan ice cream and apple pie."

"Wow, thanks, Aunt Rosie," Turner said from the living room.

"Yeah, thanks, Aunt Rosie," Michelle said in an echo.

"Thanks, Aunt Rosie," Matrina said.

"All right, all right," Rosie said. "It was on sale, and I had a coupon."

"Getting married, settling down, and becoming frugal," Matrina said. She helped herself to more salad. "What more could we ask for?"

"Not much," Rosie said. She put some mashed potatoes on her plate. "'I'm practically perfect in every way,' to quote Mary Poppins." She winked at Michelle, and Matrina knew she glanced at her to see if that got her goat. When Matrina shook her head in response, Michelle suppressed her giggles, and Rosie seemed satisfied. "And Turner is watching a Roy Rogers movie?" Rosie said. "How come an up-and-coming kid like that is interested in an old-fogy like Roy Rogers?"

"He doesn't know he's an 'old fogy' and don't you dare tell him," Matrina said. "I guess it's got enough high adventure to interest boys who don't know an 'old fogy' movie when they see one. Almost everything on the Western Channel is pretty decent, so I encourage Turner to watch their programming. He tends to just watch whatever is on that channel."

"Whatever floats your boat," Rosie said. She rose to get the pie and ice cream.

Chapter 17

The next day, Sunday spread itself across the Florida peninsula with all of its mid-July oppression that caused air conditioners to run full tilt and residents to experience heart palpitations upon receipt of their electric bills.

Matrina headed to the Trade Winds for her showdown with Kiran. Of course, this apex of effort would be more spectacular if George stood in the wings. No matter. She knew she had a winner on tap, and he could do catch up with the facts in the morning.

Matrina got out of the van, and the hot sultry breeze from the Manatee River whipped her scarf across her face. She battled her hair, and after a few swipes with her hand, gave up on it. She walked inside the Trade Winds restaurant, and had the tube-topped, flaring-skirted, red-haired hostess show her to a seat in the middle of the crowded room.

"I'm not staying right this moment," Matrina said to the hostess, who stood beside her, menus in mid-air.

"Oh?"

"No. I'm waiting for someone, so I think I'll just wait in your lounge and not take up a table until my guest arrives."

"As you wish." The hostess left Matrina where she stood beside the table and returned to the packed lobby.

Matrina noted Kiran stood at the cash register ready for action. Come on, action.

The two pots of pennies entered her line of vision. Good. The deal would go down as scheduled, and she knew she had been right all along. Why did she always doubt herself when it came to her job? Why did she always doubt herself when it came to anything? Always, when the hour of show and tell approached, she nursed nagging fears that this time, she might be wrong.

Before she left the restaurant, she noticed the same bare-footed, red-haired waitresses dressed in the same tube tops and full skirts of various pastel colors carried trays of food and drinks as usual.

Satisfied that Kiran would fall into her own trap, Matrina walked out and stood on the sidewalk and watched the marigolds do their chaotic version of *River Dance* in the swirling breeze. She checked her watch. Seven o'clock. Two hours to kill while she waited for closing and show time with Kiran. If the Haynes' yacht still occupied the same dock area, she could check that out and kill some time.

She walked out of the Trade Winds parking lot and down the grassy embankment to the boardwalk that meandered in front of the moored vessels belonging to the rich and famous of Manatee County. The *Fly-By-Night* swayed up and down where it had been moored the last time she saw it. Did people rent the same slip over and over and park their boat in the same spot every time they returned from a spin out in the Gulf? Probably.

The *Fly-By-Night* thumped gently against the padded dock in the wakes caused by other boats as they came and went in the marina. Matrina slowed her gait to a stroll as she approached the boat, about five vessels away.

Nobody lounged on the boat. The vessel looked the same as the first time Matrina had spotted her. Someone should have swept the deck. Oak leaves had blown onboard from the trees surrounding the parking lot.

Next to the *Fly-By-Night,* a boat almost twice its size bobbed and bounced in the river. Matrina noted its name, the *Empress*. Woah, Baby. She figured it must be fifty feet long, and have full living quarters downstairs. The sounds of the party going on below and the smell of steaks cooking floated into the evening air. Laughter floated up from the stairwell that led downstairs, and when Matrina paused directly in front of the *Empress* to gawk at its splendor, Andy Douglas surfaced from below. He carried a wine cooler and backed out of the hold. He stepped out onto the deck but shared laughter with the person who remained below.

Matrina freaked. Andy Douglas? Rosie's Andy? Their upstanding law enforcement type person, soon to be their family member, lounged on a yacht worth, what? Half a million dollars, give or take a couple hundred thou?

The ACS investigator had nowhere to hide, nowhere to flee, nowhere to become invisible. In sheer panic, she jumped onto the *Fly-By-Night* and pressed herself into the entranceway to the downstairs of that vessel. The protruding entranceway of about three feet on either side would protect her from Andy's view. As long as the Haynes didn't come out for an early evening jaunt down the river, she might be safe and undiscovered. If they did show up, oh well, maybe some explanation would come to her.

She nestled into the doorway to the hold and fished in her pockets so passers-by would think she hunted for the right key to unlock her cabin. Andy stood ten feet away with only the padded dock between them. The jutting entranceway obscured his view of her. The two boats bounced back and forth in their own rhythm off the dock's padding.

"Get your scrumptious southern behind up here," he said to the person who had stayed below and probably turned steaks on the grill. "Come check out this incredible sunset."

"Oh, that's a good idea," the heavy southern female drawl said from the downstairs. "Then we can have charred steaks and crunchy baked potatoes."

"You worry too much," Andy said. He took a sip of his wine cooler. "This sunset is way too much."

Matrina heard footsteps as they ascended the stairs from the cabin on the *Empress.* She wished she dared gamble a peek around the entranceway of the *Fly-By-Night* to check out this southern belle, but discovery loomed too imminent. She hugged the doorway and tried different keys from her key ring in the lock. The keys jangled in spite of efforts to keep them quiet. Jangling keys might attract Andy's attention if he had been less distracted.

"Oh, it is so beautiful," the drawling female voice said. She spoke from the deck now.

"Almost as beautiful as you are," Andy said. "How'd I get so lucky as to have you in my life?"

"I'm lucky, too," the sultry voice said. "The day you walked into the Trade Winds and ordered that T-bone and a bottle of Coors was the first day of the rest of my life."

"Mine, too," Andy said, and the silence that followed put a tender pat and a gentle kiss into Matrina's imagination. Then the sound of a timer going off from the cabin below ended the romantic moment.

"Got to go tend to the vittles." The southern drawl said with a giggle that followed. "Best come on down and eat. I have to get back to work soon."

"Don't forget to be back here by eleven," Andy said. He must have moved toward the steps as his voice drifted away. "The deal goes down at twelve." He descended the stairs to the hold.

"I'm supposed to be off at nine," the drawl said from the cabin below. "But I'll need to fold napkins, fill shakers and run the carpet sweeper before I can leave. I ought to be out by nine-thirty, though."

"You're such a good girl," Andy said.

"Ain't I though?" she laughed in return.

As soon as they left, Matrina bolted from the *Fly-By-Night* and darted

141

down the dock in the opposite direction from the *Empress*. She scurried up the grassy bank to the parking lot of the Trade Winds. Her heart pounded, and she fought tears. Poor Rosie. How could this be? Well, she planned to jolly well find out and find out soon. Andy's little midnight party would be a threesome. They wouldn't know it, and she'd be the one with the camcorder.

* * *

Matrina sat in her van until eight-forty-five. The Trade Winds closed at nine and read registers at nine-fifteen. She planned to go in now and wait until closing, order coffee and act like she expected someone to join her.

At nine-fifteen, Kiran should count the pennies in the cup. Then she should put the control key in the register and punch up the command to take the register reading. The counting of the money in the drawer would consume a couple of minutes. Removing her take would consume a couple more minutes. Then she would jot the remaining figures down on the control sheet, if she followed the same procedure as on Anna Maria. There's where Matrina would have to really watch her. Kiran should turn her back on the video behind the register, and faster than lightning, her right hand should deposit the folded bills of her take into her skirt pocket.

That 'Las Vegas' touch might make it tricky to catch her. Matrina would have to witness the movement so she could testify the money discovered in the cashier's pocket came from the register drawer. Kiran shouldn't recognize Matrina in the restaurant since she never saw that much of her at Anna Maria. Other straggling customers ought to be present in the dining room to help with the cover.

As soon as Matrina jelled her plan of action, she walked up to the front door of the restaurant and walked inside.

"We close in fifteen minutes," the hostess said. She did not carry any menus.

"I know," Matrina said. "I only want a cup of coffee, and I'm meeting someone. We'll be out by nine."

"Okay," the hostess said. She sighed and showed Matrina to a table against the wall. Matrina sat down and spotted four other tables in the room with lingering customers. Relief to not be alone and obvious flooded over her.

She sat down at the table and noted her watch. Eight-fifty.

"Well, for heaven's sake, Mrs. McCoy," a voice on her right said. A stunned Matrina looked up into the face of Frank Lowell.

"Mr. Lowell," she said. She hoped other words that made sense would surface. "I didn't expect to see you here." Ain't that the understatement of the century.

"I'm only here to pick up Kiran," Frank said. He sat down at Matrina's table as he spoke. "Since you approved her work at Anna Maria, I figured she'd be ready to send back here, since this is where the company wants her to cashier."

"Yeah, she's good to go," Matrina said. More blatant truth.

"Are you working up here now doing an investigation?" The question floated out there and waited for a response.

"Not for Trade Winds, but for a friend of mine concerning a boat in the harbor." More truth. Strange how truth worked better than any lie one could invent.

"You don't mind if I join you until Kiran is ready to go, do you?"

"Of course not." Now what? Carry on with the plan, all engines full speed ahead, that's what.

Kiran came from the kitchen, walked toward the register and stood behind the counter. She removed the control key from her pocket and inserted it into the register and turned it. The register responded and proclaimed, "ka-ching, ka-ching, ka-ching," as it spit out its totals tape for the day.

While the register did its thing, Matrina watched as Kiran dumped the pennies from the penny cup and counted them up. She plopped the pennies back into the cup. Then the cashier opened the register drawer and removed the stack of twenty-dollar bills. She counted out several, and then removed one ten-dollar bill from the next section of the drawer.

"This is it," Matrina said. She hoped she hadn't spoken aloud, but the look on Frank's face said she had. She hoped Kiran wouldn't move too far behind the register and block her view.

The red-haired cashier turned her back a quarter of a turn, and Matrina figured she thought to block the video camera. In one swift, smooth move, her right hand went from drawer to pocket and emerged again empty. She turned back in full view of the camera, began to count out the rest of the drawer and tally the figures on her control sheet.

"Excuse me," Matrina said to Frank. She left the table and walked up to the register.

"Hi, Kiran," she said. Kiran turned and looked at her, a look of confusion clouded her face. "My name is Matrina McCoy, and I've had you under surveillance for the past couple of weeks. You're going to be accused of embezzlement of funds from the Salt and Sea Corporation." As she spoke,

Matrina dashed her hand into Kiran's right-hand pocket and felt a clump of folded bills within her fingertips. She pulled the stash out and counted seven twenties and a ten, one hundred and fifty dollars. "It's over, Kiran," Matrina said. She reached for her cell phone and dialed nine-one-one.

"Oh, no, it ain't." Kiran bolted from behind the cash register counter and headed for the front door. She knocked the hostess out of the way, put her hand on the frame of the glass door and threw her entire body against it. The hostess had already turned the lock, and it wouldn't give.

Frank leaped from his seat and reached Kiran in a matter of seconds. She hammered on the door with her fists, and her screams and tears rattled Matrina in spite of her resolve. Frank grabbed both of Kiran's arms behind her back and corralled her.

As Frank walked Kiran back to the table, the cashier managed to regain her calm. She sniffled back her tears and managed a haughty glance at Frank.

She did not look at Matrina who had given the nine-one-one dispatcher the address of where to send the squad car. This involvement of Frank confused Matrina, and she had no clue where he fit into this scheme at this moment. He did not fit where she had placed him. Matrina sat down at the table with them and listened for the oncoming sirens to approach the restaurant.

"Kiran," she said, "you have embezzled Trade Winds funds. We have it all on tape." The ACS investigator pulled the hundred and fifty dollars cash from her pocket. "This money I pulled from your right-hand pocket came from the cash register. You have been tracking your take with the penny cup. When we read the register and count the money left in it, it will balance, probably to the penny. That's how good you are at this." Matrina looked over at Frank to gauge his reaction to this speech. He sat poker-faced, and Matrina needed to pull him into the net before the cops arrived.

"Frank, I think you are in on this little caper as well." She chose her words carefully. Lawsuits come from slips of the tongue.

"I am in on it," Frank said. He patted Kiran's arm and gave her an icy glance. "She was hired to work here at Regatta Pointe as the cashier. They sent her to me on Anna Maria to train on the register. So I trained her, but I knew she was stealing from us, but I couldn't catch her. That's why I hired you to catch her. She was going to get me bounced out of Trade Winds on my ear if I didn't put a stop to her."

"I saw you count the pennies in the cup," Matrina said. She had to connect the dots and do it fast.

"Yes, I wanted you to see that," Frank said. "I knew the pennies had something to do with the money she took, but I didn't know for sure how the con worked."

"You and she are romantically involved," Matrina said. "I saw you in the parking lot nights after work."

"Yes, we've had some fun, but it was all part of the game to figure her out. And when you said you didn't have anything on her, I figured she'd outsmarted you, too. I came here to try to catch her myself. Once I saw the penny pots, I knew she was doing her little gig here."

Matrina sat frozen in time. Could she believe him? She looked at Kiran and waited for her to throw Frank under the bus.

"Is that true, Kiran?" Matrina said to Kiran. The sirens came within earshot.

"I am not going to go down for this alone," Kiran said. She spoke with a snarl in her voice. "I was hired from my job in Las Vegas to come here and do what I did tonight. It was not my idea, and I will not stand by and be the patsy."

"Of course, you shouldn't be the patsy," Matrina said. She took out her notepad. "So who brought you here from Las Vegas to tap the till for them?"

Kiran cast a defiant look at both Matrina and Frank. "Ray Willard," she said, and her voice took on a new authority. "And he'll have you both in jail when he gets wind of what you've done, and Frank, you can forget working here after this. Ray will have you out on the street if you ever get out of jail. You've invaded my civil rights, and you're both going down."

"Ray Willard?" Matrina said, dumbfounded.

"Yes, Ray Willard. He used to come to Vegas a lot, and he got in over his head, and he needed to make money under the table, fast, and he offered me the deal, and I took it. End of story."

"Not end of story," Matrina said. "Beginning of story, Kiran."

The uniformed policemen rapped on the glass front door, and the hostess hurried to open it for them. They entered and walked over to Matrina and company, and Matrina rose to introduce herself. She showed her ACS credentials, and they read Kiran her rights before they handcuffed her and led her out to their squad car.

"You'll be sorry," Kiran said. "Both of you will be sorry. Just wait and see. Ray's got connections, and you guys are both going to pay." The glass doors closed behind her, and Matrina and Frank sat and looked at each other, each amazed at the other's part in this episode.

"I thought you were in on it," Matrina said.

"I thought you were dumb as a rock to not catch her," Frank said. "Ray hired me in Vegas to come here and then bring Kiran here. I thought he just wanted to help me get a job after I got canned from the gaming table at Circus Circus. So I came here and hired Kiran to follow me. I didn't come here with any references and what job history I gave, I made up. Ray said that didn't matter, that he could do the paperwork. I needed to secure this job, or I'd be back to washing dishes at some greasy spoon." Frank folded and unfolded the napkin at his place.

"I didn't know what he had in mind for Kiran until I noticed my profits sinking into the basement. As I said, I had her at Anna Maria for training, but she kept staying and staying long after she should have come back here. That's when I figured she was up to something with him, and if things went sour, they'd both toss me into the loop." Frank moved the silverware around at his place setting.

"So I figured I'd catch her before someone legit caught her. During our time together, I tried to get her to talk about Willard, but she won't budge. I wanted to get her out of my restaurant and back up here. I hoped I could stay clear of her plan."

Matrina sighed and shook her head. "Amazing," she said. She walked back to the register, removed the rest of the money from the cash drawer and recorded the totals on the control sheet. She placed the cash in the zippered bag and took the control sheet over to the adding machine.

The totaled amounts from the cash drawer appeared on the adding machine tape. She tore off the tape and compared this tape to the total of the register reading. They balanced to the penny. Relief demonstrated itself in a wave of calmness.

Matrina put the register tape and the stack of guest checks into the zippered bag, along with the pot of pennies. She knew the altered guest checks could be spotted by the extra staple markings on the checks. The thirty pennies matched the one hundred and fifty dollars she retrieved from Kiran's pocket. She carried the bag and the extra one hundred fifty dollars back to the table.

"Do we have a manager here tonight?" she said to Frank.

"Beats me. He must be in the back and deaf to boot to have missed all this."

"Could you check for me? I have to turn this cash over to someone in authority and get a signed receipt for it."

Frank walked back into the kitchen and came back with a weary manager, pencil behind his ear, apron that showed evidence of cleaning the grill.

"Mark, this is Matrina McCoy. She works for Apex Cyberspace Security, and she has quite a tale to tell you," Frank said.

"Yes, Mark," Matrina said. "Please sit down. This might take a while."

Chapter 18

An hour later, Matrina sat in her van at the Trade Winds near Regatta Pointe and waited for the southern belle she had heard on the *Empress* to leave the restaurant. She wished she knew more about the girl's identity, but while inside, Kiran keep her focused, and she forgot to listen for the telltale southern drawl. All the close-up waitresses found the excitement at work of such interest, their side work suffered, and they all clocked out late.

Several things about this twilight zone drama with Andy plagued her. How does a cop like Andy have access to a half-a-million-dollar yacht like the *Empress*? It can't be the gal's yacht. She's farther down the money chain than Andy.

The identification number from the front of the boat needed to be recorded, and Franny could run a check on it. Meanwhile, Matrina picked up her cell and phoned home.

"Hi, Mom," Turner said. Matrina figured he knew it had to be her from the caller ID.

"Hi, Turner," Matrina said. "You guys doing okay?"

"Yeah. We're watching a movie on Disney."

"Oh, good. I guess Wendy's there?"

"Yeah, she's here. Want to talk to her?"

"Yes. I'm going to be really, really late tonight, and I wanted to get her to spend the night, if she could. You don't mind, do you?"

"No, that's cool." Turner sighed. "We actually like her. She's not bossy or anything."

"I told you she was nice. So, let me talk to Michelle; then I'll talk to Wendy." Seconds of silence.

"Hi, Mom," Michelle said.

"Hi, Michelle. I was going to get Wendy to stay over with you tonight, if you don't mind. I'm involved in something, and it's going to be very late when I get home."

"That's fine," Michelle said. "She's turned out to be really fun. She's letting us stay up late to watch this movie, and she showed us how to make taco chips with melted cheese and tomatoes. They're super."

"Oh, good," Matrina said. She wondered how fast her children's veins would clog with cholesterol to have all that cheese in addition to their leftover fried chicken. "So, let me check with Wendy."

More dead air time.

"Hi, Mrs. McCoy," Wendy said. "We're fine here."

"That's what I hear. So, why I'm calling is to see if you could possibly spend the night tonight. I'm running late, and I think it's going to get later."

"Sure. No sweat," Wendy said. "We'll go to bed when this movie is over, and see you in the morning."

"Good. Thanks, Wendy. And you can call my cell if there's any problem with anything."

"Yeah. We have the number by the phone."

"Good. So, see you in the morning. I won't wake any of you when I get in."

"Okay. See you then."

End send.

Moments later, the southern belle came out of the Trade Winds and jogged down the incline to the docks of the marina. She had traded in her tube top and flowing skirt for faded jeans and a blue Mickey Mouse tee shirt. Her Adidas sport shoes clung to the dewy grass as she hurried down the hill to the docks, and her crimson locks danced in the river wind.

Matrina grabbed her camcorder and followed. She kept her distance and used the seawall that meandered through the grass halfway down the hill as a hiding place and vantage point. The camera had a zoom lens, so she could run the camera from this safe distance and still get good clarity, evidence, dirt, to send this sucker, Andy, to the moon and out of her sister's life forever.

She held the camcorder with trembling hands. The urge to get the goods on Andy and save Rosie from another romantic catastrophe spurred her on. This clown could not marry her sister. Better Rosie learns the truth now than ten years and three kids later.

Andy waited for his guest. When the redhead bounced onto the *Empress*, he embraced her, and they shared a long, lingering kiss. Wonder how long he's been seeing her? Wonder why he would want to marry Rosie when he's got this going on with someone better looking and younger? What's the connection with the expensive yacht? Whirl, whirl, whirl went the recording film. It recorded seconds and minutes of time that would smash Rosie's life into smithereens.

Matrina continued to film from her secret vantage point. She fought tears. That would only make filming more difficult. Nausea churned her stomach, and the impulse to roar screaming out of her hiding place and beat Andy to a pulp with the still-running camcorder made her heart pound.

At midnight, an older model Ford station wagon pulled onto the boat ramp about a hundred feet from the slip where the *Empress* floated. Andy's sheriff's department partner, Kenny Stephens, stepped out of the station wagon and walked down the dock to the *Empress*.

"Hello below," he called into the cabin where Andy and the girl had disappeared minutes before.

"Keep it down, will you?" Andy spoke in hushed tones from the cabin. "You want to wake the dead?"

"May as well," Kenny said. "The living, if there are any around, don't seem interested in us."

"And that's the way we want to keep it," Andy said. "Now, let's get on with it."

Andy and the girl carried blue plastic grocery bags up the stairs from the cabin. When they had put twelve bags on the deck, they divided them up. They carried four bags apiece. Andy pulled the cabin door shut, and they walked off the *Empress* and down the dock toward the station wagon. Two feet from the wagon, dock security stopped them. Here they go, thought Matrina. Whatever's going on, security will crack it open.

A conversation floated between the security guard and Andy. Andy showed the guard something from his wallet, probably his credentials, and the guard chuckled and slapped Andy on the back. They all exchanged pleasantries, and the guard walked away as the threesome got into the station wagon. Matrina listened to the conversation, and it surprised her the guard bought their story.

* * *

A half hour later, while following the trio in the old station wagon away from the marina, Matrina made another call on her cell.

"I got trouble," she said.

"Right here in River City?" John said.

"With a capital 't' that rhymes with 'p' and that stands for pool," she said.

"I didn't know you were a Meredith Wilson fan."

"Of course. Isn't everyone? *The Music Man* is one of my favorite Broadway efforts."

"So, I judge from this conversation that you're stranded in some bar, getting the socks beaten off you in a pool game, and you need me to bring my pool cue and run the table?"

"Oh, I wish it were that simple. I've got a huge, huge problem."

"What?"

"I caught Andy with another woman. Rosie's going to be shipwrecked."

"Oh, my. What's up with that?"

"I wish I knew. I had some time to kill before the big show at Trade Winds on Regatta Pointe, and decided to walk down by the Haynes yacht just for kicks."

"And Andy was making out on the Haynes yacht with Edith Haynes."

"Not quite, but close. He was on a yacht moored right next to the Haynes' *Fly-By-Night*, and he was with this gorgeous red-haired waitress from the Trade Winds. Well, being a redhead is nothing to talk about, because all the waitresses at the Trade Winds near Regetta Pointe have red hair."

"No kidding."

"No kidding. Anyway, this yacht I'm talking about; it's called the *Empress*, and it's huge. Maybe fifty feet. Brand new."

"So, whose yacht is it?"

"No clue, but I'm going back and get the ID off the front and have it run."

"Going back? Where are you now?"

"Following Andy and the gal and Kenny, his partner."

"Where're they going?"

"Don't know. We're going south on 301, just crossed the river. They're driving a clunky, old Ford station wagon. Strange. Wonder why they aren't in Andy's nice Toyota Tundra. This clunker doesn't even have a regular tag. It has a temporary tag in the back window. What do you make of that?"

"I make of that you should go home, immediately. Do not pass 'go.' Do not collect one hundred dollars."

"Two hundred dollars. When you pass 'go,' you get two hundred dollars."

"Whatever, go home." John's voice possessed an element of command that made Matrina pause and take a breath.

"Can't. I've got to figure out what's going on so I'll have a solid story to tell Rosie. I don't want her telling me this gal is his sister, or a fellow cop, and they're playing undercover, whatever excuse she might concoct. I'm doing a 'film at eleven' docudrama. I want this solid."

"Matrina, it's midnight. You can't be out there on the streets following strange people without backup. You know better than that."

"That's why I'm calling you, so someone will know where I am, and what's going on."

"In case of what? So when they find your body in Tampa Bay I can say, 'Oh, yeah, I talked with her at midnight, and she was fine.' A lot of good that'll do."

"Oh, these guys are not dangerous. They're just sneaky."

"There's more to this story that you're not saying. Give me the rest of it."

"Yes, Dad," she said. "Well, I saw them hauling stuff off the yacht and putting it in the station wagon. The marina security stopped them and asked them what they were doing. They said they had an alcoholic guest onboard, and they had to get all the booze off the boat for his own good. They had bunches of four-packs of Kahlua in blue, plastic grocery bags. The security guy made them show what they were hauling. And he looked at the four-packs, Andy flashed his cop badge, and security told them to 'carry on.' So, I guess it was no big deal."

"How many four packs are we talking about?"

"Oh, I don't know. Twelve bags with probably four four-packs in each bag. How many is that?"

"Too many. Nobody could drink Kahlua in that volume, alcoholic or not. Something's wrong. And was there an alcoholic person on the boat?"

"I don't know. I never saw any other person. I saw Andy, the girl and Kenny, his partner. Andy and the girl were smooching and fooling around. Kenny came with the station wagon, but I never saw anyone else on the boat." Matrina paused, and John made no comment. She could hear his deep sigh on the phone.

"Anyway, now we're traveling south on 301, and I want to see where they go, and get an address. Maybe Andy is living with this waitress gal and just dating Rosie on the side."

"Matrina, the guy's a cop. He'll make you in your van. Let me meet you at an intersection, and we can switch to my Jeep. He won't be as quick to recognize that."

"How can I do that? I don't know where they're going. They might turn off, and I'd lose them."

"Better you losing them, than us losing you. Now, don't be stubborn. I'll meet you at the junction of 301 and 64. Be there, northwest corner." And with that, he hung up.

Matrina took a deep breath and drove to 301 and 64, and pulled over and parked. Andy and his friends turned left on 64, and she watched the taillights dwindle almost out of sight.

John pulled up seconds later. She grabbed her camcorder and her purse, clicked the "lock" button on her door, slammed the door to the van shut, and hurried around her vehicle. She jumped into the passenger side of his Jeep, and looked over at him as he sat in the driver's seat idling the motor.

"Down 64, see? Those fading lights are his," she said. She pointed the way through the windshield and tried to curtail her bossy tone.

"Fasten your seat belt," John said. "I used to do this a lot in my youth."

"You were a cab driver? And people used to jump into your cab and say, 'follow that car?'"

He shot her a "no comment" look, jammed the gas peddle to the floor and within seconds had the taillights of the wagon well in his view.

"Wow, I'm impressed," she said. She hung onto her seat belt. "I wouldn't have thought cops from Little Falls, New York, could drive with such reckless abandon."

"I didn't learn to drive like this as a cop," he said. "I learned it bolting back to New Britain, Connecticut, from Little Falls, trying to get back to school on time."

"Whatever, good job. And I guess from this little experiment we can determine that there are no cops on the streets of Bradenton?"

"Not at this hour. Every cop knows that nine out of ten people leaving a bar at closing time, say, two A.M. is drunk. So, all they have to do is wait until two A.M., and sweep the streets to fill their quota book. But since this is Sunday night, there probably aren't many drunks on the road."

"So, where are they between now and two A.M.?"

"At Dunkin' Donuts."

"Oh," she said. She wanted to challenge that conclusion, but thought better of it.

"Be sure you know what you're doing before you rock Rosie's world," John said after several minutes of silence.

"There could be another explanation?"

"Yes. Like I keep saying, the guy's a cop. This could be an undercover assignment. You, yourself, came up with that explanation."

"And he'd have to get physical with the suspect?"

"Possibly."

"Would a cop who is involved with someone he is supposed to love take an assignment like that?"

"Not usually, but maybe it was a situation that just got out of hand."

"Oh, ppplllllleeeeaaaasssseeee," Matrina said. She leaned forward in the seat, strained against her seat belt to keep the old station wagon in sight.

"It's not something I would have ever gotten involved in, but it happens," John said.

"Did you ever work undercover?"

"Yes, as a matter of fact, I did, about six years ago, in Utica. It was a drug deal. They were running drugs down the Erie Canal through Little Falls, and I worked as a bartender in Utica on the Canal. I hung out with the bargemen, picked up little tidbits of info, helped set up the drop. It was kind of fun."

"So, what happened?"

"Not much. The drug dealers, part of a large drug cartel, had a mole in our little group who was better at clandestine operations than I was, and he ratted us out. When the deal went down, we only snared the underlings, and the big guys got away. We tried everything, and we couldn't break the guys we caught."

"Wow. If you were worming your way into a heavy-duty drug cartel, that sounds pretty dangerous."

"It was. More so than I thought when I got involved. I would've never taken the assignment had I known how dangerous. It turned out to be too big for us local yokels."

"Did your bust solve the drug-trafficking in your area?"

"For a while. The traffickers just used other means of transportation, but at least, it got them out of Herkimer County and Little Falls. That was our main goal anyway. But undercover can get out of control. You really don't know what you've stumbled into with Andy. It may be more than just a 'messing around' type thing."

"I suppose," Matrina said. "Right now, it just looks like he's dating two women who both love him to pieces, and one of them is my Rosie."

"Why do you feel so responsible for Rosie?"

"Oh, I don't know. I was eighteen when my mom died. Rosie was only eight at the time, and my dad let me assume my mother's role. He was a cab driver and worked too many hours to make ends meet. I got married at twenty, and she was ten. She stayed with us a lot when Dad worked. Mike was like her big brother, and he was strict. They would argue, and she would accuse me of siding with Mike, invading her space, not letting her live her own life, etcetera, etcetera, etcetera. Then Dad died when Rosie was fifteen. His had a sudden heart attack, like Mom. And Rosie moved in with us until she graduated from high school. Then she got out on her own, has had several live-in boyfriends, and she is so kind and big-hearted, she just gets creamed in these flaky relationships. I had such high hopes that Andy wasn't just one more. But now it seems that he's more flaky than most. It just makes me sick."

"You can't live her life for her."

"I know that. She's twenty-eight now, so it's time for me to let go. I just can't seem to do that."

The station wagon slowed down, and John backed off. He slowed to thirty miles per hour, and stayed a thousand feet behind so as not to be noticed. The station wagon turned right on a small street leading to Interstate 75. It slowed even more as it approached a Motel 6 sign.

It pulled into the Motel 6 parking lot and drove around to the rear of the building. The station wagon parked in the space that belonged to room 124, and Andy, the waitress and Kenny got out. They each retrieved four bags of Kahlua from the back of the wagon and entered the motel room. They already had a key.

"They must have already registered," John said. He made a swing through the entire parking lot, around the building, and returned to the section that housed room 124. He parked across the parking lot from the wagon and killed his motor and his lights. The crack in the drawn drapes of room 124 revealed movement in the room.

"Why would they come to a cheap motel when they have a luxury yacht at their disposal?" Matrina said.

"Because something other than a romantic interlude is going on."

"Something along with the romantic interlude. I saw their romantic interlude. Believe me, nobody is that good an actor. They're romantically involved. Something else might be going on as well, but the romance is real."

"If you say so."

"I say so."

John and Matrina sat in John's Jeep Wagoneer in the deep midnight hours of the southern night. They listened to the crickets, watched the fireflies, aware of the eighteen-wheelers that roared down Interstate 75, and wondered why Rosie's fiancé occupied a room at Motel 6 with a gorgeous waitress and his law-enforcement partner.

"You prepared to sit surveillance all night?" John said. He looked over at her silhouetted in the darkness.

"Yes, but I don't think it will come to that," she said. She looked back at him. The darkness prevented any direct eye contact. She turned her head and concentrated on the traffic on the interstate highway.

"You think they're here for something special?"

"Yes. I think you might be right. Something else is going on. If they were just going to party and spend the night, they would have stayed at the yacht. This is about the Kahlua. That's why they downloaded it from the boat."

"That's my guess," John said. "I think this is cop business, until I see otherwise." He unfastened his seat belt and relaxed back in his seat. Matrina unfastened her seat belt as well, and tried not to feel guilty that she dragged him out in the middle of the night on what might be a wild goose chase. Of course, she didn't "drag" him.

Shortly after one A.M., a white, Chevy delivery van with splashed decals that spelled "Hiram Walker" along the side, pulled up beside the station wagon. The van had no windows and two wide double doors allowed entrance at the back. A regular metal license tag hung on one rear door, but Matrina and John could not make out the numbers as the van swung past them and backed into the parking space.

"It looks like a Georgia tag," John said. "It's definitely not Florida."

The lights still blazed inside room 124. Andy appeared in the doorway, looked up and down the sidewalk, and motioned to the waitress and Kenny. They carried the twelve blue plastic bags of Kahlua out onto the sidewalk. The trio opened the two doors in the rear of the van and unloaded several cases of Imperial Whiskey, Ginger Brandy, and Canadian Club from the back of the van. They removed the four-packs of Kahlua from the plastic bags and loaded them inside the van. Then they reloaded the cases of the Whiskey, Brandy and Canadian Club. They closed the rear doors, and Andy patted the driver's side of the van. The driver, who had never gotten out of his seat, put the vehicle into gear and drove toward the exit driveway of the Motel 6.

As he paused to steer the van past other closely-parked vehicles, Matrina jotted the license number down on the notebook she pulled from her purse.

"You're right," she said to John. "It's a Georgia tag."

John nodded in agreement.

They watched as Andy, Kenny and the waitress went back into the motel room, shut off the lights and got back into the old station wagon. The waitress rumpled the twelve blue plastic bags up and stuffed them into one bag. She tossed them in the back seat of the wagon.

Matrina watched the waitress. "Sorry to see that, she said.

155

"Fingerprints?"

"Yeah. I thought if they dumped them in the trash, I could haul them out and have Franny run them for prints. I need to know who this gal is."

"You'd probably find out she's DEA undercover, along with Andy being sheriff's department undercover, and they are just playing games with each other."

"That would be silly."

"It happens. I did some undercover for the FBI when I was in college. I joined the Klan and reported on their doings. I figured out after several meetings that probably four out of every five Klan members were FBI undercover informants."

"You're making that up."

"Nope. 'Fraid not."

"So why do they let people like that operate like they do, if the authorities know all about them?"

"What good would it do to shut them down? They'd just go underground, reorganize, come up with new leadership, and new projects. It's easier to go with the group you know about and throw monkey wrenches into their plans whenever you can. It's the American way."

Matrina shook her head as John pulled the Jeep out of its parking space. He didn't turn his headlights on until the taillights of the station wagon disappeared around the building. Then he drove around the other side of the building in the opposite direction and pulled into a parking space in the front. He idled with his lights off and kept his foot off the brake so he wouldn't flash brake lights.

The wagon left the Motel 6 parking lot, and turned back on Route 64. It returned in the direction from which it had come. John waited for them to get several seconds ahead of him, turned on his lights and followed behind. He left a block and a half between them.

"This is trickier than following them here," he said to Matrina. "Lots less traffic on the road."

"Lots of no traffic on the road," she said.

"Yeah. We're going to have to compensate for that, or we'll tip them off." John pulled into a parking space on the wrong side of the road on Route 64, and killed his lights. He idled there and watched the taillights of the wagon until they disappeared.

"We'll lose them," Matrina said.

"No, we won't. Watch. It'll be okay."

"I just want to see if Andy and the girl go home together. Then I can run

156

a check on the address and find out who's renting their little love nest."

John left his parking space, and drove on the wrong side of the road with his lights off. He drove for several blocks and narrowed the distance between them and the wagon. Then he pulled over and parked on the wrong side of the road again.

After several seconds, he pulled out from the parking space and with his lights still off, he trailed the station wagon on the wrong side of the road for several more blocks. A little more than a block separated them now. The wagon rolled south on Route 301, the same intersection where John had picked Matrina up.

Andy and company cruised to a Wal-Mart Super Center that stayed open all night. They pulled into the parking lot and pulled up next to Andy's black Tundra. A red Chevy Silverado truck, which looked to be brand new, stood next to the Tundra. A temporary tag could be noted through the rear window. John pulled into a parking space at the far end of the parking lot.

Andy got out and jumped into his Tundra. Kenny got out and climbed into the Silverado, and the waitress slid into the driver's seat of the wagon. Kenny started his truck and drove out of the parking lot. The waitress drove the wagon back out onto Route 301 and continued south. Andy followed in the Tundra, and John and Matrina followed at a safe distance behind Andy.

About three miles down 301, the wagon turned right and drove into the parking lot of a used car lot called, "Jake's Reliable Autos." As the station wagon slowed down to take the turn, John drove past the wagon, and Matrina jotted down the numbers from the temporary tag. John turned at the next street and parked in the first available driveway and killed his lights. The car lot could still be watched from his rear view mirror.

The cars on the front row on Jake's Reliable Autos hailed from eight years ago, and the cars in the second row hailed from even further back in time. The cars in the last row looked like they would need a towrope to leave the lot.

The waitress parked the wagon in an empty spot on the second row of cars. She got out of the wagon, opened the back door and grabbed the temporary tag from the rear window. She grabbed the bundle of blue plastic shopping bags, slammed the back door shut, crammed the keys into her jeans pocket and walked over to Andy's truck. She climbed into the passenger seat and leaned over to give him a reciprocated kiss before she buckled up. Andy gunned the engine and drove further south on 301.

Matrina shot John a look of confusion.

"What are these guys up to?"

"Seems pretty strange, doesn't it." John shook his head. "My guess would be they stole this old wagon from this car lot and used it for whatever it was that went down tonight. Then they returned it. The car dealer probably never knew it was gone."

"Where would they get a set of keys?"

"Oh, that's easy. Just test-drive the car during the day, run back to Wal-Mart, get a key copied, return the car to the lot, come back after closing and help yourself. A car lot this shabby wouldn't have closed circuit TV or a security system. Piece of cake."

"So, you still think they're involved in undercover on something illegal?"

"Oh, youbettcha. Contraband, Baby, of some kind. Can't be high-jacked Kahlua. That would be, what, four four-packs in each bag, twelve bags, forty-eight four-packs, at what? Five bucks a pop? That's what? A couple hundred bucks? Not worth leaving the TV on a Sunday night for. No, you've stumbled into something major."

Five blocks further down Route 301, Andy turned left and pulled into the parking space in front of a lime-green stucco duplex. He and the waitress got out of his truck and walked up the front walk. She pulled out a key from her jeans pocket and put the key into the lock. A passionate kiss from Andy stopped her in mid-turn, and he held her close and nuzzled her hair even after the kiss had run its course.

"This is undercover work?" Matrina said. John pulled the Jeep into a driveway across the street and three doors down from the duplex.

"The guy's got more dedication than I would have; I'll give him that," John said. He watched the couple in his side view mirror.

Andy and the waitress entered the duplex. Lights flipped on and off in what appeared to be the kitchen area, then the bathroom area, then the bedroom area, and then, total darkness encased the duplex.

John backed out onto the street. "Seen enough?" He said,

"No," Matrina said. "I'm just getting started. Let me jot down her house number, and check the name of this street. Then I want to go back to the yacht. There's no car here in the drive that might be hers, so her car might still be back at the Trade Winds. I check that out when we get there."

"What are you looking for on the yacht?"

"Fingerprints."

"You're going to break into the yacht and look for something that's got fingerprints on it?"

"Youbettcha, Baby. Wanta come?"

"Wouldn't miss it. This'll be more fun than drowning kittens."

"You're not afraid of getting into trouble in case we get caught?"

"Matrina, I'm out on bond for murder one. How much more trouble do you think I can get into?"

Chapter 19

Moments later, John headed the Jeep north on Highway 301 back toward the Regatta Pointe Marina. He wanted to break the silence and offer Matrina solace in this arena of tangled emotion into which she had been flung, but no words of comfort galloped into his mind.

He knew the explanation, "Andy's a cop; he's probably playing undercover," didn't fly.

"What time is it?" Matrina said. She gazed out the window at the lightly-falling rain and noted the reflections of the parked cars in the pavement of the wet street.

"Nearly two," John said. He stopped for a red light and wondered why Manatee County hadn't programmed these lights to stay green when no traffic waited on the side streets.

"There's probably not going to be anyone at the marina at this hour on a Sunday night, you think?" Matrina said.

"Probably not. Have you thought about how we're going to get in if the cabin door is locked?"

"I have a nail file. You think that might work?"

"It works for Rockford. It might work for us."

"I think Rockford uses a screw driver."

"I have one of those in the glove compartment. You could get it out in case we need it."

Matrina opened the glove compartment and removed the screw driver and put it in her purse. "You've got a flashlight in here, too. Should I bring that?"

"By all means," John said. "We don't want to be turning on lights if we get into the cabin."

"I know you think this is silly," she said.

"No, actually, I don't," John said. He looked over at her and noticed the weariness in her face. "You want to know who's moving into Rosie's territory and threatening havoc in her life. You want to protect someone you love. That's never silly."

"This will be breaking the law," she said.

"Yes. But at this hour, we may get away with it with everyone except God."

"Do you think the cause justifies the means?"

"Probably not, but neither did you mortgaging your house and your future to bail me out of jail. Sometimes we do what we have to do, and wisdom gets put on the back burner. It's called loving thy neighbor as thyself while falling short of God's goal for us, or doing the wrong things for the right reason."

"I have to know who this redheaded gal is, and then figure out how long he's known her. Then I'm going to put a time bomb in his Tundra."

"As long as you don't shoot him with one of my guns and bury him in my backyard."

"That's a really good idea, but it's been done a lot lately."

"And while we're on that subject, I found out a few things about researching the purchase of nine millimeter bullets."

"Oh, good. What?"

"The registers record all the sales into a perpetual inventory system. I can find out if any nine millimeter bullets were purchased on Wednesday or Thursday before the third weekend in June. If no bullets were sold, no sense in wasting time scanning the tapes. If five boxes of bullets were sold on Thursday, for example, we scan the tapes and look for just five sales, and jot down the times of the sales, and the register number. Then we can scan the security tapes to see who made the purchase at that register at that time."

"Oh, that's great," Matrina said. John thought she tried to sound too enthusiastic about this news. "We should start tomorrow."

"I plan to. I'm going in the morning to Kmart and Wal-Mart, the stores in Bradenton anyway. If the computer shows any bullets purchased Wednesday and Thursday of that week, I'll borrow their cash register tapes. Then I'll split them up with you, and we can start the great hunt."

"Do you think they'll let you take the tapes out of the store?"

"I don't know. I'll talk to the security supervisor. Security folks tend to have a camaraderie and bend the rules for each other."

"If not, can you subpoena the tapes?"

"I'm not sure. I'll have to ask Nathan. We can subpoena the bookkeeper who is privy to the information. How we get the actual tapes, I'm not sure, but Nathan will know. Right now, I'm gambling on the security camaraderie."

"Clue me in as soon as you find out, and if you get the tapes, I'll start right in looking for bullets."

"Okay. Well, here's the Trade Winds," John said. He turned into the parking lot at the restaurant. "You wanted to see if the gal's vehicle is parked here?"

"Yes. There're six cars parked here, evidently overnight. Isn't that strange?"

"Not really. It's probably guys meeting girls they aren't supposed to be meeting, and they come here in separate vehicles, leave one vehicle here, go off together in the other one."

"And one would be Kiran's vehicle, the gal I had arrested for tapping the till."

"You had that red-haired cashier arrested?"

"Oh, yeah. You should have been here. You'd have been proud of me. She took down a big CEO of the parent corporation with her. It was quite a scene."

"And the manager dude from Anna Maria wasn't part of the deal?"

"Nope, and nobody was more surprised than me. He was here, if you could imagine that. He was on to the cashier, and wanted to stop her, and he thought I let her shenanigans fall through the cracks. He decided to stop her himself."

"Sounds like a fun evening."

"Yeah, fun. And it's gotten funner ever since."

"I think that's called multi-tasking."

"Probably," Matrina said. She scanned the six cars scattered about the parking lot. "I'll just take down all six license numbers, and have Franny run them. After I get stuff from the yacht to run for fingerprints, I'll know which car belongs to Andy's little playmate."

"That's a plan."

Matrina took her notebook from her purse and began to record vehicle types and the license numbers. After she jotted down three tag numbers, she stopped, pen poised over her paper.

"You know what?" she said.

"No. What?"

"I just thought of something."

"What?" More emphasis in the tone.

"How'd they get the station wagon from the car lot to the marina?"

"I told you. They drove it probably yesterday, had a key made, and stole it after the lot closed last night."

"Exactly. I was on the dock here around eight when I saw Andy and Miss

Chicky-poo. I went back to the Trade Winds around nine, and she came back to the restaurant minutes later. Then Chicky-poo returned to the yacht around eleven, and I followed her. Kenny showed up around twelve driving the wagon. So Kenny had to get the wagon from the car lot sometime between closing time, say nine P.M. and drive it over here by midnight. His Silverado is parked at Wal-Mart with Andy's Tundra. So, how did Andy get here, and who drove Kenny to the car lot?"

"Hum," mused John. "Well, Andy could have had his Tundra parked in the marina parking lot at eight. You wouldn't have noticed that."

"True."

"He could have left the marina when the girl went back to work, picked up Kenny, gone to the car lot, had Kenny follow him to Wal-Mart, parked his Tundra, and rode with Kenny back to the marina."

"That would work."

"Or…"

"Or what?"

"Or there's a fourth person involved who drove Kenny to the car lot and Andy rode to the marina with the waitress in whichever of these cars turn out to be hers."

"Of course. There's a fourth person. The person who drove the van at Motel 6."

"Exactly."

"And that would be who do you think?"

"Who knows? Could be another cop. Could be another waitress, or someone totally unconnected. But there is definitely a fourth person, no matter how they got the wagon."

Matrina mulled that thought over in her mind, and then finished jotting down the license numbers.

"Okay. That's that," she said. "Let's go do the marina thing."

John drove back out onto the road, and took the next quick turn into the marina parking lot.

"Not too many cars here. We'll just have to be very quiet. Tear out a few pages from that notepad you have, and give them to me. If we have to say something to each other while we're on the dock or the boat, we'll write notes back and forth. Don't talk. Sound travels further at night when you're outside, and it might attract someone, like the security guard you saw earlier. Did you check to see if the marina has security cameras?"

"No, I didn't. I should have thought of that." Matrina tore two pages of paper from her notepad and handed them to John. "If they do have cameras, we're dead in the water."

"We can check on our way down. They'll be on the light poles."

John and Matrina got out of the Jeep and walked down the ramp to the dock. John put the note paper in his shirt pocket beside his pen. He discovered two pieces of gum in his shirt pocket and handed one to her while he opened the other and popped it into his mouth.

They paused before they stepped onto the dock that ran in front of the boats. No security cameras looked down on them from the poles. That explained the presence of the security guard whom they might escape if they didn't call attention to themselves. Once on the dock, they walked through the still night air until they came to the *Empress*.

The step onto the *Empress* caused the boat to rock, and once at the cabin door John opened his hand for the screw driver and nail file Matrina had stowed in her purse. He twisted the screw driver back and forth in the lock on the cabin door, and the tumblers shifted to open the door. They walked inside, and Matrina clicked the flashlight on as they went.

The outside door opened into the salon with two long white leather couches extended along both side walls. A sweep of the flashlight revealed a big screen television embedded into another wall. A leather-topped coffee table ran between the couches and a fully stocked bar occupied one corner of the room. Empty wine cooler bottles littered the coffee table and an open bottle of A-1 steak sauce sat between salt and pepper shakers. A butter dish boasted half a stick of butter, that slithered from the dish to the top of the table. Brown and ecru marbled carpet covered the floor, and ground-in potato chips speckled the carpet. The door at the far end of the room opened into a chrome and ecru-tiled galley.

In the galley, they found a complete kitchen, with color-coordinated refrigerator, dishwasher, four-burner gas stove with oven and a stainless-steel double sink. The stove displayed the remnants of several prepared meals. Dried egg decorated the stovetop. The top of the stove and the hood over it shone with a greasy overcoat. A four-slice toaster occupied the countertop near the stove, and a puddle of bread crumbs surrounded it. The galley smelled of broiled steak. Dirty dishes cluttered the sink, and a small-sized washer and dryer filled one corner of the room. Clothes occupied both units.

In the master stateroom brown and ecru satin sheets draped over an unmade king-sized bed. They matched the brown and ecru plaid quilted bedspread crumpled on the floor. A state-of-the-art computer sat on a shelf beside the bed, along with a combination printer, scanner and fax machine.

From the master stateroom they could see the master head with an ecru-tiled counter that surrounded a stainless-steel sink. Estee Lauder makeup and bottles of Giorgio cologne filled the countertop. Thick, expensive, brown, wet towels sat in a heap on the floor.

"Must be the maid's day off," John said in a whisper as they walked through the interior of the yacht. "If you're looking for fingerprints, you've hit pay dirt, because they're no doubt everywhere."

"Good. Let me gather a few souvenirs and let's get out of here before somebody comes. I can't believe they would leave everything in this condition and not plan on coming right back."

"Oh, yeah, they would. This is their lifestyle. I'll bet this boat hasn't been cleaned since the day it came off the assembly line."

"Which probably wasn't too long ago. Everything looks new, doesn't it?"

"Yeah, it does."

"Let's not touch anything. We don't want to leave our prints here."

"True. Grab a couple of those tissues there. Use them to cover your fingers."

Matrina pulled a half a dozen tissues from an ecru-colored porcelain holder. "I don't want to take anything that will be missed. B and E is one thing. Theft is quite another."

"I was wondering when your conscience would kick in. I thought maybe God had taken a nap and left you to your own devices."

Matrina walked back into the galley and handed the flashlight to John. He shone the light ahead of where she moved. She found a box of garbage bags under the sink, used the tissue to mask her fingerprints and extracted a bag.

The full-to-overflowing garbage container under the sink provided several empty wine cooler bottles and several Coors beer bottles along with several wax-coated Dixie cups. She didn't want to take too many. She wanted the trash to appear untouched.

Matrina stopped in the galley and looked around for anything more she could take for fingerprints that would not leave an obvious hole in the decor. She spotted several books of matches in a saucer beside the stove. They advertised the Outgoing Tide Resort on Cancun. She chose a half-used book and added it to her collection. Then she picked up a new book of matches, tore out the same number of matches that had been torn from the used book, and put that book in the place where the used book had been.

"Scary," John said in a whisper. "How many times have you done this type of thing?"

"Counting this time?"

"Yes."

"Once."

"You're a quick study."

"I'd like to think so. I just don't want them to know anyone is on to them. I don't want them to start watching their backs."

Matrina peered down into her garbage bag and looked around the galley for anything else she could take that would not be missed. She sighed and closed the garbage bag.

"I guess this is all I dare take," she said. "Surely, this will be enough. That gal must have touched some of this stuff, the matches for the stove if nothing else. I know she was cooking when I spied on them."

"Okay, let's blow."

They walked out of the cabin and locked the door behind them. John turned off the flashlight, and they left the deck of the *Empress*.

The drive back to the point where Matrina's van waited took several minutes. She got out of John's vehicle and stood with his passenger's door open.

"Thank you so much for helping me tonight," she said. "I appreciate it more than you'll ever know."

"But I do know," John said. "That's how much I appreciate the help you've given me, helping post my bond, checking on the kids when I was in jail, bringing them gifts and pizza."

Matrina nodded and their words produced a warmth in her akin to the kiss that would not vacate her soul. She clutched the garbage bag that could alter Rosie's future, got into her van, cranked it up, and drove the twenty-something miles south to Sarasota and home. The contents of the garbage bag contained enough mystery to empower her.

Chapter 20

The next day, an overcast Monday morning, after five hours sleep, Matrina wandered into the ACS office. She carried her plastic garbage bag of beer cans, wine cooler bottles and Dixie waxed paper cups along with a book of matches from Cancun. She wore comfortable, old jeans, and her pink "I Love New York" tee shirt and Nike shoes. She walked through the door to the front office. "Hi, Franny," she said.

"Whoa," Franny said. The receptionist looked up at Matrina from her computer. "You must have had a rough night. No offense, but you look like the last rose of summer."

"I feel like the last car on a freight train," Matrina said. She yawned and stopped at Franny's desk. From the bottom of her purse came the notepad with the address of the redheaded waitress, the six license tag numbers from the six cars parked overnight at the Trade Winds, and the ID numbers from the *Empress*. "I have a huge, huge favor to ask of you."

"Sure, anything. What's up?"

"I need some tags run and an address checked," Matrina said. She flipped the pages of her notepad and tore out the ones she needed to give Franny.

"Okay," Franny said. "I suppose you need this stuff yesterday."

"Always," Matrina said. "Is there any other time frame for stuff like this? I have this duplex address, and six license tag numbers, and an ID from a boat."

"So, you're talking about me beating the bushes to find this info like, this week?"

"No, I'm talking about you trashing the bushes with a weed-eater and finding this info today."

"Hum. I'll have to think that one over. You're talking about me taking something that's possible, moving it into probable, then into likely, and then on into a done deal in one day?"

"For a box of Oreos?"

"A box of Oreos? I think I see 'possible' on the far horizon." Franny moved her hand as if looking off into the distance. "Two boxes of Oreos and lunch at McDonalds might move it into 'likely.'"

"Two boxes of Oreos, lunch at McDonalds, and a six-pack of Diet Coke." Matrina hovered over Franny and spoke quietly.

"You just went from 'likely' to 'done deal.'" Franny's eyes twinkled.

"You drive a hard bargain." Matrina smiled at her coworker.

"Well, you know what they say. The difficult takes a little while; the impossible takes a little longer."

"That's an axiom spoken by people who don't know about Oreos, McDonalds and Diet Cokes."

"Yes. So, I take it this little search is of a personal nature? Otherwise, I wouldn't be raking in all this booty over being part of it?"

"Yes. I'll tell George about it, and I don't think he'll mind. But it's not ACS stuff."

"He won't care. George's easy these days. I think he's mellowing with age."

"If I could get it today, that would be great."

"I'll try. Want me to call your cell if I get it together?"

"Yes, please."

"And Matrina?"

"Yeah?"

"I'm just kidding about the booty. I don't expect anything extra for running this stuff for you."

"Oh, no. A deal's a deal. And you missed your calling. You ought to be working for the State Department. You're great at negotiations."

"I thought I was working for the State Department. I'm not? What a blow."

Matrina shook her head and walked down the hallway toward George's office. He sat behind his cluttered desk and read the *Conservative Advocate* and sipped black coffee.

"Hi, Toots," George said. He did not look up. "What's up?"

"Not much," Matrina said. She sat down across from his desk.

"Where's your coffee? You look like you could use a gallon or two."

"If one more person says I look like garbage, I'm going back to bed."

"You didn't go right home and to bed after our little escapade at the Trade Winds?"

"No. I ran into a little personal crisis. I do think I'll get myself a caffeine hit, though. Be right back." Matrina got up, left her garbage bag full of fingerprint trinkets and her purse by her chair and walked across the hall into the kitchen area. "Want any coffee, Franny?" she called down the hall.

"No, thanks, Matrina," came the reply. "I'm good."

"Okay." Matrina emptied the coffee into a cup, rinsed out the pot and set up another round in the coffee maker. She carried her coffee back into George's office.

"Want to talk about your crisis?" George said.

"Not really. But I do have a favor to ask."

"Well, after last night, and our victorious landing at Normandy, you picked a good day to ask."

"I have this bag of trash," she said. She raised the bag for him to see. "There are some beer cans, wine coolers, throw-away cups and a pack of matches in here. I need to know whose prints might be found on them."

"Okay, you've been going through other folks' trash?"

"Yes."

"Is this a new hobby? You were too wired to go home last night after your big coup, so you wandered aimlessly around the beach collecting trash? You're hoping some of it might belong to a movie actor or a rock star?"

"Hardly. I wish it were that simple. I really don't want to talk about it, George, if you don't mind. I just need to know who belongs to these things."

"I can get that done for you," George said. He reached for the garbage bag. "How soon do you need the data?"

"Yesterday." Why did everyone keep asking her that question?

George eyed her over his glasses. "Okay. We'll see what we can do."

"Thanks. And I have Franny running some license tags and a boat ID number, and an address for me. I hope that's okay."

"It's okay with me, if it's okay with her."

"It's costing me a left leg."

"Good for Franny." George smiled. "And you don't want to talk about this."

"No."

"Does Franny know what's going on?"

"No."

"So there's no sense in sweating her for your secrets."

"No. I just have to work through some of this first before I can tell anyone about it. I'm not sure there's anything to tell. And, to change the subject, I guess I need a new assignment."

"Yes, you do," George said. "And I've got several little stints you would just love to jump into, like some cashier checks, time clock punching surveillance, like, looking for folks punching each other's time cards, and an undercover gig in an office supply store. The manager there thinks somebody is hiking off with paper clips and staple removers. Of course, if you take that one, you'd have to work nine to five, no way out."

"I can do nine to five, no way out," Matrina said, her tone defensive. "That's what I did at Wal-Mart, nine to five, no way out, sometimes nine to nine, no way out."

"Well, if I give you that job, you'll intercept a fax from Afghanistan and find out the manager is the brother-in-law of Osama Bin Laden. You know how you are."

"It's not my fault if I keep running into folks who are on the shady side of the law."

"True. But why do they all have to be our clients?"

"Makes you wonder just how many of those kind of folks are trotting around loose out there. Why is that, George?"

George chuckled and studied her as he sipped his coffee. "Well, in order to give me a break, from your over-zealous activities, I thought I would give you a week off with pay. Maybe you could help John with this great bullet search. He is out there gathering sales tapes even as we speak."

"Yes, I wanted to help him do that, but didn't know how I'd be able to work it in. That's nice of you, George. Do you think looking for the bullet purchase is a logical direction?"

"Yes, I do. The real killer had to get bullets somewhere, and my guess is he would buy them at some busy store so as not to be remembered. What better place to start than Kmart and Wal-Mart."

"Who do you think we're looking for?" Matrina wrinkled her brow and sipped her coffee.

"Off the top of my head, someone not connected to Christopher O'Brien, or the Disney incident. Someone who has a vendetta against John, personally. Security folks make a lot of enemies. Hard to tell."

"So you don't think this is all tied together. The threatening letters and the murder?"

"Can't be," George said. He rocked back in his chair. "The murder happened before the Disney caper."

"That's true," Matrina said. "So we have a two-front war going on? The murder setting John up as the fall guy, and the letters from the Disney incident?"

"Could be," George said. He rocked back to grab his coffee cup and took a drink from the cup. "How are you doing with the two-three-nine clue from the imprint on the notebook paper?"

"The new area code for Lee County is all I've come up with so far. Christopher O'Brien lives in Lee County, but I've been calling his home every other day since I found it out, and he must not have a roommate as no one answers."

"The area code is a good option."

"But not the only option."

"No, not the only option. Keep your eyes open and your ear to the ground."

"So, back to the tapes, what we'll have from this search is a surveillance camera shot of the person buying the bullets. Can we get a name from a photo like that?"

"I think so, if the photo is good enough," George said. There might even be a credit card slip or an ATM transaction."

"I doubt that." Matrina finished her coffee. "If I were buying bullets to kill someone, I would use cold, hard cash."

"Me, too. So that's probably what you'll find. In fact, if I were scanning the tapes, I wouldn't bother with any bullet sales paid for with an ATM or credit card. They probably won't be relevant."

"So, I have a week to get this together?"

"Yep. Tote that barge; lift that bale."

Matrina got up from her chair. "I think I'll call John and see how he's doing and when I can get my sack of tapes."

"Let me know how it's going." George returned his attention to his periodical as Matrina left his office.

Matrina left the ACS office and as she drove north on the Trail, she had to battle herself to not turn right on Magnolia Street and home, sweet home. She could drive home, pour a nice hot bath, soak her bones in bubbles, climb back into bed and drift off into a cloud of air conditioned Oz, spirited along by the whirl of the overhead fan.

No can do, the logical part of her brain said. She had to go back to that car lot and find out who drove that station wagon yesterday and had the extra key made. But it would be so nice to grab a little nap before she went, rambled the worn-out part of her brain. Just a little nap. Not a whole day in bed. No, shouted the logical segment. Nap later. Drive now. Matrina sighed as she drove past Magnolia Street.

The half-hour trip to Jake's Reliable Autos through the heavy traffic for a Monday found the establishment manned by a twenty-something tallish man, dressed in faded jeans and sporting a faded green tee shirt. The tee shirt proclaimed, "I'm with stupid," and an arrow indicated that "stupid" could be located on his left. His longish brown hair fell in his eyes, and he tossed his head to clear his vision. The movement mimicked a shampoo commercial, but his hair hadn't seen the inside of a shampoo bottle for weeks. He sauntered over to the van.

"Hi, there, cutey," he said. His drawl expanded his words. "What can we sell you'all today? Need a second car for the hubby so you can keep driving this here lil fancy pants van?"

"Well, no," Matrina said. She took a deep breath and hoped the extra oxygen would give her patience. "I just have a few questions I'd like to ask you."

"All right." He stood beside her opened driver's side door and did not leave enough room for her to get out of the van.

"Perhaps you could back up so I could get out of my van," Matrina said. She tried to conquer the icy tone that crept into her voice.

"Sure, sweetie. Anything for you." He backed up six inches.

Matrina got out of the van and closed the door.

"I want to talk to you about that Ford station wagon on your second row." She walked toward the car.

"That little beauty? She ready and raring to go." He followed her to the station wagon. "Want me to get the keys so you can drive her?"

"No, that won't be necessary." Matrina stood beside the station wagon. "Are you aware that this vehicle was stolen from your lot last night, and then returned?"

"No way. That car's right where I left it yesterday when I closed up."

"Which was when?"

"Nine o'clock. And I close at nine today too, in case you'd like to come back and visit after closing time. Maybe we could grab a few beers someplace."

"Thank you, no." All the tiny hairs on the back of Matrina's neck bristled, and she suppressed the desire to check for her Mace in her purse. "Well, sometime after nine, someone came here, borrowed that car, drove it around town, and then returned it around two A.M. What I'd like to know is who came in yesterday and test drove it. Do you remember who that was?"

"Sure do. Sharp little number dressed in pink hot pants and a white tube top. If she came back later, she was probably looking for me."

"Did she have red hair?"

"Don't know. She had her hair all done up in a scarf. Couldn't tell what color her hair was. Didn't care much. She was a fine woman, no matter what color hair she had."

"Uh-huh. How long did she have the vehicle off the lot?"

"I don't know. Don't time my customers. Let 'em drive around so they can feel comfortable with the car. Then they don't come back and gripe after they buy it."

"And you don't drive with them? You just let them drive off by themselves?"

"Yeap. Got to trust your fellowman. That's what I always say."

"Well, your fellowman, or woman, in this case, drove down to Wal-Mart, made a key to your station wagon, and then came back after you closed and borrowed your car. I think she also stole one of your paper tags. Could you check to see if you have all your tags?"

"Lady, what are you smoking? That just ain't possible. My paper tags are in the office, all of them. She wouldn't even know where to look for them."

"Was she ever in your office?"

"Of course. She was watching me write up the sales order. Then she was going home to get her old man and come back to sign the papers."

"Did she ever come back?"

"She'll be here today. She probably got busy with something."

"Could you show me where you keep your paper tags?"

"Why? So you can steal one?"

"Of course not. I just want to know if this is where she stole the tag she had on the wagon last night. Here. I have the number of it. Could you at least check to see if it is from your numbered sequence of your tags?" Matrina held out a piece of notepad paper with the temporary tag number written on it. The disgruntled salesman grabbed it gruffly from her and headed for the office. Matrina followed.

Once inside the shabby room, the man opened a desk drawer and thumbed through his paper tags. Without his comment, Matrina could see the number of the temporary tag from the wagon fell into the sequential order of the tags in his drawer.

"Thank you," she said. "I can see that the tag did come from your stack of paper tags. That's what I wanted to know. Did the girl give you a name?"

The man shuffled through a dirty, crumpled file folder. A sales sheet written up for the Ford station wagon appeared stashed amid a grimy light bill, a phone bill with a coffee ring on it, and several crumpled gas receipts.

"Says here her name is Annie Douglas."

"Uh-huh. Did you see any ID for her?" Annie Douglas. Give me a break. Why didn't she go with Andy Douglas. This clown wouldn't have known the difference.

"Of course not. I trust my customers. Why would she lie about her name?"

"You don't have to see a driver's license, insurance card, good stuff like that to make a sale?"

"Oh, yeah, the state would like all that kind of trash, but I don't mess with it much."

"So, she tooled around town last night in your car, with one of your tags on it, and if she had gotten into a wreck and killed someone, what would happen then?"

"Oh, I guess somebody would show up here and ask questions, that's for sure." He scratched his head.

"So, I'm trying to help you out." Matrina inched toward the door. "You're missing a paper tag, and she will no doubt use it again. I think you ought to worry about that."

"I ain't worried about nothing." The man slammed shut the drawer to his desk. "That ain't one of my tags, and no broad got no car off this lot last night, or any other night. I know what I'm doing, and you're asking stuff that ain't none of your business."

"That's probably true." Matrina left the office and headed toward her van. "I thought you would like to know this happened at your car lot so you could be forewarned in the future. I guess I was wrong. Please excuse the intrusion."

"So, you want to drive the nifty little wagon?" He leered at her as she opened the door to her van and tried to close the distance between them. "Make you a good deal on it." He lowered his voice to a seductive tone of familiarity.

"I thought you said it was sold to the girl who test-drove it yesterday."

"It is, but first come, first serve. You know how it goes. You snooze, you lose."

"Well, today? I think I'll choose to lose," she said.

She climbed into her van, closed the door and cranked the motor. Whatever he said after that was lost in the roar of the engine and the whirl of the air conditioner.

Come on tub of bubbles, cool sheets, blowing a/c, spinning fan and Oz.

Chapter 21

While Matrina snoozed at home under her ceiling fan while an episode of *Murder, She Wrote* droned on A & E, John sweated on the delivery dock of one of his Publix stores in Bradenton. He wanted to check on a recent delivery from the Publix warehouse. He suspected this load might be short.

John had gathered cash register tapes for the Wednesday and Thursday before the fatal third weekend in June from Wal-Mart and Kmart. He had quite a hefty bag to split up with Matrina and planned to call her to invite her, Turner and Michelle to have dinner at his house. They could spend the evening and go over the tapes. It would fill the void left by his children who now lounged on the shores of Long Lake in upstate New York.

As John scrutinized the warehouse invoices for products unloaded from the Publix truck, Vince Haynes called out to him from forty feet away.

"Fleming," Vince said, his voice icy and hostile. "Get your worthless carcass over here. I need to talk to you."

Several of the workers who unloaded the truck turned to see the target of this display of anger.

John turned on a dime, and his temper flared. He didn't usually have a temper, but Vince knew how to push all his buttons.

"Vince, you can't possibly be talking to me in that tone of voice." Get a grip. He certainly didn't need to get into an altercation with a coworker while he walked around on probation. He tried to count to ten, couldn't remember what came after five, take a few deep breaths, pray.

"I'm not kidding, Fleming. Get over here, and do it now."

John asked God to help him not to care. How could it matter what Vince thought or what he said? He walked over to Vince, and he felt calm and in better control.

"What. Do. You. Want?" he in a quiet tone of voice, one word at a time. "I'm busy."

"I want you and I to go into your office and watch this video. And then I want you to explain it to me."

"Right this minute?" His anger abated, and he felt in control.

"Yes, right this minute." Vince stood his ground with a video tape clutched in his hand. He played to the guys from the warehouse, and John looked over his shoulder at the workers, gave a nonchalant shrug and rolled his eyes to the ceiling.

"I either have to go with this clown, or I have to kill him," he said. Vince and John walked down the corridor to John's cubbyhole of an office. John turned on the television monitor and popped the video into the VCR. Vince took a seat and rocked back in his chair. A "cat-that-ate-the-canary" look swept his face.

Across the TV screen walked Matrina. She hunched down in Vince's doorway, on Vince's boat, while she listened to Andy's conversation with the red-haired waitress on the next boat.

"My security camera only kicks in film when some movement alerts it. This was last night, about eight P.M. Do you know this woman?"

"What's she doing?" John said. Always answer a question with a question when you want to avoid a dangerous answer.

"What do you mean, 'what's she doing?' You're supposed to tell me." His loud voice accompanied his twiddled thumbs and nervous movement in his chair.

"How would I know what she's doing? I'm not there, am I?"

"Not yet."

The words sent a wave of chagrin down John's spine. Lord, have mercy, ran his thoughts. He's got Matrina and I on film when we broke into the *Empress*, sure as this world is round. "Looks like she's standing in the doorway of some boat. That your boat?"

"You know very well that's my boat. That's why she's there."

"She's there to do what?"

"That's what I'm asking you. Are you deaf? What's she doing there?"

"You'll have to ask her. How would I know?"

"Because she's no doubt one of your little spies. She's snooping around into other people's business and reporting back to you every little detail she uncovers."

"This woman doesn't work for me. Anybody else checking up on you besides me? Maybe she works for them."

"That woman doesn't work in security for Publix?"

"No. Have you ever seen her in this store?"

"Well, no."

"You should get your ducks in a row before marching off to war."

"What's she doing on my boat?"

"I'm telling you, you'll have to ask her."

"Who is she?"

"Her name is Matrina McCoy. She's a friend of mine. This little excursion on your boat deck doesn't involve me."

"Well, this little excursion on the boat deck next door to me certainly involves you. Explain this." Vince cued the tape to the portion where John and Matrina walked across the deck of the *Empress*, and John jimmied open the door, although on tape, he could have had a key. The film showed they entered the cabin of the *Empress* and walked around inside with a flashlight. Moments later, they left the *Empress*, and Matrina toted a plastic garbage bag.

John sighed. Busted. He couldn't lie. He couldn't fall into sin because he got caught in a trap he should have avoided in the first place. He took a deep breath and sailed into the truth.

"Your camera covers the boat next door?" John stalled for time.

"It sweeps the dock next door. The boat just happens to be in its scope. Now, answer the question. Why were you and the broad breaking into that boat?"

"Matrina caught the guy on that boat with a woman. The guy is supposed to marry Matrina's sister this fall. She wanted to know who the woman was, so I helped her get into the cabin, and she removed some cans from the trash so she could have fingerprints run on them and learn the name of the other woman."

"You expect me to believe a stupid story like that?"

John shrugged and gave Vince his most innocent look. "Believe it or not, that's your choice, but it's the truth. The whole thing has nothing to do with you. By the way, do you know the guy with the boat next to you?" May as well rake in a little information on his own while he lingered on the rack.

"There you go again," Vince said. "Poking your nose into other folks' business. I don't keep up with the people who moor their boats next to mine. None of my business what they do or who they do it with."

"True. But if this security camera is motion controlled, it must rotate positions. You must have him and the other woman on this tape at the same time you have Matrina on your boat."

"Yes, I do. She's quite a looker."

"Yes, I suppose she is."

"So, you're not going to tell me what you were doing on that boat."

"I already told you. I can't help it if you don't believe me. I don't suppose you'd tell me how long that boat has been moored there?"

"Absolutely not. Don't you pay attention? You got to get over this snooping into everyone's life."

"Vince, it's my job. That's why they pay me the big bucks. The reason I've been snooping into your life is I couldn't figure out how you were living the lifestyle you are on the salary you make. But thankfully, I snooped, and now I know that your wife has money of her own, and you are not living on your salary, and now I'm no longer suspicious of you. You ought to be glad for that. I have to protect Publix. It's my job."

"You know about my wife's money?"

"Yes, and good thing I do. Otherwise, I'd still be trying to figure out how she could be driving a Lexus and you could be living on Key Royale, and mooring a boat at Regatta Pointe. You should be glad I snooped."

Vince made no further comment.

"It's my job, Vince. How many times do I have to tell you that.? You looked like you were living on unexplained income. Now I know that you're not. That's a positive point. It should improve our relationship."

"Maybe it should," Vince said. He got up from his chair and popped his tape out of John's VCR. "And it probably would, except I don't like you, Fleming. But now that I've got the goods on you, I have to decide what to do with it. I have so many options; show it to your boss; play it for the guy who owns the boat next door. I'll have to think about it. I'll let you know." With that, he waved the video at John and walked out of John's office and slammed the door behind him.

Chapter 22

Matrina awoke later than same afternoon to the ringing of the telephone.

"Mom," Turner said through her bedroom door. "It's Mr. Fleming."

"Okay," Matrina said. She struggled to get her brain in gear, wrapped her bathrobe around her, opened the bedroom door, yawned and shook her hair out of her eyes. "Hey," she said into the telephone.

"Don't tell me you're napping," John said. "That's not fair."

"Okay, I'm not napping, at least not anymore. And what's not fair about it?"

"Because I'm down here at one of my stores doing battle with an irate produce manager while you're snoozing under your fan and watching TV."

"How do you know I'm watching TV?"

"I can hear it in the background. Angela Lansbury?"

"Yeah, but one episode was on when I laid down, and another episode is on now, so I didn't get much out of either of them."

"So get on your glad rags, load up your troops and be at my house in an hour for supper and tapes."

"What flavor tapes?"

"Huge, thick, bulging covered with black ink, garnished with rubber bands."

"Ah, my favorite. Want me to bring something for dinner?"

"No. Mrs. Gunthrey made some potato salad, and we have smoked turkey, so it will be kind of a summer supper."

"You just miss your kids and all the frustration that goes with kids, and you want to borrow mine so life won't be so quiet."

"Seems like you've got me. I thrive on chaos. What can I say?"

"We'll be there in an hour. Michelle and Turner can help scan tapes, too. You got the recap totals from the register readings, didn't you?"

"Yes, so we know how many sales of nine millimeter bullets were made at each register on each shift. So we know what we are looking for. That's going to help a lot."

"That's true. See ya soon."

"Thanks. Bye."

Matrina sat back down on the bed and tried to wake up. "Michelle?" she called through the opened bedroom door.

"Yeah, Mom. What do you want?"

"Coffee. Hot, black, lots of it."

"Okay. I'll put the pot on. Want me to start dinner?"

"No. We're going to John's house for dinner. Just tell Turner to feed Tramp, and once I've had about twelve cups of coffee, we're out of here." Matrina took off her robe and slid into a pair of her Ralph Lauren jeans and an icy pink tailored shirt.

"Okay." Michelle ran water into the coffeepot.

* * *

John had the table set when they got there, and they sat down to paper plates, potato salad, smoked turkey, rye bread, pickles and canned soda.

"Cool," Turner said. "My kind of supper."

"It's not pizza, but I guess it'll do," John said.

Matrina noticed a huge grocery bag bulged in the corner of the dining room. She put her purse down beside the bulging bag.

"This is the bag of tapes?" she said

"Unfortunately, that's the bag of tapes. And that's just Wal-Mart and Kmart."

"Mercy me. Are we going to live long enough to go through all those?"

"Let's hope so. Wal-Mart and Kmart are the most likely sources, though, so hopefully, we'll stumble on something useful before we're through the bag. And if we come up dry, there are always sports stores and gun shops."

"What if the trial starts before we finish?"

"We can ask for a postponement."

"Oh, okay."

After dinner, John bundled up the paper plates and put them in the trash. Matrina put the leftover potato salad and smoked turkey in the refrigerator, and Michelle and Turner waited to see what would happen next. They knew about the tape search, and it sounded like a challenging game to them. They could hardly wait to get started.

"Michelle, Turner, could I get you to watch a little TV for a few minutes while I talk to your mother about something?" John said. He turned the TV on to the Family Channel.

"Sure," the kids said. "Could you put the TV on the Western Channel?" Turner said.

"Okay," John said. "That okay with you, Michelle?"

"Yeah, I guess so," Michelle said. "Some of those shows aren't too bad."

A half-finished can of Diet Coke accompanied Matrina as she followed John out into the backyard and joined him at the picnic table.

"I want to show you an e-mail I got from Dee-Dee," he said. He pulled the printed message from his pocket. "I got it today, and I wanted to talk to you about it, without the kids hearing."

"What in the world is it?" Matrina said. She took the folded paper from his hand. "Oh," she said. Her head nodded in understanding. "Yes, Dee-Dee did talk to me about Delores, and her limitations. She said she shouldn't do that, as you wanted these things kept private, with good reason, but I guess she was in a mood to need a friend. This e-mail says she's confessing all to you, and wants your forgiveness, which, I assume is not a problem."

"Of course not," John said. He took the e-mail back from Matrina and put it back in his pocket. "I just wanted to explain it to you in case Dee-Dee didn't quite get it straight."

"She said her mom was a little 'intellectually challenged.' That's all," Matrina said. She sipped her soda.

"She was," John said. He picked his teeth with a toothpick. The sun sank into the west and a slight breeze cooled the early evening. "But she wasn't retarded, or anything like that. In fact, I didn't think there was anything seriously wrong with her. I always thought her parents kept her so sheltered that she didn't get a chance to grow and expand her horizons. I love my in-laws. They're good, God-fearing people, but they hovered over Delores and drove me nuts sometimes. They didn't think she was capable of anything. I taught her to drive, and they almost had a coronary over that. I wouldn't have let her drive alone, of course, but having that little card that said she was sanctioned by the state of New York to drive an automobile was so important to her. She would take it out of her purse sometimes for no good reason and stare at it. It encouraged her so much. She was capable of so much more than her folks had imagined."

"What caused this condition of hers?"

"Who knows. Her mom said it was a birth defect. Delores was slow learning things, colors, numbers, reading, so they decided she had a learning disability. I used to wonder if she didn't have a hearing disability, as once she got something down, she understood it. Like the sewing. She mastered that. And caring for the children. She mastered that, too. The kids never, ever went unattended."

"Did you have her hearing checked?"

"We were getting into that phase when she got sick. Her folks didn't like me looking so deeply into her condition, so I had to do it on the sly, and then convince Delores not to talk about it with her folks. She didn't understand that part of it, of course. It was strange. Her folks didn't seem to mind having a daughter they thought was mildly retarded, but they didn't want anyone to think she might be a little deaf."

"Do you know what her IQ was?"

"Yes. It was eighty-five. Eighty-five is low, of course, but it's not retarded."

"What did the doctors say?"

"The doctors she saw were her parents' doctors so they were not open to new ideas. They said she should be toted around and cared for and not pressured too much."

"And you, of course, said, 'Nuts' to that."

"You've got that right. But I had to be careful not to offend the doctors and the in-laws. It was dicey, but then, I'm kind of wired for dicey situations."

"You must have loved her a lot to have tolerated the situation and tried to give her a better life."

"I did," he said. He brushed forgotten bread crumbs from a prior picnic off the wooden table. "I'll never get over her death. Maybe if she had been more normal, it would be easier to accept such an early grave. But I feel she never had a chance. Life could have been so much better for her if we'd had more time. But time wasn't on our side."

"No. Time wasn't on our side either. Mike was larger than life. He was robust, and flamboyant, and jovial, and always happy, unless I bugged him about something. He was six feet two and totally Irish. He had black hair and gorgeous blue eyes; well, Michelle looks like her dad. But more time wasn't meant to be for us either." Matrina sighed and hoped she wouldn't give in to the tears she felt swell within her. "Did Delores understand her illness?" She needed to change the subject away from Mike.

"Not completely. When they diagnosed her with cancer, she thought God would heal her, and never understood why He didn't. She's not the only one who doesn't get that one. We had prayer requests announced at church, and we even did the twenty-four hour prayer circle thing. God ignored us, and when I see Him, for sure I will ask why."

"What were you teaching her when she got sick?"

"Money. The different denominations, how to spend it, what things are worth, how to count change, things like that. That's why the purchase of the gun was so important to me. She made that decision on her own, and she did a good job. She recognized something she knew I would like, thought the price was fair, paid for it with money her parents had given her, got the right change, and beat the seller like a stepchild. It was a new plateau for her. And not long after that, she got sick, and all the games gave way to the chemo."

"I'm so sorry. I really do know how you feel."

"I know you do," John said. He covered her hand that laid on the table with his two hands. He caressed her fingers and looked into her eyes. She felt that melting emotion that enraptures teenagers and hated herself for her immaturity. "That's why I wanted to explain it to you. I didn't want you to think Delores was stupid."

"Dee-Dee didn't imply that. She explained it about like you did," Matrina pulled her hand away and finished her soda. "She's a pretty savvy kid. She has it straight how things were."

"I wouldn't want you to think I would marry someone who would be a only pawn in my life, someone I could control and rule over."

"I didn't think that."

"Delores was good, and kind, and even-tempered, religious and nice, not to mention beautiful."

"I noticed from the pictures." Matrina smiled. "She was very beautiful."

"There was only one thing missing," John said, "if I could admit to a small shortcoming in our marriage."

"What was that?"

"God said He wanted a woman to be a helpmeet for a man. That's in the Bible, you know."

"I know. I'm not churchy, but I'm not a Bible illiterate."

"Good. So husbands and wives should be like a yoked team, each having a job to do, each doing his job and not getting in the way of the other who is trying to do her job. And there should be exchange of ideas, advice and correction between them."

"Not if you're married to Mike McCoy." Matrina's eyes twinkled as she laughed out loud. "It was, 'my way or the highway.' I'm chagrined over the fights we had where I didn't like something. I'd let him know it, and he'd get mad. Then he'd have to do whatever it was to prove a point. I should have kept my mouth shut. He might have come to my conclusion on his own, if I'd been smart enough to stay out of it."

"That's what I mean," John said. "I didn't have anyone to rein me in. It would have been nice to have Delores say, 'Now, John, do you really think we need another music CD just because it's a new version of Enya?' But she never did. Everything I did was A-okay with her. It was lonely at the top, so to speak."

"I'm sure you did fine. You're very level-headed. I can't see you doing anything that would be frivolous or selfish or foolhardy."

"Unless it has to do with music. Then I'm a lost cause."

John looked into her eyes and took a deep breath. "There's something else I want to say to you," he said. Matrina waited. "Is there something going on between us we need to discuss?"

Matrina searched his eyes and wanted to lie her way out of this subject. "Yes," she said.

"I know it's wrong, but I can't get kissing you out of my head," John said. He spoke in low tones, and she wished she had let her hand stay in his. "It's like I'm sixteen again."

"Me, too," she said. She broke the control of his gaze and dropped her eyes. "I thought all those emotions died with Mike. I feel so guilty that here they are again."

"We don't have to feel guilty. But we do have to be careful," John said. "The world is careening out of control with affairs outside of marriage, but I could never do that. If this turns out to be love, I'd have to marry you before anything further happened, if you'd have me."

"I'd have you," Matrina said. "I feel the same way." Emotional commitment enhanced her voice. "I never had an affair-type thing with Mike when I was young and foolish, and I could never have an affair outside of marriage at this stage of the game, even if I were in love with the guy. I'd have to be married to him first."

"Then we're in agreement?"

"Agreement, to what?" Scary moments laced the air.

"That we should spend some time together and see where it leads us. Is remarrying a possibility in your life?"

"I haven't thought about it," she said. "Your kiss did set me on my ear, but that's as far as it's gone."

"I've thought about it, and you're the first woman I've met since Delores died that I would even consider as a wife."

"That's quite a compliment. Thank you."

"I'm glad you came into my life. You've made me feel alive again. I thought I died with Delores, as you thought you died with Mike. Maybe this is a second chance God is offering us."

"People our age have so much baggage. I had friends up north who are into second marriages and it's a nightmare. The romance seems to wear off after a while."

"That's why we need to spend more time together. Open up all the baggage. See what lurks in all the corners. That sound okay?"

"Yes." She met his eyes once more and saw in them a deep warmth that magnetized her. "I'm not Delores, you know. I have opinions on just about everything, and I have a temper."

"I know. And I'm not Mike. I'm not 'larger than life.' I'm barely, 'life.'"

"I know." She chuckled. "So, we're, what? Engaged to become engaged on the verge of becoming engaged?"

"Ah, you've captured the essence of the moment. But we do have to be careful. I can't kiss you again until we're engaged to becoming engaged, at least. Christ said we had to control our minds, and you, Matrina McCoy, my precious one, are a mind boggler. I can't risk that."

"I can't risk it either. This murder crisis we're in will give us plenty of time to be together and not become further involved. We'll see how it goes. We need to pray for direction."

"Agreed."

"Hi, guys." A new voice spoke from the opened door to the house. John and Matrina turned to see Nathan who stood there with a smoked turkey sandwich in one hand and a cup of coffee in the other. "Your Michelle makes a mean sandwich, Matrina," he said, "not to mention a meaner pot of coffee."

"You're drinking coffee tonight, hot as it is?" John said.

"Always good weather for coffee," Nathan said. He joined them at the picnic table. "So, what's up?"

"Tons and tons and tons of cash register tapes," Matrina said, "waiting to be drawn and quartered."

"Let's get to it," Nathan said. "As soon as I finish my sandwich."

"What's the latest?" John said. "You here on a social call to wolf down my victuals, or do you have news?"

"I have news, bro," Nathan said. "Strange news, but news, none the less."

"Lay it on me."

"Slats had a Rolex watch."

"Slats had a Rolex watch." Both Matrina and John echoed the comment. How could a poverty-plagued guy like Slats have a Rolex watch? Matrina turned that thought over in her mind and could come to no sensible conclusion.

By now, Michelle and Turner had turned off the TV and joined them. Each carried a can of apple juice. Matrina raised a pleased eyebrow at their sensible choice in drinks.

"Yes, and it isn't even his."

"Not his?" Dual echoes once more.

"Ever notice the echo in this backyard?" Nathan said to Michelle and Turner. "Strange phenomenon."

"What are you talking about?" John said. "Slats couldn't possibly own a Rolex. Do you know what they cost?"

"Lots," Nathan said, "but he had one. How he could afford one is the mystery."

The backyard floated in silence.

"Nathan," John said in a more commanding tone of voice. "Give."

"You remember I paid the rent on Slats' apartment for another month so I could keep an eye on the incoming phone calls and his mailbox. I wanted to see who phoned him and left messages, or wrote to him. The first week, I picked up a ton of mail from his mailbox, most of it junk, of course. But yesterday, I picked up a reminder slip from a local jeweler that his watch was ready. He had dropped it off for repair over a month ago, and never had the chance to pick it up, due to being dead, and all that."

"Nathan, out with it," John said.

"So I found the claim check in his kitchen drawer. I picked up the watch from the jeweler today, and I had the jeweler remove the watchband and check out the ID number on the casing. Guess what?"

"What?" The four voices at the table trumpeted in unison.

"The watch is registered to a Joseph Voloni with a Franklin Park address. Franklin Park is a suburb of Chicago."

"So Slats stole someone's watch?" Matrina said. Shock filtered across her voice and her face.

"You tell me. But the name sounds Italian to me, and Italian folks from Chicago might be have a godfather connection, if you know what I mean."

"If Slats stole an Italian guy's watch, and the guy was from Chicago, and connected to one of the old syndicates, the Chicago guy might be ticked off enough to have Slats killed?" Matrina stated the obvious for clarification.

"Maybe it wasn't only about the watch," Nathan said. "Maybe there were other issues between Slats and this Joseph Voloni." Nathan wiped his mouth with a paper napkin he had brought out with his sandwich. "At least now, we have a possible theory, and a name to run. We might even be able to put the guy in Florida on the third weekend in June."

"Wow," Turner said. "That would rock. This is a regular murder mystery like they have on TV."

Matrina smiled. "And this Joseph Voloni couldn't get his watch back because it was in the shop, and there would be no way he could know that, if he'd already had Slats killed."

"Guys connected to the old syndicate usually want revenge," Nathan said. "More watches they can get."

"Wait a minute, wait a minute, wait a minute," John said. He waved his hands in a manner that demanded cessation of all conversation. "So we're saying we think Slats is some kind of petty thief?"

"A Rolex watch is not petty," Nathan said. "And John, I know that you're the last word in the 'Everything's Beautiful' crowd, but what do we really know about Slats? He came here, what? Four, five years ago? From where? Never mentioned having family. Started attending church. We buddied up to him, didn't ask him many questions. We were glad he was aboard the Glory train. He could have had all kinds of secrets we never bothered to discover. If he didn't steal the watch, where did he get it?"

"I wouldn't know," John said. "It's true we didn't know much about Slats. I thought he was from Miami, but not sure why I thought that."

"Yeah," Nathan said. "I thought he was from southeast Florida somewhere, too. Not sure why. But the fact of the matter is, we didn't know Slats very well. We never knew him at all. He may have been involved in some shady deals before coming here. Maybe here is where he experienced conversion, gave his heart to the Lord, and put those evil deeds behind him."

"Here's a thought," Matrina said. She fidgeted and shifted positions at the table, "and you're not going to like it much."

"That's okay," Nathan said. "Leave no thought unspoken."

"Suppose Slats didn't give up his shady activities when he came here. He went underground with them, carefully, so you guys wouldn't find out. Maybe he was the one who stole John's gun, and someone else used it to get even with him on some unsettled score, such as the stolen Rolex or maybe something more sinister along with the stolen Rolex."

Silence bombarded her for that scenario. She knew she had tossed too much information into the mix. She shifted positions again and wished she could take the words back.

"Can you run a check on Slats' background?" John said.

"Sure. No problem," Matrina said. "And I should run a check on this Joseph Voloni as well. Here, give me your napkin, Nathan, and loan me your pen. Let me jot down Joseph Voloni's name." Matrina wrote the name on the napkin, folded it and put it in her jeans pocket. "I'll get this run tomorrow and let you know."

"I have a thought, too," Michelle said.

"Let's hear it," Nathan said.

"Did I hear somewhere that Mr. Slats, whatever his name is, put in lawn sprinklers for a living?"

"Yes," John said. "That's what he did, irrigation work."

Michelle faltered, ready to back off if she sensed any rejection from the adults at the table. "Maybe he did a sprinkler job for some rich guy, and the watch was part of the payment for his work."

Nathan pursed his lips, and squinted his eyes in thought.

"Works for me," he said. "Good thought, Michelle. We'll keep that in mind."

"Good job, Michelle," Matrina said. She reached over and patted her daughter on the arm. "That thought has real possibilities."

"Eat up, Nathan," John said. "We've got tapes to peruse."

"Gottcha." Nathan wolfed down the rest of his sandwich and took his handkerchief from his pants pocket and wiped away the remaining crumbs and mayonnaise from his lips. "Let's hit the bricks."

Chapter 23

Matrina walked into the ACS office the next day, Tuesday, around ten A.M. She wore her same Ralph Laurens and icy pink shirt from last evening.

The evening at John's had been nonproductive, except they did go through five long, long, long register tapes from Wal-Mart from the Wednesday before the third weekend in June, and accounted for the five boxes of nine millimeter bullets that the recap sheet stated had been sold. The security videos John had been able to borrow showed the shoppers as they purchased the bullets. Nathan had the crew jot down the date, time, and description of the shoppers in hopes that somewhere down the line one of these people would tie into the case.

The conversation with John about marriage fluttered in the back of Matrina's mind. She liked him, and the physical attraction to him burned in her brain, but did she want to risk marriage to him? She hoped God would provide the answers as she couldn't even come up with relevant questions.

"Hi, Franny, coffee?" Matrina said. She walked past the reception desk and into her cubicle.

"Yeah, think I will. Thanks," Franny said. "Oreo?"

"No, thanks, but I have your boxes here, and your soda, as booty for running that information on the boat and the license tags and that gal's address."

"I told you that was a joke."

"Not to me," Matrina said. She walked back to Franny's desk and placed two boxes of Oreos and a six-pack of Diet Coke on the top of her printer. "Coffee coming up."

Matrina walked back to the kitchen and poured herself and Franny two cups of coffee.

"Where's our fearless leader?" she said. She placed Franny's coffee on her desk.

"St. Petersburg. Salt and Sea Corporation."

Matrina paused and wrinkled her brow. "The Trade Winds company?"

"Yeah. That Ray Willard guy got arrested, and the board of directors wanted to talk with George about taking over their security for all their holdings, restaurants, lounges, marinas, really big deal."

"Well, hurrah for us. Think we might have a raise coming since ACS will be in high clover?"

"Don't count on it," Franny said. "Oh, I did got that stuff you wanted, you know. The ID on the boat, the six tags, and the residence information. It's all in here." Franny handed Matrina a file folder with her name on it.

"Great." Matrina took the folder and walked back to her cubicle. She booted up her computer while she flipped through the information in the folder.

The boat, a Tiara 4400, fifty foot yacht, cost $479,000.00, named the *Empress*, purchased in March of last year by Reba Panacelli Voloni. HELLO. Reba lived in Franklin Park, IL. DOUBLE HELLO. She lived with her husband Anthonio Voloni, same address. Did Joseph Voloni live with them as well? How did Slats come to know Joseph Voloni? How did Slats get his watch? Did this show a connection between Slats and the *Empress*? What's up with that?

Matrina's head reeled from the information, but she couldn't connect the dots. She moved on to the next little tidbit of data.

Four of the six cars left in the Trade Winds' parking lot overnight belonged to guys, one car belonged to Kiran Kirkland, and the sixth one, a beige Honda Civic, belonged to Sandra Marshall. The address from the license record matched the address of the duplex into which Matrina had seen Andy disappear.

A gentleman named Eugene Staple owned the duplex, address and phone number in Sarasota. Matrina picked up the phone and dialed his number.

"Hello?" Mr. Staple said.

"Hello," Matrina said. "I'm calling for a reference on a Sandra Marshall. She listed you as a credit reference."

"Yes, she's my tenant," Mr. Staple said.

"Is she reliable?"

"Oh, my yes. Pays her rent right on time. No trouble with her at all. Nice young lady."

"How long has she rented from you?"

"Oh, probably two years now. She isn't planning to move, is she?"

"No. This is just to verify her credit rating. Does she live alone, or does she have family with her?"

"She's alone. Just her. No pets, no kids, no family. Ideal tenant."

"We have her down as working at the Trade Winds restaurant. Is that the information you have?"

"Yes. She's a waitress there. Been there the whole time she's lived in my apartment, near as I know."

"That agrees with my information. Thank you for your time." Matrina hung up. Two years. So Andy could have known her before Rosie.

At that moment, George sailed into the office. He spoke to Franny and then stuck his head into Matrina's cubicle.

"Got your fingerprint information, Toots," he said. "Interested?"

"You bet." Matrina grabbed her coffee and followed George into his office. "Coffee?"

"Yes, black, large, strong." George put down his briefcase and the daily paper and looked to see why the air conditioning blew mediocre air. "Have that maintenance guy check these filters, will you, Matrina? This thing ought to be putting out more cold air than it does."

"Okay." She called back to him from the kitchen area. "I'll have Franny leave him a note."

Matrina returned to George's office, placed a paper napkin on his desk and placed his coffee on the napkin. She picked up her own cup and sat down in the chair across from him.

"So?" She said.

"So, I had to call in some heavy duty favors to get these prints run in one day, Little Missy," George said. He dug into his briefcase, found the right file and handed it to her. "I hope this is of some really great value to John's case."

Matrina slouched an inch in her chair. She neglected to tell George these prints had nothing to do with John. "We did go through several cash register tapes at John's last night," she said. She evaded the subject; better still, she changed the subject. "And Nathan came up with this thing that Slats had a Rolex watch."

"A Rolex watch?" George said, in mid-swallow. "How would a lawn sprinkler guy get a Rolex watch?"

"That's what we're all asking each other," she said. Subject changed. Good job, Matrina. "Any ideas?"

"Oh, I don't know," George said. He took another swig from his cup. "Bought it at a pawn shop?"

"Good," Matrina said. "We didn't think of that one."

"What did you guys think of?"

"Some of us thought Slats might have stolen it."

"That would be you."

"Yes, that would be me. Not a very popular notion. Then Michelle came up with the idea that maybe he got it as payment for work done, like putting in a sprinkler system."

"That's an idea. Smart kid. Anything else?"

"The watch isn't registered in Slats' name. It's registered to a Joseph Voloni from Franklin Park, Illinois."

"No wonder you thought he might have stolen it."

"Got to be a reason it is not registered in Slats' name. Voloni sounds Italian, Franklin Park's in Chicago, Italian Chicago suggests syndicate, so I thought maybe this Voloni dude did Slats in because he stole his watch."

"Maybe the watch is just the tip of the iceberg," George said. He spread his morning paper out on his desk. "Maybe ole Slats was leading a double life, good Christian guy on the one hand, syndicate connection errand-runner on the other."

"Try selling that one to our good Christian dynamic duo, John and Nathan."

"Hum. Got yourself a kettle of trouble, Little Missy," George said. He turned the pages of the paper and sipped his coffee. He adjusted the blinds behind his desk to shut out the blazing sun.

"It's my row, so I guess I'll just get busy and hoe it," Matrina said. She walked toward the door. "And you're not going to tell me what happened in St. Pete?"

"Nope. You'll get a big head for landing us this nice account all by yourself."

"They're going to go with us, then?"

"Yeah. Checker tests, surveillance, cameras, the whole ball of wax."

"Cool." Matrina smiled. "So, do Franny and I get a raise?"

"We'll talk." George turned the page in his paper and adjusted his glasses.

Matrina paused another minute in the doorway. George remained absorbed in his paper. "Thanks for the print run," she said, and then she disappeared down the hall to her cubicle.

Once in her office, she sat down and cracked the file folder. The identification of all the fingerprints soared up at her from the printed page.

The wine cooler bottles contained prints of Andy Douglas and Sandra Marshall. No surprise there. Some of the Coors cans contained fingerprints from Kenneth Stephens, Andy's sheriff's department partner. Not much surprise there either. One Coors can boasted the fingerprints of someone named Carmine Panacelli. And the Dixie cup contained the prints of— surprise, surprise, surprise—Joseph Voloni.

Matrina sat back in her chair and tried to absorb the information. Reba Panacelli Voloni owned the boat. None of the prints recovered matched either her or her husband, Anthonio Voloni. Maybe their prints would have surfaced if Matrina had taken more trash to have examined. Carmine Panacelli must be Reba's, what? Brother? Father? Nephew? And Joseph Voloni would be her son? Brother-in-law? Father-in-law? It had to be a family affair. It had "syndicate" scribbled all over it. She needed to find out how long the Voloni/Panacelli connection had been in town.

Matrina looked up the Regatta Pointe Marina in the phone book. She dialed the number while she rocked back in her chair and plopped her feet on her desk, crossed her ankles and sipped her remaining cold coffee. She made a disgusted face and tossed the empty cup into the trash can, glad the few remaining sips didn't splatter over the side of the container.

"Hello," she said into the phone. "Could I speak with the dock master?" She waited for him to come to the phone. "I was wondering if you could give me some information about one of the slips in your marina."

"Sure," came the masculine reply.

"It's the slip where the *Empress* is docked right now, next to the *Fly-By-Night*. That slip is so nice and shady. I would love to consider it for my brother's yacht when he returns from Jamaica, but I wasn't sure if the *Empress* has it all year long or what."

"No," the dock master said. "As a matter of fact, that slip is free right now. The *Empress* left port this morning."

"Really? How opportune. Has the *Empress* been in that slip long?"

"About a month, off and on. They come and go, you know. They aren't particular about which slip they put into. I could easily book that slip for your brother, and give the *Empress* another slip upon their return."

"Did the *Empress* folks say when they'd be back?"

"No. We don't ask. Violation of privacy and all that sort of thing," the man said.

"Was she in port before this? Or has she been here only during the last month."

"Only during the past month. She's a new lady to us. In fact, I don't believe she's been at sea more than a month or so. She's right off the showroom floor. Most of our clients have only the best vessels."

"I can see that," Matrina said. She tried to add a cooing sound to her voice. "That's why I'm so interested in your marina. Well, I'll tell my brother, and we'll be in touch."

"Do you want to leave your name and number?" the dock master said.

"Not at this moment. I'll be in touch. By-eee." And with that, Matrina hung up the phone.

Only in port a month, in and out, out right now, coming back? Who knows. But that might put her there over the third weekend of June. Does that tie into Slats? Don't discount it. She needed to pass this information on to John and Nathan. Maybe they could put the puzzle pieces together.

Matrina kicked her computer onto the internet and brought up her e-mail. She had one new message, from John.

"Matrina, turn on your cell phone. You're dead," it said. Aaggguhhh! How could my cell phone be off? Disgusted, Matrina fished into the bottom of her purse and hauled out her little connection to the rest of the world, and sure enough, it failed to blink back at her. She switched it back on and within seconds, it chirped in her hand.

"Hello?"

"Subway. Gulfgate. One hour. Be there."

"Okay," she said. "No meatballs, though. Something that used to cluck and lay eggs."

"Okay. I've been out collecting more tapes, this time down here in Sarasota. I'll share."

"Goody-gum drop. I have news, too. I'll tell you over lunch. Strange things have been popping up in my research."

"Okay. We'll sort it out. See ya."

"Copy that."

Could these items of information come together and begin a defense in John's case? Or had they trotted down a dead end street? She headed out to Subway and hoped they had galloped into something positive.

Chapter 24

Matrina sat down at John's table at Subway. "Hey, Kemo Sabe," she said. He wore new Levis, new Nikes and a new blue Hunt Club polo shirt. "New duds?"

"Yeah," he said. He pushed her low fat turkey breast sub sandwich in her direction. "Mrs. Gunthrey had all my old clothes stacked in a box marked 'Goodwill,' so I figured it was time. Had to do it before, heaven help us, she decided to go shopping for me. Then I'd be sitting here in bib overalls and plaid flannel."

"That wouldn't be good," Matrina said. She shook her head, and laid the file folder that contained the information from Franny's search on the table next to her sandwich.

Inside lay the data on the ID of the boat, the owners of the cars left in the Trade Winds parking lot Sunday night and her notes on her conversation with Sandra Marshall's landlord. The folder also contained the information George provided which outlined the identity of the fingerprints. "How are the kids?" Matrina said.

"They're fine," John said. He opened one of the bags of potato chips that came with the sandwiches. "I talk to them every morning and every night, and it'll probably take me years to undo the stuff they're learning from the doting grandparents."

"It sounds like fun for everyone," Matrina said. She opened her turkey sandwich. "Everyone but you."

"Yeah, well" he said, "you do what you have to do. At least, I know they're safe up there."

"That's true." She bit into her sandwich.

"Whatcha got?" John said. He swallowed a bite of his meatball sub.

"Stuff," she said. She smiled at him and sipped her Diet Coke.

"Stuff," he said. He raised an eyebrow and wiped his mouth with a paper napkin from the dispenser. "Stuff's good."

"This stuff is," she said. "Eat, then I'll lay it all out for you. You got more tapes?"

"Yes, Ma'am," he said. He took another bite of his sandwich. "I'm surprised everyone is so cooperative with me."

"Maybe it's the new clothes. They say clothes speak for the man."

"These clothes say, 'This man has been kidnapped by the Gap.'"

"Better the Gap than the Salvation Army."

"I don't know. I've found some pretty good stuff in the Salvation Army."

"We'll have to have Mrs. Gunthrey bug you more often about your attire."

"I'll put it on my 'to do' list."

"I'm sure. Speaking of Mrs. Gunthrey, I have a question for you."

"Shoot."

"Do you think her son, Jared, could be mixed up in this? You know he stole one of your guns."

"Yeah, but he didn't steal the American Luger. And I don't think he even knew Slats."

"How do you know he didn't steal the Luger?"

"Because he'd have never put it back. He'd have hocked it for crack ten minutes after he stole it."

"Oh. Well, it's nice when a person has a predictable MO. Makes him easier to figure out."

"When it comes to Jared, he's an easy read. He's a bum. He lives off his mother. He steals when Mom won't kick in. He won't get a job. He doesn't care if he lives anywhere; and when things are going well for him, we never see him."

"So, when he's AWOL, that's a good thing?"

"Right."

"Poor Mrs. Gunthrey."

"Poor Mrs. Gunthrey indeed. I have to pray about my attitude so I don't whip him within an inch of his life when he does show up. She's always so thrilled when he comes to visit. She doesn't see she's enabling him in his lifestyle."

"So you think beating him up would be helpful?"

"No, but I'd feel better about it."

They finished their sandwiches, and Matrina cleared the table, got a refill on their sodas and spread out the information from her file folder.

"Okay," she said. She passed one printout sheet to John. "This is the owner of the *Empress*, Reba Panacelli Voloni, husband is Anthonio Voloni, lives in Franklin Park, Illinois."

"You're kidding." John gave her an incredulous look and scanned the report. "So she's related to Joseph, the Rolex guy?"

"You think?"

"I think." John said. "Too obvious to be a coincidence. So, she's his mother, mother-in-law, sister-in-law?"

"Just wait. There's more. But before we get there, this is the report on the license tags in the parking lot. There was a beige Honda Civic belonging to Sandra Marshall, same address as the duplex she and Andy returned to Sunday night."

"So we have a name for the gorgeous redhead."

"Dare we go on?"

"Please do. This is fascinating."

"It's fixin' to get more fascinating."

"Fixin'? How long have you been in the south?"

"Evidently, too long," she said. "The information contained in this file will soon become more fascinating. That better?"

"Not as folksy. I'd stick with 'fixin'.' Gets one's attention." John sipped his new supply of soda.

"Okay, I called Sandra's landlord, and she's a model tenant. Worked at Trade Winds two years."

"No surprise there."

"No. Now to the fingerprints. One set belongs to Andy, one set to Kenny Stephens, Andy's partner, one set belongs to our new little friend, excuse me, our new little gorgeous friend, Sandra. And, are you ready for this?"

John nodded.

"One set belongs to Joseph Voloni."

John put his soda cup down and stared at her in total disbelief. "The Rolex guy?"

"The same. Cool, eh?"

"What's it mean?"

"I was hoping you'd know," she said. "It's just so weird. The Voloni's came down here on their yacht, got tangled up with Andy and his buddy and this waitress, somehow, and Slats wound up dead. And yet, the purpose of the boat seems to be all about smuggling something, probably from Cancun. The boat is out of dock right now."

"How do you know that?"

"I called the dock master at Regatta Pointe, and he said they pulled out this morning. He says they come and go."

"Back to Cancun?"

"Possibly, or a run to somewhere else. What do you think they're running?"

"I don't know," John said. "Drugs would be the obvious guess, or jewels, something that would fit in the Kaluha bottles, or stuffed beside the bottles in the cardboard containers."

"Or pasted to the bottom of the containers."

"That, too."

"And there are another set of fingerprints, too," Matrina said. "One of the cans of Coors had the prints of someone called Carmine Panacelli. Same maiden name as the boat owner, Reba Panacelli Voloni."

"Right out of the pages of the Godfather."

"It would seem so. He might be Reba's brother? Or her father?"

"Ole Reba wasn't onboard?"

"If she was, she didn't drink anything. No prints for her."

"Do your reports have physical descriptions on them?"

"Yes. I haven't really checked that far into that yet. But they're listed right there, see?"

"Reba Panacelli was born 1947, Arlington Heights, Illinois," John read. "Arlington Heights is a suburb of Chicago, north end."

"How do you know that?"

"Dee-Dee had a geography project on Chicago once, and we learned all the outlying areas of the city. Franklin Park is by O'Hare airport, kind of in the middle or west of the city proper."

"So Reba's an older lady."

"And Joseph was born in 1967 in Franklin Park. So, he could be her son."

"Yes, and the other guy, Carmine Panacelli was born in 1937, so he's our senior citizen, probably basking in some lake-shore condo, and probably her brother."

"He would be ten years older than Reba, but get this, he was born in Arlington Heights, too."

"Good for him," Matrina said. She sipped her diet soda. "So, Reba marries Anthonio Voloni, and moves to Franklin Park, and they have Joseph. Reba would have been twenty when Joseph was born."

"So, decades later, Reba's brother, and Reba's son, cruise on down to Florida, get hooked up with Andy and his cohorts, and start smuggling stuff? And they kill Slats for stealing Joseph's Rolex?"

"Among other things," Matrina said. "Or, as we've said before, maybe the Rolex was a gift or a payment for some deal that went terribly wrong."

"And syndicate guys are not long on patience."

"Or forgiveness."

"What's the detail on Joseph?"

"Oh, it's right here," Matrina pulled a page from the middle of the file. Date of birth, July 14, 1967, current driver's license is from four years ago, Illinois, Franklin Park address, description, six foot three, hundred and sixty pounds, brown on brown, dark complexion. Hum. That's strange," Matrina stopped and tried to digest the data. "Why doesn't he have a current driver's license?"

At that moment, Matrina and John looked at each other, and the molecules of truth bounced back and forth from one brain to the other. Neither could put the developing cloudy picture into words.

"That could describe Slats," John said. "Six foot three, hundred and sixty pounds, born in 1967."

"Is July fourteenth his birthday?"

"No. His birthday was sometime in March. Do you have a bio on Slats?"

"No. I didn't think we needed one."

"Stay right here," John said. He got up from the table. "Let me go get my briefcase and my laptop from the Jeep. Be right back." He fled out the door, and Matrina watched him hurry across the hot parking lot. She could see heat waves rising from the black pavement as she watched weary shoppers scurry from their vehicles to the air conditioned comfort of whatever store beckoned them.

John opened the doors to the Jeep, reached into the back seat, retrieved his briefcase and his laptop and returned to the sandwich shop.

"Okay, here we go," he said. He flipped open his laptop and booted it up. "You have DSL wireless?"

"Of course, my dear," he said. "I am prepared for all situations."

"A boy scout to the core."

"Actually, I'm an Eagle scout."

"Really?"

"Really."

"I'm impressed."

"You should be. For my project, I planted all sorts of perennial plants around the Herkimer County Library, and put plaques by them to say what kind of plant they were, and a little history about each plant."

"Whoa, Dude."

"You'd better believe, 'Whoa, Dude;' my mother had to drag me through the hedge backwards to get me to do it, but I'm glad she did, now. I can use it as a hammer on John and Matt to get them to do scouts."

Matrina watched as John logged onto the site where he could run a driver's license. He put in his password, and entered Robert Walker, and Robert's last address. The information popped up on the screen.

"It says, 'Robert Walker, 1240 West Indian Rocks Drive, Palmetto, Florida.' That's north of Bradenton, and it's Slats' address."

Matrina nodded and waited for more information.

"It says he is six foot three, weighs a hundred and sixty pounds, brown on brown, dark complexion, DOB March 28, 1967."

"Close enough," Matrina said. A wave of excitement filled her body. "What do you think it means? They can't be brothers. Cousins with the same general physical description?"

"Let me see where Slats' prior addresses are located. See if we can come up with a Franklin Park connection." John searched for prior addresses. "This is strange," he commented, and turned the screen for Matrina to read the words.

"It says prior addresses are Miami, Florida, but it doesn't give any exact address. It gives his social security number, and driver's license number. Look, his driver's license was issued four years ago. There should be a prior Illinois license, if he is from there."

"True. Let's check Joseph's social security number." That popped up on the screen, and no connection linked the two numbers. "Okay, Joseph dropped off the screen four years ago, and Slats didn't exist until four years ago. Do you know what that tells us"

"Witness protection," Matrina said. She dropped her voice to a whisper. "He was in witness protection, and somehow, the Chicago people found him, and they killed him over whatever it was that caused him to go underground."

"Yes. The new social security number and new date of birth were part of the cover. And the sending off of the Rolex watch for repair was probably what fingered him. Slats wouldn't be smart enough to figure that one out. Why don't the feds send people to check on these kind of situations, instead of sending people off into never-never land and hope they survive. Slats needed supervision."

"Wonder what he did that caused him to need protection?"

"I don't know. Let me bring up the archives of the *Chicago Tribune* and see what we can find." John booted up the *Tribune* web page and searched the archives for court cases. Several traffic ticket cases bounced onto the screen, a case about a husband who murdered his wife and his mistress, and several shoplifting cases. John changed his search to "Voloni" and that produced results.

"June 10, 1999: Anthonio Voloni is sentenced to life in prison for the murder of Paul Martiani, kingpin in a drug running operation on Lake Michigan. Key witness was Joseph Voloni, Anthonio's only son, who witnessed the murder. Joseph was compelled to come forward about his father's crime due to a recent religious epiphany in which he was drawn to leave his native religion of Catholicism and become part of the right-wing Protestant movement."

"So we need to prove that Robert Walker, a.k.a Slats, and Joseph Voloni are the same person."

"And do we believe that his mother allowed the use of her yacht to have her brother hunt down her son and kill him?"

"Maybe the brother didn't tell Reba he borrowed her yacht."

"Maybe. And where do Andy and his group of cohorts fit in?"

Matrina shook her head. "No idea. But let's concentrate on proving that Robert and Joseph are the same person. That might go a long ways in getting you off the hook for this murder."

"True. Nathan still has the keys to Slats' apartment. We could go there and pull prints."

"No good," Matrina said. She shook her head. "They could say Joseph visited Slats there and wanted his watch back, and that would explain Joseph's prints being in Slats' apartment."

"We need a copy of Slats' fingerprints to compare them to the prints found on the Dixie cup. That would be a start. That would put Slats on the *Empress*, and tie him to the Volonis."

"What Dixie cup?" John said. He wrinkled his brow and looked at her over his laptop.

"The Dixie cup where we found Joseph Voloni's prints."

"You didn't say they were found on a Dixie cup."

"You were with me on the yacht when I pulled it from the garbage."

"I didn't pay attention to what you were pulling. One of the items was a Dixie cup?"

"Yes. I didn't mention it to you at the time. I probably didn't think it mattered where we looked for prints. Does it?"

"Yes," John said, "big time. Slats would only drink out of Dixie cups. He used to drive us all up the wall making us keep those stupid little cups on hand for when we had Bible studies and cookouts. He said he couldn't drink out of anything else because glasses, cans, bottles and plastic cups gave him chills."

Matrina looked at John, and the amazement in her mind spread across her face.

"Then Joseph is definitely Slats."

"Yes, but we have to prove that, and then figure out how it helps me get out from under this murder charge."

"We need a fingerprint."

"Yes. A fingerprint that is defnitely from Slats." John thought this factor out, and Matrina waited for the search engine in his brain to perk. "I have it," John said.

"What?"

"I used to loan Slats money from time to time." He struggled to contain his excitement. "And I bank at Bank of America. Slats didn't have an account there, and I remember he griped and complained because they always made him put his thumb print on my check before they would cash it for him. So my canceled checks that I had made out to him would all have his thumb print on them."

"Cool. We need one of your checks, and I'll get George to run the print from it. If it comes back Joseph Voloni, we're home free."

"Except we'll have the feds down on us like ugly on alligators."

"It's not your fault his cover got blown. You had no idea he was part of the witness protection program when he was alive."

"Will they believe that, though? It might give them another motive for me to have killed him."

"Why? You are not connected to the Volonis."

"True. Hope they believe that."

"So, how fast can I get one of your Slats checks?"

"A minute and a half," John said. He reached into his briefcase and produced a bank statement. "I carry my bank statements in my briefcase so in case I have a spare minute at work I can reconcile my bank account. This is May's. I'm sure I have a Slats check in that month's."

Matrina watched as he riffled through his canceled checks and marveled at his organization. She wondered if he would freak out when he saw how she kept her checkbook and bank statements, catch as catch can. That might be baggage they would have to discuss.

"Here," he said. "Here's one for a hundred bucks, and look at the thumb print on the memo line."

"Oh, John, this is answered prayer."

"Let's hope so." John closed his briefcase and put his closed-down laptop beside it. "How quick can you get this to George?"

"A minute and a half," Matrina said, "if the cops don't catch me speeding."

"Better make it two minutes." John opened the door to the sandwich shop for Matrina to walk through ahead of him as they left the air conditioned comfort.

She paused on the hot sidewalk in front of the shop. "Let me get the rest of the register tapes to scan while we're here."

"I almost forgot about them. Good thing you reminded me." Matrina followed him to his Jeep.

She put the tapes in her van, put the canceled check in her purse, and headed back up the Trail to ACS and George. She called George on the way to outline her plan to be sure he'd wait for her. She made her explanation vague enough to riddle him with curiosity. It worked. He met her at the door when she arrived.

Chapter 25

That evening, Matrina cleared the dinner dishes away, rinsed them and put them in the dishwasher. Coffee in hand, she picked up the bag of cash register tapes from the corner of the dining room and dumped them on the table.

"All set, kids," she called to Michelle and Turner. "Come and let's look for these bullets."

"Man, this is such an huge job," Turner said. He sauntered into the dining room. "Can't we do it while we watch TV?"

"Yeah, Mom," Michelle said. She plopped down into a dining room chair. "It's so boring to just sit here in the quiet and look at tapes."

"I don't want you distracted," Matrina said. "It's very critical we look at every sale, and not take the chance of overlooking anything."

"Well, how about some music, then," Michelle said. Her voice teetered between pleading and whining.

"Okay," Matrina said, "but it has to be something soft. Background music. Something where you're going to concentrate on the tapes and not on the words in the song."

Michelle put a CD into the player and the strains of Enya filled the room.

"Is that Enya?" Matrina said.

"Yes," Michelle said. "I heard this CD at Mr. Fleming's. Her music is actually popular with kids. Most of the words are Celtic, so we certainly won't be able to sing along with them."

"Boring, boring, boring," Turner said. He sat down at the table and waited for his batch of tapes.

Matrina passed a tape to each of her children. "These are the Sarasota Wal-Mart tapes from the Wednesday before the day of the murder. The recap tape says there were eight boxes of nine millimeter bullets purchased that day. So we know how many sales we're looking for. Just go down the line of sales, and if you run across a sale for those bullets, let me know."

"Okay," Turner said.

204

They sat and listened to the haunting strains of Enya and checked their tapes. Matrina made a mental note that John and Michelle shared the same taste in music. Positive baggage? Something to think about.

The search marched on, long and tedious. Matrina often told the kids that security work consisted of ten percent excitement and discovery, and ninety percent surveillance and waiting.

"I found one," Turner said. He passed his tape to Matrina.

"Oh, good," Matrina said. She jotted down the time and the register number on her long, yellow, legal pad. It crossed her mind that security people would have nothing on which to write if the world ran out of long, yellow, legal pads.

"I've got one, too" Michelle said. She paused with her tape in hand.

Enya sang, "...sail away, sail away, sail away..."

"Great," Matrina said. "You guys are doing a wonderful job. You're going to feel really good about this when John is exonerated because of our effort here."

An hour later, the searchers took a break.

"*Get Smart's* on TV Land," Turner said. He hoped his mom would weaken to the request.

"Okay," Matrina said. "One show, that's it, then we've got to get back to the grindstone."

"Whatever that is," Turner said. He turned the TV on to the TV Land channel and plopped on the floor in front of it. Maxwell Smart chided Ninety-Nine over a misdirected phone call. Turner chuckled.

Matrina sat down at her computer and booted it up to search the net for more information on the Voloni murder conviction. Copies of the threatening letters John had received lay beside her keyboard. She scolded herself because they hadn't been filed away for safe keeping and pulled a file folder from the deep drawer in the side of her desk.

"Hey, Mom," Turner said. He turned his attention from the TV now that a commercial had begun. "Are those the letters the bad guy wrote to Mr. Fleming?"

"Yes, they are. Why?"

"Because there's something wrong with one of them," Turner said. He got up and came over to his mother.

"Wrong with them?" Matrina said. "What do you mean?"

"Well, are these supposed to be written by the guy who wanted to bomb Disney World?"

"He is one of the suspects, yes."

"And he's supposed to be a Moslem?"

"Yes. That's the thought."

"So he's not from America?"

"We think he lives in Florida, south of us, but no, he wouldn't be an American, technically."

"Then, why wouldn't he know what a jihad is?"

"I think he does know what a jihad is. He uses it in the note."

"He doesn't use it right."

"What are you talking about?" Matrina wrinkled her brow.

"He uses the expression—holy jihad, and that's redundant."

"Redundant?" Michelle said. She giggled as she spoke. "How would you know what's redundant? You been playing Scrabble with Aunt Rosie again?"

"I know what redundant means," he said. "I learn stuff you never heard of all the time."

"So, what does redundant mean?" Michelle sat erect and awaited his answer.

"It means saying stuff over again and meaning the same thing. This guy says—holy jihad—in his note, and that's redundant."

"Explain," Michelle said.

"Jihad means—holy war," Turner said in aggravated coolness. "It would be the same as if you said—wet ocean. Ocean means an area that's already wet. You don't have to say it's wet. Jihad is already holy. It's a war that's already holy. You don't have to say—holy jihad. That's redundant."

Matrina picked up the copy of the letter and stared at the words in it. She thought about Turner's comment, and it gave the words on the paper new meaning.

"I think you might be right," Matrina said. "They should have just said—jihad—period."

"That's what I thought," Turner said with a victorious glance at Michelle.

Michelle got up and joined Turner and Matrina at the computer. "You know, Mom," she said, "since we're talking about this, that other letter has a mistake in it, too."

"How's that?" Matrina said. She held the copy of the second letter in her hand.

"See? He says harm will come to—Dee-Dee. Don't you find that strange?"

"I don't follow you," Matrina said. She looked at the words on the second threatening letter. "That's her name."

"That's her name to us. But if you didn't know the Flemings, and you wanted to write them a letter, and you had to look up the names of Mr. Fleming's kids, you would come up with Delores, John and Matthew. That's what their birth certificates would say, not Dee-Dee. Especially if you were a stranger to them. Even more so if you were a foreigner and a stranger."

"Oh, my." Matrina caught her breath and touched the words on the second letter. "I think you guys have come up with something. Not using jihad correctly, and using Dee-Dee instead of Delores suggests that we are not looking for a mid-eastern person who is a stranger to John. We're looking for a person who is not familiar with mid-eastern terms and knows John well enough to know his daughter is not Delores, but Dee-Dee. This changes everything."

Matrina slumped back in her desk chair and stared at both letters. The commercial on TV ended, and Michelle and Turner sat back down to the antics of Maxwell Smart and Ninety-Nine.

Matrina logged onto the internet. She booted up her e-mail and began a transmission to John, Nathan and George to pass on this nugget of new information. "…so, I wondered what you guys thought about this letter-writing person being someone you know, John, and not our O'Brien guy. If that's true, then the two-three-nine clue probably has nothing to do with Lee County and their new area code. That would put us back to 'square one' in that department. Let me know what you think. MM"

Before she could check the rest of her messages and log off, John replied to her e-mail. He must have been on-line right then.

"That's an interesting premise," he wrote. "And Turner is right, jihad does mean—holy war. And Michelle is probably correct in that strangers would come up with the name—Delores and not Dee-Dee. But it couldn't be any of my friends. Almost everyone I socialize with is in church with us, and none of them would be involved with this."

Matrina gulped and knew she had struck a nerve with John. It bothered her she had tweaked him. He might as well know up front that tweaking came with the Matrina territory. More baggage.

"John," she replied. "How about someone you work with at Publix? How about someone you stopped for shoplifting? They might know what you call Dee-Dee, and they might not be knowledgeable about what a jihad is."

She sat at her keyboard and held her breath. She didn't want him to shut down on her in the middle of this investigation.

"Hum," he said. "Let me think about that one."

The e-mail ended without anything warm or friendly or any quick-witted banter.

A wave of discouragement pummeled Matrina. She realized John would not consider any of his friends could be involved in this. How about a list of acquaintances, not quite friends, to be considered as suspects? Of course, Jared, Mrs. Gunthrey's wayward son, topped the short list. At least Jared didn't go to John's church. That ought to be a plus in the let's-consider-new-suspects department. She thought if she logged back on and made that suggestion, John would know she had come up with a non-church person as her prime suspect. She decided against it. It sounded too apologetic and defensive. Neither case applied.

"Okay, troops," she announced, "back to the salt mines."

Moans and groans came from the troops, but they hauled themselves back to the dining room table and the great tape hunt. Tramp stretched out under the table and snored.

Turner carried a glass of water back to the work area. On his way, he passed the phone table where the land line phone and answer machine sat. He stumbled over his untied shoelace, and in his struggle to avoid his fall to the marble floor, he dumped the contents of his glass on the combined equipment. Matrina turned to see what happened and watched the water cascade over the answering machine and onto the floor.

"Ooppps," Turner said. He saved himself from his fall.

"Ooppps says it all," Matrina said. "Well, at least we don't have to worry about salesmen who clog up our answer machine with 'come buy with us' messages."

"Turner," Michelle said, "why can't you be more careful?"

"I didn't mean to," Turner said. He fought tears and chagrin for this element of gawky adolescent clumsiness that seemed to be getting worse as days went by. He brushed some of the puddles of water from the top of the machine where it had gathered around the buttons.

"It's okay," Matrina said. "Maybe it's not even broken. Who knows. I'll phone in tomorrow and see if it still works, and if not, we'll just get another one. No big deal. Glad you didn't fall. That's the important thing. The whole thing was an accident."

Turner didn't answer. He took his seat at the table and dove into the tape project. "I am sorry, Mom," he said under his breath.

"I know, Dear," Matrina said. She patted his hand. "Stuff like this happens. That's the way life is. You'll get used to it, the older you get."

"Stuff like this happens to you?" Turner said. He snuffled back his tears and wiped his nose on his sleeve.

"Oh, yeah, big time," Matrina said, with a giggle. "More than I care to admit."

"Yeah," Michelle said, softened by her brother's repentance. "It even happens to me."

"No," Matrina said. She gave her daughter a feigned look of shock.

"Yes," Michelle said. "Not a lot, but now and again."

"Welcome to the human race," Matrina said. "Onward and upward, fellow searchers, toward our current quest. Find those bullets."

Chapter 26

The next day, Matrina stood in her living room, picked up her cell phone and dialed her home number. The phone rang. The machine picked up and nothing but static came back over the line at her. She walked to the land line phone and picked up the receiver. More static filled her ear. She proved what she already suspected that they needed a new phone and answer machine.

"Did our phone and answer machine die?" Michelle said.

"I guess so," Matrina said. "I'll have to run to the store and pick up a new one."

"I figured it was gone," Michelle said. "Suzanne tried to call me today, earlier, and all the phone did was grumble."

"It grumbled?"

"Grumbled, made strange noises, whatever."

"Guess I'd better go get a new unit now. We could be missing calls." Matrina got her purse, removed her van keys and headed for the front door.

"Okay, Mom. See ya."

"You guys doing okay?"

"Yeah. Wendy's coming over. She's going to teach us to line dance."

"That sounds like fun. I'll be right back."

An hour later, Matrina pulled back into her driveway. She toted a new answer machine and phone combination and a box of jelly donuts from the Wal-Mart bakery. Strains of "Boot Scootin' Boogie" from the CD player greeted her as she walked through the front door and dropped her purse on the hall table. She put the rest of her parcels on the table in the dining room.

Wendy and Michelle stood in the middle of the living room floor, and Wendy moved to the rhythm of the music. Michelle watched Wendy's feet and attempted to follow along. Turner tagged along and copied the moves.

"What in the world are you doing?" she said. She watched the movements with interest. "That looks pretty cool."

"Oh, Mom, it is," Michelle said. She made the timely turn behind Wendy and kicked her one foot out to the side and then behind her as part of the choreographed motion. "It's called line dancing."

"That's where everyone gets up and dances in sort of a group-type thing?" Matrina said. She tried to cover the fact that she never line danced in her life, but in truth, had always wanted to. She stood beside Wendy and focused on the steps.

"It's really easy, Mrs. McCoy," Wendy said. They continued to follow the beat of the music. "See? It's just the same steps over and over, only done in a different direction."

"Yeah, Mom," Turner said. "This is kind of fun." He kept in sync with Wendy, and even managed the more intricate steps.

"You're a born dancer, Turner," Matrina said. She stumbled along beside her son in an effort to get the hang of it.

"You want to take it from the top, Mrs. McCoy?" Wendy said.

"Sure, why not," Matrina said. "Maybe with another run at this thing, I might actually grasp the concept."

"Oh, good," Michelle said. "I want to get this down pat. Once I learn it, I can teach it to Suzanne and Debbie and other kids. We'll be so smokin' at the school dances."

"Smokin'?" Matrina said. She shook her head as the music began again. "That was always my hope for you in life, that you'd grow up to be smokin'."

"It means hot, or cool, or popular," Turner said. He waited for Wendy to start the movement.

"Don't explain it to me further," Matrina said. "I already have enough information."

After an hour of "Boot Scootin' Boogie" and the "Electric Slide," Matrina collapsed on the couch and kicked her shoes off.

"Enough," she said. "You guys carry on. I need a break."

"You're catching on really good, Mom," Turner said. The three remaining dancers turned on the floor like a chorus line.

"It's catching on really well," Wendy said, "and yes, Mrs. McCoy, you are really getting into the swing of this." Wendy demonstrated little twists and kicks that added a higher dimension to the motion.

"Thanks, but I have no clue where I would ever use this new found knowledge." Matrina got up from the couch and walked over to the dining room table and her new answer machine. She pulled it from the box and laid it on the table. She opened the manual and scanned the directions. "Oh, this is no trouble. It's just like the old one," she said to the box of donuts.

She installed the new machine and picked up the phone to see if a dial tone sounded. The dull buzz sounded in her ear.

Matrina dialed her cell phone number and heard the phone twitter from her purse. Then she dialed her home number from her cell phone and left herself a message.

"All right. It works," she said out loud over the music.

She needed to be sure she could retrieve her messages from remote locations. She found the page in the manual that discussed that concept and scanned the instructions. She began the process and reprogrammed the access code from the nine-nine-nine code that came with the machine.

She decided to use the nine-eight-nine code she had used in the old machine. That stood for the last three digits from the year she and Mike had married, 1989. She used it on all her PIN digits. She jotted the nine-eight-nine down on the manual and placed it in her desk drawer.

As she jotted down those three figures, a new revelation crashed through the barriers of her mind and skidded to a stop in the middle of her brain.

Matrina sat back in her desk chair, her fingers intertwined and studied the lights in the whirling ceiling fan.

When a person installed their answer machine, they might jot their PIN down on something, like a manual, or the front of their checkbook, or a page in a spiral notebook.

If she coupled that with the misuse of jihad and Dee-Dee in the threatening letters, the writer would be someone who did not hail from the mid east and knew John personally. This someone bought a new answer machine right before he wrote those letters. He jotted the two-three-nine PIN on the top sheet of a spiral notebook. Christopher O'Brien, their Disney dude, no longer fit the profile.

This thought made the Lee County, Fort Myers new area code scenario the wrong direction. Two-three-nine could be the PIN for an answer machine. It would be easy enough to verify. She needed George in the loop to pull it off, however. John would never listen to this new idea.

Matrina picked up the walk-around phone and carried it into her bedroom.

"He's not here," Franny said. Matrina could hear the munching of cookies in Franny's voice. "He went home early."

"Okay. I'll catch him there." Matrina hung up and punched in George's home numbers.

"Hi, George," she said when George answered.

"Hi, Matrina. What's up?"

"I guess I need some help with something," she said.

She could hear Sarah, George's wife, ask who called.

"It's just Matrina," George said with his hand over the mouthpiece, but the comment sailed over the airwaves anyway. "She's probably in trouble again, or still."

"I heard that," Matrina said.

"You going to argue the point?"

"Wish I could."

"So, what's on the battleground today?"

"John. Did you get my e-mail about the holy jihad and Dee-dee issue?"

"Yes. I think you may be on to something."

"So do I. And now I'm on to something more. But John isn't going to like it. In fact, he may get mad and not even cooperate."

"John? No way."

"Yes, way. You haven't heard my idea yet."

"Lay it on me, so I can decide."

"I just bought a new answer machine. I had to reprogram the PIN digits so I could get my messages when I'm away from home."

"So?"

"So, I jotted the three numbers down just to be sure I wouldn't forget, and that got me thinking maybe the two-three-nine from the spiral notebook were answer machine PIN digits. Someone might have jotted them down on the top page of that notebook and torn the page out, leaving the impressions on the threatening letter page."

"Hum," George said. "And why is this going to send John over the edge?"

"Because it means I need his personal phone book so I can call all the numbers in it, punch in the two-three-nine and see if it gets me into their phone messages."

"What if they're home and answer their phone?"

"I'll just hang up."

"How are you going to get around your caller ID? They can tell who called."

"I already thought of that. I'll buy a phone card. People who use those cards drive me nuts as the caller ID says Denver or Atlanta and some strange number behind it. Sometimes it says the name of a strange person. No way to figure out who made the call."

"That'll work," George said. "And you don't think John will approve of your doing this."

"No, but he might if you approach him with the idea."

"That way he can be mad at me instead of you?"

"That's the plan."

"Good plan," George said. "Why do you think he'll listen to me?"

"Because he's a guy, and you're a guy, and it might work as a guy-to-guy type thing, providing you agree with me that this is a possibility."

"I definitely think it's a possibility. I never rule out any direction in an investigation."

"So, you'll talk to him?"

"I'll talk to him. I'll call him right now. That would make the Lee County area code thing and Christopher O'Brien a dead end street?"

"Yes. No connection. I've been going nuts trying to connect the dots between the Disney thing, the threatening letters, Christopher O'Brien, and the Lee County, North Fort Myers phone number, and they just don't connect. The use of the middle eastern terms like jihad and burqa in the letters were the only link, and now with this new information about jihad being used incorrectly, that flew out the window."

"It's a thought worth pursuing."

"Call me back?"

"Okay. Sit by your phone."

Matrina walked back into the living room in the middle of the rhythmic dancing, and it surprised her to see the three dancers actually in step with each other. The movements began to take on form and function. She smiled at the teens and tried to dance a little jig of her own on her way to the kitchen. She picked up the box of donuts as she passed through the dining room, and put them in the refrigerator.

A peek into the refrigerator revealed the makings of dinner, along with a tossed salad. They needed something quick so they could get back into the great tape hunt afterwards. She hated to bring the line dancing to a halt, but all good things came to an end. She'd invite Wendy to stay for dinner. That might be a Band-Aid on the gaping hole of party-dampening.

In the refrigerator, Matrina spotted two pounds of ground round that had sloppy joes written all over it. She hauled it out and crushed it up in her iron skillet, looked in her cabinets for a sloppy joe seasoning mix and found the packet by the cans of tomato sauce. Eureka. Supper's on its way.

As she dumped two cans of tomato sauce and the spices on top of the ground round, the phone rang. She had brought it with her into the kitchen, and she picked it up on the second ring.

"The eagle has landed," George said.

"How'd he take it?"

"Not well. You called that one right. He's miffed."

"He's miffed?"

"That's polite talk for—if you were a guy, he'd want to go three rounds with you at Madison Square Garden."

"Oh, dear," Matrina said. "I really like John. I hate to make him mad, but he's in serious trouble here. I can't turn my back on something that might be a clue."

"I know. Don't worry. He'll get over it."

"So, when do I get his personal phone book?"

"In the morning. He'll bring it by your house."

"Early?"

"Yes. I told him the earlier the better. This is another ring in the timeline circus. You still have tapes to search through, and now this phone marathon to manage."

"The kids are helping me with the tapes. I'll get Wendy, my neighbor college gal, to come over in the morning and help with the tapes as well. That way, I can concentrate on the phone book. If I call in the middle of the day, maybe most folks will be out, and I can check the PIN for their machine. If they're home, I'll try late at night and see how that works."

"Sounds like a plan."

"Let's hope. And I hope John gets over being miffed. I feel too strongly about this new idea to not pursue it. Surely he must understand that."

"Oh, he understands it all too well. He just doesn't like what he understands."

"Men."

"Let me know what you find out."

"I will. I hope it produces something useful."

"If not, we're back to square one, and the clock is ticking."

"Thanks, George. I'll call you and let you know how it went."

The sloppy joes screamed, "Ready." Matrina hung up the phone and called her troops to dinner. Tramp, slid into the kitchen first.

Chapter 27

The next morning, Thursday, six-twenty A.M., the doorbell at Matrina's house rang. It awoke Matrina from deep slumber. She reached for her robe and slippers, yawned her way toward the door and finger-combed her hair as she went. She peered through the peephole and noticed the sun had not yet risen. The light beside the front door showed John stood on her doorstep, a small black notebook in one hand and a plastic bag that probably contained videos in the other. She opened the door to greet him.

"Top 'o the mornin' to ya," she said. She smiled and pulled her robe more tightly around her body.

"And the rest of the day to yourself?" John said. He did not smile in return. "I think that's the proper reply to that Irish greeting?"

"Yes, it is. Pretty good for a non-Irish person."

"I hope it isn't too early to call," he said.

"No. As you can see, I've been up for hours, and I was about to till the back forty and plant corn."

"Yes, I can plainly see you're on your second pot of coffee."

"We worked pretty late last night checking out tapes. So, I guess we're sleeping in this morning."

"I do appreciate what you're doing for me, Matrina," John said, his tone somewhat softened. "I'd be lost without your help."

"That's all I'm trying to do, John, is help. Want to come in and I'll make some coffee?" She stood back from the doorway to allow entrance.

"No. I have to get down to the Sarasota store and do some damage control. One of my guys made a bad stop yesterday, and the lady is getting all lawyered up to come after us."

"Oh, my," Matrina said.

John handed the bag of video tapes to her. "Here are the security surveillance videos from Wal-Mart and Kmart. If you want, you can check out the times that match the bullet purchases we've logged. My sheet of bullet purchases is in the bag with the tapes. You can just jot down the person's description for each sale, and maybe I'll recognize someone. I should be doing this myself, but I have to put out this legal brush fire right now."

"That's fine," she said. She accepted the bag of tapes.

Then John handed her the notebook. "And here's the phone book you wanted."

"John, I know you're disturbed about this. I'm just trying to turn over all the rocks. I don't want us to miss anything."

"I know," he said. "You just don't understand that these people are my friends. Most of them are my church friends."

"It doesn't do any good to just warm a seat in church," Matrina said. She caressed the book and looked into his eyes.

"They aren't just warming seats in church. You don't understand. Our church is serious about ethics. It's not just a social club."

Matrina wanted to say all churches claim that, but controlled her mouth. She wanted to add the old saying: hanging out in a church never made one a Christian any more than hanging out in a chicken house made one a chicken. Aloud, she said, "There are Publix people in this book, too. Right?"

"Yes. But they're my bosses, and peers, not anyone who would want to do me harm. Certainly not anyone who would write those letters to me."

"After I check them all out, we will verify that, and maybe we'll find out I'm wrong. That will be nice to know."

John nodded and began to walk away down the walk. Then he stopped and turned around.

"You know what ticks me off most about all this?" he said. He walked back to her, and a scowl tainted his face.

"No, what?"

"That you didn't feel you could come to me yourself about this new idea. You didn't feel you could ask me about the phone book. You sicked George on me."

"I was afraid you'd be offended, and I was right. You are offended. The last thing in the world I want to do is offend you, but I have to be thorough in this search." She tried to meet his eyes with her own. His eyes studied the ground, and he scraped his feet on the black rubber welcome mat.

"But you should have been able to come to me with it, offended or not. If I'm offended, I'd best get over it. Shame on me for taking it so personally. I shouldn't let a personal mood cloud my judgment. This is what I mean about a woman being a helpmeet for a man. There should be no holds barred in expressing an opinion, and the man better take that opinion into consideration, or God will wonder what's going on. She's not an underling. She's a partner." John turned and walked again down the walk. This time he kept going to his Jeep and his intent to solve problems at work.

Matrina stood in the doorway and watched him drive down Magnolia Drive until she could no longer see his taillights. Then she closed the door and walked into the kitchen and made a pot of coffee.

* * *

"I'll see you around noon," Michelle said. She walked out the front door into the mid-morning sun.

"Have fun at summer school," Matrina said. She bent over the dishwasher and loaded the breakfast dishes.

"Yeah. Gotta run. I don't want to be late."

Matrina closed the dishwasher door and turned the knob to start the machine. She walked back into the living room where Turner sat in front of the computer careening his vehicle around the complicated tracks of Gran Turismo 3.

"You played out with helping me with Mr. Fleming's case?" Matrina said. She put her cup of coffee down on the coffee table and plopped on the sofa.

"No," Turner said. He concentrated on the computer screen. "I like helping. It makes me feel like Rockford."

"Good, because John dropped off the surveillance videos this morning, and what I need you to do is cue them up in the VCR and fast forward them until you come to a date and time of a bullet sale that we found on the cash register tapes. John's list in the bag with the videos, and we have our list right there by your elbow."

Turner stopped the race, and shut down the computer game.

"Okay, just show me how," he said. He turned his attention to his mother. He still wore his pajamas as he plopped down beside her on the couch.

"How about you go get dressed while I set this stuff up?" she said to him. She got up and pulled the videos out of the bag.

"Okay," he said. "I don't know why I have to get dressed. I'm not going anywhere, and nobody's coming here. What difference does it make?"

"It makes a difference to you," Matrina said. She sorted the tapes by company, register and date. "Your body will think you're sick if you stay in your pajamas. If you get dressed, your body will think you are ready to tackle the world."

"Right, Mom," Turner said. He walked to his room to change his clothes.

Matrina popped the earliest tape into the VCR and fast forwarded it to the earliest recorded bullet sale for that store and that register. She slowed down when she got within five minutes of the designated time, and rolled down to the exact time. An elderly man purchased the box of bullets and argued with the cashier over the price.

Matrina started a clean sheet of paper on her legal pad and recorded the store name, date, time, register number, amount of sale, how many boxes of nine millimeter bullets and description of the customer.

When Turner returned dressed in jeans and a Green Bay Packers tee shirt, she explained the process to him. When she thought he had grasped the procedure, she handed him the remote.

"I have to run out to the store on the Trail for a minute," she said.

Turner watched the time counter so as to not miss his goal. "Could you bring back some soda?" he said.

"Coke?"

"Yeah, and you might be out of your Diet Coke. I think Wendy drank the last one yesterday."

"Okay. Be right back."

Matrina walked out the front door and down the walk to her van. She cranked the vehicle and drove the two blocks to the Jiffy store. Once inside, her purchases included a six-pack of Coca-Cola and a six-pack of Diet Coke. She also purchased a liter of apple juice, a liter of grape juice and a gallon of milk, should her offspring find more healthy drinks to their liking. A phone card with a hundred and twenty minutes on it completed the run for the day, and she paid for the merchandise. Once home, she put the sodas, juice and milk in the refrigerator, took the phone card back into the living room and sat at her desk with John's phone book.

The phone book opened to the "A's" and a fresh yellow legal pad found its way from the bottom drawer of her desk to her phone stand. She took a deep breath and programmed the eight hundred number into her memory one in her phone. Then she programmed the ID from the card into memory two. Then she could access these memory numbers to set up the call and then dial the actual phone number.

On the first call, the phone rang four times. No one answered. The answer machine kicked on, and Matrina dialed the two-three-nine as the personal pin number. She received a recording that denied her access. She jotted the name on her yellow pad and lined through it and moved on to the next phone number. She repeated the process.

By the time she had reached the "C's," she decided she needed a soda break.

"Want a soda?" she said to Turner. She watched as he jotted the description of the latest bullet purchaser on his yellow pad.

"Yeah," he said. He concentrated on the appearance of the woman and wrote the information on the pad.

"Yeah, what?" she said.

"Yeah, Coke?"

"No. I already know it's Coke."

Turner's eyes left the screen and confusion washed over his face. He looked up at her as she stood over him, hands on her hips. She waited for the correct answer.

"Oh," he said. "Yeah, thanks."

"Thank you," she said. She patted him on the head.

When she came back from the kitchen, she handed him the soda and watched as he cued up the next time slot. As he neared the correct time, Matrina noticed someone she recognized in line behind the current customer being serviced at the register. She sat down on the couch and watched as Turner inched the film forward toward the time of the sale.

"What is it?" he said. He noticed his mother's sudden intense interest.

"I know that girl."

"Which one? The one going through the register now?"

"No. The second one back. See? She's got her hair wrapped in a bandanna."

"She's only got one item in her hand," Turner said. He inched the tape further as the man in front of the girl paid for his gallon of milk and a box of donuts.

"I see that," Matrina said. "Are they bullets?"

"I can't tell, but if the sale matches the cash register tape, then I guess they are."

"You catch on quickly," Matrina said. She touched his shoulder and patted his collar.

The tape slowed still further, and the girl Matrina recognized approached the register. The cashier scanned the box of bullets, and the girl paid for them with a ten dollar bill and accepted her change. The cashier bagged the box of bullets and gave the customer her receipt. The customer raised her eyes to the ceiling to gaze into the overhead lights to trigger an impending sneeze.

The face belonged to Sandra Marshall, Andy's new main squeeze. The bandanna served to cover her memorable red hair.

"Oh, my," Matrina said.

"What is it?" Turner said. He jotted down the girl's description.

"This might be our suspect."

"Really? How totally cool would that be if I found the suspect."

"It would be completely cool," Matrina said. "It might even be smokin.' We have to push on and do the rest of the sales to be sure we have the right person. But this little gal is definitely a good prospect."

"Who is she?" Turner said. "How's she connected to Mr. Fleming?"

"Her name is Sandra Marshall, and I wish I knew," Matrina said.

Chapter 28

Noon that same day, Michelle, Debbie and Suzanne giggled their way through the front door and into the McCoy house. They dropped their school books and purses onto the hall table and headed for the refrigerator for sodas.

Amid a round of giggles, the girls walked into the living room. Turner sat in front of the TV which played the tapes from the VCR.

"What are you watching?" Michelle said. She studied the fuzzy black and white pictures that paraded across the TV screen.

"This is very important work," Turner said. He slowed the fast forward button down to a crawl. "We're looking for the people who bought bullets at Wal-Mart and Kmart, and I found one that might be the right suspect."

"Really?" Suzanne said. "Can we see?"

"Wait, wait, wait," Michelle said. She scrutinized the screen. "Oh, look who that is in line at the register."

"Who?" The school friends moved in for a better look.

"Oh, my stars," Suzanne said. "It's Travis Walker, and look, he's stealing gum."

"He certainly is," Debbie said, "and he's not very good at it either."

"The little snot," Michelle said. "He acts so high and mighty at school, and all the while he shoplifts. How come they didn't stop him, Mom?"

"They might not have seen him," Matrina said, "or maybe they'll stop him when he gets outside, or they may have bigger fish to fry. Who knows." Matrina moved on into the "H's" as she dialed the expanse of numbers from the phone book and dialed the two-three-nine into the answer machine. So far, she had four people answer their phone, at which point she hung up. She marked her log as to who answered and who did not, and the answer machines that did not respond to the two-three-nine PIN.

"Hello, the house," came the regal greeting through the front door as Rosie entered the front hall.

Matrina got up and hugged her sister. "I'm so glad you stopped by. We haven't seen you in a week or so."

"I've been busy," Rosie said. "Me, and my man. You know how it goes."

"No, how does it go?" Matrina said. She followed Rosie into the living room.

"It goes super-duper," Rosie said. She hugged Michelle and Turner. She paused, then she hugged Debbie and Suzanne as well. They giggled and hugged her in return. "I just cannot believe life can be this happy. It is like a huge, wonderful dream, and I hope I never wake up from it. How are you guys?" she said. She scanned the faces of the girls. "What are you doing?" she added to Turner. He rolled more black and white TV footage.

"I found a possible suspect," Turner said.

"Really? A suspect for what?" Rosie said. "Could you get me a soda, Michelle? Or a glass of juice? I'm parched for a drink of something. I don't even care what."

"A suspect who might have bought the bullets for Mr. Fleming's gun that killed that guy they found in Mr. Fleming's backyard. Remember him?"

"Oh, yeah," Rosie said. "Someone stole John's gun and shot the guy; isn't that how it went?"

"Yes," Turner said. "and I found the lady who bought bullets that would fit that gun, and Mom recognized her."

"And that would mean…" Rosie said. She sipped the opened soda Michelle placed into her hand.

"Possibly nothing," Matrina said. "I recognized the girl from my little gig at the Trade Winds a few days ago; that's all. It may have nothing to do with John's case. We're not sure yet."

"So, who is she?" Rosie said. "Why was she buying bullets?"

"She's a waitress at the Trade Winds, and we haven't a clue why she needed bullets. Maybe to use in a hand gun she carries in her purse for protection."

"Here, Aunt Rosie," Turner said. He put in the tape that showed Sandra Marshall. "I know the number to cue it to. Watch."

Turner fast forwarded the tape, and Matrina held her breath as Rosie and the girls watched over Turner's shoulder.

"There," he said. "There she is. And I'll just bet she's the suspect we're looking for, since Mom knows her and all."

Rosie watched as Sandra advanced through the line at the register with the box of bullets. Matrina watched Rosie for any iota of recognition. None surfaced.

"I don't know how you can tell," Rosie said. "Her hair is all done up in that scarf. You can recognize her from that tape?"

"Yes," Matrina said. "And she does her hair up in that bandanna because her hair is very red, and that would be recognizable, and that's what might tie her into this. Why would she cover her hair to buy bullets if she planned to use them for her own gun? But she might cover her hair if she bought bullets to use in John's gun for an illegal purpose."

"Like killing someone," Michelle said.

"Killing people is pretty illegal," Debbie said with a giggle.

"So, is there some connection between her and John?" Rosie said.

"I don't think so," Matrina said. She tried to avoid the potential lie that danced around her brain and meandered to her lips. "He might have seen her somewhere, like in Publix. I'd be surprised if he knew her. She doesn't look like she would go to church. Most of his friends are church folks. You know how he is."

"Yes," Rosie said. She shook her head. "Boring, boring, boring. This little tomato looks too hot for him to handle."

"You don't recognize her, do you?" Matrina said. .

"No. If she comes into Winn Dixie, I don't remember her. However, I think I would remember the hair, if she had the scarf off. But I don't remember ever seeing her before. Why do you ask?"

"Oh, I just thought she might be a Winn Dixie customer. That's all."

"Nope."

"Do you and Andy discuss your jobs much at all?" Matrina said. She dared to test the waters in this dangerous subject.

"No, never. That's a hard and fast rule with Andy. We leave the jobs when we clock out. We never bring the work home."

"So, he doesn't tell you about the cases he's working on, and you don't complain about your cranky customers?"

"That's right. It all stays where it is when we leave the job."

"So, you don't talk about John's case or anything?"

"No, why should we? We don't know anything about John's case. That's all centered up in Manatee County. Andy's with the Sheriff's Department in Sarasota County. Why are you asking all these silly questions?"

"Oh, no reason. I was just trying to catch up with your life." Matrina wanted to assure herself that Rosie would not mention Sandra to Andy. Too many unanswered questions floated around, and she didn't want Andy alerted at this point.

"Well, anyway," Rosie said. She headed to the kitchen. "I'm on my lunch break. That means I need lunch. What's in the frig?"

"There's deli stuff," Matrina said. "Smoked turkey, cheese, corned beef."

"Corned beef?" Turner said. "We have corned beef?"

"Yes, what's so strange about that?" Matrina said. She tried to get back to her phone project.

"All we usually have is low fat turkey and Alpine Swiss cheese," Turner said. "Can I have a corned beef sandwich?"

"Of course. Do you think I bought it for Tramp?" Tramp opened his eyes and perked one ear at the mention of his name.

"I'll make you a sandwich," Michelle said. She followed Rosie into the kitchen. "Come on, girls. We'll all have lunch with Aunt Rosie."

"Be sure to put enough mustard on it," Turner said.

"Yes, tons of mustard," Michelle said. Frustration filtered through in her reply. "Piles of mustard, cups of mustard, quarts of mustard."

"Just be sure it has some mustard," Turner said.

"Mustard, what?" Matrina said.

"Mustard, please," Turner said.

Matrina cued up the phone card numbers for her next call. It all came back to her why she rarely worked from home. Work became one more element in their many-ringed circus.

"Hello?" a Mrs. Howard said into Matrina's ear, and she hung up and moved on to the next number.

* * *

Lunch time passed, and the girls practiced line dancing out on the porch. Turner finished the scan of all the videos John had provided. He laid on the floor and watched *True Grit* on the Western Channel.

Matrina walked back to the telephone after a potty break and noted the spot in the phone book where she stopped, the section under "R."

She dialed the number of David Rogers, the deacon at John's church who had moved into the area in June.

"Hello, you have reached the Rogers' residence. We cannot come to the phone at this moment. Please leave a message and your phone number and we will get back with you. Thank you, and God be with you," the answer machine said.

Matrina punched in the two-three-nine. The beep kicked in, and then a brief pause, and then the playback of messages bounced off her eardrum. She sat dumbfounded. She could not process the information. David Rogers used the PIN of two-three-nine to retrieve his messages from remote locations. Coincidence? Surely not the evidence she sought. What else would explain the two-three-nine connection?

Four messages played back. One from a dentist to confirm a dental appointment, one from a church member who wanted a counseling session, one from a lady from church who needed to know what Mrs. Rogers wanted her to bring for a snack to the Bible study to be held at the Rogers' home tomorrow, Friday evening, and a message from Andy Douglas that stated a time and place, purpose unexplained.

Andy's voice said, "Next Wednesday, eleven forty-five P.M. Get-Away Marina on the back bay, Exit 131 off I-75, San Carlos Boulevard. Later, Motel 6 in Punta Gorda. Bless us His children."

A marina. That would involve a boat. The *Empress?* How would Andy know David Rogers? Why give David this kind of information? This trip through the *Twilight Zone* scrambled her mind. When her composure surfaced again, she hung up the phone and sat in her chair for a full minute to catch her breath. It might have been ten full minutes.

What to do? Call George? She rejected her first impulse, reached for her phone and called the Publix store where John did duty today. She asked for John Fleming. The girl who answered said she would have him paged. Oh, great. That'll make his day if he's involved in something critical right now.

"Yeah?" John said. He sounded cranky.

"Hey," Matrina said. She tried to sound casual.

"Hey, yourself," John said. He sounded more friendly.

"Were you serious this morning when you said you would be happier if I came to you directly with bad news instead of getting a mediator like George to intervene?"

He paused for several eternal seconds.

"Yes."

"Okay. Can you come by my house after you finish down there?"

"Okay."

"There's a corned beef sandwich in it for you, providing I have any corned beef left after the gang that sacked my frig gets finished."

"Sounds good. If the marauders wipe you out, I'll settle for coffee and peanut butter."

"That I can guarantee. The marauders are soda folks. They don't do coffee, and peanut butter is too ordinary to consider."

"I should be finished here in a couple hours. Sixish sound okay?"

"Perfect. I'll rustle up something to go with your coffee."

"I'll stop by Publix's deli here in the store and bring something. Don't worry about food. You're in way over your head on projects now. Please don't bother with grub."

"Okay. That would be nice. See ya when you get here."

"This is bad news?"

"For you, it is."

"Does it nail the coffin on me?"

"No. It nails the coffin on someone you truly like and respect. You are not going to be happy about it."

"Oh, my."

"Yeah. You'd better believe it's an, 'Oh, my.'"

"See ya at six."

"Copy that." She hung up and wished she could reverse time and David Rogers had some other PIN for his answer machine.

Chapter 29

At five forty-five that evening, Matrina dozed on the couch in front of the TV as *Murder, She Wrote* blazed across the screen. A half-consumed cup of black coffee cooled on the coffee table in front of her. John Fleming rang the bell at the front door. Michelle heard him from her bedroom and walked to the front door to let him in.

"Hi, Mr. Fleming," she said. "Oh, you brought dinner. How nice." She carried her latest *Sister Chicks* book with her.

"Yeah. Hope you like Publix fried chicken and deli macaroni salad."

"We love it," Michelle said. She took the bags of food from him and put them on the dining room table. She hurried back to her room with her reading.

"Hey, Sleepyhead," John said. He stood in front of the snoozing Matrina. He tapped her foot with one hand and wiggled her big toe. "You just hang around here and sleep all day?"

"I must have been awake some today," Matrina said. She yawned, sat up and rubbed her eyes. "Because I certainly churned up a tub of trouble we're about to dive into. And, oh, look at this. I slept through *Murder, She Wrote*, again. And this was an episode set in Maine, too. I love those episodes, where Jessica is planting petunias and riding her bike all over town. Bummer."

"Well, let's eat first," John said. "Then we'll see what you've done to us." John walked into the dining room, pulled the bucket of chicken and containers of macaroni salad out of the bags and placed them on the dining room table. "You got any paper plates?" he called back at her.

"I don't know," she said. She stumbled in his direction. "Probably, unless our little 'Martha Stewart' clone has trashed them all so we'd have to use our China every chance we get."

She walked into the kitchen and opened a cabinet where paper plates had once been stored. "They're still here," she said to John. She removed them and carried them to the table. Another trip to the kitchen produced knives and forks and glasses of water.

Tramp appeared as if from nowhere, stood at John's heels and wagged his shaggy tail.

"Turner?" Matrina said.

"Yeah, Mom?" came the reply from his bedroom.

"Could you please feed Tramp? We're getting ready to eat this nice food Mr. Fleming brought, and Tramp'll drive us nuts hanging around and begging if he's hungry."

"He'll do that even if he isn't hungry," Turner said. He came into the dining room. "But I'll feed him anyway."

"What were you doing in the bedroom?" Matrina said. Turner's usual at-home location placed him in front of the TV or the computer.

"I was reading."

"No kidding? How neat? What were you reading?"

"A Louis L'Armour book. It's called *Treasure Mountain.* I learned in school that Mr. L'Armour was President Reagan's favorite author, so I thought I'd try one. This one's pretty good."

"Well, I'm truly impressed," Matrina said. She placed lavender flowered cloth napkins on the table beside the paper plates.

"So am I," John said. "You'll really like his books. They're great westerns." John looked at Matrina as she laid out the cloth napkins. "Cloth napkins?" he said.

"For Ms. Stewart," Matrina said, "so she won't complain about the paper plates."

"Oh."

Michelle came to the table. "We ready to eat already?"

"Yes. It's the condemned man eating his final meal," John said. He sat down and opened the boxes of food.

"Huh?" Michelle said.

"Inside joke," Matrina said. "You want coffee, John? Or if it's too hot for coffee, we might have some soda left. I think we have juice, too, although I'd have to check."

"I guess I'd better have coffee," John said. "If I'm going to be as traumatized as you say I am over this new find of yours, I'd better be a little stoked up on caffeine."

Matrina poured two cups of coffee and carried them to the table. She knew John drank his coffee black.

"I started a *Sister Chicks* book I borrowed from Suzanne today," Michelle said. She took a chicken leg and put it on her paper plate. "Paper plates? With

Mr. Fleming as our guest?" She made an appropriate face to display displeasure and looked to Matrina for an explanation.

"We have cloth napkins," John said. He passed a napkin to Michelle.

"At least, we're not totally barbaric," Michelle said. She accepted the napkin, put some macaroni salad on her plate and lifted a forkful of macaroni salad halfway to her lips.

"Mr. Fleming will say the blessing," Matrina said.

Michelle halted with her fork in midair and plopped the salad back onto her plate. Turner tried to cover a, "gottcha" snicker, received a, "not nice" look from his mother and bowed his head. John said the blessing.

After dinner, John carried his coffee into the living room and followed Matrina to her desk. She sat down in the desk chair, and John retrieved a chair from the porch and carried it into the living room and sat beside her.

"Okay, let's have it," he said. "I'm fortified with chicken and caffeine. I can take it."

"Okay." She took a deep breath. "I found an answer machine that uses the PIN two-three-nine. I know that's not conclusive, but I think we need to consider that this person jotted those numbers down on his spiral pad before he wrote you those threatening letters. It's just too big of a coincidence. Especially if you couple it with one of the messages on the machine."

"All right. Who is it? Someone in my world, no doubt, or you wouldn't be so shook up and apologetic about this news."

"Yes. It's David Rogers."

"Oh, Matrina, give me a break. No way could David Rogers be mixed up in this. He's a deacon at church, and he's only been in the area a few weeks. He doesn't even know me. Why would he write me threatening letters?"

"How can you be so sure he doesn't know you?"

"Because I would have remembered him. I never met him before he moved here."

"Okay," she said. She picked up the phone. "Just listen to this. And in case he's home by now, and has listened to his messages and already deleted them, I wrote them down, verbatim."

"Dial his number. He won't be home. He and his wife and Samuel, our pastor and his wife all went to Tampa today for a Baptist seminar. Tomorrow evening we're having a core group meeting at David's house to get a report on what they learned at the seminar. So he won't be home, but no way is he involved in anything sinister."

Matrina looked directly into John's eyes. "Yes, way," she said. She dialed the numbers, and John accepted the ringing phone.

John listened to the greeting from the answer machine and punched in the two-three-nine numbers to retrieve the messages. Matrina watched his face as he plowed through the nonchalant messages, and then she settled back in her chair for the message from Andy. John's face lost a little color, and he ran his fingers through his hair. He reached for his coffee and took a deep swig.

"So?" Matrina said. She waited for the rebuttal.

"So, this is more serious than you know," John said. He met her eyes, and she saw a cloudy weariness in them.

"And that is because…"

"Because I don't know who the caller was, but David is 'the preacher.'"

"I thought you said he was a deacon?"

"Yeah, he's a deacon at church, or he says he is, but the only person who would receive a message like this would be a guy the law enforcement world calls, 'the preacher.'"

"Who's 'the preacher?'" She wrinkled her brow and waited for more information. She wanted to reach out and touch him as he seemed rattled down to his socks.

"There's a drug lord named, 'the preacher.' He was the top dog in that drug undercover sting I helped with on the Erie Canal six years ago. Remember? I told you about it. I worked undercover at a bar in Utica, and they were moving drugs down the Erie Canal? And when we did our big bust, we netted some of the locals yokels involved, and a few medium fish, but this 'preacher' dude wasn't in the net. In fact, in a few other drug busts in New York and Canada, he'd set the whole thing up, but always manage to elude capture. He always uses enough locals to pull off his scam, and then he sets them up for the fall, if there is to be one, and he lopes off into the night free as a bird."

"How do you know it's him?"

"Because the caller used their password, 'bless us His children.' That's how they end all their communications. That way, they know they're getting the straight skinny from the right person. And 'the preacher' was constantly quoting the Bible. I never talked to him personally, but that's what I heard, that you'd think he was a preacher if you didn't know better. That's how he got the handle, 'the preacher.'"

"If you learned the password, how come they're still using it?"

"I only learned it after the bust. They would have no way of knowing it's been compromised. We kept it out of the reports so we could make use of it in the future, if there would ever be a future with this guy. He's dangerous, Matrina. I don't want you involved in this anymore."

"Oh, don't be silly," Matrina said. "He's no threat to me. He doesn't even know me."

"He doesn't know me either, but he knows about me, and the monkey wrench I threw into his Erie Canal connection. He must have gotten a profile on me, moved down here after me, and spotted me the first Sunday he attended church with me. It's all a game with him. And that would be the reason for the hokey letters. He wants me out of the area so he can do whatever it is he's here to do. He knows I'm on to his tricks. He'd be afraid I'd get in the way, and I will, if I can figure out what he's up to."

"You think he killed Slats and buried him in your backyard?"

"Could be. It's as good a scenario as any. He had the advantage of knowing who I was without my knowing who he was."

"So that would tie the murder of Slats in with the threatening letters?"

"Yes. He wouldn't have done the killing himself, however. He hires those things out."

"Would he import talent for that?"

"He might. He's connected higher up, but I never figured out with whom, or where he was from."

"He claims he's from Jamestown, New York."

"That might be true."

"Would it help to find out if he's really from Jamestown?"

"Probably. Then we could rule that area out, if he's not from there."

"If I can talk with him, I could bring up a few facts about Jamestown and see if he verifies them. My mom was from Jamestown, you know. I could set a trap for him and see if he bites."

"I just told you, I don't want you in his world anymore. He's too dangerous."

"John, I know how to play the game. I won't get into trouble. I'll pull out at the first red flag."

"Well, there is the Bible study at his house tomorrow night. You could come as my guest."

"Great. I even have a Bible to bring."

"There's good news."

"I even know a few verses."

"Hum, that will help your cover, not to mention, your life. And you'll stop the chatter when there is any sign he's becoming suspicious of you?"

"Scout's honor." She raised her hand with the two-finger scout signal.

"So, wonder who the caller is?"

"Oh, I know who it is."

"You do? So, who?"

"Andy Douglas."

"Rosie's Andy?"

"Yes. And that's not all. I have Andy's little redheaded darling on one of the security videos from Wal-Mart buying nine millimeter bullets."

"You're kidding."

"Wish I were."

"So, the redhead bought bullets, and Andy is connected to 'the preacher,' for lack of a better name, since we know he's not David Rogers. And Slats was shot with a nine millimeter bullet from my stolen gun, which could have been stolen and replaced easily by our mysterious deacon."

"That would let Jared Gunthrey, Mrs. Gunthrey's wayward son, off the hook, which is too bad. My money's been on him from the get-go."

"'The preacher' must be down here running drugs," John said. He muttered the words as if to himself.

"And he likely had Robert Voloni killed, as Robert was in the witness protection program for ratting out his father. That would involve the syndicate from Chicago, therefore we might conclude 'the preacher' has a Chicago connection."

"The body was found buried face down. That can indicate a mob execution in some circles."

"I thought the mob always shot their victims and left them in the trunks of white Cadillacs," Matrina said.

"That was back in the fifties. Now they drive black Suburbans, like the Feds, and bury their victims anywhere they please, usually face down. And burying Voloni in my backyard was a convenient bit of icing on 'the preacher's' vendetta cake."

"The other way around," Matrina said. She shook her head in the negative. "The threatening letters were the icing on the cake. The body came first."

"That's right. He figured the body would get me convicted of murder one, and that would eliminate me from ever recognizing him. Then the Disney thing happened, and that gave him the idea to write the letters. They would put more fuel on the fire. He thought maybe I'd move the kids out of Dodge and that would make me look all the more guilty of the murder."

"Wow, how are we ever going to prove all this?"

"I don't know, but at least we have a plan. That's more than we had this morning. You're positive the caller is Andy?"

"Absolutely. I'm good at voices."

"Poor Rosie. This guy's phony down to the core. Wonder why he's involved with Rosie? Wonder how he got recruited by 'the preacher?'"

"He's probably got a little bit of a checkered past 'the preacher' knows about, and it made him an easy target. We don't know much about Andy's history. And actually, if you think about it, marrying Rosie would be such a good cover. She's so open and innocent. No one would ever believe her husband is a cop slash drug runner."

"And maybe drug runner slash murderer," John said.

"So there's drugs in the Kahlua bottles?"

"You bettcha, baby. My guess would be cocaine."

"Kahlua bottles would be perfect for that. They have that twist off cap, like an olive oil bottle, and opaque glass so you can't see through it. The kahlua is white, and so is cocaine. Unless you opened the bottle, you couldn't tell the difference."

"Do you know how much money we're talking about in a drug run of that many empty Kahlua bottles filled with cocaine?"

"Have no clue. They never covered that fact in my security training with Wal-Mart."

"A million and a half, maybe one seventy five, easy."

"Whoa, baby. And they did a run last Sunday, and now they're doing another run this coming Wednesday? They're in the, "get rich quick" lane. And they must be getting the drugs from Cancun, since they were down there right before the last run, and they are gone somewhere right now."

"That's the way 'the preacher' works. He'll hit a couple of jobs here and then disappear for a few months, or maybe years, and surface again someplace totally different with a totally different agenda."

"Does he always pose as a religious person, bury himself into some church and play the role?"

"I don't know. We've never been this close to him before to know how he operates."

"We're this close to him now, so he's going down."

"Let's hope he doesn't take us with him."

Chapter 30

The next day, Friday evening, seven P.M., Matrina pulled into the driveway of the home of David and Ida Rogers, aka anyone's guess. She wore the skirt to her light blue suit and a blue dotted silk blouse with a soft bow at the neck and earrings to match. The skirt topped appropriate hose and white heels.

She carried her Coach purse, stocked with her cell phone and her container of Mace, along with a King James version of the Bible. John waited for her in the house.

"Good evening, Mrs. McCoy," David Rogers said. He extended his hand in greeting.

"Good evening to you, Mr. Rogers," Matrina said. She accepted his handshake.

"Please, do come in." David Rogers opened the door wider and Matrina walked into the vestibule and stood on the polished hardwood floors. She followed David Rogers into the living room where she spotted John who rose to usher her to the seat he had saved for her beside him on the couch. "It's a pleasure to have you join us," David said. He sat in an easy chair across the coffee table from Matrina and John. A myriad of religious magazines and pamphlets published by the Baptist church decorated the low table.

"We hope after this evening's meeting you will feel called upon to join us at church this coming Sunday," David said. "There's always room in the flock for one more lost sheep."

"Thank you," Matrina said. "It is entirely possible I will do that."

The room of fourteen members of the Baptist church board descended into a fog of silence. Samuel Hancock, the minister, and his wife, Liza, had not yet arrived, and Ida Rogers and three of the ladies put tea sandwiches and cookies out on China plates on the dining room table which could be seen from the living room.

"So, Mr. Rogers," Matrina said, to break the uncomfortable silence. "I think you mentioned before when I first met you that you and your wife are from Jamestown, New York?"

"Yes," David said. "We moved down a couple of months ago."

"Do you like Florida?"

"Yes, we do. We'll probably stay for quite a while."

"Do you still have a home in Jamestown?"

"Actually, we do. We didn't want to sell until we were sure we liked it here."

"So you'll probably sell now and relocate here permanently."

"I would think so. I remember you were from Jamestown?"

"No, not me, personally. My mother. She lived in Jamestown. In fact, I remember she mentioned to me that her parents used to take her out to eat quite frequently to the Allendale Restaurant on top floor of the Hotel Jamestown? Have you ever been there to eat? She talked about it all her life. She said they had live lobsters, and you would go over to the tank and pick out the one you wanted for dinner."

"Oh, yes." David said. "Ida and I have been there often. It has a lovely view of the Jamestown skyline. Ida could never pick out her lobster, though. She said they looked up at her with such sad eyes and pleaded for their lives. I always did the choosing of the lobsters."

Matrina laughed. "And the Allegeny River that runs through Jamestown. Did you ever fish in it?"

"No, I'm not a fisherman," David said.

"My grandfather used to take my mom fishing there all the time," Matrina said. My grandfather worked for Standard Oil New Jersey, and he ran the bulk plant on the river, and my mom would go to work with him and they would fish on his lunch hour."

"Sounds wonderful," David said.

The doorbell rang, and David went to greet Samuel and Liza Hancock. They sat down, and the meeting began with an opening prayer delivered by David on behalf of the group. Samuel stood up with his notebook and summarized their seminar in Tampa from the day before.

An hour into the meeting, Matrina rose from the couch and walked out of the living room and down the hall toward the bathroom. She reached into the bathroom, switched on the light, and closed the bathroom door without entering the room. The blond interloper slipped further down the hallway and peered into rooms as she went. At the end of the hall, she located David's office, entered the room and closed the door behind her.

Matrina took a tissue from her purse, covered her fingers and opened the briefcase that sat on the desk. Inside the briefcase lay a three ring spiral notebook. In one of the leather slots in the top of the briefcase a book of postage stamps protruded. They bore American flags as decorations, the same kind of stamps used to mail the threatening letters. Not conclusive, but not inconclusive either. The conclusive evidence proved to be the folded sheet of torn-out spiral notebook paper in the file section of the top of the briefcase with the numbers two-three-nine scrawled on it. Hello. Talk about conclusive. How about slam-dunk.

She opened the center drawer of the desk and discovered a shallow tray that ran the length of the drawer. Two black crayons sat in the tray, each worn down from use. A box of nine millimeter bullets sat by the crayons.

Matrina opened the box of bullets with her tissue and noticed one bullet gone. Beside the box of bullets lay a pair of surgical gloves. That would explain the absence of fingerprints on the letters to John.

A glass container and a wet sponge for dampening envelopes occupied one corner of the top of the desk. This house used city water, hence, lots of chlorine, lots of fluoride. Another slam-dunk. Matrina's heart raced with excitement.

She shut the desk drawer and closed the briefcase. The file cabinet beckoned, and when she got to the bottom drawer, a four-pack of Kahlua bottles presented themselves. Inside the bottles she noted a quantity of white powdery substance, not liquid Kahlua.

In the movies, the detective always stuck a finger into the substance and tasted it to confirm cocaine. Since she hadn't a clue what cocaine tasted like, that would do her no good. How would David explain such an item in his file cabinet? He supposedly didn't consume alcohol, much less cocaine.

At that moment, the office door opened and Ida Rogers stepped inside the room and closed the door. She wore a starched white sun dress with yellow daisies splattered over it. A starched yellow organdy apron served as icing on the summery dress. Her hair sat on the top of her head in a neat bun, and her face, void of makeup, should have completed the shy deacon's wife persona. However, the hardened scowl that drifted from her eyes to her lips spoiled the image.

"What are you doing in here?" she said. She moved to the file cabinet where the bottom drawer remained opened. The two women gazed at the bottles. Ida pushed the bottom drawer closed with her foot, and her eyes never left Matrina's.

"I'm sorry," Matrina said. "I was looking for the bathroom, and I guess I got turned around."

"Yes, this is a huge house, and that hallway is very confusing," Ida said. Sarcasm iced her tone.

"I said I was sorry." Matrina made her way to the door. Ida grabbed her arm and detained her.

"You have no idea how sorry you're going to be, or with whom you are messing," she said. She looked into Matrina's eyes with vehemence and anger.

"And if I tell anyone what I just found, you, of course, will sweetly deny it," Matrina said.

"To my grave," Ida said, "or to your grave, whichever occurs first." She did not ease her grip on Matrina's arm.

"You, of course, will not be inclined to mention my becoming lost and winding up in this room." Matrina did not wince under the painful grip of Ida's hand, and she met the menacing gaze head on.

"Why would I?" she said in a whisper. "You were never here. You never saw a thing. You will repeat nothing about this incident."

"How could I, since I was never here," Matrina said.

Ida relaxed her grip, and Matrina left the office. She stopped by the bathroom to check out the bruises on her arm, and although substantial, they hid beneath the sleeve of her blouse. She went back to the living room.

The meeting slid into the intermission stage, and the guests mingled around the dining room table for tea, coffee, sandwiches and cookies. John brought Matrina a cup of coffee and a cookie.

"Where were you?" he said into her hair.

"You don't want to know." She smiled up at him and accepted the snacks. "But you're gonna get to know. The Shell station, south on 301, ten minutes after we leave here."

"You're too funny." John laughed and munched a cookie.

"You don't know the half of it," she said. She giggled in return and bit into her cookie and sipped her coffee.

* * *

Ten minutes after the conclusion of the meeting at the Rogers' home, Matrina parked her van by the air hose at the Shell station south on route 301. John pulled in behind her and left his Jeep and jumped into the passenger side of her van.

"So?" he said without hesitation.

"So, for starters," she said, "David Rogers has probably never been to Jamestown in his life, much less ever lived there. The Allendale was a restaurant on Lake Chautauqua. It was definitely not on the roof of the Hotel Jamestown. And they did not serve lobster. They were a steak house. And, the river winding through Jamestown is the Chadakoin, not the Allegeny."

"But that's not the rest of the story," he said.

"No. I went into David's office, and I opened his briefcase, and guess what I found?"

"Matrina," he said. He raised his arms in frustration and slapped them down on his legs, "don't you listen to me at all? I told you specifically not to get involved with these folks. They're dangerous. They're not worker's comp claim jumpers or shoplifters like you're used to. These guys would kill you for butting in their line at the super market. Then they'd say the twenty-third Psalm over your dead body and go home and have a pizza. They're dangerous."

"You're telling me. Ida caught me in the office."

John put his head down on the dashboard and covered his ears with his hands. "She caught you?"

"Yes."

"You have to take the kids and get out of Florida. I'm not kidding. You have put yourself into more jeopardy than you can imagine. Look at what they're doing to me, and I was just a threat to a drug running operation six years ago."

"It's all right," she said. "Ida and I are at a stalemate."

"No, you're not in any kind of stalemate with anyone connected to 'the preacher.' If you're in his world, you're in checkmate."

"No, no, listen," she said. "I found evidence that directly links David to the threatening letters, and I found a four pack of Kahlua bottles in the bottom of his file cabinet. I opened one of the bottles, and it's got white powder in it, probably cocaine. Definitely not Kahlua."

"And all that will do us no good if you're dead."

"I won't be dead. We do have to get on the ball and link David to the murder, though. David and Andy are connected, and they killed Robert Voloni. They buried the body in your backyard and then David wrote the letters. The two-three-nine memo sheet is in the back of his briefcase."

John lifted his head. "Really? The torn-out piece of paper from the spiral notebook with two-three-nine written on it is in the back of his briefcase?"

"Yes. Along with the spiral notebook and flag stamps. There are black crayons and rubber gloves in the center of his desk drawer, along with a new box of nine millimeter bullets with one bullet missing."

"If you live through this, you could testify to those facts?"

"Of course. And they're not going to kill me. There's no reason to. Right this minute, I can guarantee they're burning the two-three-nine note and the rubber gloves, flushing the bullets down the commode, dumping the cocaine down the sink, sticking the rinsed Kahlua bottles into the dishwasher. They think we're going to get the D.A. to come at them with a search warrant, and they're working on being squeaky clean. Then they'd sue me for defamation of character, or something equally stupid, and that would slam the lid on any testimony I might be prone to give."

"The evidence is definitely gone by now. You're right about that," John said.

"And somewhere not far away is the place where they killed Robert, or Slats, or whatever his name was. There has to be blood traces. All we have to do is find out where they did the murder, get Nathan to talk to the D.A. into getting a search warrant, and bingo, you're off the hook. The blood samples will tie David and Andy to the murder."

"Because the cops will find traces of blood at the murder scene. And you don't think they killed Slats in my backyard."

"Heavens, no. Not even the D.A. thinks that. The cops have turned your place inside out looking for blood and DNA, and there's nothing. They killed him somewhere else and transported the body to your backyard in the middle of the night when everyone in your neighborhood was either asleep or gone for the weekend."

"So the people in Chicago located Slats, brought in David to do the job, and he involved Andy. My guess would be Andy did the actual killing. One bullet missing. Whoever shot Slats was a sure shot, like a cop. We have to hurry, though. Once David does a couple of successful drug runs, he'll disappear. This drug run Wednesday could be all he wants from Florida."

"Then he'll disappear?"

"You bet. He'll be off to California, Oregon, Mexico, who knows where. This guy leaves no traces. He's slicker than any chameleon. In the Utica area, we heard he posed as an undertaker. Here, he's a deacon. The only consistent thing about his behavior is his insistence on quoting the Bible and the 'bless us His children' closing to the messages. He has a scripture for everything."

"Then we have to move fast. I'll call George when I get home and see if he can get us a bottle of luminol. It glows greenish blue in the dark when it contacts blood."

"I know how it works," he said. "Where do you plan to look for this blood?"

"I think Andy's apartment would be a good start. And the apartment in Bradenton where Sandra Marshall lives, and the boat, of course. Maybe even the Rogers' home."

"You can forget the Rogers' home. That would be too close to David, or whatever his name is. He always keeps himself very remote from what's really going down."

"Do you think he's from Chicago?"

"Probably. He's probably connected to the Voloni family somehow. They had to trust the hit on Slats to someone they knew could carry it off. If they missed, Slats would run back to the Feds, and more of them would go down. No, they knew what they were doing when they involved 'the preacher.' They knew he would get the job done."

"And he did."

"Yes, he did. And he took me down with it. That's the way his mind works. Total destruction; take no prisoners."

"Until now," Matrina said. "We're taking prisoners, and he's number one."

John ran his fingers through his hair. "I don't like this at all."

"Oh, you'll love it when we pull it off," Matrina said. "We'll get the evidence we need, and get the D.A. to do a search warrant for wherever we find blood samples, sneak up on him, and it will be all over."

"Hope you're right."

"I am. Good night, John. I've got to hurry home and call George, and see if he can get us a bottle of luminol. I'll call you and let you know what he says."

"He's probably going to say, 'Who are you, and why are you calling me?'"

"No, he won't. He's ex-FBI. They're like old fire horses. He'll get the scent of the gig, and the biggest problem we'll have is keeping him out of it."

"If you say so," John said. "Call me." He reached over and ran his hand down the length of her hair. "Please be careful." He got out of the van and walked to his Jeep, scratched his head and muttered to himself. Matrina drove home and called George. She could hardly wait to launch the luminol connection.

Chapter 31

The next day, Saturday evening, near midnight, Matrina and John sat in John's Jeep two doors down and across the street from Andy's apartment in Sarasota.

"I can't believe I'm letting you talk me into this wild scheme of yours," John said. He sat behind the steering wheel of the parked Jeep.

"You should be glad I talked you into it," Matrina said, with determination in her voice. "When I find blood in Andy's apartment, and we get Nathan to talk the D.A. into a search warrant, they'll find out the blood belonged to Slats. That should get you off the hook and toss Andy and this 'preacher' dude right into the soup."

"Not really," John said. "They have a pretty airtight case against me, and finding Slats's blood anywhere else would prove he was there and cut himself. That's all."

"But it would show that Andy and Slats knew each other. Right now, Andy is acting like he didn't know Slats. We know that's not true because we found both their fingerprints on drink containers from the *Empress.* So, Andy's lying. And why do people lie? To protect themselves from trouble."

"That's true," John said. "And you know something else I thought of?"

"What?"

"You got four sets of fingerprints off those drink containers. You got Andy's, and the little redheaded gal, Sandra's, and the fingerprints of Slats, or Robert Voloni, since they're the same person, but there was a fourth set of prints we couldn't place. Prints of someone named Carmine Panacelli. He had the same last name as the maiden name of the lady who owns the boat. Remember? We figured she was probably the wife of the guy Slats sent up the river."

"Yeah. That's true. You think you might be wrong about David Rogers being 'the preacher,' when all the while this Carmine Panacelli might be 'the preacher?'"

"It's a possibility. Or, Carmine Panacelli and David Rogers are the same person. We need the prints of David Rogers to see if they match this Panacelli guy."

"That ought to be easy enough," Matrina said. "Tomorrow at church, pass him a hymnal, and then get it back from him and stash it."

"Good idea. That I could do. But for now, I think this blood-hunting expedition is too risky."

"We need evidence. Time is running out for us. We have to start somewhere. I want to start here. I know Andy and 'the preacher' did this. We know for sure they're running drugs. Andy called him to set that up for next Wednesday. And this Ida chick, let me tell you, she's no Christian lady. You should have seen the anger in her eyes when she was holding my arm. And she left bruises. I've confronted seasoned shoplifters, who just got out of the clink, who didn't have that kind of aggression."

"She seems so gentle-natured."

"Yeah, well, mother grizzlies should be so gentle-natured." Matrina sighed in frustration. John saw only the good in people. How could he, an ex-cop, be so naive?

"Okay," she said. She opened the passenger side of the Jeep as she grabbed the bottle of luminol George had procured for her. "Show time. I'm gone. You'll stay here? If you see anyone coming to the apartment, ring me once on my cell?"

"Yeah," he said, "Matrina, I don't like this. How do you know for sure Andy won't come home?"

"Because he's got the graveyard shift at the mall. I called and they offered to patch me through, but I said that was okay, I'd just talk to him tomorrow."

"Did they know who you were?"

"Yes. I said I was Rosie's sister and I wanted to ask him about the date for Rosie's shower to be sure it wouldn't conflict with any of his plans."

"Like drug running, or murder? Stuff like that?"

"Or tooling around town with the redhead. The guy's got a full plate of activities going on."

"So, one ring on your cell and you're out of there. Right?"

"Right."

"Promise?"

"Scout's honor."

"You were never a scout."

"You were enough of a scout for both of us."

Matrina left the Jeep and jogged across the street. She carried the spray bottle of luminol in one hand, and a screwdriver for opening the door to Andy's apartment in the other.

The overhead door to the one-car garage beside the apartment sat open. She figured the door that led from the garage to the inside of the apartment would be her easiest entry. The door gave up its lock after one insertion and jiggle of the screwdriver.

She carefully stepped inside the kitchen, locked the door behind her and sprayed luminol as she went. No bluish green smears of illumination showed the presence of blood.

Matrina walked into the living room and sprayed luminol there. Nothing. She started toward the hallway to advance toward the bedrooms and the bathroom.

Then she saw it. A shadowy figure loomed ahead of her at the far end of the hallway. It's ghostlike presence, clouded by its filmy attire, arms outstretched, power in its projection toward her filled her with panic, and before she could swing the bottle of luminol at the figure, a large object appeared in one of its hands and connected with the side of her head. She collapsed like a rag doll.

Matrina struggled to hang on to consciousness as she went down, but lost the battle as blackness enveloped her like yards and yards of drifting black velvet.

She awoke moments, maybe hours, later. Time became garbled in this arena of unreality. Andy's couch felt lumpy, and her head supported a cloth wrapped around several ice cubes. Rosie sat on the edge of the couch and dabbed the ice cubes around her sister's forehead. Matrina flickered her eyes open.

"Oh, thank God," Rosie said. "I thought I killed you."

"You? You hit me?" Matrina still lingered in the twilight zone.

"Yes. I thought you were someone breaking in the apartment."

"I was someone breaking into the apartment. What were you doing here?" Matrina sat up now, indignant, angry and in pain. She took the dish towel full of ice away from Rosie in a gruff manner and laid it back on her head herself. She noticed the towel stained with blood, most assuredly her own.

"What do you mean, 'What am I doing here?'" Rosie said. "A better question is, 'What are you doing here?'"

"I asked first," Matrina said. "You're here, in Andy's apartment, dressed in practically nothing." She waved her free hand at the filmy negligee Rosie wore.

"Matrina, this is the apartment of the man I'm going to marry. I have a right to be here. And I'm a twenty-eight-year-old woman. I can dress any way I please. Now, tell me what you are doing here, and it'd better be a good story."

Matrina pressed the ice firmly to her head.

"What did you hit me with?" Matrina said. Maybe a change in subject would save her.

"A big cop-type flashlight, and quit messing around, Matrina. I want to know what you're doing breaking into my boyfriend's apartment. This explanation better be good."

"It is," Matrina said. She leaned down over her knees and moved the package of ice back and forth where the flashlight had met her head.

"So, let's have it," Rosie said.

At that moment, the door that led to the kitchen from the garage crashed off its hinges, slammed to the kitchen floor, and left John to stand in its wake. He carried a large flashlight of his own.

"Oh, mercy me," Rosie said. "If it isn't Rambo. And all you've got for a weapon is a flashlight, too? If we're going to continue this lifestyle, we've got to invest in some serious hardware, brother."

"What happened to you?" John said. He moved toward Matrina who slouched on the sofa. He tried to piece together the scene that unfolded before him. "I waited, and waited, and you didn't come out. And then I saw the lights come on. I thought you were in trouble."

"You thought right," Matrina said. She straightened her position, and kept the ice on her wound. "I am in trouble. Rosie wants to know what I'm doing here."

"And of course, you told her," John said. "She has a right to know."

"Thank you," Rosie said.

No one said anything for a full thirty seconds.

"What in God's green earth are you guys doing here?" Rosie said again. She got up from the couch and paced the living room floor.

John and Matrina locked eyes for an instant, and then John spoke. He wondered if the truth would set him free, one more time.

"We think Andy is involved in a murder, and Matrina's here with luminol looking for blood, the blood of the murder victim."

"Are you guys nuts? You think I'm going to buy that?" She paused in her pacing, and then turned and looked at them. "Oh, I get it now," she said. "I know what you're doing here. I should have known all along. You are so transparent, Matrina, and you're so unfair."

"Because I am doing, what?" Matrina said.

"You thought Andy wouldn't be home, and I would be a nice, good little girl, and be home at my place on Lido. So you thought you'd sneak in here and see if you could find something sleazy about Andy so you could break us up. That's your game." Rosie's tone slipped into borderline ranting. "You just can't stand my finding someone you didn't pick out for me. You can't stand things going on in my life that you didn't dictate. What were you looking for? Pictures of Andy and some other woman? Evidence that other women stayed here? Evidence that he called other women on his phone bill. Evidence that he bought other women gifts on his charge cards?"

Rosie waved her arms over her head, and her voice went up a notch higher. "You were looking for his bank statements, credit card statements, phone bills. I know how your mind works. Well, you came up dry this time, Sister. Andy loves me, and we're getting married, and you'd better just get over it, Matrina. You must be nuts to go to these lengths to try to take away the only good thing that's ever happened to me."

Matrina looked at John and gave him a knowing look that said, "Roll with the flow." Rosie's explanation covered up the truth better than anything they could invent. John threw up his hands in surrender and sat down in a living room chair opposite the couch.

"We're sorry, Rosie," he said. "Matrina loves you so much, and she has a bit of a mother fixation on you, and she's so worried that you're making a mistake. That's all."

"A bit of a mother fixation on me?" Rosie said. She still paced the floor and waved her hands. "She'd have me locked in the attic until I was thirty-five, if we had an attic. She'd have me be an old maid feeding a dozen cats and learning to crochet if I'd let her."

"It's only misplaced concern," John said. He ignored the dissenting look on Matrina's face.

"Okay," Rosie said. "I guess this is just something I have to live with. I'm sorry I slugged you. I truly thought you were a burglar."

"You weren't far wrong," Matrina said. She stood up and wobbled to her feet. John came to her aid and put his arm around her to help her to the door.

"Can you stand here for a minute?" he said to her. He let go of her and watched to see that she could stand by herself.

"Sure, I'm okay." She handed the towel of ice back to Rosie.

"You sure, Sis?" Rosie said. She stood by her side and looked at the gash on her head. Rosie's anger had vented, and now a calm had set in. "Wow, that's a doozy. Here, take this towel and ice back. It's still kind of wanting to bleed."

As the sisters stood side by side, Matrina took the towel and ice back and pressed it to the gash on her head. John raised the kitchen door from the floor and put it back on its hinges. He thought one of the hinges might be broken. It snapped into place, and the door opened and closed. It would do until it could be fixed more permanently.

"Come on, Jessica Fletcher," he said to Matrina. He helped her through the kitchen door.

"I don't think *Murder, She Wrote* ever involved Jessica getting whopped on the head," Matrina said. She walked into the garage.

"Rosie followed her with the bottle of luminol. "You forgot your bottle of stuff."

"Thanks." Matrina giggled. "Can't forget that, can I."

"What is it, bug spray? You know how you're terrified of roaches."

"I don't like roaches. That's a fact," Matrina said.

"You all right?" Rosie said from the garage. John helped Matrina across the street to his Jeep.

"Yeah, I'm fine," Matrina said over her shoulder. "Nice spending the evening with you."

"Yes," Rosie said. "We'll have to do this again sometime."

"Not likely," Matrina said.

John opened the passenger side door of the Jeep for Matrina. Rosie returned to the apartment, closed the kitchen door and turned off the lights.

The streetlight bathed Matrina's hair into a shimmering halo of golden brilliance, and John moved the strands of hair away from the gash for a better look.

"This is an ER gash if I ever saw one. We're on our way to Sarasota Memorial."

"No, I'm not going to any hospital. It's not that bad."

"You don't know that. You're going, and that's that." He buckled her up in the passenger's seat, closed the door, walked around the Jeep and got into his side of the vehicle.

"I am not going." She looked over at him to drive her point home.

"Yes, you are going. I'm driving, and you're going. You could have a concussion, or need stitches. You're a parent with kids who depend on you.

You can't make a stupid decision like this and just hope for the best. You're going to the emergency room. It's not up for discussion."

Matrina put her head back on the passenger seat of the Jeep and tears cascaded down her cheek.

"Are you in pain?" John said. He pulled away from the curb but brought the vehicle to a stop halfway down the block.

"No," Matrina said. "I'm just no good at this. I thought I would be good as an investigator, but it turns out I'm lousy. I could never be a detective on my own."

"What makes you say that?" he said. "You're the best detective I know. You have deductive reasoning on a higher level than most people. And George says you're aces at your job with ACS."

"Oh, that's just busting worker's comp liars, and petty cash thieves. I couldn't make a real living as a private eye doing stuff like that. I wanted to work on real cases, like we're doing now with your case."

"And look how well we're doing," John said. He pulled out onto the Trail and headed south toward the hospital. "You're figuring this whole thing out, and getting the evidence in line. By the end of the week, we'll have me free and the bad guys behind bars."

"And me in the hospital. I'm no good at the clandestine stuff. I keep getting caught. And I didn't find any blood at Andy's. That guy doesn't even cut himself shaving."

"You underestimated your opponent, that's all," John said. He stopped for a red light. "That happens all the time in security work. You know that as well as anyone. You can't take a couple of slips in evaluating the situation and judge your whole life by it. Who would have thought Rosie would have been in Andy's apartment tonight? I would never have figured she'd be there."

"I should have figured it," Matrina said. She wiped her eyes and got the weeping under control. "I know Rosie, and I should have figured it. I messed up."

"Well, tomorrow's another day, Miss Scarlett," John said in his best southern drawl. "We'll think about all of this tomorrow."

Matrina grinned in spite of herself and fought sleep all the way to the hospital. When John parked the Jeep and walked her into the emergency room, she did not battle him. She struggled in her mind to plot their next move. Nothing made sense. They must be headed the wrong way.

Chapter 32

Wednesday morning of the next week, the day of the scheduled late-night event at the Get Away Marina Andy had mentioned on the Rogers' answer machine, John and Nathan sat in Matrina's living room and prepared to view the shoppers who had purchased nine millimeter bullets before the third weekend in June.

"Where's your mom?" Nathan said to Michelle.

"She had to run an errand. She said she wouldn't be gone long. She said to get you guys anything you want, while you do whatever it is you're doing. Can I get you anything?"

"No, thanks," John said. "We'll just scan these security videos while we wait for her."

An hour later, Matrina breezed through the front door.

"Hi, guys," she said. She walked over to the TV and looked at the shoppers who marched across the screen.

"How's your head?" John said.

"Head?" Nathan said. He looked from one to the other for an answer.

"You don't want to know," Matrina said. She touched the spot where Rosie's blow had connected. "And it's fine."

"Yes," John said. "Trust me. You are better off not knowing. Glad you're recovering," he added to Matrina.

"Don't you want to know where I've been?" Matrina said.

"Okay, I'll bite. Where've you been?" Nathan said.

"I've been out to the convenience stores that surround Myakka State Park."

Both men stopped the video scan and looked at her. "And?" John said.

"And I guess you remember when you camped out there on the murder weekend, all your flashlight batteries were missing?"

"Yes. That was strange."

"Not really. I think David took them from your survival kit. I went to most of the stores and looked at their security videos from that Friday, and guess what?"

"What?" Nathan played along.

"David went through those stores on Friday afternoon and bought every single flashlight battery in the store. So that's why you had to keep going store to store, and finally wound up in Sarasota, and put a two hour gap in your camping alibi."

"Imagine that," John said. "The guy's clever and thorough, to say the least."

"So, any of these folks on these tapes ring a bell," Matrina said. She sat down on the floor by the TV.

"We already have that one bell-ringer," John said, "the gal from the Trade Winds. I like her for our prime suspect."

* * *

After a lunch of roast beef sandwiches, made by Michelle and served on lavender flowered China plates, accompanied by lavender flowered cloth napkins, Matrina went into the kitchen to make a pot of coffee. At two in the afternoon, the only person any of them recognized on the tapes had been Sandra Marshall. It would be good for their case if she turned out to be their suspicious shopper. Anyone else who came into the picture at this late date would muddy the waters.

Matrina brought the tray of steaming coffee and set it on the coffee table. Nathan and John sat on the couch, and she had returned to the floor in front of the TV. Nathan fast-forwarded one tape and looked for the next stopping place.

"Oh, stop there," Matrina said. She pointed to the screen.

"Why, what did you see?" Nathan said.

"Nothing, really. I just wanted to point out something cute," she said.

"We could use something cute right about now," Nathan said. He slowed down the tape.

"This is the tape where Michelle and her friends spotted this boy they know in school shoplifting gum in Wal-Mart. Look, there he is now. See? Watch him pocket that gum, and nobody caught him. Can you believe it?"

Nathan slowed the tape to a crawl, and they watched Michelle's classmate put a pack of Juicy Fruit into his pocket and walk through the line.

"That's the one fallacy with the security camera being 360 degrees," John said. You get focused on the person at the register thinking that's where the deal is going to go down, and all the time it's the person at the peripheral edge of the camera you ought to be watching."

Matrina took a sudden deep breath and turned to her guests. "That's it," she said. She leaped to her feet.

"What's it?" John said. He held his coffee mug with both hands. Her excitement caused him to slosh the coffee from side to side.

"Oh, John. We've been so stupid. We could have solved this case days ago.""How so?" Nathan said. He put milk and sugar into his coffee.

"Peripheral vision," Matrina said. "It's all so clear now."

"Not to us," Nathan said. "I guess we're traveling in the slow lane."

"Vince Haynes's video, the one on his boat, the *Fly by Night.* That camera catches activity on the *Empress,* and we know from the fingerprints that Andy, Sandra Marshall, Slats and the Panacelli dude were on the boat, maybe not all at the same time, but they were all on board at one time or another."

"So?" Nathan said.

"So," John said. He set his coffee down on the coffee table, "if the video still exists from the few days before the murder, there might be footage of them all on the boat together. If nothing else, it would prove Andy and Sandra knew Slats. Andy's been acting like he didn't know Slats at all. Evidence proving otherwise would be a chink in their armor. It might even catch 'the preacher' in its wandering eye. The camera is movement activated. It only kicks on when there is something to film, so maybe the tape from that week is still around. Since it caught us on the boat, it might have caught them."

"Yes," Matrina said. "And, John, you say 'the preacher' never involves himself in whatever crimes he orchestrates, so the murder might have been committed on the boat. That would distance the crime from 'the preacher' and this entire local area.

"There was no blood at Andy's place, so if the murder was committed somewhere locally, that would leave Sandra's apartment, Kenny's, Andy's partner's place, and the boat. I don't think Kenny and Sandra are main players in this cast. That would leave the boat for the main focus of operation, and chances are they're using the boat for their midnight run tonight, since the answer machine message involved a marina."

"So we need Vince's video to check this theory out," John said, without emotion. "He'll never let us have it."

"Why?" Matrina said. She paced the living room from the TV to the couch. "Surely he doesn't want to see you go to jail for something you didn't do."

"He's not so sure I didn't do it," John said. He wiped up coffee that had slopped out of his cup. "The guy wouldn't toss me a life preserver if I were drowning."

"We have to make him see it's his civic duty to check out his videos for those few days before the murder. He'd be guilty of withholding evidence," Matrina said.

"Only if we know for sure there is evidence on the tapes," Nathan said. He put more sugar in his coffee. "You got any cookies?"

"Yeah, sure, I suppose so," Matrina said. She hurried into the kitchen and came back with a plate of Lorna Doones.

"Oh, good," Nathan said. "These are one of my favorite cookies."

"We have to go see Vince and convince him to let us view his videos," she said.

John reached for a cookie. "I'm not going to humiliate myself and beg for something he has and watch him refuse to give it up."

"Okay," Matrina said, "I'll go alone. And I'll come back with that video. You just watch."

"You go, girl," Nathan said, with conviction. "I like this gal's spirit." He nodded his head toward John.

"What store is he at right now?" Matrina said. She picked up the phone and sat on the chair beside the couch.

"The one in Bradenton. That's where he's the produce manager," John said.

"What's the number?" Matrina said.

John repeated the phone number at the store and watched her as she dialed it.

"Hi," Matrina said into the mouth piece. "Could I speak with Vince Haynes?"

Pause.

"Thanks." She gave John and Nathan a knowing grin.

"Hi, Mr. Haynes," she said. She began the conversation with confidence. "You don't know me, well, actually, you do kind of know me, but we've never met. I owe you an apology, and I'd like to come down to the store and apologize to you in person, if it's okay. Then, as incredible as it may seem, I have a huge favor to ask of you. Could you see me this afternoon?"

Another pause.

"Oh, that would be great. And it's so very kind of you to let me come down on the spur of the moment like this. I'll be there in a half hour or so. Thanks. Bye." Matrina punched the phone silent and smiled at her cohorts.

"That's round one," John said. "You don't know Vince. He'll have you beaten up and bounced out of the ring by round three."

"We'll see about that," Matrina said. "I've tossed a few guys out of the ring by round two."

She went into the bedroom, changed into her Ralph Laurens, laced on her Nikes, grabbed her purse, and walked toward the door. "The kids have gone from Scrabble to Monopoly, if you get bored. See ya." With that she marched out to her van.

* * *

Nathan ate another Lorna Doone. He sighed and looked over at John. He got to his feet.

"I get to be the hat," Nathan said. His mouth scattered cookie crumbs as he walked toward the porch.

"You always get to be the hat," John said. He followed behind.

* * *

Matrina pulled into the Publix parking lot where Vince Haynes peddled produce and got out of her van. She walked into the store. Ten minutes later, she walked up to Vince Haynes who checked in crates of fruit at the back loading dock.

"Mr. Haynes?" she said. She smiled and extended her hand.

"Yes, what can I do for you?" He smiled back and accepted her greeting.

"I'm Matrina McCoy. You were kind enough to grant me a few minutes of our time over the phone a little bit ago."

"Oh, yes," he said. He gave her his full attention now. Ole Vince seemed to be quite amiable when approached by a blond interloper whose appearance on his video a few weeks ago had sent him into a tirade with John. "What can I do for you?"

"For starters," Matrina said, "you can forgive me for invading your privacy on your boat a few weeks back. I'm the one your video caught standing on the *Fly By Night.*"

"That was you?" Vince said. He let go of her hand. "Why were you on my boat? Were you looking for me? Where was I at the time? How come I wasn't there to welcome you?"

"Good thing you weren't there," Matrina said. "You'd have shot me for trespassing."

"Never." Vince said. He put his hand on Matrina's back and guided her through the maze of newly unloaded crates and cartons. "Let's go into my office and talk about this."

Matrina allowed him to leave his hand on her back, but stayed a step ahead of him to avoid further bodily contact. She had played this game before. She knew the rules.

"Okay," she said aloud.

Vince led her down the hall from the loading dock to his office.

"Vince, may I call you Vince?" Matrina said. She sat in a chair beside Vince's desk in the cramped office.

"By all means." His smile wandered up to his eyes, and he patted the arm of the chair in which she sat. Matrina mentally located her can of Mace in the bottom of her purse.

"I am truly sorry I invaded your privacy by stepping onto your boat that night," Matrina said. She allowed his hand to stay on the arm of her chair. "You see, my sister is engaged to be married. They have the date set for September, and I spotted her fiancé with another woman on the boat next to your boat that evening. I was shocked, to say the least. I didn't want him to catch me spying on him, so I jumped onto your boat to hide myself. I guess that's when your camera caught me."

"My camera has an eye for beauty," Vince said.

"Whatever, I heard enough to know that this fellow is definitely not someone who would make good marriage material." And he's not the only person I know who appears to have a wandering eye, ran her thoughts.

"Now that I know the whole story," Vince said, "you are forgiven." He stroked the arm of her chair as he spoke. "Now, what is the favor I can do for you?" He removed his hand since she gave no response, and leaned back in his chair, laced his hands over his head and gazed at her.

"I was wondering how long this affair with my sister's fellow and his other girlfriend had been going on. Before I mention it to my sister and break her heart, I would like to have more facts. I can't approach him, for the obvious reason. He would just go postal on me and deny everything. So, I was wondering if I could borrow that tape you have from your security camera and see if there is any prior footage of them cavorting on that boat next door."

"The camera is motion activated," Vince said, "and I have had that particular tape in the camera for a couple of months or better. We don't have many intruders at Regatta Pointe so it would have everything that moved across its eye for probably two months back or so, sea gulls, squirrels, beautiful blond ladies."

"And I could borrow the tape?" Matrina smiled her sweetest smile.

"Of course. Anything for you." The comment had a leering tone.

"Do you have the tape here in your office?" She leaned toward him with the soft-spoken question.

"Yes, I do. It's right here." Vince pulled the video from the top shelf over his desk. He held it just out of her reach.

"And I may borrow it?" She did not reach for the video. The game inched toward victory, and the cheerleaders and water boys could be heard in their chant of triumph at her success.

"My pleasure," he said. He placed the video into her hand and squeezed her flesh as it grasped the cassette. Matrina got up from her chair. Touchdown.

"I am certainly indebted to you, Vince." She smiled as she walked toward the door. "I'll get this back to you in a few days."

"And then maybe we could do lunch?" Vince spoke in almost a whisper.

"We'll talk," she whispered back.

Matrina left the office and hurried down the hall, through the loading dock, through the store and out to the sidewalk at not quite a trot. She felt like she needed a shower.

She should do lunch, all right, but not with him. She should do lunch with his wife and tell her she's married to a sleaze bucket.

Back in her van and out of the parking lot, she took her cell and phoned home.

"Hello?" Turner said. Matrina heard loud, excited voices in the background.

"Is everything all right, Turner?" she said. Sudden concern shaded her voice because of the chaos that traveled over the phone lines.

"Oh, yeah," Turner said. "Mr. Fleming just got to buy Boardwalk, and he's all happy about it."

"Oh, that's interesting. Let me talk to Mr. Fleming."

"Okay. Hold on."

"Mission accomplished," Matrina said to John.

"You're kidding," John said. "How in the world did you do it?"

"I'm a woman," she said. "I know how the game is played."

"Oh," he said. "I hope the game didn't go into overtime."

"It didn't. Vince just doesn't know that yet. He thinks overtime is still coming."

"Hum," John said. "Well, take your time coming back. I just bought Boardwalk."

"So I heard. You need Park Place to do you any good. Guess you realize that."

"Nathan has Park Place, but he's an easy mark. I'll con him out of it as soon as you hang up."

"In your dreams," came the words of Nathan over the phone connection.

"Well, play nice," Matrina said. "We have to do fifteen minutes of time out if we lose our tempers or make unkind comments."

"Man, you're no fun," John said.

"Ask her to bring pizza home for dinner." Turner said behind John.

"I heard that," Matrina said.

"So you'll bring pizza?" John said.

"Yes. What do you like on it?"

"No anchovies."

"Yuck. That's a given. Be there in a little bit."

"Good. I'll have hotels on Boardwalk and Park Place by the time you get here."

"No, I'll have hotels on Boardwalk and Park Place by the time you get here," she heard Nathan shout. An uproar of four voices followed.

"What happened?" Matrina said. She turned left on the Trail and spotted a Pizza Hut ahead.

"Mr. Caldwell just went to jail," Turner said into the phone.

"He's a lawyer," Matrina said. "He can bond himself out. See you guys in a few minutes, pizza in tow."

"Hurrah," Turner said. He hung up the phone.

Matrina patted the video on the seat beside her. Would this be needed evidence, or another wrong street?

Chapter 33

After pizza, Matrina, John and Nathan plopped once more in front of the TV. They popped Vince's video tape into the VCR. Michelle had biked to Suzanne's house to do chat rooms, and Turner had biked three doors down to play Gran Turismo 3 with Buddy.

The TV screen flickered and a gull flew over the *Fly-By-Night*. The scene changed and a squirrel sat on the railing of the *Fly-By-Night* and ate a peanut.

"Wonder what this movie is rated," Nathan said. "Do they have a minus 'G' rating?"

"We have to watch the whole thing," Matrina said, "or we might miss something important."

"Yeah, the squirrel might eat the seagull," Nathan said.

The tape rolled on. More birds and squirrels flooded the screen. A dog jumped on board the *Fly-By-Night*, marked a deck chair, jumped back to the dock again, and ran off.

The *Empress* rocked in the wake of other boats since the beginning of the tape. Then came a moment when Andy climbed on board. He carried a cooler, a blue plastic bag that looked like it contained groceries and a box of large plastic trash bags.

"Wonder what he needs the trash bags for," John said.

"We know it's not for trash."

"They don't use trash bags?" Nathan said.

"They use them," Matrina said. "They just don't ever carry any trash out to a dumpster. I think it's part of their religion."

They watched as Andy carried all the parcels down into the living quarters. He stayed downstairs several minutes. Then he surfaced, locked the downstairs door and left the boat.

The next scene occurred a day later, Friday, the day of the murder. Andy boarded the boat again, still alone, opened the door to the living quarters and descended into the hold. A few minutes later, Robert Voloni, AKA Slats, boarded, and opened the door to downstairs. He disappeared into the hold.

"Oho," John said. "Now we've got it going on."

"I'll say," Matrina said.

"This proves Andy knew Slats before his dog dug him up in your backyard," Nathan said.

"Yes. Not sure what that means," John said, "but it definitely means Andy is covering up something."

A few minutes later, they watched David Rogers, AKA 'the preacher,' board the yacht. He, too, went downstairs without knocking. Then the camera flicked off. No more movement to keep it going.

The next scene, same day, nightfall had descended on Regatta Pointe, four hours later near midnight. David Rogers appeared back on deck. He descended into the living quarters, and returned to the deck again, moments later. He shut the door to downstairs behind him.

"He's coming up from the living quarters," John said. His eyes focused on the TV, and he tried to see all the visible details.

"Yes. Dollars to donuts he's our mysterious Carmine Panacelli," Nathan said.

"I gave you the hymnal from church, didn't I?" John said. He looked over at him and grabbed a piece of popcorn.

"Yes. I have the crime lab at the sheriff's department running the prints. They ought to be back any minute now."

The next frame showed Slats on deck his hands tied behind his back and his lips plastered to his face with clear plastic tape.

"Hum. Wonder why they are bringing him up on deck?" John said. "If they're going to kill him on the boat, why not just do it downstairs?"

"Andy's a good enough cop to know that would leave DNA behind. They have to use your gun," Nathan said, "so they have to do it where the blood splatters won't be findable."

"So, they're going off the boat?" Matrina said. She did not want to witness an actual murder.

"I don't know," John said. He tried to second guess the images that floated across the TV screen. "Must be a pretty dead marina at night. They don't seem worried about being noticed."

"That marina has been totally dead most of the day, up until now," Nathan said, "unless you count squabbling birds and furry critters as action."

"That's true," Matrina said. "This is the first actual people we've seen triggering the motion of the camera."

David Rogers led Slats by the elbow to the edge of the vessel. Slats did not seem to struggle. David brought him to the edge of the boat, and leaned him over it, face first, toward the water.

"They can't be going to drown him," Matrina said. "We know he was shot."

"No, this should be Andy's cue to shoot him right here," John said. "That would leave blood splatters on the outside of the boat to be washed off by the waves, and no blood on the boat at all."

As soon as John stated that fact, the camera picked up Andy as he stood on the roof of the living quarters. He aimed John's Luger with both hands, and got off one shot with exact precision as Slats slumped over the railing. David had to struggle to prevent him from falling overboard into the water.

"Oh, my," Matrina said. She put her head into her hands. Her shoulders shook, and she collapsed onto the cool marble floor and wept. Her blond hair made a halo around her head, and her knees curled up in a protective curl.

John knelt beside her, picked her up and held her in his arms while he rocked her and smoothed her hair.

"I didn't think the actual death would be on the tape," he said. "I should never have involved you in getting this video, and certainly not in viewing it. Please forgive me."

Matrina buried her head in his shoulder and clung to him. Her sobbing slipped out of control.

"I'm so sorry," he said.

"It's not your fault," she said. She sniffled, pulled away from him and dried her eyes with a tissue she pulled from her jeans pocket. "I don't do death well since Mike. I don't do anything well since Mike. Thank heaven the kids are out of the house."

"Thankfully," John said. He held her at arm's length while she blew her nose and wiped her eyes.

"I'm sorry this is so hard on you, Matrina," Nathan said, "but we have to check out the rest of this scene on the tape." Matrina and John turned their attention to the tape, but the scene in question had passed from view.

Nathan rewound the tape to the shooting section. "And looky here," Nathan said. "That Andy must have calculated the ballistics and the travel of the bullet as he knew it had to stay in Slats' head in order to implicate you. Look, he's standing on the roof to get enough distance to do the job and leave the bullet in the target."

"Let me catch my breath before we continue," Matrina said.

"Why don't you go out on the back porch and just pass on this part of the tape," John said.

"No, I have to see all of it, so we don't miss anything," she said. She blew her nose again and sat up ready to continue.

After Andy shot Slats from the roof of the cabin on the yacht, he climbed back down off the roof and grabbed the box of large trash bags and the clear plastic tape. He hurried over to David who kept Slats from going over the railing, and together the two men wrestled a large trash bag over Slats' head and pulled it down as far as it would go. Then they took tape and wrapped it around his torso and brought the body back on the deck of the boat.

They took another large trash bag and brought it up over the lower portion of Slats' body and taped that bag around the torso. Then they carried the body off the boat and met Sandra Marshall as she walked up the dock toward the *Empress.*

When they rendezvoused on the dock, they walked out of the camera range, and the scene clicked off. Nathan and John sat and looked at each other, speechless at what they had witnessed.

"You're off the hook," Nathan said. He nodded his head toward the video.

"Yes. God's answered my prayers," John said. He shook his head in disbelief.

"This tape is good," Nathan said, "but it would be better if we had some physical evidence to support it. In this day and age, you know, tapes can be doctored to show anything you want, so it might not be conclusive."

"We need blood samples or DNA from the yacht," John said.

"Yes," Matrina said, "and I know how we can find some."

"How?" the men said in unison.

"They shot him over the edge of the boat, so there wouldn't be any blood inside the boat. But there would be splatters on the exterior of the boat. There would be DNA from Slats on the inside of the yacht, but that wouldn't prove anything except that Slats was onboard, and probably no one would care about that."

"How could blood be on the outside?" Nathan said. He dug back into his popcorn. "Wouldn't it be all washed away by now?"

"Most of it would be all washed away," John said. "But all they would need to find is a drop or two. There might be that much left up under the railing above the waterline."

"The yacht isn't even in Manatee County, so we can't get the D.A. to issue a search warrant," Nathan said.

"And if we get him to issue a search warrant, and they don't find any blood, that will blow our case all to blue blazes," John said.

"I'll tell you one thing we can do," Matrina said. She finger-combed her hair and stood by the couch. "We know where the *Empress* is right now. We could drive down to Lee County and spray luminol on the place where we know the murder happened, and see if it shows any spots of blood. If it does, we can call you tonight, Nathan, and you can get the wheels rolling for Lee County to go out and do the search before dawn tomorrow. We have to work fast, as this may be their last drug run, and then that boat will be in Cancun by Friday, and probably be sold and gone forever."

"Meanwhile, what about 'the preacher?'" Nathan said.

"He'll get off scot-free, like he usually does," John said. "I can't believe he was involved in the actual murder. He must have tried to get Andy's partner, Kenny, to help, and he chickened out. They were in gear to do the deed while I was camping, so he had to step into the gap. They got Sandra to drive the getaway car where they drove Slats over to my place to bury the body."

"How'd they get away with that?" Nathan said.

"It was a beautiful June weekend. Most everyone on my block was gone. Piece of cake."

"Would there be blood or DNA in whatever vehicle they used?"

"They probably did their ole 'borrow a used car and then return it,' trick," Matrina said.

"Or, they could have used Andy's Tundra, knowing that there would be no blood or DNA with the body wrapped in the trash bags like that," John said

"I could get the D.A. to sweep the Tundra, if you find blood under the railing of the *Empress*," Nathan said. "That would give us probable cause."

"I wish the camera extended to the ramp where the vehicle Sandra drove was probably parked. Then we could see what they drove to my place," John said. "If it was a borrowed used car, the link will be lost."

"We should get on the road to Lee County and the Get Away Marina," Matrina said. "It's a good hour and a half drive. They said on the answer machine that the deal at the marina was going down at eleven forty-five. It's eight-thirty now. Let me call Suzanne's mother to see if Michelle can stay over with Suzanne and Debbie tonight, and then I'll call Buddy's mom about Turner staying there. After that, I'll be good to go."

Matrina picked up the phone and punched in the numbers.

"Let me call my pal at the sheriff's department and see if they got the results of the prints from the hymnal yet," Nathan said. "If they belong to Carmine Panacelli, that will tightened the net."

"Yes. That would mean Rogers was Slats' uncle. And he borrowed his sister's yacht to sail down here and find her son after the information on the Rolex watch surfaced in Chicago."

"Slats seemed to take the execution well," Nathan said.

"They know the rules," John said. "Slats broke the cardinal rule of being unfaithful to the family. He would know there was no forgiveness for that. It was just a matter of time until they found him. He was probably surprised he lasted as long as he did."

"Was it religion that made him turn on his family?" Matrina said. She hung up the phone after her two calls.

"I guess so. We'll never really know," John said. "That's what the paper said, that he couldn't be part of the family crime wave anymore."

"Where do you think 'the preacher' is right now?" Nathan said.

"You could check up on him back here," John said. He carried the bowl of popcorn into the kitchen and waited for Matrina to get her purse and her luminol so they could leave for Lee County. "He's probably headed to the airport even as we speak. Check all the flights leaving the Sarasota-Bradenton Airport, and all the fights leaving Tampa. He and Ida will be leaving the country for somewhere to lay low."

"I can do that," Nathan said. He got up to leave. "I'll call you on your cell and let you know about the prints and the airports."

John paused halfway to the door. He looked at Nathan, "And check the taxis from airport to airport," he said. "Like, if a cabby remembers picking them up at home and driving them to the Sarasota airport, see if a cabby at that airport took them to Tampa after that. And visa-versa. 'The preacher's' clever. He's never been caught clocking out before. I am sure he has planned their exit down to a farthing."

"A farthing?" Nathan said. "You expect me to catch someone who thinks in farthings?"

"A six-pence. Think along those lines. And we'll call you about the blood, if we find any. Then you can find a judge who is a late-night owl and get him to sign a search warrant."

"How about our church brother, Judge Barry Newton?" Nathan said.

"Good choice," John said. He followed Matrina out the front door. "Are we finally on the right track?"

"God only knows," she said. "Your car or mine?"

"Mine." They headed for John's Wagoneer.

Chapter 34

Interstate seventy-five stretched before John and Matrina as John's JeepWagoneer covered the ribbon of highway that meandered down the western coast of the coral reef that liked to think of itself as Florida. The mile markers zipped past, and silence ruled the vehicle.

The trip south to the San Carlos Boulevard exit in Lee County took about an hour and a half. They passed Fema City in Charlotte County where acres and acres of mobile homes stood as temporary dwellings for people who found themselves homeless after recent hurricanes. As John careened off at the exit, Matrina finally spoke.

"I have a question," she said. She smoothed the nonexistent crease in her jeans. "We saw that Slats didn't seem to put up much of a fight when they executed him. But he must have wanted to get away with testifying against his family, as he went into the witness protection program. Why do you think that was?"

"Oh, sure," John said. He stopped at a red light on the Boulevard. "He wanted to get away with betraying his father, and I'm sure if he had known that turning in the Rolex watch for repair would lead the family to his new whereabouts, he would have never done it. But once he was caught, he knew the game was over."

"That's so bizarre," Matrina said. "If 'the preacher' turns out to be the unaccounted for Carmine Panacelli, and the boat is in the name of Reba Panacelli Voloni, and Slats was really Joseph Voloni, Reba's son, then that would make 'the preacher' probably Slats' uncle."

"Yes. Carmine is probably Reba's brother. And the testimony of Slats would have sent his dad, Anthonio Voloni, up the river. So, Carmine, 'the preacher,' got sent to avenge the family honor by stamping out the renegade. It is standard mob procedure. I'm sure Slats felt he had it coming."

"There's no consideration for the fact that Anthonio was a criminal, murderer, drug runner, thief, and needed to be taken off the streets, and his son did an honorable thing by helping do that?"

"Oh, mercy no. You've got to watch more Al Capone Chicago crime movies. If you're a kid born into a crime family, you just salute smartly and charge up the hill. You don't ask questions, and you very definitely do not cooperate with the feds. That's a major no-no."

"Hum," Matrina said. She took a deep breath. "So, they stole their philosophy from Ollie North?"

"No. I stole the expression from Ollie North. They stole the philosophy from General Patton."

"There's a lot of stuff out there that we have no clue about, isn't there."

"You bettcha, thankfully," John said. "Okay, the Get Away Marina is just ahead, on the back bay. Watch for the signs."

"Is that it there?" Matrina said. She pointed to the entrance.

"Yeah," John said. He pulled into the parking lot. "We have to park as far away from the water as we can so we don't risk the chance of Andy recognizing my Jeep."

"Or, 'the preacher,' in case he's here."

"He won't be here. He never is. But if this is their last drug run, he's probably headed for ports unknown, if not right now, for sure tomorrow. Last time I was in a skirmish with him, he got away with drug running. This time, he'll get away with murder. Really irks me that he's so much smarter than all of us. He keeps pulling off these capers and vanishing like the wind."

"He must be an incredibly evil man," Matrina said. She watched John park at the end of the brightly-lit parking lot.

"Evil and cagey," John said. He killed the engine. "He played the role of the newly-transported deacon with flawless determination. I never had a clue he wasn't who he said he was."

"Yes, he even knows the Bible. That's the mind-boggling part."

"I told you, he's always quoted the Bible. That's how he earned the handle—'the preacher.'"

"How scary."

"How blasphemous." John opened his door and stepped out onto the pavement. Matrina opened her door and joined him. She brought her purse that contained her cell phone and carried her bottle of luminol.

"You think that makes God mad?" she said. "That a person uses religion as a cover?"

"I certainly hope so. And maybe that's why we're so close to him this time out."

"Maybe that's why we'll catch him this time out."

"Would that we could."

They crossed the parking lot, and John checked his watch.

"It's eleven-thirty," he said. He looked around the large parking lot for sight of any other human beings. A dozen cars dotted the lot, but they contained no drivers. "We'd better find a spot to lay low, if this thing is to go down at eleven forty-five. Then when we're sure they're all going with the Kahlua bottles, we can do our luminol thing."

"Sounds good," Matrina said. She fell in step with his long gait. "There's a seawall over there. We could duck down behind that."

"That'll work," he said. He walked in the direction of the pink, concrete block wall. "There are hibiscus bushes along the wall. They'll provide pretty good cover."

Matrina and John walked into the hibiscus bushes, which spread red and pink flowers across the seawall. They squatted down on their knees, settled back and waited.

The southern night sky shone with bright stars. A loud sonic boom thundered from overhead, and the squatters jumped with the sound.

"The shuttle," John said. "Coming in for a landing at the Cape."

Matrina nodded affirmation. That had been a worrisome sound when she first moved to Florida. New Floridians experienced trauma at the telltale sonic boom upon the entrance of the shuttle into the earth's atmosphere and the breaking of the sound barrier. Now it fell into just another fact of Floridian life like afternoon thundershowers and unrelenting heat, and no-see-ums, a naughty little gnat that you felt but truly could not see. Matrina brushed her arms to rid her skin of the invisible gnats, and wished she had remembered her can of "Off."

At exactly eleven forty-five, they watched Sandra Marshall, Andy's other woman, walk down the dock of the marina to the *Empress*. Andy met her on deck, embraced her and kissed her with passion. Matrina's eyes rolled toward heaven, and she shook her head in disgust. John focused on the drug run as he scanned the deck of the boat for the blue shopping bags that contained Kahlua bottles full of cocaine.

Kenny, Andy's partner, appeared from below, placed the blue shopping bags on deck, came topside and locked the door behind himself. He, Andy and Sandra divided up the bags and walked off the *Empress* and down the dock, as they had done the last time Matrina watched them in this maneuver.

They probably have another borrowed car from ye ole local used car lot, Matrina figured. The spies from Sarasota watched as the three subjects of their attention loaded the twelve bags of Kahlua bottles into the back seat of an old station wagon. Andy and Kenny got into the front seat, and Sandra got in the back with the bottles. The car cranked and moved back down the ramp, turned around in the parking lot, headed out to San Carlos Boulevard and turned toward Interstate seventy-five.

Matrina and John waited another ten minutes. No headlights splashed around the parking lot. No motors marred the midnight silence. No footsteps could be heard on the dock.

"Come on," John said. He left the seclusion of the hibiscus bushes and walked toward the *Empress*. Matrina followed in silence, purse in one hand, luminol in the other.

They moved down the grassy bank on the back bay side of the seawall. They leaped the railing that surrounded the *Empress*, and put foot to the deck.

"Over here," Matrina said. She walked to the side of the boat she estimated the murder had occurred on the video tape. "Isn't this the spot?"

"Pretty close," John said. "Spray under the bottom of the railing and see what you get."

Matrina leaned over the railing and aimed the luminol at the underside of the boat's railing. She sprayed an even layer of the liquid along the edge of the boat.

"Hot dog," she said. "Look at all the pretty bluish green speckles. Some of Slats' blood survived two trips to Cancun, or wherever."

"We've got to get out of here and phone Nathan. He's got to get a search warrant going, *muy pronto.*"

"Will your judge friend get out of bed to sign such a thing?"

"Oh, yeah. He'll be excited to help prove me innocent, after he approved my bail. He's been holding his breath, waiting for some nosy reporter to figure out we go to the same church and make a big deal out of it. This new piece of evidence will thrill him to death."

"It has to be Slats' blood, right?"

"Unless they're in the habit of icing folks in that same spot."

John and Matrina jumped back onto the dock and jogged at a steady lope back to the Jeep. They climbed in, and John dialed Nathan on his cell.

"Haul Barry's legal backside out of bed. We have a winner," he said into the phone. "We need a search warrant to look for blood on the *Empress* moored in Lee County, the blood of Joseph Voloni. Use the video as probable cause."

Silence, while John listened to Nathan's response.

"Wow, great," he said into the phone. "Call your buddy in the Manatee Sheriff's Department and get him to swear out a warrant for the arrest of Carmine Panacelli. I think they can make murder one stick. He's on the tape holding Slats down. How much more involved in a guy's murder can a person get? You'll probably have to find Carmine yourself, and sit on him until the cops show up. Go over to his house, and see what's up. If his car is in the garage, check to see if the house is empty. I'm betting it is, and they're long gone. Then call all the cab companies in the Bradenton phone book. See who picked up a couple of fares at that address. Then, like I told you before, see where they got toted, and then see if they switched cabs and went somewhere else."

"What?" Matrina said.

"Guess who shared a hymnal with me last Sunday?" John said. He turned out onto San Carlos Boulevard.

"Carmine Panacelli?" Matrina said. She fastened her seat belt.

"None other." John smiled. "Nathan just got the report on the fingerprints from the hymnal. We're going to catch that slime ball this time. I can just feel it."

"Wouldn't that be neat? He must have overshot the runway with God by posing as a religious official. God's going to get him for that."

"Yes, God can only take so much, then He gets even. This is neat, stupendous, mind-boggling, incredible, and I hope I'm there when they read him his rights. Makes me wish I were a cop again. I could type out the Miranda rights on a sheet of heavy brown paper and make ole Carmine eat every word."

Matrina smiled into the darkness of the moving Jeep. "I have another question," she said. She noted the information sign along the Boulevard that stated how far it was to the Interstate.

"What?"

"How'd they ever recruit Andy? Where did they find Andy in the first place? Do you think Andy is a distant family member?"

"Probably not," John said. He stopped for a red light. "'The preacher' usually moves into an area, puts the word out on the street that there's fast money to be made, and like moths to a flame, the marks show up, crooked cops, greedy politicians, desperate waitresses. You name it; they're out there. Then 'the preacher' recruits them, trains them, uses them and leaves them behind for the legal nets to scoop them up, while he waltzes off into the sunset."

"So, 'the preacher,' Carmine, and his wife, lady-friend, whoever she is, are where, right now?"

"I would guess they're halfway to Mexico, Guatemala, Brazil."

"Nathan can check the airline rosters once he finds out which airport they're at, if they actually left the house tonight."

"Yes. But they're too smart to use their own names," John said. He turned onto Interstate seventy-five and headed north. "They have some kind of alias all prepared, passport, travelers checks, driver's licenses, etc." He paused in mid-thought, and tapped his fingers on the steering wheel. Matrina waited for him to speak. She figured he had some kind of deep revelation that careened around in his brain. He passed his cell phone to Matrina. "Could you dial Nathan again?" he said. He gave her Nathan's cell phone number, and Matrina punched them into the phone.

"What's up?" came Nathan's voice on the phone.

"John wants to talk to you," Matrina said. She passed the cell phone back to John.

"Hey, I just thought of something," John said into the phone.

Matrina could hear Nathan's reply. "Talk to me. I'm driving down 'the preacher's' street to his house even as we speak."

"When you figure out what airport he's using, check the roster for the planes flying out of the country. I think he's got to put miles between himself and the mounties. And when you check the roster?"

"Yes?" Nathan said. "I'm here at his house right now."

"Good. Check for the names—John Fleming and Matrina McCoy."

"You think?" Nathan said.

"I think," John said. "That would be his style and make him think he's beaten me one more time."

"Gottcha," Nathan said. "Then you'll get to have a 'flight to avoid prosecution,' when the cops arrest John Fleming."

"Only this time, it won't be me," John said. "I can live with that. Gotta go. Catch ya later." He ended the call.

"Using our names?" Matrina said. She struggled to grasp the concept.

"Yes. It's a definite possibility. You have to think like they do, or they keep having this criminal edge on you."

"That's the trouble with people like us tracking people like them," Matrina said. "We're so clueless about what makes them tick."

"Yes, we have to get inside the dark abyss of what these guys laughingly call their minds," John said.

Matrina nodded and put his cell phone down into her purse so it wouldn't slide to the floor and get lost in the shuffle.

Ten minutes later, both John's phone and her own phone rang from the bottom of her purse.

"Heavenly days," she said. She scooped both chirping phones from their confinement. "No way they could be calling each other, right?" She handed John's to him and answered her own.

"Hi, George," she said into her phone. "Where? No kidding. Wow, we'll be up there in a minute or two; we'll check it out. Thanks, George." She clicked off the phone and put it back into her purse. When John clicked off his phone, he handed it back to her. She put his phone back into her purse, too, and waited for him to tell her the latest.

"The house is empty," he said. "Everything's gone, furniture, dishes, vehicles, all gone."

"So, where are they?"

"Nathan's checking. They might have driven to an airport, bus station, wherever, and then they would leave the car and call a cab. They'll leave no trace. I wish we were up there. I'm not sure tracking bad guys like this is one of Nathan's talents."

"We can't be two places at once," Matrina said.

"Two places at once," John said. "That's it. You're a genius."

"Oh, good," Matrina said. "What'd I say?"

"Dial Nathan back," John said. Matrina took his phone one more time from her purse and dialed Nathan.

"Here's John," she said into the phone and handed it to John.

"Hey, Nate. Check the airports for 'the preacher' and the woman to be flying out separately, John Fleming from say, Tampa, and Matrina McCoy from, say, St. Pete or Sarasota. Check the cab companies for single fares, rather than couples."

Matrina heard Nathan's response. "Okay."

John shut down his phone and handed it back to Matrina.

"So, what did George want?" he said. He changed lanes to get out from behind a semi that swerved land to lane.

"Oh, George couldn't hang with all this excitement going on," Matrina said. "What did he do?"

"He paid back a couple of favors he owed DEA."

"By doing…"

"By giving them a free collar at the Motel 6 in Punta Gorda."

"For real?"

"Yeap. We'll be in that area in just a minute. We can see for ourselves. Look. Up there. Pretty blue and red lights. That's probably where the party is going down."

John slowed down and pulled off at the exit across from the Motel 6. Six police cars blinked in the motel parking lot, and lawmen wearing DEA jackets ushered Andy, Kenny and Sandra into waiting vans. "See?" John said. He slammed his hands down on the steering wheel. "This is a typical 'preacher' operation. He leaves the underlings to twist in the wind while he flies off, free as a bird."

"But this time, we have fearless Nathan on the hunt," Matrina said.

"I hope that's enough."

Halfway back to Sarasota, John's phone rang from Matrina's purse. She brought it out and answered it. She handed it to John.

"Nathan," she said.

"We won," Nathan said loud enough for Matrina to hear.

"You're serious?" John said. Hysterical euphoria laced his voice. He leaned toward Matrina, "They got them. They actually got 'the preacher' and the lady friend, and the lady friend is saving her backside by slam-dunking ole Carmine. Couldn't happen to a more deserving guy."

"That's what that Kiran did at Trade Winds," Matrina said. "She was fine in sharing the profits from the creative bookkeeping, until the scene got dicey, then she couldn't wait to throw her partner under the bus."

"The fickleness of women."

"Thank goodness." Matrina smiled into the darkness.

John handed his phone back to Matrina.

"So, they were flying out under the names John Fleming and Matrina McCoy?" she asked. She put the phone back into her purse.

"Not quite," John said. "They picked up Matrina McCoy in Orlando, and Nathan Caldwell in St. Pete."

"Nathan Caldwell?" Matrina laughed out loud.

"How'd that make Nathan feel?"

"Kind of honored, I think." John chuckled. "He didn't know the guy knew enough about him to steal his ID."

"I have one more little scene to play in this drama."

"Really? What's left?"

"I have a video to play for my sweet little sister."

"Tonight?"

"Yeah. If I wait for tomorrow, I won't be able to do it. I'd just let her think that Andy succumbed to the money, and leave the extracurricular fringe benefits out of it. I can't do that. She has to have a reality check for future reference."

"Ouch."

"Yeah, double ouch."

* * *

Two hours later, if someone had been a fly on the wall, they would have seen two sisters piled up in front of the TV at Rosie's apartment. One wore a pink chenille robe and slippers; one wore jeans and a tee shirt. A pot of raspberry zinger tea sat between them. The robed, younger sister collapsed into the arms of the older, jeaned sister. No words filled the air. The fly would witness sobs and rocking, and caressing of hair and tears streaming down both sets of cheeks. It would take more than raspberry tea to cushion this pain.

Chapter 35

A week later, John, Matrina and Nathan sat in John's backyard. They drank iced tea from tall frosty glasses and lamented the Floridian August heat. Dee-Dee, John and Matt had returned from the grandparents in upstate New York.

"*Andy Griffith* is too a good show," John, Junior, said, from the living room "We should watch that."

"Yeah," Matt said. "It has Opie in it. He's a good little kid."

"It's not as good as *Home Improvement*," Dee-Dee said.

"Oh, yeah?" John, Junior, matched her tone and her determination. "What makes it so much better?"

"Because it's got a mother in it. I like shows that have mothers in the family."

"That's what makes Opie's show better," John, Junior, said. "Their family is like ours, and they get along just fine."

"They have Aunt Bea," Matt said. "And we have Mrs. Gunthrey."

"It's not a sin to want to watch a show that has a mother in it," Dee-Dee said in her louder tone of voice.

"It must be some kind of a sin to want your own way all the time," John, Junior, said. His voice climbed a half an octave.

John got up from the picnic table. "Got to go referee. Excuse me a minute."

"I have the same scene playing at my house, I'm sure," Matrina said. "Only it would be over watching the Western Channel or the Hallmark Channel, and only two kids, not three. At least with three, you could come up with a *quorum*. At my house, we have to toss a coin."

"I hope I get to be married and have a family some day," Nathan said. He sipped his tea and munched from a plate of oatmeal cookies Mrs. Gunthrey had placed on the table.

"Did you ever have a serious girlfriend?" Matrina said. She swirled her long tea spoon around the bottom of her glass.

"Yeah, once," he said. He wiped his mouth with a paper napkin. "Her name was Loretta. I loved her a lot. I bought her a ring, and she said she'd have to think about it."

"That's not good," Matrina said. She moved the citronella candle closer to their end of the table to keep the mosquitoes away.

"No, it wasn't good," Nathan said. "The next week, she ran off with her supervisor at work. He was six foot two. She said I was too short to marry."

"Count your blessings you avoided that trap." Matrina said with emotion. "What a shallow woman. Judging you on your height? What kind of person does that?"

"Women I fall in love with," Nathan said. He grabbed another cookie.

"How long ago was that?" Matrina said.

"Oh, I don't know. Four, five years ago."

"And you haven't dated anyone seriously since then?"

"I haven't dated anyone at all since then."

"Nathan, that's terrible. Don't you have a singles group at church?"

"Oh, sure. It's full of all the Alice Toney's you can handle. Who needs that?"

Matrina rolled her eyes and wondered what to say next. "You're a lawyer. You're very successful, and you're very good at your job. You're a very good catch. Any girl would be lucky to land you. You shouldn't let one bad relationship get you down."

Nathan smiled and sipped his tea. The theme from *Andy Griffith* came from inside the house.

"The boys must have won," Matrina said. She looked toward the closed glass patio door for John to return and update the battle.

"John keeps track," Nathan said. "Dee-Dee must have won the last time."

"Makes you wonder why the kids couldn't keep track," Matrina said, "and give the choice to the one who lost the last time."

"If that philosophy ever caught on in human nature, it would put all us lawyers slap out of business," Nathan said. He grabbed another cookie.

John came back and sat down at the picnic table.

"You'd think they could figure out some of this out for themselves, wouldn't you?" he said .

"It's a personal favor from God to Nathan," Matrina said. She sipped her tea.

"Excuse me?" John said.

"Inside joke," Nathan said. "Now, back to the business at hand. The court will have the bond money ready to refund to us probably tomorrow."

"Oh, good," John said. He smiled at Matrina. "We can all pay off our mortgages and have our houses back again."

"What do we do with the money Carmine kicked in, back when he was being the good deacon, David Rogers?" Matrina said.

"'The preacher' actually kicked in some money to bond me out?" John, shocked by that news.

"Sure," Nathan said. "Didn't I tell you that part of it? He kicked in fifty thou."

"Fifty thousand? Like in dollars?" John's mouth dropped open. Matrina handed him a cookie, and he put it into his mouth.

"Yes," Matrina said. "I guess he thought it would be a good cover to secure his position with all of us."

"He'd be right," John said. He tried to keep cookie crumbs from falling onto the picnic table. "Fifty thousand dollars. How incredible."

"The incredible part of it is," Nathan said, "what do we do with it when we get it back?"

John connected the dots. "No choice. We have to give it back to him."

"Give it back to him?" Matrina said. Shock shaded her tone of voice. "Syndicate money, that came from who knows what evil source?"

"Not our job to judge," John said. He sipped his tea and swatted a mosquito. "The guy coughed up the money; he gets it back. Done deal."

"I agree," Nathan said. He jotted a note on his yellow legal pad.

Mrs. Gunthrey came out into the yard and emptied the grounds from the coffee pot around John's rose plants. She shook the filter to get all the grounds out, and thumped the grounds container against the rose bush.

"Coffee grounds on the rose bushes?" Matrina said. She watched the elderly lady's maneuver.

"Yes," Mrs. Gunthrey said. "The grounds have caffeine in them. Good for growth, keeps ants away. My mother's secret for growing good roses."

"It's evidently working," Matrina said. "You have roses even now, when they should be slowing down until fall. I'll have to remember that. Does it have to be one special brand of coffee, or will any brand do?"

"I think any brand will do," Mrs. Gunthrey said. "We always buy Yuban, but I don't think it matters."

Mrs. Gunthrey walked past them back into the house. She sighed and wiped her brow as she went. She brushed imaginary grounds from her white apron. She muttered to herself. Matrina overheard her to say she wondered why these three supposedly responsible adults sat all piled up outside in the heat and left her alone in the house with the three dueling darlings and the time bomb that ticked away until their next disagreement.

"The biggest problem at hand is we need more physical evidence against Andy and Carmine," Nathan said.

"The video isn't enough?" Matrina said.

"We knew that wouldn't be enough when we came up with it," Nathan said. "In today's age, videos can be created. A good lawyer could blow it all to smithereens. I'd hate to see them walk due to lack of evidence."

"Can the D.A. have it verified by an expert to state that it hasn't been altered?" Matrina said.

"He's already done that," John said. "But the lawyer 'the preacher' hired will no doubt produce another expert who'll swear by all that's holy that the tape has been tampered with. We're not playing on a level field with this group, you know."

"And then there's the blood found on the *Empress,*" Matrina said. "Doesn't that count for something?"

"Yes," John said. "The blood turned out to be that of Slats, of course, but they know we were down there. They could accuse us of planting it."

"Time element," Matrina said, undaunted. "The experts can time-date the blood to the June murder weekend."

"Already done," John said, "by the D.A., of course. But once again, the legal charlatans from Chicago will try to discount that."

"So, we need something that ties the death of Slats to Andy and by association, 'the preacher.'"

"Exactly," Nathan said. He walked back into the house for another glass of tea. "More tea?"

"No, thanks," Matrina and John said, a beat behind each other.

"How about blood?" Matrina said. "I swept Andy's apartment, but did anyone luminol his Tundra truck?"

"Yes, they did. Nothing. Clean as a whistle."

"They probably used a borrowed car from a used car lot for the transporting of the body anyway," Matrina said. "How about Andy's garage? They had to bring shovels here to bury the body. Blood on any of his tools in his garage?"

"They looked. Nothing. There were shovels and tools in his garage, and some looked like they had been used to dig with, but no blood. Remember, they brought the body here in a couple of large trash bags. When they dug the hole, they probably dug it before the body was near it so there would be no blood.

"They would have removed the trash bags from the body, dumped Slats down into the hole, and shoveled the dirt back on top, being careful not to have the shovels come in contact with any DNA or blood. Then they no doubt dumped the trash bags in the nearest shopping center dumpster on the way out of here. There might have been dirt still on the shovels, but there wouldn't be any blood. We're dealing with a cop here. He knows how to do this stuff."

Nathan came back with more tea. They sat at the table in silence as the sun slipped more deeply into the western sky, however, it refused to take the heat of the day with it. Matrina fanned herself with a napkin.

"Want to go inside in the AC?" John said.

"No, I'm fine. I kind of hate to discuss these issues in front of your kids. I wouldn't want them to worry about anything."

"Yes, they think it's all over, now that I'm not being accused anymore, and I let them come back home."

"The D.A. should have enough evidence with what he has. All he needs is motive, means and opportunity, and he certainly has that," Nathan said. "The problem is the clowns from Chicago will lie and create reasonable doubt in the minds of the jury, and that's all it will take to mess up this prosecution."

"I'd hate to see 'the preacher' walk because the case is too weak," John said. He looked over at Matrina and smiled. She did not smile back at him. "What's the matter?" he said.

"The coffee grounds," Matrina said. "Nathan, can you call your buddy at the sheriff's department and get a search warrant to go back out to Andy's apartment, and this time, don't look for blood. Scour the shovels, other digging tools, and the garage floor for traces of Yuban coffee grounds. Check the bed of the Tundra, too. Even if they used a stolen car to bring the body out here, they would have to put the tools back into the bed of the Tundra after they returned the car."

"Yuban coffee grounds," Nathan said. "That would definitely tie Andy to John's backyard. Good work, Matrina. You'll be a Rockford yet."

"Oh, we don't want that," John said. "Then she'd have to move to Malibu and live in an old, beat up trailer."

Chapter 36

Saturday, Labor Day weekend, seven P.M., Matrina, Rosie, Michelle and Turner walked up the wooden ramp to Casey's Lounge on Lido Beach.

"Are you sure you want to do this?" Matrina said to Rosie. She stopped her with a hand on her sister's arm before they entered the main entrance.

"Yes. I have to do this. This is my last hurrah in putting Andy out of my life forever."

"But you were going to marry him tonight, and have your reception here. Isn't that going to be really hard on you?"

"Matrina, I'm twenty-eight years old. I have to face life head-on. You have been mothering me forever, and don't think I don't appreciate it. Well, okay, I haven't always appreciated it. Sometimes it drives me plum nuts, but I know you mean well. But there are some things I just have to do. I met Andy here. We used to go here lots. I like this place. I have to be here without him and enjoy it again on my own."

"You're sure it's appropriate for kids," Matrina said. She fell in step behind Rosie as she opened the front door to the restaurant.

"Yes," Rosie said. She drew out the word in frustration. "It's a family place. They have food, and a pool table, and computer games. And there will be other kids. You'll see."

Matrina sighed and exchanged concerned glances with Michelle. Turner held the door open for the ladies, and they walked into the restaurant that had a distinct western flavor to its ambiance.

"At least, there's no chance of running into Andy here," Rosie said over her shoulder.

"There's no chance of running into Andy anywhere," Matrina said. "It's going to be a long, long time before that man's goes anywhere again, if ever."

"Which proves there is a God, and all's right with the world," Rosie said. They followed the hostess to a table for five. Wooden armed chairs surrounded the table, and peanut shells covered the table and the floor.

"Don't they ever clean the tables and sweep the floor?" Michelle said.

"No," Rosie said. "It's part of the old west charm." She opened the menu handed to her by the hostess who wore a fringed western skirt, a checkered western shirt and a wide brimmed cowboy hat. She handed menus around to everyone, then left to get the waitress. The western-clad waitress returned with a fresh bowl of roasted peanuts and a tray full of glass mason jars and a pitcher of water.

"Just push the peanut shells off onto the floor if they bother you," Rosie said. She opened her menu.

"This place rocks," Turner said. He shelled a couple of peanuts and tossed the shells on the floor. "I love it here. Maybe we could use their idea and live like this at home." Matrina and Michelle shot him out of the saddle with glares over the top of their menus.

"I don't think so," Matrina said.

"Heavens, no," Michelle said. "This would drive a normal person nuts."

"They will never learn to think outside the box," Rosie said in a hushed whisper to Turner. "But they're family, so we're stuck with them."

"Guess so," Turner said. He opened his menu. "They have Reuban sandwiches here, Mom. Can I have that?"

"Sure," Matrina said. "Have anything you want." She scanned the menu and looked for something in a grilled chicken, found it, and closed the menu.

The waitress returned to take their orders. Michelle had a taco salad, and Rosie had a steak and baked potato, loaded with butter, sour cream and chives.

"And for dessert, cheese cake," Rosie said.

"Oooo, that does sound good," Michelle said. She looked to her mother for approval.

"I told you," Matrina said, "have what you want. This is a celebration of sorts."

"Yes, it is," Rosie said. She raised her mason jar of water in a toast. "To me, and the rest of my life."

"Here, here," Matrina said. They clinked jars with each other and the kids.

"And then there's the other reason we have to celebrate," Rosie said.

"What's that?" Matrina said.

"The Yuban coffee grounds," Rosie said. "Andy thought he had covered his backside so completely, and he got done in by old, stale coffee grounds. How's that for justifiable karma?"

"Yes," Matrina said, "or intervention by God. It's a miracle that clue finally dawned on us." She ran her finger around the top of her water-filled jar. "I have to admit, that was pretty cool. They found coffee grounds not only in the garage and on the shovels, you know, but in the bed of Andy's Tundra, too."

"To reborn Rosie and sure-shot Sherlock," Rosie said. She raised her jar in another toast. Matrina clunked Rosie's jar with her own and smiled in deep satisfaction.

After dinner, Matrina had coffee, the children had another soda, and Rosie had a wine cooler.

"I like the sign they have over the bar," Matrina said. "We reserve the right to limit alcohol to three drinks per person. Do they stick by that rule?"

"You bet," Rosie said. "That's what I keep telling you. This is a safe place to come and bring kids. No drunks tolerated in here."

"Can we go play computer games?" Turner said.

"Sure," Matrina said. She dug in her purse for coins and dollar bills. She handed him four ones and a few quarters. "This should hold you a while."

"Come on, Michelle," Turner said. He took his Coke with him. "They have one of those motor cycle games. We can each ride a cycle and race."

"That would be no race," Michelle said. "I can beat you any ole day of the week." She followed behind Turner to the game room.

"In your dreams," Turner said. "Come on. Let's see who beats who." The kids walked in front of each other to the game room.

"You okay?" Matrina said. She patted Rosie's hand.

"Of course, I'm okay," Rosie said. She sipped her wine cooler. "I'm always okay. I'm like a cat with nine lives. I keep landing on my feet."

"I'm just so sorry you had to go through all this," Matrina said. She sipped her coffee. She took a peanut, shelled it, and dumped the shells on the floor. The action brought a touch of laughter to her eyes. "Look at me. I can't help myself."

"Sloppiness is addictive," Rosie said. She took a peanut herself and tossed the shell over her shoulder.

"Well, I don't believe it," Rosie said. Her eyes wandered to the front entrance.

"You don't believe what?" Matrina said.

"Looky there," Rosie said. She motioned toward the foyer where two men and three children chatted with the hostess.

Matrina turned around and looked over her shoulder.

"You're right," she said. "I don't believe it either. I can't believe John would ever come to a place like this."

"Maybe he's not such a 'stick in the mud' as he seems," Rosie said. Rosie

279

raised her hand and waved to John. John caught her eye and waved back.

"Who's the cute guy with him?" Rosie said

Matrina looked again. "That's Nathan Caldwell, John's attorney. Nice guy."

"A little on the short side, but he's got kind of a little jaunt to his gait. Looks like he'd be a lot of fun."

"He is," Matrina said.

"How come he's friends with John?"

"Rosie, that's not nice. John can be fun."

"No, Matrina, I've never seen the man in a 'fun' mode."

"I think you make him nervous. You're a little too much 'fun' for him."

"Apparently, I'm a little too much 'fun' for just about everyone."

John, Nathan, Dee-Dee, John and Matt approached Matrina and Rosie at their table.

"I can't believe you're actually in a place like this," John said to Matrina.

"I was just saying the same thing about you. This would have been my last choice for a place to run into you."

"Nathan likes to hang out here. He likes the food, of course. You know Nathan. Food's always high on his 'to do' list. And he's not above having a beer now and again, but we don't tell the Baptist board about it. We just pray he'll see the light and repent."

"There's nothing wrong with an occasional beer," Nathan said. "And three's the limit here, so no chance of getting snockered."

"Bummer," John said.

"Are your kids here?" Dee-Dee said to Matrina.

"Yes, they are," Matrina said. "Over in that game room, racing motorcycles."

"Oh, cool," John, Junior, said. "Can we go over there with them, Dad? Please?"

"Okay." John looked over his shoulder to check out the proximity of the game room. He reached into his back pocket and took out his wallet. "Here's a five. See if there is a machine to break it for you."

"Thanks, Dad." The duet of boys, and Dee-Dee hurried toward the game room.

"Mind if we sit down?" Nathan said.

"Sit yourself down," Rosie said. She extended her hand to Nathan. "I'm Rosie, the evil twin," she said. "Matrina and I are sisters, but we are sure that one of us has to be a genetic throwback. We're nothing alike, but we've learned to cope."

"Thank goodness," Nathan said. He took Rosie's hand. "One of Matrina is quite enough." He winked at Matrina.

"What are you drinking?" he said to Rosie.

"Wild strawberry daiquiri," Rosie said. She turned the bottle for Nathan to read the label.

"Smokin'," Nathan said. "I'll have one of those," he said to the waitress who had walked up to the table.

"I thought you just drank Coors," John said.

"I'm open to new ideas," Nathan said. "This chick looks like she might have a lot of interesting new ideas."

"You can probably count on that," John said. He smiled at Rosie. "I'll have a cup of coffee," John said to the waitress.

"And I'll have a refill," Matrina said. "Are you having dinner here?" Matrina said to John.

"No, we did Burger King on the way down from Bradenton. Then Nathan wanted to come here to shoot some pool. I've been here with him before, so I knew it was okay to bring the kids, so here we are."

"You shoot pool?" Rosie said over her wine cooler bottle.

"Do I shoot pool?" Nathan said in an incredulous tone of voice. "Does the sun slide into the Gulf every night?"

"I might give you a chance to pick up some pointers," Rosie said. She got up from the table and carried her bottle with her.

"You, teach me?" Nathan said. He chuckled and sipped his newly arrived cooler. "I think not, my fair maiden."

"Right this way," Rosie said. "Class is about to begin."

They walked the fifty feet to the pool area, and Matrina watched as they chose their cues. Nathan struck a stately pose with his arm over his head and his pool cue extended in the standard fencing position. Rosie struck the same pose, and crossed her cue with his.

"On guard," she said. They batted cues back and forth several times and then moved to the pool table. "Rack 'em up," Rosie said. Nathan put the brightly-colored balls into their triangular guide and moved the group to the starting position on the pool table.

"Oh, mercy," Matrina said. She watched them over John's shoulder. "What have we done?"

John turned to watch them as well. "Probably struck the biggest match to hit our lives since we were at Disney in July."

"Will we live through it?" Matrina said. She shelled another peanut and tossed the shell on the floor.

"Probably," John said. He sipped his coffee that had just arrived. "Or not." He shelled a peanut and tossed the shell with Matrina's. "At least the journey won't be dull."

Matrina watched Rosie and Nathan and an air of sadness and concern clouded her face.

John picked up her hand and held it between both of his hands. "Let it go," he said. "She's a grown woman. You're not her mother. Let it go."

"Funny, that's almost what she said coming here tonight. That I mother her too much."

"You do," John said. He caressed her fingers. "That's not wrong. It's just fruitless. Rosie's like a fresh breeze off the Gulf. You can see where it's been, but you haven't a clue where it's going."

"Amen to that," Matrina said. She put her free hand on top of his hands and looked into his eyes. She really liked this man. He made her feel grounded.

"I think I love you," he said.

"I might love you, too," she said. She heard the words and wondered if she really said them.

"We'll give it some time and see where it goes. No more kisses," he said. "Christ had plenty to say about what that does to a guy's mind."

"Women have minds, too, you know. Christ wasn't talking just to men." She smiled at him, and he smiled in return. "That's good news."

At that point, a three piece combo began to play country music near a waxed, shell-free dance floor.

"They have dancing here?" Matrina said, honestly surprised.

"Yes," John said. "Line dancing."

"Line dancing? Oh, Michelle will get into that. She's been practicing all summer." Strains of "The Electric Slide" slithered across the room.

"Mom," Michelle said. She approached the table and danced a few steps as she came. She had Dee-Dee in tow. "It's 'The Electric Slide.' Can you believe it? I've got that one down perfectly. Come on, Dee-Dee. I'll show you how it goes. You're gonna love it."

"I guess the boys are still in the game room?" Matrina said to John after the girls darted off to the dance floor where a group had formed to began the steps.

"Oh, yeah," John said. "You can bet on that. Come on. Let's us give this a go." He got up from the table and held out his hand to Matrina.

She accepted his hand and walked toward the dance floor. "You know how to line dance?"

"Of course," he said. He led her into the line close to the edge of the floor and dropped her hand. "Delores loved to line dance. She used to drag me to a club in Little Falls that had line dancing every Saturday night."

"I would have never known that about you," Matrina said. She watched his feet and tried to get into the rhythm of the music. She wished she had paid more attention to Wendy's lessons.

"There are lots of things about me you don't know," John said. He watched her feet and moved closer to her to make it easier for her to follow his feet. "Right foot, left foot," he whispered into her hair.

"I've got to write that down," she whispered back. After a few repetitions of what she had seen performed in her living room the past few months, she got the hang of it, sort of. She struggled to ignore the laughter that drifted from the pool table area. Rosie and Nathan leaned over the pool table and the crack of colliding balls mingled with the laughter.

"Rosie does seem to be putting up a brave front," Matrina said. She watched John's feet so she could stay in sync.

"Yes. Nathan's not a bad guy to hang out with on the day of your supposed wedding to a philandering murderer."

"He seems to have gotten her mind off the situation," Matrina said.

"He doesn't even know there is a situation," John said. He turned in place and began the dance sequence over again. "I never mentioned anything to him about Rosie and Andy. It's up to Rosie to tell people, if she wants them to know. This 'party animal' spirit is normal with Nate."

"She sure seems to be having fun," Matrina said. She added some arm movements to the steps of the dance. "This is the happiest she's been since all this happened. Maybe there's hope after all."

"There's always hope," John said. "As long as we draw breath, there's always hope."

"Right foot, left foot," Matrina said.

The End

Printed in the United States
68357LVS00008B/117